Sleeping Tigers

Holly Robinson

For Diane &
Suzanne —
Such a lovely,
loving pair — it's
always so good
to be around
you!
xo Holly

Chapter one

On my second night in San Francisco, Karin took me to a bar on Valencia Street. The place was the size of a trolley car and oddities were displayed along its walls in glass cases: shrunken heads, a stuffed alligator, ancient eyeglasses, women's lingerie, and a flea circus. I looked closely, but I didn't see any fleas.

"You deserve to celebrate your freedom," Karin declared once the bartender served our Cosmopolitans. The drinks looked as pink as Kool-Aid in this light.

"I'm not sure there's a whole lot to celebrate," I said.

Karin patted my hand. Her nails were long and painted an elegant mauve; mine were short and bare, the tips of my nails as ragged as a child's. I curled them under.

"I never did understand what you saw in Peter," she said. "It's better that you ended things before you actually married the guy. Peter was as stupid as soup."

"Peter's sweet," I countered. "I never saw him get angry, not in three years. He paid for his sister to go through college. He helped his mom buy a house! And he always remembered my birthday with flowers. Once, he even made a Valentine's Day card for me stuffed with little paper hearts that fell onto the table when I opened it."

"Yeah, yeah. Mr. Excitement. Hold me back."

"Oh, come on. You can't tell me you're immune to that sort of thing."

Karin shook her head. "One does not live by Hallmark moments alone."

"My parents liked him," I offered. "Dad gave Peter the seal of approval the day I brought him home. Said he was glad I'd found a decent, hard-working Republican with good tires on his car."

Karin howled, showing the row of big teeth that Peter thought kept her from being truly beautiful. "She looks like she bites," he once said, but I'd always liked Karin's teeth. Big and square and white, her teeth were a metaphor for the fact that Karin was just what she seemed: a woman who knew what she wanted and went after it. None of my mother's, "You catch more flies with honey," philosophy for Karin. Whether she was going after a job or a man, Karin favored the flyswatter approach.

We'd known each other forever. It was Karin's idea to marry our hamsters in a back yard ceremony when we were eight years old, mine to run a neighborhood babysitting monopoly in high school. I became a teacher and Karin studied nursing; when I moved to Boston from our small, central Massachusetts town to earn my master's degree, Karin followed and worked at Mass General before moving to San Francisco. Now an operating room nurse, she went through lovers the way most women go through lipsticks.

"Remember how you and I always imagined that we'd be brides on the same day?" I asked her now. "We thought we'd marry movie stars and have mansions next door to each other. Even in college, we were sure that was the plan." I licked sugar from the rim of my glass. "Well, maybe not movie stairs," I amended. "But we thought we'd be wives and moms together, like our mothers were friends."

"Yeah, well, forget that plan," Karin said. "You already broke Rule Number One: never get serious with a guy your parents think is good for you, or you're doomed to repeat their mistakes. And do you really want to be married to a guy who spends the whole weekend mowing the lawn?"

I laughed. My father once said I could work for money all my life, or marry Peter and earn it in five minutes. I told Karin this and about how, on the first morning after I'd left Peter and moved back in with my parents, Dad shook a fork at me and sent a sliver of egg sailing through the air. At my advanced age of thirty-three, he assured me that I was more likely to meet a roof sniper than another potential husband.

"Was Peter any good in bed, at least?" Karin asked.

"That's the thing. He's so great looking, so sexy! Much better looking than I am," I conceded. "But he had so little interest in sex after the first few months! Peter tracked our lovemaking on his iPhone so that he could print out a spread sheet if I complained, just to prove we were above the national average of 2.5 times a week."

"Twice a week? That's for married couples with kids, or maybe people in body casts." Karin shook her head. "Will you please quit feeling guilty for leaving him? Peter was good looking, sure, but like a Ken doll is good looking, with all of that tidy black hair and his manly jaw. Boring. Besides, from what you've told me, it sounds like Peter would've left you first, if he'd only had the balls. Face it, Jordan. Your relationship wasn't just fizzling. It was a flat line."

I sighed and nodded, too exhausted to argue. I had driven alone from Boston to San Francisco, choosing this city as my destination because it was the farthest place I could drive and still know people: Karin and my brother Cameron. Once I'd announced my intentions, Karin magically pulled an affordable apartment out of thin air for me to sublet. I hadn't been able to reach Cam at all. This worried me, but it wasn't a surprise. My younger brother was a drifter, and other than one Christmas, he had been particularly incommunicado since moving West two years ago.

I stayed in one cheap motel after another during my solo drive cross-country. Each was gussied up in the same oranges and browns and then forgotten, as if one person bought the linens and carpets for every hotel under $60 on Route 80. Two of my stopovers were equipped with massage beds. One had a lava lamp. And every motel room had burn rings from coffee pots on the dressers. In my Denver motel, a man tossed beer bottles out his window all night long, so that I stepped outside onto a shimmering crystal carpet the next morning.

When I finally arrived in San Francisco, I stalled my car several times on the roller coaster hills. I blamed my poor driving on the strangeness of the houses, which bloomed like children's crayoned drawings, pink and orange and purple and terrifying yellow. I had two more days until I could move into my apartment, so Karin had offered me her couch; when I got to her place last night, she fed me chocolate bars and sourdough bread with a bottle of beer.

Now, Karin was asking about my plans. I reminded her that the school had renewed my contract for next year and my teaching salary carried through the summer, so I wouldn't have to work. I could just stay in San Francisco until August, when I'd head back to Boston to prepare my classes and crash with my parents until I found an apartment. "I don't know what I'll do, other than spend time with you and Cam. I'll probably just go nuts." I wasn't joking.

"Oh, poor you, with too much money and free time."

"I don't know. I might really blow a fuse with no structure to my days. I usually teach at one of the private schools during the summer."

"You're not sick of teaching?"

"Never. They even let me put together the science curriculum last year for the entire elementary school. Should have seen our fossils lab."

Karin tipped her head back to finish her drink, then said, "You know, we do have schools in California. There's no law saying you're doomed to go back and live in the same state as your parents your whole life."

"I've already signed a contract," I said.

I didn't bother adding that I just couldn't see myself ever fitting into San Francisco, which might as well be a foreign country to a staid East coast woman like me. Here in the Mission District, open air Hispanic markets and burrito bars vied for space with cafes where men wore berets and women scribbled in journals with the intensity of second graders mastering cursive writing. Earlier today, I'd spotted a Chinese restaurant sandwiched between a Vietnamese grocer's and a Salvadoran pupusa stand, and passed a thudding alternative dance bar.

The people were just as diverse. Tanned skate boarders and joggers sped along the streets, homeless people hunched over shopping carts of possessions, business people squawked into cell phones, and Hispanic women clutched cloth bags of groceries.

As I shouldered through San Francisco's version of the American Dream, anything seemed possible. But where did you begin a new life?

"With a party!" Karin said, as if answering my question.

"What?"

"That's it! You need to start right in and meet people. I'm planning the Party of All Parties to welcome you to San Francisco. We'll have it tomorrow."

"Tomorrow?" I squeaked. "How can you give a party on a day's notice?"

She gave me a pitying look. "That's why they invented social media. Will you come?"

"I'm staying at your place, remember?"

Karin grinned. "Good. That's settled, then."

She paid the check and we left the bar. The air was balmy and smelled of oranges and the sea. As we rounded the corner onto Church Street, a trolley car rattled past, sparks flying from its wires like manic lightning bugs. It seemed like all of San Francisco had decided to stay up late. Through the windows of the houses I could see blinking television sets, Chinese lanterns, red and purple curtains, and silhouettes of people sitting, gesturing, eating, even dancing.

"Doesn't anyone ever sleep in this city?" I asked.

"Sleep's overrated. That's an East Coast obsession."

On our college campus, Karin's housekeeping was legendary. That hadn't changed much in twelve years. Karin now lived on the top floor of a triple decker, and the windows were so smudged that at first I thought it must be raining. The walls of the living room were painted a medicinal pink with orange trim; the kitchen's violet counter tops were so splattered with food that they looked speckled by design. Unwashed glassware and stacks of plates competed for sink space and a pyramid of empty beer cans formed a centerpiece on a drop-leaf table, where the remains of a pizza were arranged like flower petals around an overflowing ashtray. I'd been cleaning since late morning, about the same time that Wally, Karin's disgruntled boyfriend, slammed out of the house, gym bag in hand.

"What's wrong with him?" I had asked, watching Wally's stiff back retreat through the door.

"Oh, he doesn't want me to have a party on a night he's working." Karin waved a hand.

"Should we be doing this, then?" Karin had been seeing Wally exclusively for nearly six months–a record length of time for her to keep any man in her sights–yet all I knew about him was that Wally worked as a bellhop in a big hotel, played in an emo band, and lived on a steady diet of cigarettes, coffee, and tuna straight out of the can. This morning I had collected the tuna cans to prove it.

Karin had raised an eyebrow at me. "Honey, the minute you start letting a man tell you what to do, you might as well give up on yourself and wear elastic-waist jeans, too."

By now, it was late afternoon and I had filled seven garbage bags–the hefty size. I tripped over a pair of wet running shoes and lined them up neatly in the hall closet despite my temptation to stuff them into a garbage bag, too.

"I just don't get it," I sputtered. "How can you be an OR nurse and live like this? The doctors must always be sewing misplaced sponges and scalpels into your patients."

Karin sniffed. "I have an impeccable nursing record. And, let me tell you, after sterilizing and organizing all of those shiny little tools all day, I don't want to clean when I get home, too. Now find me a can opener. I'm making us some dinner."

"Where is it?"

"Over there." Karin gestured vaguely towards the drawer beneath the oven.

I performed an archeological drawer dig, unearthing nail clippers, pens, a dog collar with tags, packets of neon condoms, sheet music for Christmas carols, rubber bands, and a man's athletic sock. Finally, I laid my hands on a rusty metal can opener that looked positively toxic.

"Maybe you should try keeping your can opener with your cooking tools," I muttered.

"Oh yeah, I will, soon as I have my personality makeover. Now get back to that dusting! I'll make us some fabulous spaghetti sauce and you can do the dishes."

"Oh, there's a good deal. A year's worth of dishes and all I get is a canned dinner."

I washed while Karin cooked, taking a break to phone and text my brother. Still no answer. I hoped Cam hadn't left the country again without telling us; last year, I received a postcard from India just days after sending a birthday present to his address in Oregon.

After dinner, Karin insisted that I take a bath and relax. I started filling the tub and studied my face in the mirror. Karin's bathroom was wallpapered in tilting blue sailboats, and my face floated like a giant white buoy among them.

Maybe Dad was right and I was on a downward spiral toward a raggedy, husbandless future. Should I have stayed with Peter? At the very least, I could count on Peter to come home for dinner on time. As an added plus, he always remembered to pick up the dry cleaning.

Over the past three years, our relationship had crossed one commitment threshold after another without stumbling: dating, engagement, then living together, a process that forced us to whittle down our glassware and linens to fit into a single apartment's built-in shelves.

As Karin saw it, I'd stepped onto a conveyor belt to matrimony, moving along without thinking because it was all so easy, and because I had celebrated my thirtieth birthday in a subdued state of panic three years ago, the month before Peter and I met. She was right. Yet, I already missed elements of my sensible life with Peter. Days with him were calm. Predictable. Sweet. Contented, mostly.

We played Scrabble and chess, held dinner parties, spent weekends exploring Vermont, talked about getting a dog. It was almost as if we'd already put our courtship, wedding, and children behind us, and were now companionable retirees in our golden years. Without Peter, I was afraid that I'd become that quintessential stereotype, the old-maid teacher with chalk on her sweater, ink on her upper lip, and seasonal dangling earrings—bats, candy canes, bunnies—to complement my embroidered holiday sweaters.

To distract myself from this dire thought, I read the labels of Karin's mind-boggling array of bath oils lining the shelves: Eucalyptus Dream, Peppermint Pep, Calming Camomile. "What about Lascivious Lime?" I yelled at Karin from the bathroom, stripping off my clothes. "Got any of that?"

"Coming right up, Toots!" a man shouted up from the yard below.

I scrunched beneath the window and yanked the shade shut, then ducked into the tub. I settled for two caps full of Peaceful Plum.

"How do you look in red?" Karin popped in, dangling a sleeveless dress the size of a tube sock.

"I'm not wearing that. I'm a respectable elementary school teacher."

"Doesn't mean you have to look like one," Karin scolded. "What were you planning to wear tonight?"

I nodded at my neatly folded khakis and t-shirt, which I'd left on the chair in the bathroom. She wrinkled her nose and plucked the clothes off the chair between two fingers, removing them from the room like a dead rat.

"Hey!"

"Hey, yourself!" she shouted back. "I'll return these in due time. For God's sake, Jordan. You dress like a woman on safari studying elephant dung."

"What's wrong with that?"

Karin reappeared in the bathroom, shaking her head. "The only women in San Francisco who dress the way you do are the ones in the Marina, and they can't help themselves. Trust me on this one. I'm going to hide all of your clothes until after the party. And promise me you'll use the condoms I'm putting in the pocket of your outfit."

"I will not have sex with a stranger!"

"They won't be strangers. Every single person at this party tonight will be a friend of mine. Did you reach Cam, by the way? Can he come tonight?"

"No. What's going on with him, anyway? Have you seen him? My parents are frantic."

Karin shook her head and reminded me that she'd only spoken to Cam once last year, when he got back from India. "He called to see if I knew of any jobs at the hospital, but he never followed through. That's not surprising, though. I've never been Cam's favorite person. I'm too abrasive for a dreamy pot head like him."

I piled bubbles up to my chin and let my arms float upward. "Is he still, do you think? A pot head?"

"Who knows? So many people are on Klonapin or Zoloft these days, I don't think nearly as many need to smoke dope." Karin left the room again and came back a few minutes later to display a black knit jumpsuit for my inspection. "How about this? Very chic! Very retro!"

"Very Catwoman. Very not me."

"Well, you'd have to wear a body shaper to smooth out the profile," she admitted.

"Forget it. I enjoy my oxygen too much."

Karin sat on the toilet and arched her back, her thick black hair moving like an animal curling along her shoulders. She had on tight jeans and a black tank top. Suddenly, I felt self-conscious and vulnerable in front of her, sitting naked in her tub. My own hair was the pale brown of underdone toast and hung below my shoulders, its bushy tendencies tamed only by headbands. Soon my face would sag beneath the weight of all this hair, like an ornament hung on a Christmas tree branch too scrawny to support it.

I was taller and thinner than Karin, but curvier, too. My breasts bobbed about in the water like a pair of tennis balls and it was all I could do not to cover the left one, the breast that still bore the scar of my surgery six months before. I'd gone in for a routine mammogram that turned out to be anything but. The radiologist had outlined little white flecks on the film, raising his eyebrows in a way that made me think I might be in for something.

I was: the white flecks were actually calcifications clustered in a pattern around a small tumor, he'd said. "Maybe benign, maybe not."

Two weeks later, I was in the mammography room again, having what the radiologist breezily called "a needle loc" in preparation for a biopsy. This procedure made me feel like a radio-controlled car, with a long wire shot straight through the side of my breast and technicians controlling my every move.

The mammography staff, perhaps determined to take my mind off the wire, explained the hazards of their profession, like the time one of them flicked the switch to squeeze the mammography machine's plates shut, and accidentally trapped the head of another technician between the plates instead of the patient's breast. Meanwhile, the two women opened and closed the metal plates against my breast, flattening it up and down, side to side, working the machine like some sort of exotic sandwich-maker.

Afterward, one technician patted my arm. "There, now. That wasn't so bad, was it?" she asked.

"Only when I imagined kissing my breast goodbye," I replied, just to see her wince.

There followed the biopsy, more waiting, and then the diagnosis–yes, breast cancer; no, it hadn't spread outside of the tiny pinpoints of light in the milk ducts–and surgery. Then more waiting for the results of the lumpectomy. Five interminable days later, the call had come.

"We got it all," the surgeon crowed over the phone. "Clear margins all around!" No need for radiation or chemo, he said, going on to pronounce me "cured" before hastily adding, "Well, not that there's really any such thing as a 100 percent cure, is there? With cancer, we can only say 99 percent. Still, pop the champagne while you can."

That one episode had lasted just a few short months of my life, yet I had gone from 0 to 60 mph during that time, looping through the entire Rocky Mountains of my emotions. Of course I was terrified of dying. At the same time, I felt newly awake: things that had mattered so much to me before—PTO meetings, fund raising for the school science trip—shrank to gnat-like proportions, while things I hadn't thought about in ages—like my brother, and why he'd dropped off the family radar screen—suddenly seemed vitally, achingly important. I felt relieved to be in the clear, yet oddly guilty about dodging the breast cancer bullet this time, while others in more difficult circumstances—a neighbor down the street with three young kids, for instance—hadn't been able to beat it.

Now, scarcely six months later, there was nothing left to show for my experience on the outside but this ugly scar: a raised line half as long as my palm and still red, like a dogwood branch laid against the side of my left breast. Inside, however, I felt that I might never be the same.

When it was all over, Peter wouldn't touch that breast at all. He simply treated me as if I were the one-breasted woman we were both afraid I'd become. What had prompted me to leave Peter in the end wasn't boredom or the fact that he wasn't as interested in me physically, but the idea that, if he couldn't handle this kind of scare, what would happen to us if the breast cancer returned and a surgeon couldn't tell me to pop the champagne?

I explained this to Peter as I broke off our engagement. He accepted the ring I returned with a curt nod, no argument. He was probably relieved.

I had told Karin all of this through weekly phone calls coast-to-coast. Her response was as pragmatic as I had expected—one reason I loved Karin was that she always, always told the truth, as boldly as possible.

"I understand that you're upset, but really, Jordy, did you think you'd be the one person in the whole world who never got cancer?" she had asked. "Don't you dare wallow! The surgeon says you're clean, which is as good as medicine gets. It's a lesson in mortality, sure, but use it to toss the dead-wood and get on with your life."

I knew that, by "deadwood," Karin was referring to Peter. I also knew that Karin was busy with a single woman's preoccupations, just as I had been before. Love, work, and everything else in Karin's future still stretched before her like a straight, smooth highway.

Despite being my best friend, Karin had yet to realize what I now knew: each of us carries a sleeping tiger inside, and we can't predict when that cat will wake, stretch, and sharpen its claws. Having to face the tiger's presence inside myself was what made me finally leave Peter. It was also what drove me to seek out Cam and Karin: I felt an intense need to recon-nect with what little family I had, and to live a bold, truthful life that went beyond the carefully orchestrated domestic existence I'd shared with Peter.

Karin was still talking about Cam. As far as she remembered from their last conversation, my little brother was working a part-time job in Berkeley and sharing a house with a group of people she'd never met.

"Cam always was different," she said, reaching into the medicine chest for a pair of tweezers. "He's nothing like my three brothers, all gung ho about sports and money."

It was true. Cameron was the family dreamer and video gamer, while I carried the itchy mantle of Responsible Oldest Child. Cam had earned better grades than I did in college, but he dropped out senior year to travel and work odd jobs.

Meanwhile, I went on for my master's degree and found a job, pre-paring to marry, provide grandchildren, and show up for Sunday dinners. Eventually, I would be called upon to puree my parents' dinner in a blender and push their wheelchairs around the block. I didn't resent Cam, exactly; I only wondered why he'd turned out one way, while I was another.

Oh, for heaven's sake! Stop thinking! Leave yourself alone! I commanded, and sank into the bath water until I wore a crown of bubbles in my hair.

Karin made me leave her apartment an hour before the party. "Take a walk or grab a coffee. You can't be both the guest of honor and the first arrival."

"I'm not just the honored guest," I reminded her. "I'm also the cleaning crew and caterer." Still, I humored her and left the apartment, aimlessly wading into the inky purple night. I wore the outfit Karin had loaned me—tight black leather pants, high black leather boots, a turquoise leotard top, and beads that clacked against my breast bone—only because she had hidden my suitcase.

I followed Dolores to 24th and then turned left into Noe Valley, where I was soon mingling with the wine bar crowd. The feathery tops of the palm trees were etched black against the sky. A few lights glimmered in the houses, and I saw a woman moving about in her second-floor kitchen. A man read his newspaper by kerosene lantern on the rooftop garden just to the left of her.

From Noe Valley, I continued up a hill so steep that it made my calves ache, then descended into the Castro, where the gay bars were buzzing and the windows were flung open to the night. The sight of so many beautiful men snuggled together on the benches in one ferny bar sent me into a deep gloom.

What was I doing here, walking alone in someone else's ill-fitting clothes, with only a plastic tourist map for comfort? I wondered where Cam was, and fervently wished that my brother would miraculously appear to save me from showing up solo at the party. I checked my text messages again, but still nothing.

I stopped to catch my breath in front of a diner surrounded by drag queens in fantastic wigs, long eyelashes, and short skirts. Their horsey muscular legs tapped impatiently on the sidewalk as they waited in line on the sidewalk for dinner booths. No doubt about it, they had more fashion sense than I did. Better make-up, too. And where did they get earrings that size?

I studied my map in order not to stare, and was suddenly reminded of the Treasure Map game that Cam and I had played as children. We drew our treasure maps on white construction paper, elaborate scrawled illustrations in smudged pencil, then deliberately chewed the paper's edges to dampen it before we rolled the maps into scrolls and left them to yellow in the sun for that authentic treasure map look. I always felt slightly bored during this game, but my brother leaped into full character every time I agreed to play. He'd pretend to hobble along on a wooden leg as a pirate, or sneak like a stowaway behind the kegs of gunpowder disguised as living room furniture.

Whatever his role, Cam's mission was to steal the treasure map. And I was always the captain of the pirate ship, except for the one time we convinced our father to play this game with us. Our father had roared and swung an egg beater inside his sleeve like a fake metal arm. Cam and I fled, shrieking, into the garage.

Just as my father came flying out the back door, the screen slamming behind him like a musket firing, Cam yanked me to safety into the dark space behind the furnace. We hid there in the oily smelling dark, hearts pounding, until our father tired of looking for us and retreated.

"We fooled the Captain," Cam had giggled. Where my brother was concerned, it was always us against the scary outside world.

"Well, brother," I whispered, pocketing my map and turning back towards Karin's apartment. "Where are you hiding now, in this scary, scary world?"

Chapter two

I 'd worked myself up into such a state of anxiety by the time I arrived at Karin's that I nearly ran back down the stairs when she opened her door. I had to remind myself that a party is just a sandbox for grownups.

This particular sandbox was already crowded. It pulsed with people and music and flashing lights that made the guests look like jerky marionettes. I certainly would have retreated if Karin hadn't caught me by one arm.

She wore a thigh-length black satin dress that revealed the pale tops of her breasts. Around her neck, Karin had wrapped a white scarf studded with gold stars, and her earrings were enormous gold moons. She embraced me in a musky hug.

"No hiding," Karin whispered in my ear. "You look too fabulous. Now listen: there are at least a dozen single straight guys here. They've all got good jobs, and I've tried two of them out personally, so I know they're hot."

"Jesus, Karin." I didn't know whether to laugh or call Animal Control.

She giggled and led me into the living room, announcing my arrival with the subtlety of a talk show host. "Hey, everybody! This is my best friend from back home, Jordan O'Malley!" Karin elicited a cheer from the crowd, then left me while she greeted more guests at the door.

I had a strategy for surviving any party: graze. There was plenty to nibble. I'd seen to that myself; I even knew where to find the extra bags of tortilla chips if we ran out. I gravitated towards the dining room table, but Karin reappeared before I could fill my plate. A man followed in her wake.

"This," Karin said, docking in front of me, "is a friend of mine from the hospital, David Goldstein. He's a pediatrician and you're a teacher, so you both must like kids, right? That should be a good ice breaker."

Certainly, nobody could ever accuse Karin of procrastinating. I shook hands with David, the first contestant in Karin's private Dating Game, wondering whether she'd had the chance to, as she put it, "try him out." The only thing I knew for sure was that he was employed.

Karin embraced us both, pulling us together like salt and pepper shakers, then zoomed off. David shifted his feet. He wasn't much taller than I, which made him short in a man's world, and he had the slightly stooped shoulders and slender frame of an academic. I could have looked him in the eye if his gaze hadn't been focused on the floor. Instead, I studied his hair. The curls were as silver and metallic as my mother's favorite brand of kitchen scrub pads. He was probably about my age, but his hair made him look older.

And what was he looking at? My boots? Or, rather, Karin's boots. I had the urge to squat down and peer into his face, which is what I did with students whenever they felt too overcome to look me in the eye. But no. Let him rise to the occasion. I waited him out.

Judging from David's wire frame glasses, baggy jeans and pocket t-shirt, he was the sort of boy who had coached the high school math team. He had been laughed at in gym class. And he had probably gone straight from college to medical school, then completed a residency in a clinic for the poor.

I deduced this last bit from David's shoes, which were the thick leather sandals worn by teachers I knew who had done Peace Corps stints in countries with more dust than rain. They were the shoes Moses must have worn to lead the way through the Red Sea, and David Goldstein wore them with frayed socks. All in all, David looked like someone I could talk to. I was sorry he couldn't possibly think the same thing of me, since I was dressed in Karin's Whore of Babylon ensemble.

It was too loud to talk in the living room. I led him out onto Karin's porch, where at least there was a decent breeze. We leaned against the railing and David told me that he did work in a clinic for the poor, as I had suspected. He also served as a pediatric emergency physician in the same city hospital where Karin worked. He'd recently spent a year working abroad, he added, and was having trouble readjusting to life here.

"Where were you?"

"Nepal," he said, sounding wistful. "Right up until last month, I lived in a mud hut and practiced medicine in a converted cow shed."

I conjured up dirt floors, dung heaps buzzing with flies, and bloody sheets. "Why there?" I spun my mental globe and found Nepal: Land of Sherpas, yaks, Mt. Everest, and yetis, according to one of my fourth grader's oral reports for social studies.

"Not for the noblest reason," David said. "I went for the mountains. Ever since I was a kid, I'd dreamed about climbing Everest."

"And now you've done it? That's wonderful!"

David shook his head and made a face. "Not quite. Weak knees," he explained, pointing down at the betrayers. "The curse of being in my thirties and spending my whole life lifting books instead of weights."

"I bet you saved a few lives, though, even if you didn't climb mountains."

"Not as many as I would have liked." David set his beer bottle on the railing and turned to look out over the rooftops. I did the same, our shoulders comfortably touching. A jet flew overhead, silent and twinkling.

"Once, a villager brought me into his house," David said, "and begged me to look at his daughter. I went upstairs, where the whole family was gathered around a heap of wool blankets. The only light was from this smoky little fire, so it took me a minute to realize that my patient was actually under those blankets. She was a little thing and skinny as a stick. Her temperature was soaring, up to 105 degrees. She had a severe pelvic infection. A pelvic infection!" He shook his head. "In our country, sulfa drugs could snuff that out in a week, but that kid was on death's door."

I could imagine it all: the shadowy figures, the smoky room, the moaning child, David huddled over her. "So what did you do?"

I never found out. Our conversation was interrupted by a loud beeping from David's pager. He grabbed it off his belt and grimaced at the number. "Sorry. I need to make a call."

"Karin's room is quiet," I suggested. "Down the hall, last room on the left." As I watched David make his way through the dancers, I wondered whether he already knew where Karin's bedroom was.

I lingered on the porch, listening to the night sounds of the city. For the last party I'd gone to with Peter, I'd bought a tight little black dress, the sort that would give a dead man an erection. Peter had looked me over and only asked if I could please blow-dry my hair straight, just this once.

Karin materialized at my side. "Why are you moping out here?" She took me firmly by the elbow, leading me back into the apartment.

"I was waiting for David. We were having a nice talk."

She rolled her eyes. "That figures. Takes a nerd to know one. Listen, David's as dull as dirt and piss poor besides."

"But you're the one who introduced him to me!"

"Just as a warm-up exercise. You said yourself that you're through with nice guys. Peter was nice, remember?"

"That's mean."

"Look, David's got a billion stories, every one of them sad to the bone. That's the last thing you need right now. Besides, he had to leave for an emergency room consult. If you really want to pursue things, I'll give you his number later. Now mingle!" she ordered.

Karin drew me into the brightly lit, crowded kitchen and pointed. Next to the table, which was barely visible beneath six-packs and wine bottles, stood a man whose freckled face was haloed by a cloud of blonde hair. We watched for several minutes while he performed tricks with a tiny Frisbee for several female groupies. He was tall, with a lanky runner's build and a face that might have been handsome if it were plumped out a little. As it was, his small dark eyes, flat nose, and pert mouth looked stamped onto his skin. He was dressed in a blue Hawaiian shirt, baggy green shorts, and running shoes.

"What do you think?" Karin breathed into my hair. "Wouldn't you rather frolic with a feral Frisbee player than ponder the world's woes with a pensive pediatrician?" Karin waved and the man grinned, flexing one arm like Popeye. "Isn't he amazing?"

"He's coordinated," I said, as Surfer Boy shot a miniature Frisbee into the air and caught it on his forehead, where it balanced on edge.

Karin elbowed me in the ribs. "You don't know the half of it," she moaned, fanning her face theatrically. "Come on, what do you really think?"

I studied the guy more closely. "Sorry. There's not enough beer in the world."

"Oh, give him a chance. Break loose for once," Karin said, and abandoned me again to join the dancers in the living room.

I wandered over to the dining room table, loaded down a plate with food, then hovered in the kitchen doorway, watching the object of Karin's admiration spin a palm-sized red Frisbee across his shoulders. The man saw me watching and advanced. When we were scarcely a foot apart, he pulled an even smaller Frisbee out from behind my ear, rolled it down his arm, then balanced it on one finger. He lifted my hand to pass it to me; the Frisbee continued spinning on the tip of my forefinger.

I had to laugh. "Now what?"

The man shrugged. "Keep it. Consider it your Welcome to California gift." He flashed a grin and made his way back into the kitchen.

I eyed the Frisbee uncertainly. It seemed a shame to stop the spin, but how long could I stand here like the Statue of Liberty, especially with a plate of food in my other hand?

"Neat trick," said a woman beside me.

I turned to look at her and dropped the Frisbee, but caught it in midair. I hastily slid it into one of the many pockets of my leather pants. "Too bad I couldn't keep it up."

"Bet he could, though." The woman gestured with her sharp chin in the Frisbee player's direction. She was attractive with the anemic, alien good looks of a super model. In her rayon pink dress, pink leggings, and black Chinese slippers with embroidered roses, however, she looked like a little girl playing Cinderella. Her hips were slight, but her breasts held their own against an enormous metal necklace that might once have been part of a chain link fence.

"He certainly has energy to spare," I said.

The woman examined me with huge, kohl-rimmed dark eyes and introduced herself as "Anna, Anna Mendez," exhaling each time on the final "a" of her name as if she were doing abdominal crunches: "An-ah, An-ah!"

"I work with Karin and wanted to meet you, Jordan. Karin thinks the world of you," Anna said in a voice so ragged and small that it wafted in my direction like a scrap of paper caught on a breeze.

"Are you a nurse with Karin at the hospital?"

"A nutritionist."

Ah. Hence the death-by-starvation appearance. I'd seen more fat on a ribbon snake. "That must be interesting work," I said.

Anna shrugged. "Not really. People are bent on killing themselves through excess in this country."

I glanced down at the paper plate in my hand, which sagged in its greasy middle under the weight of artery-choking cheese, pastries, and chips. My leather pants squeaked and wheezed as I shifted my weight and slid the plate onto the tiny folding table beside me, where the fats could congeal in peace. I struggled to think of something to say. "So, how do you encourage people to change their habits?"

"She terrorizes them." A man joined our conversation. "Our little Anna is a real Discipline Diva with a crop in her boot."

The speaker was dressed like someone on the cover of a romance novel, in a billowy white cotton shirt, black jeans, black cowboy boots, and a black scarf wound in a complicated way around his neck: testosterone on the hoof. He had a sturdy handlebar mustache and shoulders so broad that Karin must have turned him sideways to fit him through her bedroom door. I had no doubt that he'd been there. She would not have let this one go untouched.

Anna introduced us. "This is Ed," she breathed.

Ed: a name meant to be stitched on a mechanic's overalls. He had kind dark eyes, but looked too much like a cartoon villain to be truly appealing. Anna, however, devoured his beefcake proportions the way I'd go after a brownie.

"I do not ever terrorize anybody!" Anna was protesting, speaking in the lilting cadences of uncertain women. "You can't scare anyone into anything? Not really, when it comes to changing their eating habits? Because people have to motivate themselves?"

I was glad that Anna wasn't my nutritionist. I was also happy that nobody was standing behind us. My butt would look like a beach ball next to hers, which was as small and tight as two clenched fists.

Our conversation meandered. Anna, it turned out, was from Minnesota. "Horrible, horrible place," she said. "Bleak skies, lots of snow, and nothing but white bread in the bakeries."

"What about you?" I asked Ed. "How did you end up in San Francisco?"

Ed smiled handsomely. How else could he smile? "I'm an anomaly, a native San Franciscan. Third generation!" He pulled a wallet out of his pocket and displayed a photograph to prove it. A collection of at least two dozen people, all ages and sizes, smiled into the camera. Like Ed, they had strong chins, hairy forearms, and broad shoulders. Even the girls.

"That's really something," I said.

Anna looked stricken. "I always wanted to come from a large family. But I was an only child, the spackle on my parents' marriage."

Uh oh. Here it was: The California Confession. One thing I'd learned in my two days here was that Californians could bring out the big guns of personal pain on a moment's notice. Just today, I'd been in the corner market buying party supplies when I overheard one woman emphatically tell another that she was learning to honor her clitoris after her divorce.

"Are your parents still together?" Ed asked, proving his true California colors by forging ahead fearlessly with the conversation.

Anna shook her head, her satiny black curtain of hair swinging around her elfin face. "They got divorced five years ago. That's when my repressed memories of the emotional abuse first surfaced enough for me to own them," she explained.

Ed folded Anna into his arms, then cupped her chin in one hand and tipped it towards him. "I want to say one word to you. Just one," he said. "It's a word I want you to repeat as you process your past and progress with your life's work."

Embarrassed but fascinated, I stepped closer, anxious to shoplift any soul-saving secrets I could use for myself.

Anna's eyes brimmed. "What is it?"

"*Forgiveness*," Ed murmured, stroking Anna's hair the way you'd calm an anxious horse.

"That is so beautiful," Anna told him.

That is so much hooey, I thought, as a commotion broke out behind us. Dancers were skipping to the left and right, the women climbing onto the sofa and chairs, the men spinning around, flapping red paper napkins.

"Look out! A rat!" a man cried.

It was a mouse, actually. The terrified rodent scooted between feet and furniture legs. A bearded man in a black t-shirt and black jeans stepped forward with a dish towel held in front of him like a fireman offering a net. "Jump up here, little guy!" he coaxed. "Jump!"

The mouse ignored this invitation and continued to zip around like a wind-up toy. Various people squealed and shrieked, including the bearded man.

Finally, Ed dropped to a crouch, scooped the mouse into one hand and flipped it into his shirt tail. He toted the mouse in this cozy shirt hammock down the back stairs.

A minute later he was back, not even breathing hard. "Dance?" he asked.

I looked for Anna, but she had disappeared in the stampeding herd of mouseophobes. "Maybe just one," I agreed.

Three, five, then seven dances. I lost count after that. I would never wear leather pants again, I vowed, as sweat streamed down my thighs. Ed didn't dance like anyone else I knew. He gyrated, strutted, twirled, and even took me in his arms for a number that left me upside down and seasick.

When we finally retreated to the kitchen for more beer, he told me about his family. Ed grew up on a houseboat in Marin with his two sisters, two brothers, artist mother and carpenter father. His father had died five years ago; Ed took his mother out every Sunday for dinner, wrote poetry for love, and made money by taking carpentry and modeling jobs.

"Remodeling?" I shouted over the music.

He shook his head, dark eyes dancing beneath the thick brows. "Modeling."

"You mean for magazines? Department stores?"

He shook his head again. "Artist's model." He struck a manly pose: Atlas on one knee, holding up the world.

"Oh, no!" I laughed.

"No? Well, how about this, then?" Michelangelo's *David* was next.

It was easy to imagine these poses in their unclothed entirety. I held the cold beer to my forehead. "Where do you model?"

Two art schools used him on a regular basis, Ed told me. Occasionally he did private sittings as well.

"But doesn't your construction work interfere? What if you bash your thumb with a hammer or take a two-by-four to the forehead? Do they still want to draw you when you're all bruised and splintery?"

Ed grinned, teeth flashing beneath his mustache. Seeing Ed smile was like unwrapping a turkey sandwich when you're hungry: its appeal was its simplicity. "You bet. The more bruises, bumps, tools, and dust I bring to my modeling jobs, the more they love me," he said.

The imagery was taking me by storm. I closed my eyes and felt Ed's breath on my face as he leaned close to kiss me. I let him, and it was better than just all right.

Karin chose to appear at that instant. "Oh good. I'm glad to see that you're hooking up." She patted my back pocket meaningfully, to remind me of the condoms she'd put there earlier, hard-rimmed tokens of good luck. A look of confusion crossed her face when she felt the Frisbee instead.

"I'm about to invite Jordan to my house, if you don't mind the guest of honor leaving early," Ed said.

"Mind?" Karin rubbed her hands gleefully. "Not a bit. As long as you both PROMISE not to do anything I wouldn't."

Ed shrugged. "That should be an easy promise to keep. What do you say, Jordan?"

What could I say, but yes? Here was my golden opportunity to act impulsively for a change, instead of planning my next move. That's why I had come to San Francisco after all.

∞

Ed drove a filthy Saab with a muffler problem that prohibited all conversation. His apartment was just south of Market and flaunted the same inattention to detail as his car. A couple of webbed lounge chairs stood on either side of the fireplace, a battered chunk of redwood served as a coffee table, the bookshelves were swaybacked wooden planks separated by cinder blocks, and a pair of ancient snowshoes hung on the wall.

"My father's snowshoes," Ed said, as reverently as if he were presenting a cremation urn.

In the kitchen, I began to doubt my own intentions as the beer wore off and reality set in. Was I ready for this? There had been a few other men before Peter. (I could still count my lovers on one hand, something that Karin found hilarious.) To varying degrees, I'd been in love with each one. But Peter was the only man who had ever seen the scar on my breast. I thought I'd keep my top on tonight, avoid the issue entirely, then remembered I was wearing a body suit beneath Karin's leather pants. I'd have to convince Ed to turn off the lights if we got that far.

Stalling for time, I asked Ed to put a kettle on for tea. He lit the stove and plopped a couple of herbal tea bags into a pair of oversized pottery mugs. Tan linoleum curled beneath my boots and the speckled Formica table teetered on the crooked floor, its surface not quite leveled by a wad of newspaper. I could only hope that Ed's carpentry skills, like Karin's talents as an OR nurse, weren't represented by what I saw in their apartments.

I sat down. The leather pants cut grooves into my thighs. My earrings, silver hardware also borrowed from Karin, angled into my neck. I might as well have worn a straight jacket and fish hooks.

I gazed into the mug when Ed put it in front of me. The tea bag puffed and floated like a jellyfish, yellow gradually seeping into the steaming water and sending the aroma of spring grass into the room. What was I doing here? I didn't know this man. And I hated herbal tea. What was the point of a hot beverage without caffeine?

"So talk to me," Ed said. His broad shoulders dwarfed the chair.

"I don't know what to say."

"Do you want to go back to Karin's?"

"I'm not sure." I sighed. "I don't even know what I'm doing in San Francisco, much less here in your apartment." Ed was watching me closely, his eyes kind. Now that I saw him in good light, he looked older, closing in on forty. "I thought you were interested in Anna," I confessed.

"I am interested in Anna."

"So why didn't you dance with her?"

"Because I'm not interested in Anna the way I'm interested in you."

"She's prettier."

"Debatable."

"Skinnier!"

"True. But skinny isn't necessarily a good thing. Anna strikes me as someone who would be very high maintenance. Anyway, why are you trying to get me interested in Anna, when you're the one sitting in my apartment?" Ed took my hands in his. My hands felt small, safely enveloped, warm. "Are you hoping I'll ask you to leave? Let you off the hook, so you won't have to hurt my feelings? Sorry. That's not going to happen."

I started to cry. A steady stream of tears rolled down my cheeks, as salty as the San Francisco fog. I sniffed, wiped my nose on a paper napkin and crumpled it. I tossed the ball into the trash basket near the window, banking it off the wall.

"Good shot," Ed observed.

"Hours of playground basketball."

"I bet you're a great teacher."

"You don't know anything about me," I sniffed.

Ed's gaze was steady. "Oh, but I do. You love to dance. You're a terrific listener. You're a good friend to Karin, who's one of the dearest people in the world to me. Your left blue eye has a very interesting spot of brown. And you've got a luscious body."

I blew my nose on another napkin and tossed that one, too. The shot went in again. "You're right. I'm a good teacher. My fourth graders love me. The parents love me. Even the principal thinks I walk on water. But get me out of a classroom, out of those four walls where I can plan every minute on paper, and my life is a wreck. Karin told you, I guess, that I'm just out of a relationship? That I was engaged, but broke it off?"

Ed nodded. "I think what Karin said was, `Thank God she's out of that one.' But listen, Jordan, most people almost get married. A lot of us even go through with it. And then a lot of us get unmarried."

"Have you ever?"

"Yep. You can't get to my age and not be married at some point in your life."

"Why, how old are you?"

"Forty-two."

Pretty old to be a poet and a model, I thought, never mind scampering around on carpenter's scaffolding like a monkey. In my circle of friends back home, the fortysomethings were lining their ducks in a row to put children through college.

"You don't look that old," I said.

"I don't feel that old. But I'm that experienced."

"Where's your wife now?"

Ed ran a finger around the edge of his mug. "She found herself a house and a man to keep her in it, so she left me. We don't talk any more."

"How long ago did you get divorced?"

"Eight years."

"What was she like?"

He smiled, playing some private reel in his head. "The tough kind of woman you never realize is soft and hurting until it's too late."

"Have you been in love with anyone since then?"

Ed laughed. "You ask the worst questions. You must be a relentless elementary school teacher. Yes, of course I have." He cocked his head at me. "You know, just because you're here doesn't mean that we have to hook up.

I can take you home. Or you can just spend the night with me and we'll see how things go. Would you like that?"

"I don't know." I was shivering slightly.

Ed rose from the table, washed out the cups at the sink. "Stay with me tonight. I promise you won't come to any harm or do anything against your will."

"Have you got a couch?"

"Afraid not." He led me into the living room. "Just the lawn chairs or the bed. You choose. Though I'll tell you right now that the lawn chairs have been known to swallow my guests whole and spit them back out on the floor."

Ed's bed was inside a closet in the living room. The bed filled the entire closet, and it was a cozy place, covered in a red flannel quilt and lined with blue flannel pillows. "I'll tell you what," he said, coming up behind me and resting his hands on my hips. "Let me entertain you."

"What do you mean?" I looked around for a TV, saw none.

He guided me onto the bed gently. "Lean back against the pillows."

"Mind if I take off my pants first?" I rubbed the leather seams along my thighs. "I feel like I'm sewn into a sausage casing."

"You're asking permission to remove your clothing?" Ed leaned against the closet door, grinning.

"Just my pants," I warned.

"Sure. And anything else, if the mood should strike."

I tugged off the leather an inch at a time while Ed pretended to busy himself with the stereo. My legs were creased and dented with the memory of every seam and metal rivet; the leotard had worked its way uphill in a most unattractive way. "Could I borrow a t-shirt? And maybe some boxers?" I asked. "And would you mind if I took a shower, too?"

"Yes, yes, and a most emphatic no." Ed gathered things out of his bureau and showed me to the bathroom.

This room was clearly the showpiece of the apartment. The new tiles were red, and inside the shower a black bench ran the length of the wall. I turned on the water and perched on the bench to massage my feet, which still ached from Karin's high-heeled boots.

It all felt so good that I found myself humming by the time I got out and examined myself in the mirror. Ed wouldn't necessarily notice the scar on my breast if we did go to bed. I'd just keep the lights low. Or off, better yet. I pulled on his green V-neck t-shirt and a pair of plaid boxers, feeling almost relaxed.

Back in the bedroom/closet, Ed told me to get into bed. I propped myself up against the pillows and waited. He disappeared into the kitchen, put on slow reggae music, then began to dance for me.

He was a good dancer. No surprise there. But then Ed began to strip off his clothes, slowly, unwinding his scarf and draping it over the floor lamp before he undid the buttons of his shirt. The shirt fell to the floor and Ed moved about the room, wordlessly inviting me to admire his broad, smooth back and muscular carpenter's shoulders.

As he danced, Ed touched himself with his hands just enough to make me shiver. I tried not to think about who else had seen this particular mating ritual. But a part of me stayed on alert and wary, observing the action instead of being fully engaged in it.

Perhaps that's why I reacted the way I did when Ed unfastened his trousers. His pants were held together by a Velcro strip, and he ripped them open with such deliberate flair, such noise, that I gasped. As his pants puddled around his ankles, Ed's penis reared its head like a prairie dog popping out of a tunnel.

That's when I laughed. Uncontrollably.

"I'm so sorry," I wheezed, once I'd stopped snorting. Ed's proud manhood had shriveled to thumb size and now dangled despondently. "You just surprised me, that's all. I've never seen anything quite like that."

Ed hurriedly hiked up his trousers and fastened them again. "It's all right," he said with dignity. "Some women like something different, that's all. I just wanted to please you."

The phrase "some women" got to me. I didn't want to be one more mare in the stable. On the other hand, Ed had honestly been nice, hadn't he? Trying to please me in bed had to count for something. For a lot, after Peter. After all, wasn't that why I was here? For the joy of sex without the ponderous weight of love? To leap my own life's boundaries?

"I'm really sorry," I said again.

"Don't worry. It's fine," Ed said, waving a hand, but we both knew it wasn't.

Ed took a shower then, and I lay miserably against the pillows. Would it be better if I left? Or worse?

He seemed cheerful enough, though, when he came back, toweling his hair. Ed slid into bed naked beside me, hiking the covers up over his bare chest. "I hope you still feel comfortable enough to stay what little is left of the night," he said, turning on his side to face me.

Ed smelled now of the night outside, as sweet as the sea. The covers had slipped to reveal one brown shoulder. I traced it with one finger, then touched his collar bone. His bulk was comforting. "I might," I said.

"I hope you will. You're a wonderful surprise," he added, lifting the covers up to look at me.

"Why?"

"All those wonderful curves. Much nicer than I expected. And I expected to like you a lot." Ed's voice was drowsy and his eyes were at half-mast. I touched his dark hair, which was thick and soft and just long enough to tug between my fingers.

He didn't stir. He was sound asleep.

I slipped out of bed and dressed again, then let myself out of the apartment.

Chapter *three*

I crept barefoot into the early morning fog and walked back to Karin's apartment. I still had traces of eye makeup ringing my eyes, I carried Karin's tall boots because my blistered feet screamed when I tried to put them on, and I was once again wearing the squeaky leather pants. It didn't matter, though. The only people I passed on the street looked worse than I did. And at least I wasn't relieving myself in the gutter.

I had left Ed a note with my phone number, after debating the etiquette of thanking a man for a night of lovemaking that had, in the end, fizzled. I hoped he wouldn't be hurt that I'd left as soon as his head hit the pillow.

Karin's apartment looked like the site of an earthquake. She and Wally were still sleeping; I could hear Wally snoring like an asthmatic spaniel. Miraculously, though, she had put my suitcase on the couch, and on top of that an envelope with the key to my new apartment and instructions for finding it.

I washed my face, changed into jeans and a t-shirt, brought the suitcase down to my car, then drove the four blocks to the corner of Dolores and 28th Street. The fog was starting to lift. I admired the pastel houses shouldering in along the sidewalks. It was quiet enough for me to hear the rumble of a trolley on Church Street.

I paused uncertainly in front of my new home, a modest, two-story green clapboard house with a steeply-pitched roof. There were two front doors and three doorbells, not one of them with a name. I'd just have to guess which apartment. I pressed the lower bell.

A skinny, scruffy man cracked open the door on the left and slithered outside, blinking like a mole in the bright light. The man's nose twitched beneath his crooked glasses, which were held together with a piece of fine wire wrapped around the left eyepiece. Behind him I glimpsed computer monitors, circuit boards, and tiny metal drawers stacked on racks around the dim living room.

"Hi!" I said brightly. "I'm Jordan, the new tenant." I sounded like an Avon Lady. "Is this Louise's place?"

The man grunted and managed to look as though he were viewing me from a great distance, even though we were only inches apart. "Upstairs," he said, pointing to the top bell.

"Oh. Well. See you around, then."

My new neighbor folded his arms, considering this proposition. Then his voice rumbled forth from somewhere deep within his body. "I don't work the usual hours," he informed me, and retreated behind his door again.

I rang the top bell. Karin had warned me that Louise, who worked from home translating hospital brochures into various languages, was the oddest person in San Francisco. This man could give her some competition. Still, I was grateful to Karin for having found an apartment I could sublet for the summer.

Louise answered the buzzer, her voice a series of squeaks on the intercom. "State your business and make it snappy."

I spoke with my mouth close to the speaker, feeling ridiculous as a group of chattering teenagers bobbed past on the sidewalk. "It's me, Jordan O'Malley. Your new tenant. I brought you a rent check."

"Oh, I know all about you," Louise assured me. "No need to come upstairs. Just slide the check into the mail slot. You have the key, don't you?"

"Yes, but don't you want to meet me?"

"Not necessary. I've only ever rented that apartment to wonderful tenants. You'll be no exception. Your door is around to the right. No kids, no pets, and no noise after midnight. Enjoy!"

I slid the rent check through the mail slot, feeling rejected, and opened the side door of the house with my key. The studio inside wasn't much larger than the living room of the condominium I'd shared with Peter. A counter divided the galley kitchen from the main living space, which was furnished with a bed, a bookshelf and a desk, all natural pine. The bathroom was so narrow that I could touch the opposite walls without straightening my arms.

The walls of the apartment were painted a pale salmon with cream trim; someone had stenciled a grape vine onto the wall behind the bed, adding bunches of green grapes to the vine. The vine extended onto the ceiling, too. I liked the effect, which was that of being outside even when enclosed in this small space.

And the garden, as Karin had promised, added another dimension. I opened the French doors and stepped into a garden lush with fleshy jade plants and herbs. Bougainvillea snaked up the walls separating my garden from the yards around it, the scarlet blossoms fluttering like hummingbirds in the sun.

"I can live here," I announced.

I spent the rest of the afternoon unpacking the boxes I'd kept locked in my car since my arrival, the French doors thrown open until afternoon, when the fog rolled back into the city. In San Francisco, fog didn't appear as wispy strands, the way it did in Massachusetts, but was tossed into my garden in thick, soggy pillows that soon made it impossible for me to see the bougainvillea. I made a bowl of instant oatmeal and tried Cam's cell again before falling onto the bed and napping in my sweaty clothes.

When I woke, I studied the path of light from the bathroom window, wondering again why my brother wasn't answering any of my messages. Maybe he'd lost his cell phone, but that didn't explain why he hadn't even checked in with our parents. How could Cam have disappeared so completely?

The light filtering into my apartment reminded me of being underwater, and of the time Cam saved me from drowning. It was the summer after my freshman year of high school. I had invited my boyfriend, Dominick, to meet me at the town lake, beneath the water ski jump. I asked him on the telephone, calling after breakfast on a Saturday morning in July while my mother was safely out of earshot, since she was so bent on ridding me of Dominick that she had once shooed the boy off our back steps with a broom.

"He's just white trash," my mother told me. "And you're not."

Of course, one woman's trash is another woman's obsession. I was still a nice kid at fifteen, a polite, Catholic schoolgirl who paid attention in class and never mouthed off to the teachers. However, my adolescent aim was to ruin any possibility that I might end up like Mom, a woman who relished every opportunity to operate a Dust Buster, even whisking sandwich crumbs off the table before you'd finished lunch. I was sure that Dominick, with his black buzz cut and cigarettes and hand-carved ink tattoos, could show me the way.

Dominick introduced himself by grabbing my butt beneath my plaid school uniform as I walked by his desk in algebra class to sharpen a pencil. In response, I clocked him with the full force of my open hand against his skinny neck, knocking him sideways onto the floor, desk and all. But Dominick only laughed. That's what got me: there he was, lying on the floor with his long body still trapped in his desk, and the guy guffawed like he'd just won the pot at a church Bingo game.

We were inseparable after that. Dominick sat next to me in the cafeteria that day, waving away my only two friends in school—Karin had already defected to the public high school—and took charge of my life. When Dominick banished my friends from our usual table, the girls waited for me to signal them to sit anyway, but I didn't. The girls moved away, whispering like my mother and her friends did during Mass, hands hiding mouths pure of lipstick, smug with the self-righteous satisfaction of women whose behavior is above reproach.

Within a month, Dominick taught me everything my parents had warned me about, and I went wild for the first and only time in my life. I rolled my skirts high above my knees and smoked dope even at school. I drank a great deal, too, sneaking down to the town common at night to meet Dominick and his friends, where we swilled beer until the only cop in town chased us away.

Best of all, Dominick took me snowmobiling that winter. My mother referred to snowmobilers as "Hell's Angels on runners," but I was enthralled by the face-numbing speed of those machines. My favorite snowmobile run was through the State conservation land, up a series of steep hills and across a frozen river. I wore a snowmobile suit that Dominick gave me to slip on over my clothes. Sometimes we stopped and switched off the engine in the middle of the woods.

Alone at last, we'd unzip our suits and warm our hands, giggling and gasping, on whatever flesh we could grope through the layers of clothing. Sometimes Dominick lay on his back in the snow, a dark angel in his blue snowmobile suit, while I pulled the zipper down and took his penis in my mouth. It felt like a rubber hose and scared me with its angry purple snout. Gradually, though, I became fond of Dominick's cock, thinking of it as my very own sweet, secret pet. By that summer I was ready, I thought, to go all the way, to prove my love to this boy who had expressed his claim over me with a metal ID bracelet heavy as a bike chain.

I told Dominick to meet me at the water ski jump. I didn't tell him that I had decided to give myself to him under water, under the ski jump, in a place where I imagined no one would see us, and in a way that would allow his sperm to be washed out of me like a school of tiny white minnows.

Unfortunately, I couldn't have declared my love for Dominick even if he had shown up to meet me. I came up for air in the wrong place under the water ski jump and whacked my head on one of the wooden supports. Luckily, Cam saw me swim beyond the lifeguard's rope and followed out of curiosity. When he saw me floating face-down in the water, Cam pulled me onto one of the support beams in the dark watery cavern beneath the jump, wrapped his arm around my shoulders and pressed his skinny, smooth, eleven-year-old body against mine to ease my shivering.

"Come on," he said. "You've got to swim back."

"No. You go without me. I've got to wait here. Go!" I was crying. My head hurt and my teeth were chattering.

"Wait for what?" Cam looked confused.

"Dominick's meeting me." Even then, with a lump the size of an egg on my forehead, I planned to give myself to love.

Cam sighed. "He's not coming, you know."

"What? You don't know that!"

"Yes, I do," my brother answered calmly. "I saw Dominick." He hesitated before adding, "With Cathy Prefontaine. They were making out on the town common this morning."

I hated Cam at that instant. "You're lying!" I yelled, though I knew he wasn't. "Go away and leave me alone!"

"I can't leave you," Cam said calmly. "You might drown and Mom would kill me. I'll stay here until you swim back to shore."

I saw that Cam meant what he said. I also saw, in the sharp rise of his collarbones and in the angle of his chin, the man lurking within his boy's skin.

It was the man within my brother who talked me into going back under water. Even though I cried and said I couldn't hold my breath and swim beneath the water ski jump again, for fear of coming up wrong, I knew that with Cam I'd be all right. So I let my brother lead me, holding his hand until we surfaced where the water was suddenly filled with light that grew like thick yellow tree trunks from the floor of the lake to its dappled green surface.

Even here, lying on my bed in San Francisco, I could still conjure up clear memories of plotting that swim, of how it had felt to move sensuously beneath a membrane pricked with rain, and of later coming to consciousness in that dark space with its eerie shadows, coughing on the stink of boat fuel as I opened my eyes and saw Cam's anxious frown. "Just breathe," were his first words when I came to. "Just keep breathing. You'll be okay."

I had silently repeated Cam's words during the biopsy for breast cancer, just before they gave me a light anesthetic and took out the core of tissue to send to the lab. I had also repeated them again, over and over—"just breathe, just breathe, just breathe"—while I showered on the morning before my lumpectomy, feeling my breast whole for the last time and imagining what might be there afterward, the dent, the scar the surgeon might leave as a reminder that all is not necessarily well, no matter how orderly and calm your life might seem.

Now, I repeated those words in my new apartment, trying to motivate myself to get out of bed, shower, dress and go to the grocery store. "Just breathe," I whispered, but I couldn't get up off the bed. Not yet.

Instead, I lay there a few minutes more, remembering the last of my relationship with Dominick, the way I'd stalked him and Cathy on my bicycle for days until I discovered them holding hands in Dominick's dusty yard, inside the husk of a derelict car. I hit Cathy across the cheek, so that welts rose on her skin as pink as a lipstick kiss. That was the end. And that was why I'd always associated falling in love with drowning, with losing all sense of perspective until you finally whack your head on something and come to your senses.

I got up, walked across the room and parted the curtains. The sun was starting to set. In the dusky light, the flowers in my garden looked like smudged thumb prints against the fence. I should go grocery shopping, but Cam wasn't here to hold my hand, to make me breathe, to lead me out into the sun. I didn't have the courage to go outside alone. I decided to have another bowl of instant oatmeal and go to bed.

It took me a week to settle into the apartment. I spent the time exploring San Francisco, usually meeting Karin for drinks after her shift at the hospital. I went to the movies, too, once alone and once with Ed. Ed held my hand and kissed me, but didn't ask me back to his apartment, much to my relief; I found his kisses too calculated, too deliberate, but didn't know why. It didn't matter. I had bigger worries now: my brother still wasn't returning my messages.

"Why do you think Cam isn't calling me back?" I asked Karin at the end of that first week, over pizza in a North Beach restaurant with low ceilings and huge bunches of shiny black plastic grapes dangling ominously low over our heads, like bats. "Why can't Cam just call or text me like a normal person?"

Karin laughed. "Jordan, I hate to break this to you, but lots of people go for months at a time without calling their sisters. I'm sure Cam's fine."

"I don't know." I took another piece of pizza. "Wouldn't you think it was weird if one of your brothers just dropped off the face of the planet?"

"Oh, I don't know. People get busy."

"Maybe that's the problem," I said. "I'm not busy enough. I don't even feel like me anymore. It's like I'm in another woman's body, going through the motions, pouring cereal for breakfast while my mind careens out of control. I thought I was taking charge of my destiny by leaving Peter, but I don't know what the point of my life is anymore."

"Nobody's in control of destiny!" Karin snapped. "Cancer, brain tumor, car accident, terrorist attack: you get what you get, and it isn't always up to you. Whether your life means anything or not in the end is entirely subjective anyway."

I shook my head. "I don't know, Karin. Other women have husbands, kids, even divorces at my age. I know you don't think we're old enough to be grownups. But sometimes I wish I'd stuck it out long enough with Peter to at least get a child out of the relationship." I twisted my napkin. "On the other hand, having cancer scared me into thinking I shouldn't have kids, in case I'm not around long enough to drive them to preschool."

Karin shook her head, dark curls gleaming red in the candlelight. "Will you please stop? You don't have cancer! Not anymore, okay? Hell, I have as much of a potshot at the cancer lottery as you do. Everybody does. The one thing nursing has taught me is that there's always a rock with your name on it, but no guarantee you'll see it whizzing towards your forehead. And if you'd stayed with Peter and had a child, then what? Kids don't solve a thing! In fact, for women the two biggest predictors for poverty are kids and divorce."

Glumly, I stared at the tidy row of uneaten pizza crusts on my plate. At least if Peter were here, he would have eaten those crusts. "Don't you ever think about getting married or having kids?"

"Whenever I do, I put a cold cloth across my forehead and lie down until the thought goes away." Karin raised her wine glass and touched it to mine. "Here's to your new freedom, Jordan. Enjoy it while you can."

Two days later, I woke early and vowed to make it to the laundromat before my jeans stalked out of the apartment without me. I gathered my things and stepped onto the brick walk outside, then wavered. I should really meet the landlord. I didn't like being this anonymous.

I walked around to the front of the house and leaned on Louise's intercom bell. My only witness was a woman walking her dog, a black Scottie.

When I turned to smile at her, I realized that the woman's flannel trousers were covered in tiny black Scotties. Her socks were, too.

"State your business," Louise said, "and make it snappy."

"It's Jordan, your new tenant. Look, sorry to bother you, but I just wanted to come up and say hello."

There was an audible sigh through the metallic speaker, and then the door buzzed. I opened it, deposited the laundry bags in the hall, and climbed the stairs.

Louise shouted, "Open, Sesame!" when I knocked. Inside, I was greeted by the stench of cigarette smoke. The room was so dimly lit that the furniture appeared as hulking animals. A four-legged table and two chairs had been herded into the middle of the room, where a vacuum cleaner stood guard with its hose snaked around the furniture legs. A brilliant red cloak hung on one chair and a romance novel with a lurid cover lay on the table.

"Pay no mind to my hell hole of a kitchen, Hon. Just pick your way through the mess and pray you don't break a leg." Louise's accent was Southern. I followed her voice into the next room, expecting to find a seductive blonde in a filmy black gown, lounging on the couch with a pearl-tipped cigarette holder until the arrival of her next gentleman caller.

I was partly right. Louise's hair was cheesecake yellow and she was dressed in a black rayon gown clasped shut at the neck by a cameo brooch. However, my landlady was no ordinary seductress. Louise lounged, one thick arm spread along the back of the couch, with the sleepy gaze and beefy torso of a Roman emperor reclining after a post-battle feast.

"Hello, Jordan-My-New-Tenant," she said. "Need something? Or just couldn't stand the suspense of not meeting me?"

"I'm fine, thanks. I just wanted to say hello."

She fluttered a hand in my direction. "And now you have."

So much for that myth about pathologically friendly Californians. "It's a nice apartment. I'm really glad you let me sublet it."

"I actually thought that nice nurse friend of yours was going to rent it," Louise said. "It was the old bait-and-switch, as far as I was concerned. I was hoodwinked."

"Oh! Sorry," I fumbled.

"No worries. You're only here for three months. How much can you trash the place?"

"I promise I won't do that," I said, taken aback.

My landlady waved an arm, flesh rippling inside her gauzy sleeves. "That's fine, then. So long as we understand each other. You have a nice day, now, doing whatever you need to do."

I shook my head as I went downstairs, feeling dismissed and irritable. I had left my cell phone on top of the laundry bags; now I saw that the message light was blinking.

I had two messages. The first was from my mother, anxious about my whereabouts despite the fact that I had called her just a few days ago. The second message, amazingly, was from my brother.

"Hey!" Cam's voice blared. "Super sorry it's taken so long to connect. Let's do Ocean Beach, all right? Come to our Lie-In! That's L-i-e, as in lie down." He snorted. "Sounds weird, but what doesn't? Anyway, we're going way early, like 10 o'clock tomorrow morning? Ocean Beach, okay? Be there, or be square."

I grinned and played the message again, relieved that my brother had surfaced at last.

Chapter four

The next morning, I drove through Golden Gate Park, smelling the heady scents of eucalyptus and pine. Ocean Beach was completely fogged in. I heard the water long before I saw it, tall green humps feathered in white as the beast breathed along the shore. The beach was empty except for a few dozen shapes lying on the sand. I thought they were seals at first. Once I'd parked the car and started walking towards them, though, I realized that the shapes were people.

I walked fast. The sensation was a strange one, walking with the fog hovering all around, the unseen waves grumbling along the shore. The water shone every now and then, glinting like glass whenever an occasional needle of sunlight pierced the fog. I was acutely conscious of the patterns in the sand beneath my feet, where circular ridges rose like tiny mountain peaks, as though I were flying above the earth.

One of the bulky shapes on the sand turned out to be Cam. Wrapped in a blanket from head to foot, he lay on his side facing the water. He had dug a depression in the sand so that he was cocooned there, nested. My brother's eyes were closed and he looked just as he had when I last saw him, two years ago at Christmas. He still wore a mustache and the scraggly whisk broom of a beard that made him look like an Amish farmer. His skin gleamed bright pink between the whiskers. He looked so young! But he wasn't. Almost thirty by now, I reminded myself. Practically middle-aged, like me.

I nudged his backside with the toe of my sneaker. "Hey. Wake up, Sleeping Beauty."

Cameron stretched, but didn't bother to stand. He squinted at me, his blue eyes bright, and flashed a crooked grin. "Hey yourself. Join me."

"Doing what?"

"Lying down."

"Doesn't sound like much fun." I hovered over him, uncertain. Now that Cam was actually there in front of me, I realized how little I knew about how his life had gone for the past two years.

"Uh, Jordan? The fog's breaking up and you're blocking my rays."

"Sun's bad for you."

"Don't believe everything you read. Here." He nodded towards his backpack. "Look in there. I brought you a blanket so you can try this."

"Try what?"

"Dig a sand bed. Make yourself a little sand pillow, wrap yourself in the blanket and lie down. Give yourself over to the rhythms of the planet. You'll love it."

"The rhythms of the planet?" I repeated. My brother really had been in California too long. "Oh, come on. Get up!" I nudged him again, harder. "Let's go for coffee."

The shapes around us stirred. Cam shushed me. "Later! Lie down. You're disturbing the moment."

"Forget it. I didn't travel 3,000 miles to take a nap with you. I want to talk. You've been a real jerk, not calling. We've all been worried sick." I bent down and tugged at his blanket.

Cam caught my wrist. "You didn't come to San Francisco just for me. And it's been two years. What's another few minutes?"

We glared at each other. My brother's hand around my wrist reminded me of how Cam used to challenge me to an arm wrestling match almost daily when he was in seventh grade and I was in tenth. He didn't beat me until three years later; he kept trying until he succeeded.

"You've made your point," I said now.

Cam let go. "Fine. Don't lie down. Don't relax. Don't do anything!" His voice drifted and he closed his eyes again. "But let me do my thing."

I couldn't very well lift him up and carry him off the beach. "Oh, all right," I grumbled. "As long as we can talk later."

That grin again, and then my brother's face went still, all expression extinguished.

I tugged the extra blanket out of the backpack and followed Cam's instructions. It was surprisingly comfortable. I soon fell asleep, lulled by the sound of the ocean and the warmth of the sun and sand.

I woke to the smell of baking bread. Only it wasn't bread I smelled; it was me. The sand, my cotton blanket, the sweat trickling down between my breasts: the smells were a combination of sweet, musky, and yeasty. The fog had lifted and the sun-drenched beach was so noisy now with surfers and families, joggers and dogs, that I could scarcely hear the waves. I sat up, shook my hair free of sand and looked around. Cam was still asleep.

I studied his peaceful silhouette. Who, after all this time, had my brother become? My firsthand knowledge of him stopped, really, after Cam's senior year of college, when he had invited friends to our house for a blow-out college weekend party that had included a live band.

Cam's girlfriend at the time had appeared in an outfit she'd made herself by drilling holes into nickels and stringing them together. She writhed and shimmered to the music like a shiny fish just pulled from the lake.

Dad had whistled appreciatively at the sight of her. "That little girl's the one damn thing Cameron has ever done right in his piss poor life," he said, and my mother ran out of the house at that point to ply the girl with coffee.

Later that night, there was an argument in the garage. Cam, drunk as I'd ever seen him, struck my father, clipped him hard enough on the jaw to send Dad reeling backwards into the neat row of rakes, shovels, and push brooms hanging along the far wall. It wasn't the first time that Cam, cornered, had lashed out at Dad. Nothing extraordinary, other than the fact that this particular time it was Cam who was drunk, not our father, who had finally sobered up five years before that.

The event had stayed with me as some sort of turning point. After that night, Cam really "managed to drop off the family radar screen," as he put it the next Christmas. My brother dropped out of college during the last semester of his senior year without explanation. After that, he stumbled through odd jobs whenever he wasn't traveling. His few postcards to me were limited to quotes from philosophers, literary figures, and musicians, conveying little about his life other than geographical locations: Wyoming, Oregon, India, Thailand, Bali, and, finally, California. The last post card he'd sent was postmarked on my birthday and showed San Francisco's sky-line at night, with the Trans Am building lit up like that Egyptian hotel in Las Vegas.

"Yo!" Another sand cocoon sat up suddenly and faced me over Cam's inert body, studying my face closely. "Jordan?"

"Yes."

"You look just like your brother. And I mean that strictly as a compli-ment. Cam's one of the beautiful people."

"Are you one of his roommates?"

"I own the house." The man nodded, his arms still wrapped in his blan-ket. "I'm Shepherd Jon."

I laughed. "And these would be what, your sheep?" I gestured around the beach, where I counted three other blanketed cocoons besides Cam's.

Jon gave me a tolerant look. "Housemates of like mind and spirit. I rent out rooms to a chosen few. The house used to belong to my parents, but now it's mine."

Something about this man made the hairs on the back of my neck prickle. He was being civil. Even friendly. Yet, I didn't trust him. "This lie-in was your idea?" I asked.

"Sure." Shepherd Jon grinned. "And not a bad one, was it? You looked like you weren't hurting any. Snoring away."

I was snoring? Well. So very gallant of the good Shepherd to tell me. The man might as well have pointed out the drool on my chin, too, which I now hastily wiped away with one hand.

"I needed a nap. Jet lag." My voice sounded cranky. Elderly.

"It's the negative ions in the air that does it."

"Does what?"

Jon shrugged. "Whatever you need." He stood up, dropping the blan-ket in a heap on the sand.

Jon began walking around the beach, tapping the others on their shoulders. He had a swimmer's build and a rock star's swagger. His blonde hair was caught at the nape with a piece of rawhide and snaked over one shoulder in a thick ponytail. He wore ordinary clothes—a gray t-shirt and blue jeans—but, on him, the clothes looked alive, electric as an animal's fur coat. His eyes were the same green as the glassy sea.

Shepherd Jon was in his early thirties, judging from the lines on his face, but he was so tightly wound, bouncing on the balls of his feet as he walked across the sand, that he appeared much younger. Must be all those negative ions. Either that, or no mortgage. He was free and clear. Probably scrounged a good living from boarding his flock of sheep, including my brother.

"Coming?" Jon touched Cam's shoulder, but he was looking at me.

Cam sat up and let the blanket fall to his waist. "Absolutely."

"Where to?" I stood up and shook out my blanket.

Cam scrambled to his feet and looked at Shepherd Jon. "We really gonna make this thing happen, Bro, or what?"

"You bet your ass." Shepherd Jon grinned and unzipped his jeans. Within seconds, he was undressed and so was Cam. The two women did the same, as did the fifth member of the Lie-In party, a chubby man.

Now I was surrounded by naked, shivering people. I kept my eyes averted from my brother, who I hadn't seen naked since we bathed together as children. Jon did a few stretches, standing on one leg like a heron, still watching me. Probably waiting for a reaction. He was like that kid in my fourth grade class last year who liked to set fire to trash cans: any attention was better than none.

"Coming for a swim?" Jon challenged me.

I laughed. "Are you nuts? That water's about 50 degrees!"

"You don't know what you're missing."

"Oh, I think I do. Cam and I used to go swimming in Maine."

I was having trouble not looking at his penis, which sprouted like a dark mushroom from a tangle of hay-colored pubic hair. Then again, I didn't know where else to look, since the five nude lunatics on the beach around me were whooping and spinning like tops, arms outstretched, while the Sunday family strollers and picnickers scattered away from us like seagulls.

Where were the cops? Who was going to order these people to put their clothes back on? But no, this was San Francisco. The human whirligigs sailed themselves into the water with shrieks of pain as a few teenaged surfers, sensibly enveloped in wet suits, paused with their boards to watch, yelling, "All right, oldsters! Go for it!"

The sheep didn't last long in the water. I barely had time to shake out Cam's blanket and fold it. The women came out first, bellies jiggling, nipples blue with cold, hair as slick as seal skin. They rubbed themselves with towels, ignoring the cheering surfers, and didn't speak to me. Their teeth were chattering too hard.

Jon, Cam, and the third man came out together, holding hands and shouting, doing a sort of high-stepping jig over waves that threatened to catapult them back under water. Jon and Cam were streamlined, all stringy muscles along their tanned arms and legs. The plumper man plodded between them. They dressed hurriedly, their balls as shriveled as dried figs, their penises as tiny as crunchy cocktail pickles.

I drove Cam to his house in Berkeley, following Shepherd Jon's battered orange van. "Is that your van?" I asked. "I don't remember it being that vegetable color."

"Nah. That's Jon's. Mine blew up in the desert on the way to Baja. It was good 'til then. I made many a fine meal of radiator rice and had zero problemas fitting in the hitchers. I had, like, fifteen people in that baby when it blew. We got busted by the Mexican policia, though, and it wasn't pretty. That's why I wasn't around when you first called me." He shuddered slightly. "Cost us everything to cut loose from those bastards."

This was the most I'd heard my brother speak since seeing him, or maybe ever, I thought, slowing for a stoplight. Cam was always quiet, even as a young child.

The only time I ever saw him speak freely was to Grammy, my mother's mother, after she had her stroke and came to live with us. She was eighty by then, a woman built like a fireplug with a pale yellow mustache. Dad called her hillside mobile home "that Tinderbox on wheels," but it had been a childhood paradise for my brother and me. During one of our visits, for instance, Grammy offered us jewelry boxes full of crispy locust shells. She helped us spray paint them silver and stick them to the curtains, saying, "There, now doesn't that add a bit of sparkle to the room?"

By the time she came to live with us, Grammy's cataracts were bad, her hearing was shot, and she was paralyzed on one side. She had trouble making herself understood, chewing through her words. I was shy around her, afraid to look into those rheumy eyes, but Cam spent entire afternoons curled up beside Grammy on the couch. While our grandmother huddled in a nest of quilts, Cam kept up a stream of chatter, explaining his television shows or video games to her.

"How can you stand to talk to her so much?" I asked Cam once, as we both said good night to our grandmother and climbed the stairs to bed. "I never understand a word she says. And she can't even see the TV, you know."

My little brother gave me a look that stopped me cold. "I do it because once Grammy told me she feels like she's sitting alone in a dark tunnel," he said. "I don't want her to be afraid."

Cam's reticence had been his best defense against our father, I thought now, glancing at my brother's profile as we approached the Bay Bridge. Dad began drinking off and on early in his twenties. My mother had once told me that he even drank in the waiting area when she went to the hospital to deliver Cam. By the time the nurses told my father he had a new son, he'd already passed out on a plastic chair. When he came to, he tried to belt one of the doctors, rushed past the orderly who tried to restrain him, and fell to his knees beside Mom's hospital bed, weeping.

"He called me his Madonna," Mom sighed, telling me this story. "It was difficult to stay angry with your father, because he was always so sorry for the things he did."

Dad's drinking escalated slowly. I mostly remembered him being like the other fathers in our neighborhood who came home and had a couple of highballs. His real drunken, raging fits didn't begin until I was in high school, after Dad was laid off from the lumber sales job he'd held for fifteen years.

I remembered one of those early rants clearly: I was a sophomore in high school, talking to Karin on the phone one Saturday when Dad told me to hang up. Typically, my father would have called me more than once; I counted on those warnings, eking out every moment of phone time. But this time Dad stormed into the kitchen, his face scarlet, the veins on his neck bulging.

"It'll never be `wait a minute' again. Not from you, Missy!" he bellowed, and slapped me so hard across the face that I dropped the telephone receiver and fell to the floor, my knees buckling beneath me like a doll's.

My mother and Cam ran into the kitchen, Cam with his hands balled into fists. I was sixteen, so my brother must have been thirteen then. Mom knelt down and held me in her arms until she realized that I refused to cry. Then, as if on cue, we both stood up, brushed ourselves off and walked into the dining room with Cam silently dogging our heels, turning our backs on the volcano behind us.

Lucky for me, my mother had taught me how to mostly dodge or sweet talk my father, how to be all smiles and tiptoes whenever the man was in a mood. That was the only time my father ever struck me.

Cam, though, had it much worse. His adolescence coincided with the peak of Dad's melancholy drinking, and he spent his teen years ducking my father's noisy, sloppy moments of affection as fervently as he dodged the blows when Dad started careening towards him, shouting at Cam to cut his hair or bring up his grades. Dad didn't sober up completely until Cam left home for college. Cam had never been able to forgive him.

We'd come to the end of the Bay Bridge. "So, do you have a job?" I asked.

Cam laughed. "You sound like Dad. Sure I have a job. Not a career. Just a job that lets me come and go."

"A job doing what?"

"I'm a falafel man."

"Well, thank goodness your college classes prepared you for something."

"College taught me that I wanted to avoid the ol' nine-to-five ball and chain. What about you? Still wiping snotty noses for a living?"

"Funny. Fourth graders wipe their own noses, thank you very much. It's one of the first things we teach them."

"Suppose somebody has to."

I thought back, trying to remember what Cam might have been like in fourth grade, but failing. "It's really good to see you. I'm sorry we've been so out of touch."

Cam was leaning against the seat, his eyes closed, occasionally reaching up to scratch his scalp. His damp hair hung to his shoulders, and every time he scratched his head, another handful of sand tumbled onto his shirt. He wore a tattered flannel shirt over sweat pants cut into a pair of shorts. Blue plastic thongs dangled from his bony feet. It occurred to me for the first time that Cam might be broke. He might really need Jon, not just to tell him what to do, but to help keep a roof over his head. How much money could a falafel man make?

Now Cam tugged his beard. "Huh. I always thought we still were in touch." He caught my look of disbelief and grinned. "Missed me, huh? Well, now you've got to kiss me." He leaned over and gave me a wet, salty smack on the cheek. "There. Feel closer now?"

I smiled. "Remember that time you came to live with me in college?"

"Sure." Cam rearranged his long legs and whacked his knee against the dashboard. He rubbed it. "Ow! Fucking piece of shit Japanese cars! Made for midgets. Yeah, you were living with that weird girl with the Cleopatra hair. She was a wildcat in bed, man."

"What?" I was so shocked that my voice came out as a squeak. "You went to bed with Debra Shriner?"

"Hey, watch the road! Yeah, sure I did. Well, to be exact, she went to bed with me."

I tried to think back. How could it have happened? The year Cam visited, I was a junior in college and he was threatening to drop out of high school. My parents were, as my father so diplomatically put it, "at the end of our tether with this damn kid."

During Cam's spring vacation, my parents sent him to me. He had been skipping classes and my mother had caught him smoking dope in the garage. She had searched the house and found baggies of grass everywhere, she told me, weeping into the phone.

"He must think we're too stupid to notice our son's an addict," my mother said. "Talk to him, Jordy. You're the only one he's ever listened to."

So they put Cam on a bus to Amherst and I collected him at the station. My brother looked like every other stoned kid wandering around the University in a hoodie and sagging jeans. I didn't want to set him loose on campus, not knowing what he might get himself into, so I drove Cam straight to my apartment and parked him there under the eagle eye of my roommate, Debra, while I went to classes.

The apartment was cheaper than living in a dorm, but there was a reason for that: the only source of warmth was a cranky space heater in the living room. Karin was doing a semester in Ireland and my other room-mate, Debra, was someone neither of us knew very well; she had answered an ad. Her biggest vice was singing, which Debra did every afternoon with her headphones on, weaving her head like a cobra's as she sat cross-legged in front of the gas stove.

"Well, was Debra nice to you, at least?" I asked Cam now, keeping an eye on Shepherd Jon's van as we wound our way up through the Berkeley hills.

"Sure. For a horny sixteen-year-old boy, it was a heavenly fate."

I shuddered and tried to put the image of Debra devouring my skinny, stoned brother out of my head. "Is this your street? I lost Shepherd Jon."

"Yeah. Keep going straight to the top of the hill. On the left, that blue turd with the dog shit brown trim. Can you believe that color combo? Jon's parents were definitely color challenged."

"So that was it with Debra? That once?"

"Hell no! I must have screwed Debra Shriney Hiney a million times that one week. Sure got me off drugs in a hurry. Now I had a new addiction, and it was way more fun."

True enough. Cam did ease up on the dope after that. He aced his SAT's and was accepted into one of the small independent colleges in Maine.

"And all this time I thought I was the one who turned you around, when it was really Debra the Predator," I teased. "But that still doesn't explain why you crashed and burned your senior year of college." I glanced at him. "I never really understood what happened, you know. One minute, you were Dean's List. And then Dad was tearing up your tuition check and burning it with the trash. What happened?"

Cam drummed his long fingers on the dash. "I figured out that college is a fine fucking fantasy life, but has no bearing on reality."

"That's absolute crap," I snapped. "You wouldn't be frying falafel if you'd only put in three more measly months. You had a 3.8 grade point average! You could have coasted right on up to the podium to get your degree."

"Maybe it was more important for me to piss Dad off than graduate," Cam said mildly.

"But why, when it cost you everything?"

Cam picked at something on his flip flop. "Jesus, take a chill pill, Jordy. What did it cost you, what I did? You chose the high road, I chose the low. You've got your little life, your little job and your steady paycheck. Meanwhile, all I have to worry about is nothing but me, myself, and I."

We were in Jon's driveway now. I bit my lip to keep from lashing out. So Cam wasn't ambitious. So what? Everyone knew too much ambition caused heart attacks.

The neighborhood smelled of that cocoa-scented mulch that everyone in Berkeley scattered in their gardens to control the weeds. At least Cam was living in a decent area; this was a suburban neighborhood of professors' homes and swing sets. A group of men whizzed past on bicycles, hunched low over the handlebars and wearing goggles that made them look like insects.

Across the street, a scrawny blonde teenager toted a baby in a backpack, striding purposefully to the corner until she saw our car and stopped to stare. Cam was already walking towards the house, so his back was to her, but I smiled at the girl and waved. She didn't wave back.

Shepherd Jon's house was a Victorian, all turrets and porches and odd round windows. It had fanciful gingerbread trim beneath the eaves and the porches sagged.

"Quite the Gothic abode," I commented, following Cam up the walk. The door gaped open. Shepherd Jon and the others were already inside; I could smell coffee.

"Cool, huh?" Cam said. "And cheap."

I brushed the sand off my jeans before stepping through the front door. Not that it mattered. There was so much sand in the front hall, it looked like someone had deliberately laid a gritty path to the kitchen. Cam ran his hands through his hair. Now that it was dry, it was the same color as mine, with the same wiry, wavy texture. I'd lost my hair band somewhere on the beach, so both of us had tangled tan manes.

A chipped mirror hung in the front hall. In its reflection, Cam and I looked like a pair of shaggy lions. Our eyes were the same bright blue in our narrow faces.

I followed Cam to the kitchen at the back of the house. The floor was black and white checked linoleum, the walls lime green, the trim pomegranate red. Oven mitts shaped like stars hung from hooks near the stove; the salt and pepper shakers were bunches of bananas danging from tropical glass trees. It was like the illustration of a kitchen in a children's book.

One of the women from the beach, a bloated looking blonde dressed in a colorful caftan, was seated at the kitchen table. Her hooked nose was accentuated by mirrored sunglasses that reflected the checkerboard floor.

Cam introduced us, using first names only: "Valerie, Jordan. What's up, Val?"

"It's the flesh, the flesh!" Val moaned, nodding in the direction of the stove, where Shepherd Jon was frying bacon. "I can't bear the flesh."

"Val's a vegan," Cam explained, handing me a cup of coffee that smelled like burning tires. "Won't touch meat, eggs, or anything else that comes from the exploitation of animals." There was a note of admiration in his voice.

"Vegan Val? Really?" I lifted my chin in the direction of the other woman's leather belt and shoes.

Cam gave me a look that said, *Don't start.*

"I love your necklace," Val breathed, tipping her head like a bird, so that the reflected floor in her glasses shifted. "What are those black stones?"

I lifted the beads between my fingers and bent down to show them to her. "Hematite."

She nodded. "That's good for grounding."

I had to assume that she wasn't talking about lightning storms. "It used to be my grandmother's." I smiled, imagining what Grammy would have to say about this crew. Grammy had survived on beef jerky, beer, canned hash, and television in her metal trailer for seven decades.

Cam led me through the kitchen, ignoring the chaos. Jon had several things going on the stove. The dark-haired woman from the beach had thrown on a sarong and faded t-shirt; she was pulling plates from the cupboard while the chubby man slipped a coffee cake into the oven. They must have prepared most of the food before going to the beach; it was like being in a restaurant kitchen, frenetic yet carefully orchestrated activity. These people must have been living and cooking together for a while.

"Can I help out?" I asked.

Cam waved a hand. "Nah. We're better off out of the way. They know I'd just burn the house down."

As we continued through the kitchen's back door and into a steamy attached greenhouse, I bristled at my brother's refusal to take responsibility for even the most mundane aspects of his own existence. So typical!

"Good thing you have slaves for roommates," I said, "since you're so helpless."

"Fuck you." Cam's voice was mild. "You don't know jack shit about my domestic arrangements." He settled himself in a wooden rocking chair in the greenhouse. The chair was stenciled with moons and stars. "I've got KP duty. Shepherd Jon doesn't let anybody off the hook."

I pulled up a matching chair next to his. "And he makes the rules?"

"It's his house."

"But you pay rent, right?"

"A token." Cam stretched out his long legs and meditated on the steam rising from his coffee. "Without him, I'd probably be living in People's Park. So, how are things with you? I take it you wised up and never married that petty bureaucrat with the great hair?"

"No, I took a lesson from you and ran like hell," I joked, then hesitated, wondering just how much to tell Cam about Peter and me, or about what I'd been through.

I hadn't told Cam anything at all about the breast cancer. I had started several letters, but gave up. My explanations sounded too self-pitying, even when I tried joking about the Barbie doll wigs I planned to buy if I had to go the chemo route, or how I'd be sure the plastic surgeon took inches off my hips if I needed a hunk of flesh to replace a missing breast.

What could I possibly tell Cam that would sum up my current state of mind, when I wasn't even sure what it was anymore? That I was scared and lonely? That I could scarcely even look at my breasts in the mirror, because the scar reminded me that someone had sliced and diced my body, taking out a melon ball or two of flesh?

Sitting next to a brother who had become a stranger over the past two years, I realized that I couldn't say any of these things. My guard was up against both his pity and my own. I would have to wait and work up to that conversation gradually. I babbled instead about my teaching, the break-up with Peter, and friends we both knew back home, until at last Cam put a hand on my arm and forced me to take a breath.

"You did the right thing, leaving that guy," he said softly. "He wasn't worthy."

I sat up straighter in the chair, automatically ready to defend the man who had once been, mistakenly or not, the love of my life. "You hardly knew Peter!"

Cam shook his head. "I didn't have to. Remember the wet money?"

And I did, so suddenly it was as if Cam had suddenly opened a pair of drapes across a window: I saw Peter on a blustery summer day two years ago. Cam was visiting my mother, home from a trip to India, so Peter and I had driven to my parents' house from Boston to see him.

Cam and I borrowed a sailboat that weekend to take Peter out on the lake. Peter had dressed the part of "an old salt," as he put it, in a bright blue striped shirt and khaki shorts, new Topsiders and blue visor. He'd even bought new sunglasses with a braided plastic rope to hang them about his neck. But then we'd come about on the water and started scudding, and Peter had forgotten to duck beneath the mast. He was knocked clean off the boat and into the water, arms outspread and waving like a great blue heron flapping onto the water's surface.

Cam and I laughed, but Peter climbed back aboard with a grim, set mouth. Once we were back in my parents' house, he immediately asked my mother for the ironing board and iron. Peter changed his clothes, stuffed his wet things into the dryer and then stood in the kitchen to iron his money, bill after bill of it, until the green rectangles were smooth and dry and warm on the kitchen counters, laid end-to-end like an enormous chain of green chewing gum wrappers.

"Peter was a little compulsive," I admitted now. "But he kept me organized."

Cam rolled his eyes. "You need somebody to help you jump fences and whistle in the dark, Jojo, not keep you confined to your safe little sawdust cage," he said. We sipped our coffee in silence for a minute. Then Cam finally asked, "So what's with the 'rents? Is Mom still up to her eyeballs in handicrafts?"

"She's onto crocheting now."

"What, like afghans?"

"And hats. Lampshades. Toilet paper covers."

"You're shitting me."

"Nope. Cows, Santas, the Virgin Mary, fleecy lambs with pink tongues. They're amazing, really. You'd never guess there was a roll of toilet paper under them."

Cam cracked up, tipping his head back. "Amazing? Yeah, Jordy, that's one word for it. Jesus. And how about Dad? Still mowing down the roses?"

"He took a pretty good chunk out of the big lilac bush the day before I left."

We were both laughing hard by now. Dad had mowed the lawn every Saturday for thirty years, even on the weekend after his hernia operation. Four years ago, everyone in the family–even Cam, though minimally–had chipped in to buy him a riding mower for his fiftieth birthday. Our father had kept it buffed and shining: Dad's chariot, we called it. Unfortunately, the mower had more horsepower than our tiny yard could withstand. So far, Dad had flattened the knee-high boxwood hedge, Mom's flowerbeds, a neighbor boy's bike, and even the mailbox. It was like launching a speedboat in a duck pond.

"Can you believe our gene pool?" Cam shook his head. "There's Mom, vacuuming up sandwich crumbs around our lunch plates, always in her pearls, like June Cleaver on Speed. And then there's Dad in his recliner, soaking up Fox News. Christ, Jordan. Remember that time on the town common? Our perfect All-American Fourth of July picnic?"

I had just taken a sip of coffee. Now I laughed and snorted the coffee up my nose. I'd nearly forgotten about that. My father had become increasingly patriotic through the years, obsessed with war because he hadn't served in Vietnam. During that Fourth of July picnic, Dad spotted a trio of young men lounging on a blanket made of American flags. Without warning, he had risen from our family blanket and stormed the group, my mother shrieking after him to stop.

"Those guys scattered like pigeons, didn't they?" I gasped. "It was horrible. Dad was out of his mind."

"He always was a pissy drunk. Mean as a snake," Cam reflected.

"At least he eventually quit," I reminded him. "AA or not, that must have taken guts."

"Jesus, Jordy!" Cam shook his head. "Why do you always defend the guy? He was a bastard. Dad quit drinking only because his doctor said his liver was blowing up like a balloon. So what if he lost his job? Lots of people don't have jobs, and they don't take it out on their kids."

I flicked my brother's wrist with two fingers hard enough to sting. "You're never going to forgive Dad for being human, are you, Cam? Even if he's the guy who always found a way to keep food on the table and a roof over our heads? Even if he's the one who taught you how to ride a bike and throw a ball? He drank and he made mistakes. He wants to apologize to you for that, if you'd ever let him."

Cam snorted. "Oh, really?"

"Yes, really! He keeps telling me so. And maybe you don't want that, but Cam, if you hang onto this kind of anger, you'll die with it eating a hole in your heart."

Cam poked a finger into his own chest. "What's that you say? A hole in my heart? And here I thought it was from a bullet!" He grimaced, mimed writhing and dying, then said, "Sorry, but the old man's going to have to go to his grave without me making it easier for him to pass through the pearly gates. I've never been the saint in the family. That position was already filled when I was born." He pointed at me.

We finished our coffee in silence, then sat with Cam's roommates and ate eggs, potatoes, toast, bacon, and coffee cake in the greenhouse on a rickety picnic table painted white and stenciled with moons and stars. Whoever did the artwork around here had a thing for night skies. The stars were sloppy; they looked more like a child's hand prints. Vegan Val and the other woman, Melody, sat on either side of me, across from Jon, Cam, and Domingo, the third man. Val, of course, nibbled on a separate breakfast of fruit and nuts.

"You grew all of these orchids? They're amazing," I said to Shepherd Jon, staring at the plants hanging above us and stacked in clay pots on metal shelving. We were seated in a forest of flowers, the scent of so many orchids overpowering, cloying.

"My father started the collection. I've just kept it going," Jon answered. "He was a botany professor at Berkeley. Took I don't know how many trips to the Amazon. Even had a couple of flowers named after him. When he died a few years ago, I decided to keep things going as a tribute to him. I've been collecting orchids in Nepal, working with a conservation group there as a volunteer."

"Doing what?"

He shrugged. "Whatever. Last time I was there, I was mostly helping them train the customs officials to spot orchids being smuggled out of the country. There's one in particular, *Panch Aunlle*—means 'five-fingered'– that's very valuable because people believe it can give you more energy."

I looked around the greenhouse. "It must take a huge effort to keep so many plants alive."

"Not really. Orchids are a common vascular plant, and they're hardier than you'd think. Just give 'em humidity and they're happy campers."

I craned my neck to see the plants hanging at the far end of the green-house. We were surrounded by blooms of every color and size; many had leathery leaves that looked like dry green tongues. "I never knew there were so many different kinds."

"Sure. They're one of the most adaptive plants on earth, so orchids are pretty good at carving out special niches where they won't have to com-pete so hard for food and light." Shepherd Jon tossed his blonde ponytail over one shoulder and gestured at various plants. "Some smell like rotting meat to attract certain flies. Others are designed to attract mating beetles by emitting the scent of a female beetle. Then there's that one in the far corner. See it? Looks so much like a female wasp that male wasps actually mate with it."

The others at the table were watching Jon silently, their upturned faces almost reverent. Next to me, Melody's sarong had ridden high and she kept shifting her pale, fleshy haunches on the bench. I suddenly realized that she was trying to reach Jon's feet under the table with her own. He kept talk-ing, either oblivious to her seductive efforts or determined to ignore them.

"Are orchids edible?" I asked.

"Yep. You're eating one right now." Jon pointed at the slice of vanilla-frosted coffee cake on my plate. "Vanilla beans are the pods of an orchid plant."

We all contemplated my cake until I felt obligated to take a bite. Jon smiled slightly, watching me chew, then said, "What's really cool is that orchids are so sexual looking. It's a real turn-on, sitting here among all of these sweet little vaginas." He reached up and stroked a petal between two fingers. "My beauty girls," he crooned.

The chunk of cake seemed to expand in my throat. I gulped a glass of juice to get it down. Val giggled. She still wore her sunglasses.

"What do you do when you're not growing orchids?" I asked.

"A little of this. And even less of that." Shepherd Jon studied me with his eyes half shut.

"Where do you work?"

Jon tapped his temple with one forefinger. "Right in here."

What a pompous jerk. What was so difficult about answering a sim-ple question? Talking about your job was standard, getting-to-know-you brunch fare. In this company, though, it appeared to be an invasion of privacy. Too bad. I pressed on. "And just what do you do in your home temple?"

"Try to make peace with myself and the world. The world has enough type A's," Jon said. "Why add to the world's woes? I had a job on the outside once upon a time. A job with an office, health benefits, a retirement plan."

"He was the marketing manager for a pharmaceutical company," Melody said, shaking her head as if this tragedy had taken all of Jon's courage to overcome. "They even gave him a company car."

"That's right," Jon nodded. "But I dropped out after 9/11. Saw where I'd been and where I was going, decided to eject myself from my own life. I'd rather inflict no harm on this cesspool of a planet and simply enjoy what little beauty is left." He caressed the orchid above his head.

"Nice work if you can get it," I said. "Especially if you have a house handed to you on a silver platter. But what are you accomplishing?"

Jon leaned forward, his ponytail spilling down one shoulder, his green eyes unblinking. "Whether I accomplish anything hardly matters, since the world's likely to go up in a ball of flames. So I laid to rest Jon Clemmons, Marketing Director of Salient Pharmaceuticals, and became Shepherd Jon, traveler and thinker. Someone who knows that one life is all we have to live."

The table burst into applause. I felt like I was at an amateur dinner theater, trapped between soggy appetizer and bland entree before the tired opening number. I laughed. "That was your big deal epiphany? That we have but one life to live? I hate to break this to you, Shepherd, but a few other people have been there, done that. There's even a soap opera by that name."

Jon straightened in his chair. "The difference between my decision and the cliche," he said, "is that others talk the talk, but I walk the walk. I quit my job. Scissored my suits. Shredded my credit cards. Now I use every moment to inhale life's sweetness, to live in the present without contributing to humanity's demise, and to volunteer my services to people and countries in need where possible. It's an example that I hope others will follow." He looked meaningfully around the table.

"Amen," Val breathed.

"You go, Bro," Cam said solemnly.

"And what happens if everyone does follow you, like sheep?" I asked. "What then? We all go back to living off the land? Is that your grand scheme?"

"In fact, yes. I've already got my urban garden out back, if you'd care to look, and I spin my own wool. I've converted the van to using biodiesel fuel and I heat the house with wood. And, when I'm not here, I'm try-ing to help save the world's remaining species of plants." Jon clasped his hands around his coffee mug. "You have a better idea for changing the world?"

"Maybe I like the world the way it is."

He looked smug. "Oh, yes? What is it you like about our world, Jordan? The nuclear tests in remote villages in India? The terrorists who strap explosives to their own bodies? The mothers right here in Berkeley who sell their bodies and souls for another pipe?"

I had to struggle to put my thoughts into words; hadn't I, in fact, just kicked aside the scaffolding of my own life, with the possible excep-tion of knowing that I loved children and teaching? Didn't I volunteer, too, even if it was only on projects within a ten-mile radius of my home in Massachusetts? Soup kitchens, beach cleanups, recycling drives: okay, I hadn't traveled to Nepal to save rare tigers and orchids, but I'd always made a point of giving back to my community. Were Jon and I so different, really? Why was I even bothering to argue?

"Those things you're talking about aren't the whole world," I said, my face hot with the frustration of trying to explain my thoughts before I'd had time to fully mull them over. "Just pieces of it gone wrong. Who are you helping by dropping out, besides yourselves?"

There was an uneasy titter from Melody, a warning look from Cam. I ignored them and focused my attention on Domingo, whose head was drooping over his plate. I leaned forward and tapped him on the back of his hand. He jerked awake. "What about you, huh? Are you in the world, or out of it?" I demanded.

Domingo showed me the whites of his eyes. "Me?"

"Yes, you! What do you do, when you're not busy taking sand naps or eating?"

Cam nudged my foot under the table. "Ease up, Jordan." He nodded at the rest of the table. "My sister's always been the motivated one in the family. The big success story. Master's degree, teaching job, the works. She's our Go Getter Gal. Jordan hasn't ever had time to understand the world's essential truth."

I fixed him in my sights. "Which is?"

Cam grinned. "Which is that it can take a whole lot of time to drink a cup of coffee."

The others laughed, and even I had to smile. I wasn't going to change these people, and that was okay. I was only here because I wanted to be part of my brother's life again. No point in alienating Cam. I could let the conversation slide for now, and Cam and I would have another chance to talk alone later. I'd see to that.

Jon lit a joint and it went around the table, slowing the talk as Cam's roommates, sated and stoned, pushed back their chairs. I declined the joint and told them a bit about my teaching, then asked about their lives, keeping myself on a short leash.

This group made the Vienna Boys' Choir look rowdy. Domingo consulted on occasional software jobs. Melody had a rubber stamp business, designing stamps to order. Val catered vegan meals at private Berkeley parties.

"What we mainly like to do is get high and night skate," Cam said. "That's how I met this crew."

"Night skate?"

"Yeah, there's a whole gang of us. The Holy Rollers. Everybody here, and maybe another dozen across the Bay. We meet in Golden Gate Park on Tuesday nights and skateboard or bike the hills around Pacific Heights. Fun as hell."

Domingo was grinning, nodding so hard that his dark hair bounced around his shoulders. "Yeah, suicide is a definite possibility if you don't count right between lights."

"Let me get this straight," I said. "You take your skateboards and bikes into the city at night? On streets with traffic?"

"Not much traffic at night," Cam pointed out. "And this city's like one big skate park. We've done every hill, ramp, tunnel, you name it. Even Twin Peaks. Man! What a rush. Fifteen of us zooming down that sucker, barely making the corners."

"Fifteen of you with a suicide wish," I pointed out.

"It's a bitchin' good time," Cam said. "Funner than fun."

Fun. Fun was the point. Cam and his housemates were like those fourth grade kids who refused to wear jackets at recess, even if it meant flying headfirst into walls because they were so cold that they'd pulled their arms inside the sleeves of their t-shirts, as if they were wearing straitjackets. I was torn between wanting to scold Cam for playing Peter Pan and envying his freedom.

Just then Melody, who had carried a stack of dirty plates into the kitchen, returned to the greenhouse and said, "Cam? She's here again."

Melody stood between me and the greenhouse windows on the street side, blocking my view of the driveway. Her back was stiff with tension. Cam immediately disappeared from the room, his bare feet surprisingly soundless on the stairs.

A moment later, the front doorbell rang. Shepherd Jon excused himself to answer it.

"What's going on?" I asked, trying without success to see out the windows.

Val leaned close to me. She had removed her sunglasses; the whites of her eyes were shot with red around the blue irises. "Cam has a stalker," she whispered.

"Oh, lighten up, Val," snapped Melody. She began collecting more plates from the table.

I followed Melody into the kitchen. "Lighten up about what?" I demanded. "Who's at the door?"

She sighed and started rinsing dishes. "Just this insane girl who's got some screwed up idea that Cam still wants anything to do with her. She comes around every now and then, makes a scene, and Jon has to scare her off."

"Oh." I automatically started lining up the rinsed plates in the dishwasher, conscious that Cam had somehow gotten out of kitchen duty while here I was, ever my mother's dutiful daughter. "Is it a woman Cam was involved with for a long time?"

"I don't know. What's a long time?" With her hands still submerged in bubbles, Melody wiped her forehead with one arm, a gesture I remembered my own mother making at the kitchen sink. She didn't wait for me to answer her question. "Long enough, I guess," she said. "But believe me, this girl is nobody for you to feel sorry for. She's an operator."

"Why? What does she do?"

Melody rotated her shoulders. Standing this close to her, I could see the fine lines in her skin. She was an attractive woman; I wondered how long she had been pursuing Jon and whether her feelings had ever been reciprocated. For a moment, I felt a kinship. Why did she stay? What was a long time for her to be in a relationship? For any of us? Our lives were going by, one sink full of dishes at a time, and yet we didn't see the moments, the days, passing.

"The thing is," Domingo said from the doorway behind us, "there's a kid involved."

I whirled around. "*What?*"

"Stay out of it," Melody warned, turning to face Domingo and scattering droplets of water at him with her damp hands. "This thing is nobody's business but Cam's."

"And mine," I added. "If there's a kid, that makes me an aunt."

I shot out of the kitchen and into the greenhouse again, where Val now sat cross-legged in a square of sunshine at the far end, meditating with palms upturned on her knees. I peered out every window between the plants, but the street was deserted.

I crossed back through the kitchen, this time searching for the stairs leading to Cam's room. Shepherd Jon was returning from the front door, his footfalls echoing on the wooden floor as decisively as a soldier's marching to a snare drum. He blocked my path, draped an arm around my waist, and spun me like a dancer away from the door.

"Problem solved," he said. "Let's finish our discussion. I was enjoying myself."

I shook him off. "Where did the girl go?"

"Back where she belongs. People's Park."

"What's that?" I remembered Cam saying he would be living there if not for Jon.

"A place near the University where the homeless camp out."

"Is this woman homeless?"

"Let's just say that she's choosing the street for now."

"Where's my brother?"

He sighed heavily. "Don't blame Cam. None of this is his fault."

I glared at Jon, barely resisting the urge to grab his beard and give it a good tug. "If Cam's in trouble, I'd rather hear it from him."

"Suit yourself. Top of the stairs, turn right. Last room on your left. But don't expect him to be coherent."

"Cam doesn't have to be coherent. He's my brother."

"Lucky him," Jon said.

Chapter *five*

U pstairs, away from the heady scent of the orchids, Jon's house smelled like every other college house I'd ever been in, of damp towels and rotting food and cranky radiators. The wallpaper was an old woman's choice, bouquets of roses tied in pink ribbons. The floral carpeting on the stairs had faded to pale blooms.

Clearly, this part of the house hadn't been touched since Jon's parents died. I had a brief image of Jon as a boy, towheaded and energetic, running up these stairs ahead of me, his green eyes snapping a challenge: catch me if you can!

All of the bedroom doors were open but one, and nobody had bothered to make a bed. Untamed plants hung in the windows, some with dead brown tendrils mixed among the green. Several of the bedrooms had clothes scattered over the pine floors, arms and legs spiraled outward.

Two of the bedrooms were further crowded by bicycles standing like horses in dim stalls. The upstairs bathroom was painted a garish purple;

it had a claw-foot tub with a clear shower curtain gone green with mold around the edges.

I knocked on the only closed bedroom door. "Hey. Can I come in?"

Cam didn't answer.

"Open up! Come on, Cam. I'm not going away until you do."

Still nothing. I nudged the door open with my foot.

My brother was sprawled on his back across the double bed, staring at the ceiling. "Don't," he said, but his voice was toneless, drained of energy.

"Too late."

Cam covered his face with both hands. I surveyed the room from the doorway. One side of the ceiling slanted down above a desk heaped with books and papers. The headboard of the bed was pine and an old pine bureau stood in one corner. Both pieces of furniture were heavily scarred, as if they'd not only been dragged upstairs, but across town, too.

I couldn't help myself. "Palatial abode you've got here."

"I've always lived in shit holes. What makes you think now would be any different?"

Truthfully, I had expected just what I saw here, knowing my brother as well as I did. There was nothing on the walls to liven up the peeling yellow paint. My brother's dirty laundry was heaped in a plastic hamper with a cracked rim.

The only thing in the room I recognized was the blue terrycloth bathrobe flung over the foot of the bed. My mother had bought that robe. I knew this because she had given me the same robe, crowing later about the 2-for-1 sale and how I wouldn't mind a man's robe, would I?

Two years ago, the last Christmas that Cam and I had both spent at home, Mom called us down to breakfast. We stepped out of our bedrooms at exactly the same time and happened to glance at each other as we tied on our identical robes. This mirror image caused us to laugh so hard that we collapsed on the stair landing.

And then suddenly Cam and I were sliding feet-first down the stairs the way we had as children, as if we were riding down a waterfall. We landed in a tangle at the bottom, hooting, where Mom stood over us, shaking her head. "You two," she said.

I nudged Cam's leg with my knee to get him to make room on the bed. "So what gives?" I asked, plopping down beside him and giving him a good bounce. "I can comfort you with platitudes until I break you. Smile and the world smiles with you! That which does not kill you makes you stronger!"

A glimmer of a smile. "That which does not kill me only postpones the inevitable."

"The harder you try, the more likely you are to succeed!"

"The harder I try, the dumber I look," he moaned.

"Ah, but it's always darkest before the dawn."

"It's always darkest before it's pitch black." Cam grimaced. "Things are really that bad, Jordan. Black, black, black. Things are fucked. I'm fucked. Like, completely."

"Please, my virgin ears. What things? With this woman?"

"You saw her?" His voice was suddenly anxious.

"No. She never made it past the front door. Why didn't you talk to her yourself, instead of letting Jon do your dirty work?"

"Jon's better at dirty work than I am."

"I'll bet."

"Don't say it like that. You don't know what he's done for me." Cam plucked at the bedspread. "Jon says he's going have her arrested for harassment if she keeps coming here."

"Is that true? Is this girl harassing you?"

"No idea what to call this, except to rule it out as fun," Cam said. "I'm betting the cops wouldn't do jack shit anyway. It's not something cops take seriously, a woman stalking a man. Even in the People's Republic of Berkeley."

"But nobody should be allowed to do this to you, Cam. My God! You're up here cowering like a child."

"Wish I was a kid again. Things were easier."

"Not always." I searched the room, looking for proof of this, and spotted Cam's flip-flops. Beach shoes. "Remember the time we went to the beach with Mom and you cut your foot on that bottle? You were just a kid then, maybe ten years old, and it was awful." I shuddered, remembering how the glass had shattered on the boardwalk, spraying Cam's blood onto the splintery weathered boards.

"Sure." Cam had thrown an arm across his face; his voice was muffled. "Mom about fainted. You were the one who carried me all the way to the car. I still don't know how you did it. I was almost as tall as you were by then."

"Yeah, but you only weighed about five pounds." I laughed. "You were one skinny kid."

Still, I remembered the discomfort of it, how it was so hot that the asphalt parking lot sank like a sticky sponge beneath my feet as I half-carried, half-dragged Cam to the car. We bundled Cam's foot in beach towels and drove him to the emergency room to have the fragments of glass removed.

As the doctor numbed Cam's foot with needles, my brother asked to hold my hand. He acted as if our mother wasn't even there. That hadn't surprised me, though; whenever Cam was frightened, he sought me out for comfort, not Mom, since wherever Mom might be, Dad was likely to follow. And Dad was unpredictable back then.

"You looked like a spirit, all wrapped in white," I told Cam now. "I imagined you rising right up off the table, like Jesus after the resurrection."

My brother smiled. "You really are a warp job. They never should have let the nuns near you. You're scarred for life. Completely delusional."

I was relieved to see him lighten up a little. "Hey, you're the one who thought God was like the Boogeyman under the bed, ready to grab you by the ankles and set you on fire any time you touched your willy."

"I still think that sometimes."

I poked his side. "Tell me what's going on," I said. "I'm your big sister! I carried you with superhuman strength over blazing asphalt when you were bleeding to death! Who's that woman out there, harassing you?"

"She's not a woman, exactly. More like a girl."

"What! How old is she?"

"I don't know. She never told me. Well, she told me, but I don't believe her."

A chill ran up my spine. "What did she tell you?"

"Eighteen. But, after things heated up, it was pretty obvious she wasn't more than sixteen." Cam lowered his arm and studied my face for a reaction.

He got one. "Christ, Cameron! You're almost twice her age! What were you thinking?"

Cam rubbed his face. "I don't suppose I was." He sat up and thumped the back of his head against the wall. "You know me! I'm no expert on women. Completely clueless, in fact. And that girl came on to me like somebody who knows the score."

"No sixteen-year-old girl knows the score, even if it's printed on her forehead!"

Cam's face was closed; it was the same expression he used to wear during Dad's drunken tirades. I took a deep breath. If I slammed him too hard about this, I'd get nothing.

"Okay," I said. "I'm sure you didn't intend to hurt this girl. How did you meet her?"

"At a party." About a year and a half ago, Cam explained, one of the San Francisco night skaters held a three-day party in the Fillmore. "Music all day, all night. He rubbed his temples. "And this girl was there, high as a kite and dancing like a demon."

"Does she have a name, your dancing demon?" I kept my voice light. "And were you high, too?"

"Nadine. And yes. That was before Jon helped me clean up my act."

"And what's this about a child? Is that true? Is it yours?"

Cam mumbled something that I couldn't quite catch.

"What?" I poked him again. "Is it or not?"

"Probably."

It felt as if someone were squeezing my temples, my head was pounding that hard. How could my brilliant brother be this incredibly stupid? If that girl was really only sixteen, he could be charged with statutory rape, never mind the issue of child support. Part of me wanted to pick him up and shake him. Another part wanted to smooth back Cam's hair and tell him that everything would be fine. Except, of course, that would be a lie.

"How did this happen?" I asked. "Didn't you use protection?"

"She said she was on the Pill. And, she wasn't just with me, Jordan." Cam was pleading with me now, but I wasn't sure for what. Understanding? Forgiveness? He'd have to wait a while.

"So how do you know the baby is yours?"

"If you saw her, you'd know."

"*What*?" I stared at him, incredulous.

"It's true. She looks just like me, that baby. I didn't even go for a paternity test." Cam scrubbed his face with both hands.

"Isn't there some way you can work with the mother, maybe help her out a little so that she can raise the baby?"

"I'm not talking to her. She's a cranked up meth addict, Jordan! Easy come, easy go."

I caught my breath. "I'll assume you had an AIDS test."

Cam paled. "Yes. Two tests, both negative. I was lucky." His eyes looked wild. "Nadine's a fucking drug addict, Jordan. A street person!" He barked a laugh.

"Yeah? Well, like you said, without Jon, you'd be a street person, too," I said, hating myself for lashing back, but still wanting to knock some sense into my idiot brother. "Cam, you can't just duck out of this one. You have to face up to the fact that you have a child."

Cam's face had broken out in a sweat. "Why should I? It wasn't my choice to bring a kid into this crap life, with deadbeat parents like us," he said. "Nadine's crafty. She probably scoped this place out and got pregnant just to score child support. I was honest with her from day one. When Nadine told me she was pregnant, I told her no way did I want a kid. I would've paid for an abortion. Or, if she wanted to have the baby, I could have hooked her up with an adoption agency. White babies are easy to place, right? Nadine could maybe even make some money on the deal. But she gives me this total bullshit about not being able to kill it or give it away. Kill what? Give away what? She was, like, two months along. It was a thimble full of cells, and she talked like it was headed for kindergarten!"

I was silent during this rant, dizzy and panicked. My brother was a father. I was an aunt. I had a niece. None of these sentences made any sense. I wanted to lie down beside Cam head-to-toe the way we used to do during thunderstorms, when he'd sneak into my room because our parents wouldn't let us come into theirs no matter how scared we were.

"Did you kick Nadine out of the house?"

"I wouldn't do that." Cam sat up. "Nadine took off before the kid was born, probably hooking to score some shit because I kept trying to get her to clean herself up while she was pregnant. I didn't see her again until a couple of weeks ago." He scrubbed his face in his hands. "It's so fucking unfair, having her lay this on me."

I stared at my brother, at this mangy, skinny, wild-eyed man, and fury rose in a tight ring around my temples. "You selfish bastard," I shook my head. "Tell me this isn't you talking, Cam. Tell me you do feel a drop of compassion for this girl."

He narrowed his eyes. "Fuck you!" he yelled, springing to his feet with surprising speed. "I didn't ask you to come here and mess with my head!" He grabbed my arm, yanked me off the bed, spun me towards the bedroom door, and shoved me through it. He slammed the door between us and I heard the lock turn.

I hammered on the door with my fist. "Me, mess with your head?" I yelled. "Come on, Cam! You've done that all by yourself!"

I heard footsteps behind me and wheeled around. Shepherd Jon stood there, leaning against the wall. His green eyes were serene but I could see a muscle twitch in his jaw. "So that went well."

"You're encouraging my brother to act like an idiot and ditch his responsibility!"

Jon shook his head, his expression still calm, his voice placating. "Your brother was a terrible mess when I met him, Jordan. I'm trying to give him solid ground to stand on so that he can own up to his mistakes. He's just not strong enough yet. And the girl is, as he told you, crafty. Don't let her fool you into thinking she's vulnerable."

"I don't even know her," I said. "How could she fool me?"

He cocked an eyebrow. "Aren't you going after her now? I was sure that would be your next move."

I pushed past him and ran down the stairs. "Tell Cam I'll be back!" I yelled, hoping that my brother would hear me and know it was true.

❀

I hated it that Jon knew I was determined to find her, but that was the truth. Nadine had to be that scrawny blonde girl I'd seen across the street from Cam's house with the baby in the backpack. I drove too fast down Telegraph Avenue, dodging skate boarders, bikes, and scooters until I was close to the University, my knuckles white on the steering wheel, my jaw clenched as I scanned the streets for her.

Cam had acted without thinking, under the influence of whatever substances he was abusing. He had slept with a homeless drug addict, he hadn't used precautions, and he had fathered a child. I lined these facts up in my head over and over again, until I could accept them all. Still, I was furious that my brother, whose single greatest quality had always been his compassion, would act cowardly instead of assuming responsibility for his actions—and for the new little life he'd brought into the world.

I was also struck by the gross unfairness of this situation. Why had Cam, who had never wanted children, as far as I knew, and who could barely look after himself, managed to produce a child, while I had not?

Shortly after Peter and I were engaged last year, I thought I was pregnant. My period was several days late, my breasts were heavy and sore, my back ached. Peter and I were on a weekend trip to upstate New York when I told him, and he bought me an Amish rocking chair to celebrate. Then we'd come home and, before I could buy a pregnancy kit, I started bleeding.

I was devastated. Peter had comforted me with a series of brotherly pats, saying that we would be better off getting married and buying a house before becoming parents. I had almost believed him. Then I was diagnosed with breast cancer several months later. My first agonizing thought, as the surgeon clipped the mammogram to a light board and used a sharp wooden pointer to outline the defects in my breast, was this: I will die before I ever get to be a mother.

I parked the car on Telegraph Avenue and asked an elderly man in a beret for directions to People's Park. "Hide your wallet in your sock," he advised, sketching a map on the back of a tattered envelope.

Another block later, I was swallowed up by a flock of Hari Krishnas flailing under orange robes and rattling tambourines. I slowed to let them swarm around me like migrating Monarch butterflies, my feet moving in time to their chanting, "Hari, Hari!"

By the time I could see clearly again, I'd arrived on restaurant row. In three blocks I traveled from Ethiopia to Mexico. Between these ethnic eateries were head shops, garden pubs, coffee houses and bookstores, all just a backdrop for outdoor vendors whose tables carried everything from Chinese herbs to African jewelry.

Berkeley was caught in a time warp, and this city was all about sensation: heightening it, mellowing it, broadening it, or stamping it out altogether. Oh, there were the MBAs and the cell phones and the kids in Urban Outfitter clothes, but mostly I was aware of people on the street in various states of awareness who had transported themselves back in time by swathing their bodies in psychedelic prints and ethereal gauze, much of it adorned with tinkling bells. Berkeley was a world populated by madmen and angels. Cam definitely belonged here.

When I finally turned off Telegraph, I discovered a student ghetto, a narrow street of shabby houses with porches groaning under the weight of damp furniture, bicycles, and tattered boxes of books. People's Park was across the street. I wandered its narrow paths, glancing over my shoulder now and then as I threaded my way through dense vegetation.

Eventually I found an encampment of moldy looking tents and sagging cardboard houses, some with shopping carts parked alongside the temporary shelters like minivans in driveways. Laundry was spread over the bushes to dry and the ashes of last night's fires blew about like black moths. The grass had been trampled down. There was a vegetable garden with lettuces the size of my head and fantastic carrot tops that looked more like feathers than anything edible.

I heard voices over the sound of the breeze through the trees. My heart started pounding and my throat went dry. I should have brought someone with me, Ed or even Karin. What defenses did a suburban East Coast elementary school teacher have in a place like this?

Besides the fact that I probably wouldn't be able to find Nadine, nobody knew where to look for me if I got mugged or murdered. Who would even know I was missing? Karin might call, or my mother. But it would be days before either of them thought something was wrong. The curse of living alone was that nobody but you knew when you were tucked into bed at night.

Too late for second thoughts. I tracked the voices to another clearing, where smoke rose from a small fire surrounded by people removing their clothes and piling them haphazardly in a casket, shouting, "Off with the Emperor's Clothes! Off with the Emperor's Clothes!" while a group of onlookers murmured approval.

For crying out loud. Twice in one day! What was it with Californians and this pressing need to parade around nude?

I sidled up to a broad-shouldered woman who was still dressed. She wore a Hawaiian shirt held together with safety pins. "What's going on?" I asked.

The woman gestured with one hand; she wore a cuff of bright plastic bracelets. "We're burying our inhibitions and airing our vulnerabilities," she answered in the chatty tone of a mother reporting her son's Little League line-up.

Sure enough, the dozen or so participants now stood around with their inhibitions completely buried, or at least removed. Every crack and dimple of vulnerability exposed, they lowered the casket of clothing into a shallow grave and started chanting.

I waited until the casket was out of view before asking Miss Hawaii if she knew Nadine. The name wasn't familiar to her, but when I described the blonde teenager and her baby, she nodded with enthusiasm.

"Why, that baby's just getting out of the pickle stage!" the woman chortled. "Can't imagine how that girl will keep that tiny peanut away from the fires, now she's startin' to crawl."

Ages and stages. But from pickle to peanut? "Do you know where they are right now? I'm the baby's aunt, actually." The words didn't exactly roll off my tongue, but my admission certainly got results. The woman put two fingers into her mouth and whistled like a football coach. "Yo, Star!"

A man as knobby-kneed and pink as a flamingo left the chanting group around the fire to amble towards us, his penis swinging like a pendulum. "Isn't this just too cool?" Star asked me, sweeping his arm toward the new grave. "We are totally free. We've taken control of our destinies. We are the lucky ones."

Mighty lucky Berkeley doesn't have mosquitoes, I thought.

"Star, honey, you seen that little blondie girl with the little bitty baby?" Miss Hawaii asked.

Star nodded. "She's at the playground now, seeing as there's a bonfire today in the garden." He shook his head dolefully. "Can't keep no babies around no fires."

They pointed me in the direction of the playground. I followed another path, this one more overgrown, until I reached another clearing.

There, standing next to a battered metal swing set that looked as though it had been thrown out of a truck, was the blonde teenager I'd seen across the street from Cam's. She was holding the baby that might be my niece. From this distance, the baby looked like any other baby: bald as a cue ball, a halo of blonde fuzz standing out from her ears and forehead.

I approached them slowly. I could tell by the way the girl stared hard at me that the recognition was mutual. "Are you Nadine?" I asked, stopping several feet away from her.

"Who wants to know?"

Nadine was as narrow-hipped as a boy and wore low-slung jeans. Her stained t-shirt hung on her bony shoulders and her blonde hair stood out in sporadic clumps around her head. Nadine screwed up her face at me, defiant and and frightened all at once. Cam was right. No way was this girl more than sixteen. Fifteen, even. How could I have such a clueless moron for a brother?

"My name is Jordan. I've been looking for you."

"Let me guess. You came to piss me off too, right?"

"Why would I want to do that?"

"You tell me." Nadine gestured with her little ferret chin at the baby, who she clutched close to her bony chest. The infant was dressed in a faded t-shirt and diaper. Her little toes were as black and round as dried beans. As Nadine lowered the baby into the infant swing, I saw that the child's diaper was so full that it hung like Gandhi's dhoti between her legs. Nadine wrapped a flannel shirt around the baby's scrawny torso to wedge her into place and gave the swing an unenthusiastic push.

"I really don't know what you're talking about," I prodded. I wanted to see what she'd tell me on her own.

Nadine shrugged her narrow shoulders. "You're tight with that bastard Cam now. I seen you at his house. Ask him."

"That bastard Cam's my brother."

She glanced at me sharply. "Okay. I can see that," she admitted.

Nadine bent down to retrieve a can of generic cola out of a tattered canvas backpack. Next she fished out a baby bottle encrusted with the dried remains of formula and filled it with cola. She stood up and handed the bottle to the baby, then plopped down on an enormous boulder while the baby dangled in the swing beside her like a puppet.

"So you know the score," Nadine said, noisily chugging down what was left in the can.

"I'd rather hear your side of the story." I deliberately avoided looking at the baby with her crusty cola bottle, for fear I'd snatch the bottle away.

She laughed. "That's a new one. What do you want to know?"

"Well, for starters, are you really sure this is my brother's child?"

"Shit, yeah."

I finally took a good look at the child. Up close, the baby's resemblance to Cam, and to me, was uncanny. Our gene pool might be funky, as Cam said, but it was powerful. The child's blue eyes were tipped at the corners, and one of them was flecked with a brown spot like mine. She had the same long, narrow nose we did. Even her hands, broad but long-fingered, were tiny copies of mine and Cam's.

Looking at this baby, I felt dizzy with recognition, slightly sick, as if someone had sucked me in the stomach. This child was family. The next generation. And yet, here she was, guzzling soda out of a baby bottle, smelling like a sheep barn, and carrying a month's worth of grime between her toes.

I blinked back tears. "So what are you going to do, Nadine? Sue my brother for support? You can do that if he's the baby's father. Have you talked to a lawyer?"

Nadine squawked at this idea. "Do I look like the type a fucking lawyer would take on?" She tossed her oily hair. Along Nadine's cheeks and narrow jaw ran rows of festering sores. It didn't look like an adolescent's ordinary acne. Was it something to do with drugs? Nadine certainly had an addict's rolling eyes and edginess.

"Anybody can see a lawyer," I told her. "There are probably free legal centers right here in Berkeley. Or you could get a lawyer who would get paid later, out of your back child support."

"Oh, right. Like Cam has fucking shit for money." Nadine scratched at the bumps on her face. She was missing one of her bottom front teeth and her gums were tinged green. I thought of the moldy shower curtain in Cam's house. "Nah. If Cam won't play, screw him. We'll get by. Right, Girlie?" She tweaked her daughter's toe.

"What's the baby's name?"

"Paris." Nadine tossed the cola can into the bushes and pulled a cube of chewing gum out of her jeans pocket. The gum was purple; she chewed with her mouth open, exhaling grape. "I always wanted to go there."

"She's a pretty baby."

Nadine shrugged. "She's butt ugly. A little monkey face. But look who she has to take after." She glanced my way. "No offense."

"Look," I said, exasperated, "you can't just live out here in the park with a child. It's dangerous! Don't give up on Cam. Keep after him until he helps you."

"Fuck that!" she flared. "I'm done with Cam and his house of freaks. Me and The Admiral, we're going to Oregon to pick apples. Make some real money, fast."

She was a fine one to call my brother a freak. I said, "You can't take a baby with you to pick apples."

"Oh, I'll figure out something." Nadine cut a sidelong look at me. "Course, it's hard to think straight when I've been up three nights straight with the baby. Something's wrong with her. Barks like a seal at night." Nadine tapped the baby's foot again.

Paris had been dozing with her bottle in the swing; now she started and her face wrinkled up. She did look a little like a monkey. I wondered if something serious really was wrong with her, if her mother had been doing drugs all through her pregnancy.

"You should take her to a doctor. Has she had all of her immunizations?"

Nadine snorted. "Like I've got the money for doctors, either."

The baby started to fuss. Nadine continued to sit there, oblivious to the piteous cries. I finally took the child out of the swing, wrinkling my nose at her rank smell, and eased myself down to sit on the big rock next to Nadine.

I had expected the baby to reach for her mother, but Paris wrapped her skinny arms around my neck and pressed against me, curving herself around my breasts and shoulder and hanging there like a purse, heavy and damp. If she'd had such a chaotic existence, I supposed it was possible that Paris hadn't ever bonded with her mother; maybe at this point, the baby figured that one pair of adult arms was as good as another. Or was she just not old enough yet to care? I didn't know much about babies, only mouthy fourth graders.

I patted Paris's bony back awkwardly and let her dig her toes into my thighs. The combination of the shock of seeing Cam's child, the rancid stink, and the baby's tight grip on my neck was making it hard for me to breathe.

"Look," I said in my sternest, no-nonsense teacher's voice. "Don't you dare leave California without giving me time to talk sense into my brother. He'll come around."

Nadine's eyes were gray, and she had the steely, flat expression of someone used to bargaining with whatever scraps she had. In this case, her highest card was my apparent interest in the baby. "I guess I could wait around some," she acquiesced slowly, "if only I had a little cash to, like, tide me over, maybe buy us a little food and pay for a doctor."

I eyed her suspiciously. "You know, you could always take Paris to an emergency room. They're bound by law to treat anyone who walks through the door, no matter how poor."

"Yeah, right!" She rolled her eyes at this. "Those fucking Nazi social workers would take my baby away before I could sneeze. Shit!" Nadine reached over and stroked one of the baby's legs in a hypnotic way, her fingers tracing the curve of Paris's skinny calf. "She's a little monkey face, isn't she?" The baby grew heavy on my shoulder as she sank into sleep, her cheek sticky against my neck.

I felt stunned, almost immobilized by the weight of my brother's child. "All right," I said at last, looking Nadine in the eye. "I'll give you some money if you promise to buy food and stick around here for at least a couple more days."

"What else would I buy?" she said, pouting in a way that almost made her look like a normal teenager.

After counting out the bills in my wallet—over seventy dollars–I took a scrap of paper and a pen out of my purse and scribbled my name, cell phone number, and San Francisco address on it. "This is where I am. Please. Don't just take off with the baby. We have a deal, right? I'll work something out with Cam. Can you meet me here tomorrow at the same time?"

"Yeah, okay. That's cool." Nadine wadded the paper into her jeans pocket along with the money and plucked the baby out of my arms. Paris's head snapped back and she let out a startled yowl. My skin burned a little where the baby's head had rested against it. It was all I could do not to snatch the child back.

"Take it easy!" I said, alarmed. "You've got to support her head better than that."

Nadine slung the baby over one shoulder. "Don't get your panties all in a bunch, now." She grinned. "I'm a pro after seven months of this motherhood crap." She nodded at me as she stood up. "Come on, Baby," she said to Paris, suddenly cheerful. "We've got places to go and people to see."

She disappeared like a deer, noiselessly sliding into the shrubbery behind the boulder and leaving me feeling wounded and bereft.

Chapter *six*

Furious at my brother, I drove back to Cam's house, but it was locked up tight and the van was gone. Where had they all gone? Having another lie-in? Cavorting on skateboards?

No answer on Cam's cell, of course. There seemed to be no choice but to go home and think things through. I was suddenly exhausted, and I could hear my bed calling me from across the Bay.

I made my way back across the Bay Bridge into San Francisco, let myself into the apartment, sent Cam a text, had a good cry, and fell asleep with a pillow over my head. I woke to the music on my cell phone—a Bollywood tune–and snatched the receiver off the cradle, willing it to be Cam returning my call.

It was my mother and she was on a roll. I carried the receiver over to the refrigerator, where I listened to her rant while I pulled a hunk of cookie dough off the store-bought log on the top shelf and poured a glass of milk. Mom was still going off on me for not calling as I flung open the French doors to the garden and, munching doughy goo, dragged myself out to the deck.

I sat cross-legged in my private square of afternoon sunlight until my mother finally inhaled. The gist of her tirade was that she was worried sick. First Cam disappeared and now me, how could any daughter of hers be that thoughtless, etc. Highway accidents, city muggings, apartment fires, earthquakes: her only daughter could fall victim to all that and more.

"Sometimes I think you left home to escape reality," she accused finally.

"Mom, believe me. I'm wallowing in reality," I assured her. "But you're right. I should have called. I really am sorry. How is everything?"

"Oh, status quo. Status quo." She covered the phone receiver on her end and spoke in a muffled voice, presumably because my father was somewhere within earshot. He had probably told her not to call me. "Have you talked to your brother?"

I gave her a brief sketch of Cam's job, house, and roommates but left out any bits about meth addicts and babies. Still, my mother knew from my voice that something was up. She started fishing for clues.

"Has your brother been in an accident?" she asked. "Is that why we haven't heard anything? I worry about that boy's reckless driving."

"No, Mom! Cam doesn't even have his van anymore. The engine gave out when he took it down to Mexico."

"Mexico! You can catch diseases in Mexico!"

"You can catch diseases anywhere, Mom," I said patiently. "Anyway, Cam's using public transportation these days, so you don't need to worry about his driving." I refrained from mentioning her son's new passion for night skating.

"Is he involved with someone? Is that why he hasn't called?"

"Kind of. But you know Cam. It's nothing that will last." I gulped down a chunk of cookie dough with the white lie. "He has a job, though. That's a plus."

"I'm sure he's still in debt," my mother snapped. "That child never could manage money. Honestly, Jordan, I wish he'd been born with half your common sense." She sighed heavily. "What about his health? Is he eating enough? He isn't still on drugs, is he?"

"Mom, will you stop? Cam's health seems fine. In fact, he went swimming at the beach when we were there this morning."

"You've actually seen him! Oh, Jordan." My mother was crying in that way that people cry on the phone when they don't want the person on the other end to know. She was breathing fast, *huh huh huh*, like a stubborn lawn mower engine that won't catch.

"You okay?" I asked.

"Of course not!" she spit out. "God, Jordan, you've no idea what it's like to be shut out of your child's life."

"Please, Mom. Try to relax. Cam will be fine." Of course I could convey no specific assurances; I didn't quite believe, myself, that my brother would be fine. But there was no point in worrying my mother. "He's just, you know. Asserting his independence."

Bad choice of words. "Why would your brother want to be so independent that even his own mother can't reach him?" she demanded.

"You know what Cam's like," I said helplessly. "He's always been evasive. Hey, where's Dad right now? Can I say hi?"

"Oh, he's out." Her tone was dismissive.

"Out, where?"

"Watering the roses, weeding. It's Sunday, you know. Yard work day."

I knew from her suddenly distracted tone that my mother was probably checking out the window to see if my father—a barrel-chested ex-Army captain who owned a machine shop–was still outside. I pictured Dad as he always looked in the yard: his forehead sunburned, the v-neck t-shirt slightly yellowed from sweat, the determined look on his face as he held his weekend showdown with the overgrown grass and weedy edges of the lawn.

Dad was apparently out of earshot. Mom's voice relaxed, turned more conversational. "So how's your apartment?"

"A postage stamp with a bed in it," I admitted. "But I've got a great garden."

"And you've introduced yourself to the neighbors, I hope?" Mom's theory was that tragedies could happen to anyone, but mostly to people who didn't mind their manners.

"Oh, sure. I've met everybody in the building." Not that anyone wanted anything to do with me, but I didn't tell her that. "And Karin had a party so that I could meet some of her friends," I added, knowing my mother would seize on this as evidence that her daughter wasn't friendless out here in the Wild West.

"You know, I should come out there," Mom proposed suddenly. "I'd love to see your apartment and Cam's house. I can stay in a hotel if you don't have room for me. Or maybe Cam could find a place for me in his big house? I've never been to California," she added, sounding wistful. "And you see so much of California on the television. The palm trees, the beautiful mansions."

"What? You can't do that! Anyway, that's Los Angeles you always see on TV."

"Of course I can come if I want," my mother countered. "I could leave tomorrow, get on a plane and be there in six hours. I'm sure you could use the help getting unpacked and settled."

I glanced around my apartment and its sparse furnishings. I'd unpacked the boxes, hung towels in the bathroom, and put sheets on the bed in less than an hour's time. What could my mother find to do here? Put plastic on everything, crochet a lampshade or two?

Her visit could potentially throw a wrench in the works before I'd gotten Cam to admit he had a new obligation in his borderless life, that's what she could do.

"This really isn't the best time," I said gently. "Why don't we talk about a visit next month? By then, I'll know my way around. Besides, Dad wouldn't know what to do without you."

"I'm sure he'd manage," she said stiffly.

My mother, whose longest solo voyage to date was a bus trip with her sister to Atlantic City the month after Grammy died, had never flown on a plane. I tried to imagine her on one, offering coupons, tissues, aspirin, gum, and hand cream to the businessman or college student trapped in the seat beside her. Mom would knit fruit-shaped hats out of the yarn she carted about in her knee-high flowered bag. She would make friends with the flight attendants, too, quizzing them gently about their children and face creams. The fruit hats would be handed out to anyone with babies: blueberries to the newborns, strawberries to the older babies, watermelons to the toddlers, each hat with a green stem on top. Picturing Paris in one of those strawberry hats made my head pound with anxiety.

"I'm not saying it's a bad idea," I amended to avoid bruising her feelings. "I just think we ought to wait until later in the summer."

"Well, it was just a thought," she said. "Forget I said anything."

Perversely, I hated to hear my mother sound so easily defeated. "I'll talk to Cam," I said. "We'll come up with a plan to see you soon."

We hung up with promises on my side to call her daily, and then I dialed Karin's cell. "Can you meet me for dinner at the Church Street Cafe?"

"Sure," she said. "Give me ten."

I walked the five blocks to the cafe, where I bought an uninspired chicken sandwich and chose a high table near the window. Karin arrived minutes later. She had put her hair up in a neat French twist and was wearing her nurse's uniform. The blindingly clean white dress on Karin was like seeing a push-up bra on a nun, given her housekeeping and party habits.

Karin spotted me immediately and plopped down in the free chair, picking up my sandwich and taking a bite. "So what's up?" she said, chewing. "How's it going with Ed?"

I was about to answer, when something stopped me. I don't know what it was–the uniform, the hunch of her shoulders, the overwrought makeup–but something felt off. What was going on with Karin? And why was she asking about Ed again? I'd already told her about his striptease and me chickening out of the final act, then skulking home.

"We saw a movie a few days ago, but I haven't talked to him lately," I told her. "Are you going to eat something besides my sandwich?"

"I don't know." Karin waved away the fronds of an enormous fern hanging in the window above her head. "You need a damn machete in here," she said. "So tell me. Did you turn Ed down out of panic, or because you really meant no?"

I rolled my eyes. "When have I ever been smart enough to do anything deliberate in a relationship? Nothing happened because I didn't want anything to happen. Not that night, and not when I went to the movies with him, either. There's no spark! Which is fine, believe me. Don't feel bad about it. I've got other things on my mind, actually."

I waited for her to ask what those things might be, but Karin took another bite of my sandwich and said, "I'm not at all surprised that Ed tried to hook up with you."

"Well, you shouldn't be, since you practically shoved me out the door with him," I pointed out. Then it dawned on me. "You two had a thing, didn't you?"

Her face clouded. "Long, long ago, in a place far, far away."

"When and where?"

"Three years ago in Marin. Ed had a houseboat there. He built it himself," she said with pride. "He's really clever with his hands." She winked at me. "But you knew that."

I touched her arm. "Drop the jokes. Why didn't it work out? What happened?"

Karin's eyes brimmed with tears, blurring her liner and only making her look more exotic. "Ed's the marrying kind. I'm not." She blew her nose noisily into a napkin. "Plus, Ed's much nicer than I am. He deserved better."

"Stop it. You're the nicest person I know."

To my surprise, Karin began crying harder. "It's nothing to do with you and Ed, this breakdown," she said when she could catch her breath. "I'm really happy for you two."

"You're clearly not listening to me!" I said. "Ed and I didn't even spend the night together. Nothing happened between us! He's a nice guy, but not my type. Now what's giving you the breakdown? Wally?"

At the mention of her boyfriend's name, Karin scowled. "I've had it up to my neck with that toad."

"Are you going to break up with him?" I asked in surprise. I hadn't seen this one coming. Then again, I seemed to have completely lost the ability to see what was careening around the corner and crashing into my own life, never mind beyond that.

Karin blew her nose on a napkin. "I already did. This morning. He's history."

"Oh." I didn't know what to say. "Well, are you sorry?" I ventured. "It didn't exactly seem like true love. Whenever I saw Wally, he was in a crappy mood."

"That's his M.O.," Karin said. "Much cooler to be a moody man than a cheerful one, right?" She sighed. "Wally will go down in my Lovemaking Hall of Fame, if only for that time we did it in the shower and the glass door broke and we kept right on, just threw a towel over the mess so we could finish. But whenever I tried to talk to him about my feelings, he started tossing out one-liners like a stand-up comic."

"You'd be better off with a dog," I comforted her. "At least a dog would stay home at night and wouldn't joke about your feelings."

"Yeah, well. I don't know why I'm so upset. I'm the one who kicked Wally out. I guess I'm afraid I'll end up like that woman." Karin nodded toward a middle-aged, big-bottomed woman huddled over what appeared to be an entire head of lettuce on her plate. "Always asking for a table for one in restaurants."

"You won't, though." I took Karin's hand in mine. "You'll always have me. We can have a table for two."

Karin suddenly looked contrite. "Jordan, what kind of friend am I? You're the one who called me. You sounded upset. Did you see Cam? How is he?"

Now it was my turn to break down into a pile of napkins as I told her about meeting Cam on the beach, having brunch at his house of crazies, and tracking down Nadine and the baby at People's Park. I couldn't help but be vaguely aware at the same time that I was becoming more Californian by the minute, with this level of public confession. Ouch.

"I can't believe I let that girl take off with the baby and a fistful of cash," I finished. "Do you think she'll head north before I talk to Cam and find her again?"

Karin frowned. "I don't know. But do you really think you can convince Cam to get involved with the baby? I know your heart's in the right place, but he's such a perpetual adolescent and always broke besides."

"He could at least work full-time and cough up child support." My throat and head hurt. I knew that Karin was probably right about it being difficult to get Cam to do the right thing. I sucked on a piece of ice for a minute, then said, "What a mess. I don't know what to do. On the way home, I even wondered whether I should try for legal guardianship of the baby. But what if I get cancer again?"

"Will you quit with the death dirge?" Karin said, exasperated. "How about if you just recognize that you beat the cancer crap shoot and get on with your life."

"I want to, you know?" I fiddled with the ice in my cup. "I've tried telling myself that. But there's a woman I know who teaches at our school. She had breast cancer two years ago. Now she's got ovarian cancer. How fair is that? She's dying, Karin, and she has two little kids. That could be me some day."

"But it isn't you today," Karin said gently. "Look, we're all scared of dying. But that's also the best thing about life: our ability to put one foot in front of the other and find joy in the here and now, no matter how scared we are. Follow your heart, Jordy, and then you won't have to regret missing all of those things you wanted to try but didn't." She glanced at her watch. "I have to get to work. I'll see one of the social workers on my break, see if she has any advice about Cam and the baby. You might as well be armed with information, because nothing you do will be easy."

"I know."

Karin rested a hand on mine. "I know you know. And that's why I love you, because you always try to do the right thing, even if it's not the easy thing." She hugged me before leaving, her brisk white form disappearing quickly into the foggy night.

I was awakened at dawn by a cat's noisy, pitiful meowing. On and on it went, until I clutched the pillow over my head to muffle the sound.

It was no use. I was fully awake, even though the first fingers of sunlight were just now reaching beneath the curtains. I sat up and studied the swirling pattern of dust motes in the pale light, listening hard. There it was again. Only now the noise had quieted to a soft grumbling.

The sound was definitely coming from outside. With a sigh, I climbed out of bed and padded to the front door, curling my bare toes into the thick tan carpet as I unbolted the door and opened it, squinting into the fog.

There was another cry, this one right at my feet. I stepped back and stared at the bundle of old towels on my doorstep. It wasn't a cat after all, but a baby.

Of course I knew who it was even before I uncovered Paris's pinched little face. She was bundled in the towels so tightly that she couldn't squirm out of them, and she was mad as hell.

At the sight of me, my niece's grumbling exploded into an angry howl. Nothing pitiful about that cry. She struggled inside the cloth, thrashing her scrawny limbs, but nothing happened. That baby was wrapped like a burrito. I loosened the towels, trying not to gag at the stink.

I patted Paris on the back and draped her over my shoulder the way I'd seen Nadine do. The baby's nose rested like an ice cube on my neck and she was hiccuping now. Between hiccups, she drew ragged breaths. I stood there stupidly staring into the fog for several minutes, the baby molded against my chest and neck, wondering how long she'd been lying on my step. I had to figure out what she needed, fast.

Paris started nuzzling my neck, rooting for something to put in her mouth. Back in the apartment, I unwrapped one of her hands so that she could suck on her fist, saw the state of those fingers, and quickly held them under the kitchen tap.

Afterward, as the baby stuffed her fist into her mouth, the towels loosened a little more and a scrap of paper fluttered to the floor. I picked it up and peered at the childish scrawl.

I'm splitting. Thanks for the $$$. The Admiral says I can't take the baby so please take care of her and love her like she is yours. This is a legal note and The Admiral is hereby my witness when I say you should adopt her, my only baby. Always tell Paris her mother loved her and this was the best thing. And also say goodbye to Cam for me. Officially signed, Nadine Charlotte Mortimer.

My knees were trembling. I wanted to sink to the floor, to read the note again until I could absorb what was happening. But Paris's whimper had bloomed into a wail, her diaper weighed as much as she did, and her stench, now that the towels were unwrapped, was unbearable. I had no idea what time it was, but I had to find her something to eat and then get her cleaned up. After that, maybe I could think.

My refrigerator was empty. I'd finished the milk with the cookie dough. I didn't even have any eggs to scramble. I scanned the counter and saw one banana left in the wooden bowl. Working with one hand, I split the peel, put the banana in a bowl and mashed it up with a little warm water. Tentatively, I put a spoonful of mush in front of Paris's mouth.

She went after it like a snapping turtle, clamping her hard rubbery gums on the spoon and sucking off the banana. The baby ate the entire bowlful while I stood there, feeding her on my shoulder and trying not to mind the juices spilling down my neck.

When she'd finished, Paris whimpered for more. What should I do next? I wanted to call Karin, but it was too early. She'd be incoherent at this hour. I dressed with one hand, since Paris screamed whenever I tried to set her down on the bed. Then I sponged off the baby's face, held my breath, stripped off the old towels, and slid her into a clean pillowcase. I'd have to change her diaper and deal with the rest of her needs after I had the right supplies.

Thankfully, the tiny corner store was open. The young Indian woman who managed it was sweeping behind the cash register with a whispering sound as regular as breathing, her blue sari sparkling in the dim store. I had seen this woman daily since my arrival in San Francisco, usually when I stopped in for coffee and the paper.

Seeing the baby brought a broad smile to the woman's narrow face. "Hello to you, Baby!" she crooned. She glanced at me shyly. "Girl or boy?"

"Girl."

"You are indeed blessed!"

I knew this woman had two small children of her own, a pair of boys who played behind the counter with wooden blocks or a fleet of tiny metal cars. "She's not mine," I said hastily. "I mean, she's my niece, not my daughter. I'm just taking care of her. So I'm blessed, yes, but clueless. What should I buy for her?"

It took the woman only a moment to adjust her expression from good cheer to sympathy. "Ah, but she is loved and you are needed, so that is a double blessing." She flashed me another brilliant smile before beckoning for me to follow.

Colors gradually emerged from the dun-colored recesses of the shop as my eyes adjusted. Together we patrolled the aisles, collecting diapers, baby wipes, jars of applesauce, a carton of eggs, oatmeal, and a gallon of milk. Paris twisted about in my arms and reached for the shelves as we walked, screeching nonstop. My ears were ringing by the time we reached the cash register.

"She has a good pair of lungs, that one," the woman remarked, ringing up my purchases while cleverly dangling a set of keys to distract the baby.

"I guess that's a good thing," I grunted, trying to extricate money from my pocket without dropping the squirming baby. Holding Paris was like hanging onto a panicked rabbit. My arm had gone numb below the elbow, yet I didn't dare put her down in the store. It was too easy to imagine Paris speed-crawling away and disappearing under the shelves.

I thanked the woman, found out her name was Kanchan, and promised I'd bring the baby by to visit.

Back in my apartment, I dropped the bag on the counter and plunked Paris on the carpeted floor, where I pinned her down with one arm while I took off her diaper. The diaper disintegrated into stinky lumps of sodden pulp. I scooped these into the trash while Paris crawled around the room at top speed, butt in the air, until she collided headfirst with the bookshelf. More howling. I picked her up, ran water in the kitchen sink, dunked her into it for a quick wash, then diapered her haphazardly.

The baby didn't stop screaming until I'd balanced her on one hip, singing snatches of lullabies as I cooked oatmeal on my two-burner stove, all the while marveling at how much complaining a person this small could do. People who thought they were practicing for parenthood with their Golden Retrievers had a big surprise in store.

When the oatmeal was ready, I perched on a counter stool with Paris on my lap. I gave up feeding her with a spoon when I realized how efficient this child was with her hands. She cupped her palms into little shovels and snorted like a rooting pig as she moved the food from container to mouth at top speed. We were both soon splattered with oatmeal, but at least the baby was quiet.

When my cell phone rang, I didn't even consider answering it. My hands weren't just full; they were gluey. I waited until the phone stopped ringing, then pushed the button to play the message on speaker phone.

Ed's voice boomed through my tiny apartment. "Hey, Babe, I know you're probably still sleeping, but it's a beautiful morning and I was thinking about driving up to Point Reyes. Call me."

"Ha." I stared at the phone. My life had completed its transformation from surreal to sticky. "Looks like I'm not going on any dates for a while," I murmured to Paris. "I don't even have a car seat. I'll have to tell Ed there's someone else in my life."

Paris ran her gluey fingers through my hair. I was too stunned and tired to put her down on the floor until she grabbed a metal spatula out of the jar of cooking tools and began thwacking it on the counter like she was killing bees.

"You need a real bath this time," I announced and carried her into the bathroom.

I could use a bath, too. I shut the door, filled the tub and stripped off my own clothes before undressing Paris. Her t-shirt felt stiff with grime. I put it in the bathroom trash with the diaper, tied the trash bag shut, and climbed into the tub.

"Come on in, the water's fine." I held out my arms.

Paris crawled away from the tub as fast as her skinny knees would carry her.

Maybe she'd never had a bath, since Nadine was homeless. "Come on in," I coaxed gently. "Don't worry, I'll hold you the whole time." I talked on and on.

Nothing I did made a positive impression. Paris pressed herself against the bathroom door, naked and shrieking. And, when I shampooed my hair, Paris fell strangely silent and sat absolutely still, like a forgotten garden statue against the wooden door.

Not a cherub statue, though. Much too skinny. More like a gargoyle. My niece was the boniest baby I'd ever seen, outside of famine pictures in the newspaper. Was this due to Nadine's absent-minded parenting, or to the secondhand drugs Paris was exposed to during Nadine's pregnancy? What if something was really wrong with the child? How would I know?

I stared into Paris's enormous eyes. They were the same bright blue as mine and Cam's, with the same brown spot in one iris. There was no escaping those eyes, that solemn glance, or what it meant: this baby and I were connected by blood, and she knew as well as I did that I was in charge of her life right now. I only hoped that she didn't also know how terrified I felt.

I climbed out of the tub and slipped into my bathrobe. Then I knelt down close to Paris and began combing my hair, staring into the baby's eyes and talking to her about anything—palm trees, oatmeal, the birds we could hear out the window—to calm her. Even so, Paris knew her number was up. When I reached for her, she made a final dash for freedom, skittering back and forth under the sink like a mouse until I finally hauled her out.

"Sorry, Kidlet. But I'm not dressing you until your skin is at least one shade lighter," I apologized, realizing only then that I had no clean clothes for her.

Well, I couldn't worry about that now. I couldn't think about anything. Bathing this child was like washing a cat. Paris clawed and scratched and scrambled up the sides of the tub, howling in frustration. I gave up trying to pacify her and concentrated on simply not drowning her, holding the baby's scrawny squirming body in the tub with one hand while I trickled water over her head and washed her fine hair with a dime of shampoo.

When the water was grayer than the baby, I scooped Paris out of the tub and wrapped her in a towel. Only a wet tuft of hair and a pair of furious blue eyes showed over the towel's hem. Paris thrashed around inside the cloth for several minutes, then let her body relax against mine with a final shudder.

I had brought a rocking chair with me from Boston, a red wicker chair I'd picked up at a yard sale near my parents' house and tied to the top of my car at the last minute. The wind almost sent that chair sailing clear across the Rocky Mountains, but the ropes held.

Now I opened the curtains across the garden doors and sat in it, rocking Paris slowly as the sun's warmth filled the room. When the baby was asleep at last, her body heavy against mine, I got up and slipped into bed with her, pulling the quilt high around both of us.

Chapter *seven*

I woke with a start when I felt something pressing against my face. Paris had wriggled up against me so that her body was curled like a puppy's on the pillow, her hot, rounded back against my nose.

Outside, I could see the papery red bougainvillea blossoms gleaming and plastic looking against the bright white fence. There was no trace of morning fog. I guessed that it must be well after noon. I shifted my weight away from the baby an inch at a time, tugging my hair free of Paris's hand as I lifted my head off the pillow.

I was terrified of waking her and not knowing what to do next. Gradually, though, I managed to sneak out of bed. I pulled the blanket up to cover her and then stood there, breathing in the baby's presence.

In sleep, Paris's face was pink and relaxed. Her sparse hair was tinged gold in the morning sunlight. She looked more like a baby and less like a monkey. She was almost pretty, really. I could see Nadine in her high, flat cheekbones and wide mouth, but my brother and I were there too, in her arched brow, long nose, and sharp chin. Paris's fingers were slightly curled, the nails like tiny iridescent seashells. I had to resist the impulse to pick her up and hold her again.

But this whole situation was impossible! What was I going to do with a baby? In theory, helping Cam with his daughter's care had seemed like the most logical thing in the world last night, while I was sounding off to Karin like Mother Theresa. In reality, it was a terrifying prospect. In eight short weeks I'd be back in Massachusetts, working full-time. What would I do with a baby?

No need to dwell on that yet. Cam probably didn't even know that Nadine was gone. I'd tell him, and he would have to decide Paris's future. She was his child, after all.

I propped the pillows around Paris to keep her from rolling off the bed, then tiptoed across the room and dressed. I opened the front door and scanned the steps and sidewalk. Had I missed some magical clue to Paris's appearance? Had Nadine left anything else, like a scrap of paper with a forwarding address or cell phone number?

As I stood there with my bare feet going numb on the cold cement, I heard the front door of my building open and slam shut again. I trotted up the short walk from the side of the house, where my door was located, to the front sidewalk, where Louise was regally descending the steps in her bright red cloak.

When I greeted her, my landlady stared at me with unblinking doll's eyes. "What are you doing out here?" she asked. "Waiting for a bus?"

"Just checking the weather. Chilly, huh? But it looks like another nice day." I don't know what prompted me to lie. Louise could hardly evict me for having a child in the apartment, even a screeching one, for just one night.

Louise shrugged, and the folds of the cloak rustled around her massive body. "It's always a nice day here. But that's the whole point of California, isn't it?"

"Looks like you're ready for any weather opportunity." I gestured at her layers of red and gray.

"I hope to be," she replied with dignity.

Where was Louise off to now, in that opera diva rig? This was San Francisco. Anything was possible. "Off to work?" I ventured.

She swiveled her head, owl-like. "Work? I'm going to church!"

Who went to church on a weekday afternoon? And in a red cloak? But I nodded as if this made perfect sense. "Of course. Sorry. Anyway, I was just wondering if you heard any strange noises last night."

"What kind of noises?" In their layers of fat, Louise's eyes were as dark as currants sunk in pastry.

"Like a cat, maybe?"

"Not so I noticed. Of course, there all kinds of noises in a city," Louise said. "Cars, cats, sirens, dogs, birds. People talking. People laughing. People we'll never meet, living lives we'll never know."

Amen to that, I thought.

Louise was gliding away, moving so smoothly down the sidewalk that I imagined roller skates under that cloak. "Things happen in cities," she murmured. "Every day," she added with a wave.

Things happen. Every day! Huh. My new mantra.

Inside, Paris was still sleeping peacefully in her nest of pillows on the bed, one impossibly skinny little arm showing above the blankets. Seeing her pale, smooth skin reminded me that she had nothing clean to wear. I could buy her an outfit, but what would she wear to go shopping?

Somewhere in this mess I had a sewing kit. I hadn't planned on bringing it to San Francisco, but Mom had thrust it into my hands at the last minute.

"You never know when you'll go missing a button," she'd explained, trying to look at the flowered enamel box and not at me as we stood in the driveway of her house, saying goodbye after my last day of teaching in June.

Both of us had pretended not to notice that Mom's eyes were red because she had cried all through breakfast, standing at the stove with her back to me, frying bacon I didn't want to eat.

"There's nothing worse than needing a pair of scissors and not having any," Mom had sniffed, handing me the sewing kit as I packed the car.

My mother had devoted the spare hours of her life to creating things for other people out of yarn, fabric, needles, and thread. I had never so much as darned a sock. But I brought the enameled sewing box across the country anyway, feeling comforted because it was almost as if some part of Mom had joined me.

Now I dug the kit out of the rubble in my closet. Everything was just as I remembered: the spools of colored thread arranged in a rainbow of possibilities, the velvet packets of silver needles, the strawberry wrist pin-cushion leaking sawdust.

I rummaged in the closet again, this time for my softest t-shirt, an ancient beach coverup with magenta stars on a white background. I found it tangled on one of the hangers and laid it on the floor.

Finally, I dug Paris's t-shirt out of the trash, spread it out on top of mine, and began cutting the fabric, feeling like a pioneer woman two steps ahead of the coyotes.

Just before two o'clock, Paris and I stood outside Karin's building and rang the buzzer to her apartment. Karin lifted the screen of one front window and hung her head down, her face glowing pink in the tangle of dark hair falling like a shawl over her bare shoulders.

"What?" she hollered, then spotted us standing on the steps below. "Oh, it's you. I was hoping it was Wally."

"You were? Why? Did you two make up?"

"No. I just wanted him to know that he's locked out forever."

"Doesn't he have a key?"

"I've always got spare locks around. And I'm pretty handy with a drill." Her eyes widened as Karin fully comprehended the fact that I was carrying a baby. "Cam's, I presume?"

"So it would seem," I said.

"Okay. Hang on and I'll buzz you."

I shifted Paris to my other hip and marveled at Karin's calm. She'd greeted me as if it were perfectly normal for me to show up on her doorstep with a baby.

Nothing was normal about this. Carrying Paris around this morning had made me feel like an actress in a play–an actress who keeps fumbling with the props. Yet, having a baby in tow did have its up side: I'd apparently earned an honorary membership in some sort of secret Mothers Club. I'd lived in this neighborhood for almost two weeks, yet I hadn't met a single person. Everyone who passed typically shifted their eyes away from me in that typical city survival mode.

Today, however, as I walked to Karin's with Paris on my hip, nearly every person said hello. Two women stopped to compliment Paris's halo of yellow hair, the dress I'd made for her (crooked but cute), and her two-toothed grin. An older man had even offered to let Paris pat his dog, a waddling Corgi that looked like a pot-bellied pig.

It was unnerving to be so suddenly approachable. I didn't know whether people were talking to me because I now seemed safe, or whether babies just brought out the best in people. I was bone tired, though, after carrying Paris just four blocks. I put the baby down in Karin's front hall and let her climb the stairs on her own.

Even going uphill like this, Paris managed to crawl with her tail end pointed up like a dirt-scratching hen's. She grunted as she conquered each step.

By the time we reached the landing, Karin was standing there with her arms folded. She had thrown on a shimmering gold slip, tucked her feet into fuzzy pink mules, and twisted her black hair up with red chop sticks.

"You look fabulous," I told her.

"Thanks. I have to look good since I feel like crap. I can't stand it that Wally hasn't called to beg me to take him back. Life is so boring. Thank God I have you and your little friend to distract me," she added, watching the baby's steady progress.

"Maybe it's good to be bored," I suggested. "Beats a crisis."

"Being bored *is* a crisis at our age, honey." Karin stepped back and Paris scuttled inside the apartment like a crab.

"Then my life is as serene as can be."

"She looks just like you," Karin said. We both watched the baby race-crawl toward the coffee table, her makeshift dress up around her waist. "She's definitely got Cam's go-for-it personality, though." She squatted down to get a better look at Paris. To my amazement, Paris shrieked and crawled over to my leg, where she attached herself like an ankle weight.

I picked the baby up and cuddled her. "Wow. Did they teach you that bedside manner in nursing school?" From the safety of my embrace, Paris grinned at Karin and wound one hand in my hair.

"This always happens. That's why I like my patients best when they're fast asleep," Karin said softly, passing one hand in front of her face to play peek-a-boo until Paris grinned at her.

Karin's kitchen was in its usual state of chaos. While Karin somehow made tea amid the rubble, I told her about the baby being left on my doorstep. Paris sat on the floor playing with a couple of pots and a wooden spoon. The baby alternately gummed on the spoon and used it to bang on the pans.

"What's your game plan?" Karin shouted over the noise.

"I have to get hold of Cam, obviously. I called him twice before leaving my apartment, but he's not picking up and I didn't want to spook him by leaving a message. I'm hoping Cam can help me track down Nadine, see if she's sure about giving up the baby. Even if she has already left, how hard could it be to track her down? There's a finite number of orchards in Oregon, right? I could just drive up there."

Karin looked skeptical. "Orchards, maybe. Workers, no. Those pickers come and go, sometimes daily, and get paid under the table. Nadine would be just another faceless pair of hands. You'll never find her." She nodded towards Paris. "Anyway, why the hurry?"

"What do you mean?"

Paris crawled over to my feet and plopped down on her rear, sucking her fist with the slurping sound of someone walking in mud. I lay my hand gently on her silky head.

"You know the baby's better off with you," Karin said, "even if it's only for a little while. She can get her immunizations up to date and beef up a little before she hits the road with her crazy mother or moves into that Berkeley flophouse with your brother. I bet this kid's never even seen a pediatrician. She's how old?"

"I'm not sure. Seven months, maybe?"

Karin shrugged. "Your guess is as good as mine. Babies all seem like puppies to me until they're upright. She looks little for seven months, but who knows if that's because she's malnourished, or if it's because her mom sniffed, shot, and gobbled up all those fun drugs during pregnancy?"

My throat tightened. I didn't want to find out something was wrong with Paris. "Well, whatever I do, I've got to find Cam first. You can see by looking at her that he's the father, right?"

"Oh yeah," Karin said. "He might as well have tattooed his name on that kid."

As I continued to stroke the baby's hair, I felt her head lean heavily against my leg. "Maybe having to face up to parenthood will help Cam decide to turn his life around. He was using drugs, but he's clean now."

"What kind of drugs?"

Mentally, I slapped myself. I hadn't even asked him. "Pot, I assume, since that was always his self-destructive tool of choice. I'm betting he'll stay off it if he's got a kid around, though."

Karin gave me a hard look. "Yeah? How likely is that?"

"Pretty likely. Cam says he tried to get the mother to clean herself up, and that's what made her take off when she was pregnant. Plus, I plan to camp out on Cam's doorstep until he admits he has a child and takes action."

"Sounds like you have it all worked out," Karin said. "You turn the baby over to Cam. He'll sell her to pay the rent, maybe buy himself a new pair of skates or a fix. And I'll go back to bed and finish moping about my love life."

"Cam wouldn't do that!"

Karin stood up and put the tea cups in the sink, then faced me with her back against the counter. "Look, I know he's your brother, but guys like Cam are navel gazers. They can't see anybody's needs but their own. You love Cam, so you can't really see how useless he is. The guy barely has a pulse, Jordan! Even Nadine understood that. Cam's doorstep was a lot closer to People's Park, but she chose yours instead. If you don't want this baby, you'd better find somebody else who does. Somebody with more on the ball than your loser brother."

"You mean give her up for adoption."

"I do. I don't know why Nadine didn't do that in the first place, frankly. Any hospital emergency room or church would take in the baby, and there would have been no legal action taken against her." Karin studied her nails. "Of course, if you decided to give Paris to social services now, she'll probably spend some time in foster care until she's legally free for adoption. You wouldn't believe the red tape in these cases."

I pulled Paris onto my lap. The baby leaned against my shoulder and promptly fell asleep. "I don't want her with strangers," I blurted.

"Oh, come on. There are lots of really great foster parents," Karin said, but I could tell by her smug expression that she knew she'd won the argument.

I sighed. "Don't I need somebody's permission to get medical care for Paris? There must be some legal procedure involved in becoming a child's guardian, even temporarily."

"You've got a head start on that with Nadine's note. Meanwhile, I don't see a logistical problem. You and Paris even have the same last names.

Who'd bother to ask questions, anyway? You won't need a birth certificate until Paris goes to school, and by then everything will be resolved."

Karin tugged open a drawer and, amazingly, pulled a business card out of the stew of stray objects. "I've got just the doctor for this girl. Remember David from the party? Dr. Dull-as-Dishwater?" She turned the card over and scribbled something on the back with the stub of a pencil. "He'll help you out. Here's his clinic address and home phone."

I'd nearly forgotten about David. Now I remembered his kind brown eyes and curly mop of hair, and felt comforted. He wouldn't judge my brother's actions—or mine.

Karin rested her hand on the baby's back. Paris sighed but didn't stir. "Besides," Karin added softly, "it doesn't really matter if you want to adopt this baby or not. Paris has already adopted you."

❦

While Karin showered and dressed, I telephoned Cam again from her kitchen. Shepherd Jon answered.

"Cam's working," he said. "What do you need? Tell me and I'll relay the message."

Below Jon's slow, deliberate Western twang, I detected a strangled hint of New York accent. "I need to speak with Cam in person," I said. I didn't dare offer more information. If Cam knew I had Nadine's baby, he might refuse to see me.

"Yes, Ma'am," Jon said. "Soon as that boy drags his sorry ass home, I'll make sure he reports to duty."

I hung up, fuming. If I didn't hear from Cam by tonight, I'd go over there first thing tomorrow. By then I hoped to have a car seat for the baby.

Paris was still sound asleep, curled against my chest like a puppy. My shirt was damp and I stank of milk and bananas. What to do next? Well, I couldn't go anywhere without a car seat. I'd check out the area thrift stores for baby gear, then make that appointment with David.

I heard Karin emerge from the shower, singing, and felt suddenly envious: I'd already forgotten what it was like to have the freedom to close a bathroom door with nobody but me inside. Finding time to shower was a strong argument for parenting with a partner.

The front doorbell buzzed. I crossed the room, still cradling Paris against my shoulder, to lean on the intercom button. "Yes?"

"Hey, it's me," a man's voice replied.

"Me, who?"

"Funny girl. Me for you, that's who."

I didn't recognize the voice, but the man sounded friendly. I buzzed him in. Maybe it was the mysterious Wally, returning for a last, dramatic scene, and I'd get to watch. Good. Karin would be happy to do battle, especially with an audience.

But it wasn't Wally. I opened the door to Ed, bearing a bouquet of mixed flowers and a box of chocolates.

"Well, if it isn't Cupid," I said.

He shifted his feet and looked sheepish. "That's me. Your neighborhood Cupid on winged feet."

"If you're traveling on winged feet, I think you mean Hermes. But he didn't do much for love. I think he was more like Federal Express. Any package, any time."

"There you go again. Always the teacher, drowning the rest of us in your well of knowledge."

"Sorry."

Ed smiled uneasily, and pointed. "What's that?"

I'd had Paris on my shoulder for so long that I'd forgotten I was holding her. "My brother's daughter."

"You're babysitting?"

I nodded, unwilling to explain and suddenly confused. What was Ed doing at Karin's place with such classic courting gifts?

Ed was rocking from one foot to the other. "You going to invite me in?"

I laughed and opened the door wider. "Sorry."

He started to reassure me the minute he was inside the door. "You're the one I've been trying to call, Jordan. I only came here because I couldn't reach you. I thought I'd stop in and visit Karin while I was in the neighborhood."

I suspected Ed was relieved that I wasn't home, offering him a handy excuse for visiting Karin. "It doesn't matter why you're here," I told him truthfully. "I'm glad to see you."

It was true: I *was* glad. I liked Ed. On the other hand, even with Mr. Testosterone standing close enough for me to rub his bulging blue jeans like a genie's lamp, I felt nothing more than a vague affection for him. The chemistry just wasn't there.

As I watched Ed find a vase on Karin's cluttered bookshelf, fill it with water, and fuss over arranging the flowers, I was aware that dancing with him, being in his apartment, and sitting next to him on our one movie date already seemed like distant memories.

Karin emerged just as Ed took a seat on the couch. She was dressed in tight black jeans and a black t-shirt, a shadow of Ed's outfit. In my khakis and stained white sweatshirt, and with Paris on my shoulder, I felt like a mother chaperoning a first date as Ed scrambled to his feet again and embraced Karin.

She exclaimed over the flowers and waltzed over to the table to open the box of chocolates before turning to me. "I called Ed, like, ten times this morning to cry over Wally," she said, popping a chocolate into her mouth. "He always knows how to comfort me."

"I'm kind of like Karin's relationship hot line." Ed added.

"I don't know why I'm still moping over Wally, that hairy dog," Karin said. "I guess I should have waited."

"Until what?" I asked. "That relationship was a flat line."

"Until I had someone else in my sights! Then this process wouldn't be so painfully tedious."

Ed shook his head. "You've always been one foot out the door with Wally anyway. Now we're going to carry you over the threshold for good."

I didn't comment on the obvious marriage metaphor, or on the foreign concept to Karin that it was possible to live without a man.

"I don't know, Ed," Karin sighed. "I botch every relationship." She sank down onto the couch and buried her face in her hands, crying softly.

Ed and I exchanged a look and then, as if on cue, settled down on either side of her.

"Maybe you subconsciously pick men who can never match your ideals, so you won't have to worry about getting married," I suggested.

Karin peered at me from between her fingers. "God, how pitifully self-indulgent. But maybe so. Remember Mexico, that last vacation we took together?"

I patted her with my free hand. Paris was snoring slightly in my ear. "Of course. I've never been so sick in my life!"

Karin shuddered. "I blocked out the sick part. But remember that guy, the waiter in Puerto Vallarta with the spaniel eyes?"

I thought hard. There had been so many men. In the United States, Karin and I were over the hill, nothing to turn heads. But, on vacation in Mexico three years ago, just before I met Peter, we caused stares and whistles everywhere we went, simply for being women without husbands who had money to spend and wore bikinis on the beach. Which waiter could she be talking about?

Then I remembered. "You mean Ernesto? The head waiter who took you to his village by boat while I went to the museum?"

"Right! What was he, maybe twenty years old?" Karin smiled. "Ernesto took me to his village, and we ate armadillo soup at his mother's house and took a walk out on the fishing docks. And then, I don't know what came over me, but the moon rose over the water and I had to have him. So I did, right there on the docks."

"On wooden docks? Ouch." Ed made a face.

Karin dropped her hands. "Well, on ropes, to be exact. These thick damp fishing nets. I felt like I was making love to all of Mexico in a single moment." She turned to me, her eyes suddenly anxious. "I never saw Ernesto again. I never even saw Mexico again. Do you think I'm horrible, Jordan?"

I smiled at her. "No. Why would I? Think about it. There I was, moldering away in a museum, while you were making love to Mexico. Who has more to remember?"

"And more to forget," Karin said, making a face. "But I guess that was the point. To make love with the moment."

"You'll have more moments," Ed said, then turned to me. "So how long are you babysitting, Jordan? Can you go up to the beach? We can hike at Point Reyes, maybe grab some barbequed oysters and a couple of beers. You come too, Karin," he added hastily. "We've got plenty of daylight left. Sound good?"

"Sounds impossible," I replied.

Ed looked startled. "Why?"

"For one thing, I don't know how long I'll be babysitting," I hedged, giving Karin a warning look so that she wouldn't intervene or explain my situation. "Besides, I don't have a car seat or anything to carry the baby in if we go hiking."

Ed considered this, chewing on the end of his mustache. "Some other time, then?" he said at last. "It would be a shame to go all the way up there and not hike."

Karin and Ed were both watching me closely; I didn't need a psychic hot line to read their minds. "Why don't you two go without me?" I suggested obediently. "Karin, you definitely need to think about something besides Wally."

"Oh, I don't know." Karin glanced at Ed, whose face had brightened.

Aha, I thought. So he had brought those flowers to the right address after all. Well, Karin wasn't the only one who could play matchmaker. "Come on," I said. "It would do you good."

"Are you sure you don't need help with the baby?" Karin's dark eyes searched mine. I knew what she was asking, and it wasn't permission to go to the beach.

"I'll be fine," I promised. "Go!"

Shortly after that, we left Karin's apartment together. Karin set off with Ed in his rattling orange car, blowing kisses, and I walked towards the Mission to shop at the thrift stores with Paris on my hip, trying Cam's cell phone again.

◐◑

There was still no message from Cam by the time I returned late that afternoon by taxi, with a car seat, a portable crib, a high chair, a stroller, and two plastic bags of baby clothes. Once inside, I made up the crib, fed Paris and settled her in the crib for nap. Then I stripped off my jeans and fell into bed without bothering to shower.

My cell phone sounded just as I was drifting off to sleep. I snatched it up and carried it into the bathroom, grateful that Paris was now in a crib and couldn't fall off the bed. It was Karin, asking innumerable questions about the baby until I realized that she was stalling.

"So, " I interrupted. "How was the beach?"

Karin waxed poetic about surf and fog, seals and barbequed oysters. Then, unexpectedly, she began to cry. "I feel sick," she said.

100

"Why? Bad oysters?"

"No! I hardly ate or drank anything!"

I frowned, studying my bare feet against the tiled bathroom floor, then said, "You're probably just feeling guilty because you and Ed slept together and you don't know how to tell me." I opened the medicine chest and rummaged for my moisturizer. When I found it, I began rubbing it into my face.

"Would you hate me if I did?"

Bingo. I wiped the excess face cream off my eyelids so that I wouldn't look so much like I'd contracted a terrible, oozing eye infection. "There's nothing you could do that would make me hate you, Karin."

"Well, Ed and I didn't have sex," she said.

"You didn't?" I squinted disbelievingly at the rust stain on the sink, which was shaped like Italy. "Why not? Was it the sand in your suit or high tide?" I teased.

"I suppose it was the tide. The tides of time, the way people come and go in my life. Except you." She caught her breath. "I didn't want to hurt you, so I didn't have sex with him."

"How would you being with Ed hurt me?" I was truly puzzled.

"Don't you like him? Even a little?"

I considered this. "Well, I like him better than Wally," I said. "But, honey, I like Ed for you, not for me. What does Ed want?"

Karin blew her nose, honking on the other end of the phone like a bus in traffic. "Oh, he's Mr. Romance, says we should give love a chance. But he doesn't want to do anything that might screw up my friendship with you, or take the risk that I'll bust him up with a hammer again."

"Is there that risk?"

"Of course. I'm completely unreliable as a lover," Karin pointed out. "Look at my track record!"

"Maybe you should think of Ed as a friend," I suggested. "You might be unreliable as a lover, but as a friend, you're a Hall-of-Famer."

"Oh, Jordan." Karin honked again. "Thanks for that. I owe you."

"I owe you back. Go for it."

Chapter eight

P aris hated the car. More precisely, she hated the baby seat in the car. When I tried strapping her into the seat to drive to the grocery store the next morning, she fought and hissed like a cornered wolverine. I had to pin her into the seat with my forearm while I pulled the strap over her head.

We suffered a repeat performance of this as we left the market's parking lot, with the added challenge of Paris's glass-shattering shrieks of fury. I'd been to rock concerts quieter than this. To make matters worse, a dozen onlookers gathered, probably ready to demand that I hand Paris over to someone more competent, like that woman in the minivan next to us whose three children remained placidly strapped into place while Mommy, not a hair out of place, packed the van with enough groceries for Armageddon.

Paris's howls escalated as I pulled out of the parking lot, white-knuckled and sweating. I spotted a pet shop across the street and toyed with the idea of stopping there to buy an animal crate. I could put the baby in that instead of the car seat and give her a few toys to maul.

Later, I decided that a dog crate might come in handy at home, too. While I unloaded groceries, Paris pulled the maple syrup out of the cupboard and poured herself a sticky skating rink. As I mopped that up, she hauled herself to a standing position on a counter stool, then wailed in horror when the stool toppled onto its side. Moments later, I discovered my niece ingesting half a tube of lipstick she'd managed to fish out of my purse.

"She probably ate $7 worth of my favorite lipstick," I complained when Karin telephoned. "This kid is a cross between Houdini and a chimpanzee."

"Don't look to me for sympathy. Caretakers like you keep us nurses employed," Karin reminded me. "Are you going to Berkeley today to see Cam? I can come over and help you wrestle Paris into the car. We'll just throw a towel over her head, the way my mom used to do to our cat when we took her to the vet's."

I declined, since I still hadn't heard from Cam. "I'd rather invite him to come over here, anyway."

"Oh, I get it. You're thinking turf wars. Like, if Cam's on this side of the bridge, he's more likely to own up to the fact that it takes two to make a baby?"

"He might."

"Dream on."

Things went better once I got the baby outside. Paris loved riding in her stroller and giving everyone the Queen's wave. We hung out in Dolores Park, watching the druggies, the other children, the ants on the sidewalk, the martial artists, and the wind through the leaves. I'd even thought to bring along a juice box and crackers.

When the afternoon sun began to lick the tops of the palm trees, Paris fell asleep and I walked back to the apartment.

Still no message or text from Cam. I couldn't wait any longer. I'd have to drive over to Berkeley the next morning with Paris.

I imagined surprising Cam at the falafel cart, the two of us embracing with the baby between us in one of those happy cinematic endings where onlookers applaud. But, no, Cam would be more likely to flee the scene as we approached, his Falafel Man apron flapping around his legs as I chased him down with the baby stroller.

The sky darkened and a late fog drenched the clothes I'd hand washed and hung on a line I'd strung from the back of the house to the garden fence. Why wasn't Cam returning my calls? He couldn't possibly be making falafel 24 hours a day. I had telephoned him before dinner, and again every hour after that, but nobody answered. I left more messages, brief but urgent. "Call me now. I need you." "Don't wait. Call me."

Finally, I bathed Paris in the sink, sparing us both the ordeal of the bathtub, and sang her to sleep. I tried Cam once more at 9 o'clock, gazing down at the baby as I left yet another cryptic message for my brother. The baby lay on her back across my lap, her mouth slightly open, a single blonde wisp over her forehead. I could drive to Cam's place right now, I decided; I could probably transfer the baby to her car seat without waking her.

I rose and reached for my purse, but Paris immediately squirmed into the tight crook of my arm and grabbed a handful of my hair, whimpering. Get her into the car without a struggle? Ha. Fat chance. And I was too tired to cope with anything more tonight. I'd let her sleep and track Cam down in the morning.

෧෧

I was awakened later that night by the sound of a terrifying bark. The sound turned out to be the baby wheezing for breath.

I sat up and snapped on the bedside lamp, my heart pounding, remembering what Nadine had said about Paris's strange cough. Surely this was it. The baby was sitting up in her crib, gasping for air, her narrow chest concave with the effort of sucking in oxygen.

Paris saw me and struggled to stand, but the effort made her hiccup and bark and gasp until her lips turned blue. She didn't have enough breath in her to cry.

"Shh, it's okay, it's okay," I murmured, but it wasn't. Paris managed a faint, raspy howl, broken by that inhuman seal's cough at the back of her throat.

I was terrified to pick up the baby, afraid she'd turn even bluer and die in my arms. Had I fed her something wrong? I rapidly catalogued what she'd eaten. Could she be allergic to milk, apples, cheese?

But I hadn't given her anything new to eat today. And this wasn't an allergic reaction; it was some sort of respiratory failure. I'd seen enough of those as a teacher to recognize them. But from what? Cystic fibrosis? That might explain why she was so skinny. Pneumonia? Had I kept Paris outside too long in the fog?

Did she have some horrible side effect from her mother taking drugs during pregnancy? No, no. I would have seen signs before. What, then, could cause her such distress in the middle of the damn night? I could go online and look up symptoms, but that would be even more terrifying. I couldn't do any of this alone.

I scooped Paris up and dialed Karin's number. "Pick up, pick up," I muttered, but there was no answer. Of course there was no answer. It was 3 o'clock in the morning, and Karin turned the phone off at night. Or maybe Ed had come around with another bouquet.

I couldn't risk taking Paris over there. I'd be better off driving to the ER, which was the same distance as Karin's house—except that I was afraid Paris would carry on about the car seat like she did before and somehow choke in panic. Or I'd have a car accident listening to Paris in the back seat while I drove.

By now, Paris had gone limp against my shoulder, except when her tiny body was in the throes of a coughing spasm. Then she flopped about like a rag doll. I pressed my ear against her ribcage and heard bubbling through her lungs. When I lifted my head again, I spotted David's business card, the one Karin had given me, on the counter where I'd left it. I had meant to make an appointment at his clinic for the baby's checkup, but I'd forgotten.

I flipped the card over, found the cell phone number Karin had scribbled there for me, and punched in the numbers. He was a doctor. He was Karin's friend and a pediatrician; he must be used to dealing with emergencies and panicked parents.

David answered on the second ring. He seemed not the least surprised to hear from me. Karin must have seen him at work and told him about the baby. David asked me to describe the baby's symptoms in detail, then told me to sit in the bathroom with her.

"Run the shower," he said. "Crank up the hot water. Hot as you can get it. Keep the shower curtain open and the bathroom door shut. You want steam, lots of steam. Wait! Tell me how to get to your house. Leave your apartment door unlocked and give me fifteen minutes."

He was with me in ten, carrying a comforting looking black medical bag. David slipped into the bathroom so quietly that Paris didn't startle, and perched on the tub. I was sitting on the toilet seat with Paris on my lap, the shower going full force. David's flannel shirt gaped open over his red t-shirt and his curly hair was matted flat on one side. I'd definitely gotten him out of bed, yet he seemed fully alert. So was I, high on adrenaline.

"Her lips are blue," I said desperately.

"What's her name?" he asked softly, taking a stethoscope out of his bag.

"Paris."

"Hi there, Paris," he greeted her solemnly. "I'm Dr. David." Then, to me, "Can you turn her on your lap, please, so that her left side is to me?"

I did as he asked. David's fingers were gentle as he listened to the baby's heart and lungs, took her temperature, checked her pulse, and peered into her throat and ears. I relaxed slightly as David took charge. He talked not to me, but to Paris, who watched him warily and, for one split second, smiled when David said, "You've got a birdie in your ear, I think, Miss Paris. No, wait, it's only a kitty!"

Her breathing eased gradually, and Paris pressed her head against my shoulder, moving her head slightly as she tracked David's movements. When he was finished examining her, David pulled a final magic trick out of his bag: an orange Popsicle. It had already started to melt, but he pushed the frozen end between the baby's lips and coaxed her to taste it.

"What's wrong with her?" I asked finally, as Paris tentatively tongued the frozen orange.

"Croup," he said. "Fairly common in infants, but scary as hell, isn't it?"

I burst into tears and blubbered something about how I'd been certain she was dying.

David's glasses had fogged over. He removed them and wiped the lenses on the tail of his flannel shirt. "Everyone thinks that when their kids have croup. And sometimes it can be very serious, if there's a complete obstruction of the airway. Most of the time, though, croup is something that a little hot steam can fix at home."

"But what is croup, exactly?"

An infection, he explained, of the voice box, windpipe, and bronchial tubes, usually viral, though there was a bacterial croup, too. Very rare.

"Typically, a child has a cold first, but not always, and the first night of croup is always the worst," he said. "She'll wheeze for a few more hours, maybe, but it'll ease up. See? She's already breathing better. You did a great job of keeping her calm."

"Are you kidding? I didn't do anything but panic! It's just dumb luck that you're a neighbor and Karin gave me your home phone. And I'm not her mother," I added, blowing my nose on a scrap of toilet paper.

David raised a bushy eyebrow above his glasses, but his lenses had fogged up again and I couldn't read his expression. "Really? She looks just like you."

"She's my niece. My brother's child. A long story," I apologized. "I didn't even know I had a niece in San Francisco, or anywhere else, for that matter. This is a recent development."

"A nice surprise, I hope?"

"An ongoing saga. Look, aren't you on call, or something? I feel awful now, getting you out of bed for nothing."

"Don't. It's my night off. I don't have anywhere I need to be."

"Oh, God. I got you out of bed on the one night you could have slept? I'm so sorry! I just didn't know who else to call. I don't know anyone here except Karin and my brother, and neither of them answered their phones."

"It's really okay." David grinned, his foggy lenses glinting in the flourescent light. His hair had curled into tight ringlets in the steam. "I'm glad you called. I wanted to see you again. I tried to say goodbye to you at Karin's party, but you'd left the porch and I couldn't find you. I was planning to call Karin to find out your status."

"You make it sound like I'm a plane about to leave and you're a late check-in."

He rolled his eyes. "The story of my life."

I smiled and stroked Paris's hair, which clung to her head in damp yellow threads. The baby was really getting into the Popsicle, and the Popsicle was getting all over me. I pulled a washcloth off the rack and started swabbing the sticky orange goo off one thigh. That's when I realized what I was wearing: a tattered blue t-shirt and faded red bikini underwear. When would this guy ever see me in normal clothes?

"Oh, no," I moaned. "I forgot to get dressed!"

David laughed. "Where's the rule that says you've got to be dressed in your own bathroom? Besides, it's a hundred degrees in here. You're the smart one. It's time I joined you."

He stood up and pulled off his sandals, jeans, and flannel shirt, dropping each item into an untidy heap at my feet. I couldn't help but compare his hasty, comic performance to Ed's carefully choreographed striptease, and David's slim, wiry frame to Ed's muscular bulk. I grinned.

"What?" he asked.

"Not fair. You're wearing boxers. And in San Francisco that pretty much passes for clothing."

"Yeah, but I'm also wearing socks. That definitely gives you the fashion edge. How attractive is a man in underwear and socks?" David perched on the edge of the tub again, his hairy knees bumping against my own smooth ones.

I giggled. "Why keep them on, then?"

"Didn't want to give you the wrong idea. I'm not easy, you know. I'm a highly trained professional. Tell me about your niece."

Paris's coughing had stopped, and her hoarse breathing had settled into a slight rattle deep in her chest. She was asleep. I shifted her weight to one arm and took David's glasses off with my free hand. "If I'm going to bare my soul as well as my legs, I want to see your eyes." I laid the glasses on the edge of the sink.

David blinked at me. Beneath his mop of curls, his dark eyes were sleepy and long-lashed, warm.

He's beautiful, I thought, and started telling David everything.

"You slept with David?" Karin shrieked.

I held the phone away from my ear until she'd calmed down. "Yeah, but that's it," I said then. "We slept together. As in sawing logs. Triple Z's."

It was late morning, and Paris was asleep again after getting up briefly to eat a bowl of oatmeal. I was sitting on the floor of my bathroom, my new home away from home, the phone cradled against my ear while I folded laundry. Lots of laundry. Thank God baby clothes were small enough to wash in the sink. Paris went through more costume changes than Lady Gaga.

Karin was still laughing. "Are you positive we're talking about the same guy? You actually had a one-night stand with David Goldstein?"

"It wasn't a one-night stand in the biblical sense. We just happened to fall asleep together..."

"...in the same bed..."

"...in the same bed, yes, but for only three hours, and with a baby in the same room. That hardly counts as a one-night stand." I sighed. "He's amazing, Karin. Heroic and kind. And he has beautiful eyes."

"Oh boy. You must be punchy from lack of sleep. David's a great doctor and a nice guy, but within an hour of being in his company, most people want to give away their dirty money and join the Peace Corps."

"I think he's sexy," I insisted, then held the phone away from my ear again while Karin howled in disbelief. When she'd finished, I added, "Anyway, I'm glad that I had his number. Thank you for that. Paris probably would have been okay, but it sure felt like an emergency."

I smiled, staring down at the tiny cotton t-shirt in my hands. The baby had fallen asleep on my shoulder after finishing her orange popsicle, and David helped me sponge the worst of the syrupy mess off my legs and her face before we transferred her to the bed. Then the two of us sat at my kitchen counter, and I told him the whole Cam story while we ate cheese sandwiches and drank what was left of a bottle of tequila. David had started to leave, but I convinced him to stay with me after we both realized he had to be in the clinic in just three hours. Besides, I felt safer with him there, in case Paris had a relapse.

Spooning on my bed, David behind me with an arm about my waist, we had fallen into a deep, comforting sleep. When the alarm on David's watch went off, he had dressed and stroked my hair as he whispered good-bye. Almost as good as an orgasm, that caress. But Karin would only laugh if I told her that.

"I just don't get it," she was saying now. "I thought you were done with nice guys and ready to just have some fun."

"I guess I lied."

She sighed. "Okay, go ahead and pursue things with David. For all I know, the man could be a smoking volcano in the sack. When are you seeing him again?"

"Today. I'm taking Paris into the clinic for her shots. Pretty romantic, huh? Then I'm going to Berkeley to find Cam."

Karin offered to take the baby while I went to Berkeley. "Babies almost always run a fever after those shots."

"Think you can cope?"

She snorted. "Don't forget that I'm a trained professional."

"Just promise that you won't make Paris wear leather pants and high-heeled boots to the playground."

It was a couple of miles to the clinic, but I put Paris in the stroller rather than try strapping her into the car seat. As we walked, the neighborhoods got progressively less chic until we were in a part of San Francisco you never saw in the movies. The buildings were crooked multistory tenements in washed out colors. Men stood around cars shipwrecked on cement blocks. Women chased small children through dusty yards or sat on the front steps of buildings, their haunches broad and shiny in rayon dresses. Broken glass sparkled like the sea.

Paris clung to my neck in the dreary cement building that housed the clinic. I was the only non-Hispanic woman in the waiting room. I was also the only woman with a single child.

One woman, her legs as solid as tree trunks beneath her stained pink cotton dress, had brought along four. When she sat down on one of the orange plastic chairs, the children fought for space on her lap. The woman brought a box of doughnut holes out of her enormous cloth bag and handed them around. The children's faces puffed like hamsters hoarding seeds, their mouths soon sticky white rings.

I waited for an hour before a male nurse called my name. By then, the waiting room had taken on the companionable, chaotic atmosphere of a ferry crossing choppy water, one where nervous passengers make the best of a bad trip. Two of the mothers offered Paris graham crackers and handfuls of cereal; of course I hadn't thought to bring snacks.

The nurse, a dark-skinned man with a gold stud in his nose and black hair slicked back from his high forehead, wore a name tag that read

"Enrique." He wrestled with Paris to get her to lie on a baby scale. The scale looked too much like a car seat for Paris; she thrashed about as if she were being stuck with pins.

"She's a real little wildcat," Nurse Enrique pronounced, and helped me pin her down on the table so that he could measure her height. Then he left the room, saying the doctor would be right in.

Finally, David appeared. He was dressed in the same clothes he'd been wearing when he left my apartment, but he'd thrown on a white lab coat. He greeted me with a nod and played with Paris, moving her limbs around like a doll's and encouraging her to crawl on the table. Then he had me sit the baby on my lap while he examined the curve of her spine.

Why didn't he look at me, I wondered, or make conversation? I didn't get it. David was even more reticent here than he'd been at Karin's party. Was he embarrassed about sleeping with me? Was he involved with someone else, and didn't know how to bring up the subject? Or was he just being professional? I wondered how to put him at ease.

Nurse Enrique returned and threw a loving arm around David's shoulders. "You gonna come play with us tonight, Doc?"

"Wouldn't miss it," David said.

Enrique giggled. "Watch this guy, *guapa*. Doc's got himself some fast hands. And rhythm! Ooh la la."

I felt like I'd had the wind knocked out of me. David couldn't be gay, could he?

"Is your nurse a close friend?" I asked David casually, once Enrique left us alone again.

"Very," David said, then glanced at his watch and got down to business. Paris was thin, but we couldn't determine where her weight fell on the growth curve, he told me, since we had no actual birth date or previous medical history. But there was good news, too: her heart, lungs, muscle tone and reflexes all seemed normal.

"We'll start catching her up on immunizations today, and we'll keep an eye on her weight gain over the next few weeks," he explained. "We want to make sure that her failure to thrive has been the result of poor nutrition and nothing more."

"Thank you," I said. Hearing the phrase "failure to thrive" made me feel sick with anxiety.

On top of that, I now felt confused about David. Was sleeping with me last night just another good deed for him? A California sort of welcome? A favor for Karin? And how was it possible that I had once again fallen for a guy who found me as desirable as plywood?

David flashed a smile, softening his professional cool. "Hey, want to join us tonight? A bunch of us are going to play at a club called Aunt Mary's. It's near your house. Can you get a sitter?"

"You want me to go with you?" I asked. "I thought you were going with Enrique."

David studied me over his glasses, drawing his bushy eyebrows together in a slight frown. "Sure, Enrique will be there, too, but so will a lot of other people. You know where Mary's is? Near the Bart station on 24th?"

Right in my neighborhood, but definitely not right up my alley. I didn't really think David was gay. But I couldn't imagine myself competing for David's attention among a group of swinging singles as hip as Enrique, me in my khaki pants with a baby on my lap. "Sounds fun, but I can't," I said. "I'm going to Berkeley to talk things over with my brother."

"You sure?"

Did David look disappointed? No way to know. I reached out to shake his hand. "I'm sure. Maybe I'll go out with you and your friends another time," I said. "Thank you for everything."

David patted my arm awkwardly. "Okay. We'll be there until pretty late if you change your mind. Enrique will come in to give Paris her shots in just a minute. Good luck with Cam."

Paris was running a slight fever after her vaccinations, so I took Karin up on her offer to watch the baby while I drove to Berkeley that afternoon. I should have been relieved to be driving without a screaming banshee in the back seat, but instead I felt bereft, as if part of me were missing.

I reminded myself that I was looking for Cam not just for my sake, but for Paris's, too. Even so, by the time I crossed the Bay Bridge and saw how the fog was wrapping itself around San Francisco like a moist towel, I had to fight the urge to turn the car around. I was exhausted on top of every-thing else; who knew that babies were this tiring?

It was easy to find the outdoor food vendors near the main campus gate on Telegraph. There were salad carts and fruit carts, hot dog stands and fruit smoothie trucks, pretzel vendors and one enormous stand that special-ized in Chinese food. Among this cornucopia of student cuisine, I spotted The Falafel Man truck.

Cam wasn't there. A tiny brunette, maybe twenty years old, stood alone in the cart. The tattoos on her neck and arms were so vivid that at first I thought she was wearing a long-sleeved shirt beneath her halter top.

"What's your pleasure?" the woman lisped around a silver tongue stud the size of a June bug.

"I'm looking for Cameron O'Malley. Do you know him?"

The woman dug her hands into the front pockets of her jeans. "Cam, he's the man," she said, flashing a mouthful of silver.

A tongue stud and braces? With this much hardware, the woman could receive her favorite radio stations. I asked her if Cam was working today, but she squinted at the question, suddenly suspicious, and didn't answer. She just stood there, her metal bits sparking in the sunshine.

"I'm his sister," I explained. "I was just passing by, and thought I'd say hello."

"I haven't seen you before," she said.

"I haven't been living in the area." I smiled, playing the polite guest at a dinner party. "I just moved here from Boston. That's where Cam and I are from."

"I knew that."

She did? Now it was my turn to look suspicious. "How long have you known Cam?"

The woman shrugged and dug her hands deeper into her pockets, safe-guarding whatever secrets she kept in there. Not that much would fit. Those jeans had to be a size 0. "Oh, me and Cam, we go way back," she said. "Since right after him and that Nadine split."

"You knew Nadine?"

"Yeah, she hung out. Cam, he was always good to her. Gave her free falafels. Sometimes she had the humus plate, though," she added judiciously.

"My brother's a generous man," I agreed.

A young Asian man stepped up to the counter and rapped on it with his knuckles. "You got the Falafel Special today?"

"Every day," the woman replied.

"Okay, then. I need one of those specials and a large lemonade."

The woman got busy. She was surprisingly efficient. After the man had walked off with his meal, she swiveled towards me, chatty again. "Cam's like, my main squeeze. Or he was," she amended. "That was like, ancient history. A month ago."

I nodded, trying to look sympathetic. Boy, Cam really knew how to pick them. What was wrong with him, that he couldn't date a woman his own age? Or his own IQ, for that matter. I asked when she'd last seen my brother.

"We usually tried working the same shifts so we could hang out," she said. "Then, two days ago, Cam suddenly turns on me, says I've been this major drag. 'So go,' I says to him. And he did. Just like that! Said something about there being a journey within himself, and he could only go it alone. I couldn't tell him what to do anymore, he says. Huh. Like he ever fucking listened to me anyway." She plucked a piece of lettuce out of one of the metal bins and munched on it.

Two days ago? Cam must have broken up with this woman right after getting my message saying I wanted him to come see me in San Francisco. "He hasn't been to work since then?" I asked.

"Nope. And I've been swamped."

I glanced at the empty counter. Well, all things were relative.

The woman was still talking. "Boss says we gotta replace Cam, but Cam always knew when to order inventory and stuff. Nobody else can do that. So I told the boss to hold off on firing him. Your brother's done runners before. He always comes back. Only this time he can kiss my ass." She pouted, perhaps in anticipation.

"Any idea where he went?"

The woman began haphazardly swabbing down the counters with a gray rag. "No. All he told me was this job was his ball and chain." She scrubbed harder.

If this job was Cam's ball and chain, Nadine must have felt like a dungeon. "Look," I said finally. "If you see my brother around, tell him that his sister needs him. Say it's urgent, okay?"

The woman's gaze drifted in my direction. She had clearly lost interest. "Yeah," she said. "Okay. Real urgent."

I drove back to Cam's street and parked a block away from the house so that he wouldn't spot my car. If I entered through the greenhouse, nobody could spot me and warn him that I was coming.

The plan was nearly perfect, except for the high metal fence separating Jon's back yard from the yard next door. I hadn't counted on that. Years of playground duty paid off, however: I got a toe hold in the wire and climbed the fence, swinging myself over the top and landing with a soft thud in the mossy shade of a rhododendron bush.

The greenhouse door was unlocked and the house was silent. A forlorn yellow tea cup sat on the kitchen counter near the empty sink. There was no sound other than the rattle of the eucalyptus leaves in the tree outside the window. The house had the musty, abandoned feel of a house whose owners are on vacation. Where could they all be? It was nearly six o'clock in the evening.

"Hello?" I called. I wandered from the kitchen to the foyer and stood beneath the teardrop chandelier. The glass shuddered slightly above my head as I moved to the foot of the stairs and called again. "Hey, anybody home?"

There was a faint shuffling sound. Val appeared at the head of the stairs. She was swaying slightly, wrapped in a tattered Navajo blanket, droopy-eyed and snuffling. She was either sick, coming down from a high, or suffering from her vegan diet. Maybe all of the above.

"Who's there?" she said.

"Oh, hey, Val. It's just me. I'm looking for Cam."

Val clutched the blanket around her neck, but it gaped open from the waist down. She was naked beneath it, the V between her legs so light with blonde hair that at first I thought she was wearing pink leggings. "You're too late," she said.

"What do you mean?" My skin prickled with alarm.

"Cam's gone." Val leaned on the wall. The blanket fluttered open, her body emerging from within its fraying folds like a pink pupa sliding out of its cocoon.

"You'd better sit before you fall down," I coaxed, ascending the stairs slowly until I stood on the step beside her. "What's wrong? Are you sick?"

Val sat down but misjudged the distance. Her butt met the step with a painful sounding thump. "Not sick. Alone again," she moaned, dropping her head into her hands.

"You're not alone. I'm here." I touched Val's hand. "And the others will be home soon, won't they?"

Val scuttled away from me, sliding her rear along the landing until she was hunched against the wall. Her blonde hair was matted close to her head. She had a tiny skull beneath all that hair and her face had seen too much sun. The skin was dry and slightly wattled beneath her double chin.

"Nobody's coming home," she insisted. "I'm alone again! Just like last time."

Now I was really feeling panicked. Val seemed so certain. "Val, what are you talking about?" I kept my voice light. "You live with friends. Of course they'll come home."

Val started pounding her fist on the wall. A small dent appeared in the plaster as the ancient wallpaper gave way. "I! Am! Too! Alone! Again!" she shrieked with each punch, then collapsed, folding her body forward and pressing her face against her knees.

I stroked Val's back while she cried, wondering how she stood the itch on her bare skin. Val's story oozed out: Jon had bought everyone plane tickets. But Val had no passport. And that was just too bad, Jon said, since he'd advised everyone to keep their passports up to date, always, in case of emergencies like this one.

"What emergency?" I frowned, my heart pounding.

"Cam's emergency. Cam was in trouble, Jon said." Val raised her head and glared at me. It was dawning on her that, since I was Cam's sister, this latest twist in her life could be my fault. "Cam had to leave the country. They all did, to save him."

"Save Cam from what?" I could hardly breathe.

"That girl coming around here with his baby! She catches up to him, Cam's going to be screwed, Jon said. He won't be able to stay clean."

"Where did they go?" I stood up and gripped the railing, as if I could leap down the stairs and start chasing Cam right now, the way I had when we were kids playing tag.

"To the mountains. The Shepherd wants everyone to cleanse themselves in the purest air, especially Cam. And he wants them to serve the earth.

He bought them all tickets to Nepal and everybody signed up to be an eco volunteer."

I had no idea what an "eco" volunteer was, but it must have something to do with plants, knowing Jon's passion for plants over people. "Are you serious? Nepal? That would cost thousands of dollars!"

Val nodded, morose. "Jon bought them all tickets," she repeated. "All except me. And I'm the one who needs cleansing more than anybody."

She wept while I rubbed my temples and tried to focus on what to do next. Why did it surprise me so much that Cam had pulled this disappearing act? Irresponsible, self-absorbed brat. What kinds of drugs did he use, to make him behave this way? Even his homeless girlfriend had been thoughtful enough to leave me a note.

Well, I wouldn't make things easy for him. I'd find a way to contact him. I wouldn't leave Berkeley without making one last attempt to find Nadine, too. There was a slim chance that she hadn't gotten her act together to leave for Oregon. I reached down and touched Val's oily hair. "Look, I've got to go. Will you be all right?"

"Sure. Why shouldn't you leave? Everybody else does."

"Is there anyone I can call to come over? Do you have friends here in town?"

Her voice was muffled, exhausted. "You've met my friends."

"Maybe it's time to get new ones," I said gently.

"Oh yeah?" She raised her head and curled her lip at me. "And maybe you should just piss off."

By the time I arrived at People's Park, the light was fading. It would be dark in another hour. I made my way slowly into the thick brush edging the park, following a narrow path towards the scent of cooking fires. The shadows were long, the grass was damp around my ankles, and the clacking of the tree branches made me jumpy.

Small knots of people were gathered around a bonfire in the same spot where I'd first talked to the naked flamingo man and the woman in the

Hawaiian shirt. I searched for them among the faces flickering in the fire-light, lingering on the fringes of the crowd, reluctant to draw attention to myself. Everyone was drinking, the bottles glinting in the firelight as they were passed around.

I finally approached a bull-necked woman standing on the sidelines. "Hi," I said, feeling the terror of every new child on a school yard. "I'm looking for someone, and I was wondering if you've seen her."

The woman wore fingerless wool gloves and a frayed tweed jacket; she was missing a front tooth. She drew back when I spoke, startled. "I don't hear so good out the left side," she apologized.

I repeated myself and described Nadine. "I think she was staying here with a man called The Admiral."

The woman nodded. "The Admiral, he and your girl packed up two, maybe three days ago. Ain't been back since. You can check with Sister, though. Sister keeps track."

"Who's Sister?"

The woman gestured towards the opposite side of the fire, where I spotted the woman I'd spoken to that first day. She wore the same Hawaiian shirt and remembered me, too, when I squatted beside her and asked if Nadine had left the Park.

"Packed up to go north," Sister answered. "Went off with a truckload of folks. There's a farmer comes around here every few weeks. Says he gets tired of pissing money across the border to Mexicans when he can get red-blooded American workers with college degrees. He comes here to fetch people and drives them far as Portland, sometimes."

I thanked her and turned to leave, but Sister grabbed my wrist between two fat fingers. "Nadine weren't a bad girl," she added. "She found a good home for that baby with family, she told me. Knew better'n to try and raise it up herself."

Talking about Paris made me miss her. I thanked Sister again, and told her that I was the one who had the baby now. Sister beamed. "Nadine's nobody's fool," she said.

I hurried out of the park. Several hundred feet into the brush, though, I realized I had taken a different path. Well, it had to lead out to the street. I kept walking, ducking my head to avoid the branches, my heart beating hard as cracking sounds popped in the undergrowth all around.

Finally, I heard the comforting, belligerent honks of the fog horn in the Bay. I forced myself to stand still and focus on the sound until I was certain of my direction. But then I heard the sound of footsteps behind me and panicked. I dashed through the brush, pinwheeling my arms to clear away the branches until I burst out onto the sidewalk.

There was nobody following me. I looked around, panting, and recognized one of the houses by its creative paint job of aqua trim, pink clapboards and lime green door. My car wasn't far away. I limped towards it, holding my side with one hand until I could lean against the car's solid, comforting hulk and search for the keys in my purse.

What had I been thinking, taking my purse into People's Park at sunset? Jesus, what an idiot.

I glanced around, relieved to see that the only other person on the street was a tall, broad-shouldered blonde in a short skirt. She walked towards me with brisk strides, her heels clacking along like horse's hooves.

I turned my back on the woman to unlock the door. Within seconds she was on me, clutching my head beneath her arm in a muscular half-Nelson while she grabbed my purse and shoved me down onto the sidewalk. This was no she, I realized by the size of his feet and legs. My mugger wore platform shoes, but black stubble poked through his pale stockings like the bristles of a nail brush.

The assault was over in an instant, my little car speeding away from the curb before I could scramble to my feet. My purse was on the passenger seat. I brushed myself off, silently cursing my own stupidity. If this were a TV show, I'd want to turn it off. I'd been alone on a dark street and broken the cardinal rule of city dwellers everywhere: get into your car fast and lock the doors.

Miraculously, a patrol car rounded the corner. I bounded into the street and stood there like a deer trapped in headlights, waving my arms. My saviors were a pair of Berkeley cops, a black man and a white woman, both with bellies they carried like sacks over their belts. They approached me with hands on their guns and I blubbered out my story. Within a few minutes they'd whisked me to a police station lit up like a bus terminal.

"And you say the perp was wearing platform shoes?" The officer taking my statement on the computer was an older man with a scar across one eyebrow. "Any other identifying features?" he pressed.

"He had on a blonde wig and a red miniskirt."

The officer in the cubicle behind us snorted, but my man remained professional. He poured a cup of sludge into a styrofoam cup and handed it to me, then tapped a few notes into a computer. "You seem pretty sure this was a male assailant."

"He had a five o'clock shadow around his lipstick and his legs were covered with black stubble."

A muscle in the cop's jaw twitched. "You got anything of value in the car to report?"

"You mean my purse and car aren't enough to lose?"

He shrugged. "This is the time to give your insurance company a full report of anything you lost." He kept his eyes on the screen. "Anything at all."

I sighed. "Nothing but my purse and an old pair of sneakers." Luckily, I'd left the baby seat with Karin in case she had an emergency with Paris. I ached to call Karin. What if the baby had panicked in my absence, had another bout of croup, or suffered a bad reaction to those shots? I'd already left her longer than I'd promised. Not that Paris could understand about time at her age, of course, but still: a promise was a promise. Enough people had already let her down.

The cop delivered a pat speech about procedures, asked me to sign some papers, then offered me his phone. I called Karin. She was appropriately appalled and I felt instantly better. "Oh, poor you. That sounds horrible!"

"Well, it was my own damn fault," I said. "I should have known that area wouldn't be safe at night."

"That's ridiculous. It's not your fault you were mugged. Look, give me half an hour and I'll be there. I'll bring you back to my house, and we'll cry over spilled milk. You should see how your kid trashed my kitchen!"

Like anyone would notice the difference, I nearly said, but was stopped by the words "your kid." Was that what I really wanted, for Paris to be mine?

Right now, I wanted Karin to rescue me. But that wouldn't be the best thing for Paris, waking her and driving over here at night. I told Karin that I'd borrow subway fare from the police, and she encouraged me to go straight home instead of picking up the baby.

"You need a good night's sleep," she insisted. "Paris will be fine here until morning."

So much for feeling essential. I hung up on the verge of tears, begged a few dollars from the cop, and walked to the BART station around the corner. The train arrived and departed with merciful efficiency. It was well after eight o'clock, yet the train was still clogged with evening commuters, mostly in suits and headphones, hypnotized by their phones. I couldn't believe there was this much normalcy left in the world.

Half an hour later, I arrived at my station. No car, no purse. Just me and a pocketful of loose change. I started trudging towards Noe Valley, dreading the idea of my empty apartment.

I hadn't walked more than two blocks before spotting a blue neon sign—Aunt Mary's—outside a bar with a bright pink beaded curtain fluttering across the doorway. I fingered the change in my pocket. This was where David was meeting Enrique and the rest of his friends.

With luck, I could get them to buy me a drink before I went home. That might take the edge off the fact that I'd lost not only my wallet and my car, but my brother, too.

Chapter nine

Entering Aunt Mary's was like wading into a city swimming pool on the Fourth of July: lots of blue light and standing room only. This was an affluent, intellectual looking crowd, people in their twenties or thirties who dressed like Berkeley but had Silicon Valley money.

The band was working a noisy rhythm and blues set. I threaded my way through the crowd, noting the bits of car fenders, tires, and steering wheels comprising the giant mobiles dangling ominously above the crowd. Nobody could ever accuse San Francisco artists of wasting materials.

I felt claustrophobic and discouraged. I had as much chance of finding David in here as stealing my car back from that high-heeled mugger. I resigned myself to spending my last few dollars swilling a beer alone before going home to bury my head under a pillow. At least I could look forward to seeing Paris in the morning.

This accidental longing to see the baby left me feeling just as terrified of losing her as I'd been, only days ago, of raising her. That was scary: every baby belonged with her parents, if possible. I had to give Cam the opportunity to do the right thing, no matter what my feelings.

The room shuddered with bodies in motion. I spotted another doorway and angled towards it. This opened onto a swimming pool enclosed in a courtyard. The water was eerie, green lights gleaming from beneath its surface like cats' eyes shining through the fog. The pool was covered with a thick sheet of plexiglass.

Dancers cavorted on top of the pool with the sweaty abandon of pagans celebrating the rites of spring. I half expected the men to have hooves. They certainly sounded as if they had hooves, stomping on the plastic like that. The band was playing a blues tune I recognized as "Got My Mojo Working," and the pianist kept up pretty well with Otis Spann's famous finger work on the keys.

Above the swimming pool, a crowd observed the dancers. It took me several minutes to realize that the onlookers weren't people, but mannequins dressed in tropical tourist gear: Hawaiian shirts, Bermuda shorts, sundresses, and sunglasses. I climbed the stairs to the balcony and scanned the club for any sign of David. I was excited to see him but anxious, too. Maybe he had only invited me along because Enrique mentioned it, and David was being polite.

The stage was directly below. The musicians were all men except the drummer, a black woman with bright red beads braided into her hair like ladybugs marching down her neck. The pianist, who had his back to me, was announcing the next tune.

"This here's the *Gravier Street Rag*, made famous by the untouchable Champion Jack Dupree," he shouted into the microphone, moving his fingers over the keys in a rapid blues shuffle.

The singer sauntered up to the piano. A tall, thin man with slick black hair and an enormous gold hoop in one ear, he choked the microphone with one hand, waggled his hips and howled like a wet cat. The singer's rendition of wine-headed Sue made the crowd hoot in return. This was clearly a regular.

I laughed, drawn into the music despite my own blues. Or perhaps because the music fit my mood and hit my gut. There were sad blues and happy blues, I'd once heard Billie Holiday say in an interview. This was definitely the happy kind.

I gripped the railing and bobbed to the music. I still couldn't believe the audacity of Cam's vanishing act. And to Nepal, of all places! How many people even knew where Nepal was, much less flew there on a whim?

Jon must be rolling in dough, if he'd flown the coop and taken the others with him like a flock of geese. I imagined them in a perfect V formation, Jon in the lead, the rest frantically flapping their arms to keep up, as I leaned down over the balcony between a pair of mannequins and tapped my foot to the music. Then the pianist turned his head toward the microphone again, and my foot froze mid-tap.

That was David below me, playing the piano, his hands hopping across the keyboard. And Enrique, David's nurse, was singing, all flexible hips and gleaming grin as he played to a cheering, hooting crowd. Impossible, but there they were.

It took me several minutes to make my way back down from the balcony. Once in front of the stage, I was drawn onto the floor by a group of dancers who gestured for me to join them. I did, working my way up to the stage that way, and began dancing in front of the band.

They finally broke set. Sweat was pouring down my face and neck by the time David stood up behind the upright piano and knocked back a bottle of water. Enrique, laughing at something the saxophonist shouted in his ear, spotted me first. He tapped David on the shoulder and pointed. David's grin was all the invitation I needed. I reached up, and Enrique grabbed my hand and tugged me onto the stage.

"Told you she'd show!" he shouted to David before waltzing off with the saxophonist, their arms draped about each other's waists.

I stood next to David at the piano. "I can't believe that was really you playing!"

"It wasn't. That was my alternate persona. The one who grew up in Chicago instead of a white bread suburb of Milwaukee. Want a drink?"

"Sure." Then I remembered. "But I don't have any money. I was in Berkeley and got mugged and car jacked. And my brother has disappeared! Left the country!"

He raised an eyebrow. "Sounds like a busy night. What about Paris?"

"Karin took the baby to her house while I went to Berkeley. Then, when things got complicated, we thought it was better to leave her there overnight."

David's grin broadened. "So you're a free woman."

"I guess so. Relatively speaking, anyway."

"In this life, everything is relative," he reminded me.

◑◐

I danced until midnight, when the band brought down the house with "Who's Gonna Be Your Sweet Man When I'm Gone." After that, so suddenly that I scarcely knew how we'd arrived, David and I sat alone on the summit of Bernal Heights Hill, admiring the city's necklaces of lights and sharing a bottle of wine.

David was slightly hoarse after the gig, so he encouraged me to do most of the talking. I recounted the day's events, then backtracked to tell him about Cameron, Boston, my parents, the break-up with Peter, and teaching. Finally, I asked how he'd become both a musician and a doctor.

"Most people are lucky to be good at one thing, and here you are, Mr. Talent, pulling off two fabulous careers and putting the rest of us to shame," I said.

"That's Dr. Talent to you," he said with a laugh, and lay down on the grass beside me.

I wanted to kiss David, to feel the length of him against me the way I had when we slept together. But did that mean I wanted sex with David, too, or just comfort? And was David only keeping me company because I was a friend of Karin's?

David was telling me how he had studied classical piano but learned blues by ear, taking a bus to visit bars on Chicago's south side whenever he could. "Music lessons were my mother's idea," he said, "but Dad wanted me to be a doctor. He used to tell me the names of bones at night instead of reading me stories."

"So which do you like better? Music or medicine?"

"I'm glad I don't have to choose. Both jobs feed my belly and spirit. I like my volunteer work, too, like what I was doing in Nepal."

Nepal again! You'd think that was the only destination on earth. "My brother's in Nepal now," I said, "doing God knows what."

"He'll have lots of company. Kathmandu attracts people who go there, then try to figure out why."

I plucked nervously at the grass between us. "Let's not talk about my brother right now. Tell me how, if you're out late every night playing music, you manage to get up early every morning and work at the clinic."

"Easy. I just don't sleep." David yawned and stretched his arms over his head.

We both laughed. "Come on," I said. "We'd better go home. You live around here, don't you?"

"How about if I take you home instead? It's right around the corner. We can just walk."

I swallowed, trying not to show my disappointment. Why didn't he want me at his place? Was David involved with someone? Not attracted to me? Maybe it was a bad thing that he hadn't tried to have sex with me the night we slept together.

We wound our way down the narrow streets of Bernal Heights and crossed Dolores Street to my place. It wasn't until we had reached my apartment door and I began fishing the keys out of my pocket that I realized they were probably still dangling from the ignition of my stolen car.

"Oh, God," I moaned, and told David. Inwardly, I brightened: now David would have to take me to his place. I could see how he lived—and whether he lived alone.

"No key? No problem!" David fished a complicated tool out of his pocket, a knife with dozens of tiny attachments, and picked the lock in under a minute.

"Wow," I said. "You're a little scary."

He looked pleased. "Am I? Why?"

"You broke into my house just like that, and you're not even a jewel thief!"

"There's really not much difference between musicians, physicians, and jewel thieves," David pointed out. "We've all got good hands." He gave me a steady look that nearly made my knees buckle. "If I ask you a question, will you say yes?"

"I don't know. What's the question?"

"Oh, it's a very long question. Might take me all night to ask it."

"And here I thought you'd never ask."

David smiled. "I almost didn't. As a general rule, I don't take advantage of women who have just had babies dropped on their doorsteps, lost their brothers, gotten car jacked, been mugged, and downed more alcohol than three lumberjacks. Might just be the wrong time to ask a woman anything. Hell, she might do the wise thing and say no."

"Or a woman might say yes." I leaned over to kiss David's neck, tasting salt, and he wrapped his arms around my waist. We stood there for a long time, swaying in the dark.

I only had toddler food in my kitchen: bananas, peanut butter, oatmeal, apple juice, and milk. David didn't seem to mind. He rummaged about in my galley kitchen and slathered a banana with peanut butter for breakfast.

It was seven o'clock. We had only fallen asleep a couple of hours ago and I wanted David to come back to bed so that we could make love again. This surprised me. With Peter, sex was such a rote activity, a task to be crossed off our lists, that by the end of our relationship we were both relieved when it was over.

David, though. Oh, David. With David, sex was the best sort of conversation, the kind of exchange that covers all the bases and lets each of you say what's on your mind. I didn't want to miss a word.

Our love making had included actual words, too. Everything from simple questions, like, "Do you like that? Do you want this?" to phrases that would have made me blush if I had read them online. We talked, we moved, we rested, we talked and moved some more, each of us tender and frenzied by turn.

I hadn't even flinched when, halfway through, David had stopped to touch my scar, tracing a finger along the curve of my breast and then kissing it. "What happened here?" he asked solemnly. I told him, and he kissed my breast again.

"You don't mind it?" I asked. "It doesn't put you off?"

"Of course not. It hardly shows."

He meant it. Still. I had to be able to tell him this one thing. "I feel flawed," I ventured. "Like a teacup with a chip in it."

He smiled. "They look more like soup bowls to me."

I punched him lightly on the arm. "The thing is, I keep wondering if the whole handle will break off next, you know?"

David looked at me with those dark, kind eyes and then kissed me full on the mouth. "We all get to be new once," he said. "And then we all have to survive the dishwasher. You're a beautiful woman, Jordan," he had added, and I believed that he meant it.

"You all right?" David asked now, leaning down to kiss me good morning.

"Sure." I propped myself up on the pillows, bleary from lack of sleep and cotton-headed with a throbbing hangover. I wished I had a comb and a mirror, or that I could at least brush the sweaters off my teeth before David kissed me goodbye.

I took his hand and held it to my cheek, hoping to persuade him to stay a little, but then the doorbell rang. It had to be Karin with Paris. Who else would appear at this hour?

It was as if someone had thrown a switch from forgetting to remembering. Immediately, I was conscious again of Paris, of how much I missed her. Her blanket was still tucked beneath my pillow, where I'd stashed it after David fell asleep, just to have her smell nearby. Now the waiting was over. Hangover momentarily forgotten, morning lust shoved to the back burner, I sprang out of bed and pulled on my underpants and a faded t-shirt.

"Need these?" David held up the jeans I'd stripped off last night. "I can hide in the closet if you want."

I tugged on my jeans. "No need. I'm sure it's Karin, and she'll want full credit for you being here."

I stepped outside, wincing at the feel of cold cement on my feet. I was dimly aware of Karin's presence, and of her car idling at the curb beyond her, but I had eyes only for Paris. I caressed her silky head. "Hey, baby," I murmured. "I missed you!"

Paris squealed, clapping her hands.

"Hey, yourself." Karin sounded grumpy, so unlike herself that I looked at her more closely. I didn't like what I saw. Karin looked stunned, as if she were the one who'd been up all night. Maybe she had. Her face was pale, devoid of makeup, and her hair was tangled. Even her clothing, a gray sweatshirt and a pair of matching sweat pants, didn't look right. I urged her to come inside. "I'll make you tea."

"I really can't stay." Karin rolled her eyes and jerked her chin toward the street. "Prepare yourself."

Was she having a seizure? Exercising her facial muscles? "Oh, come on. Just for a minute. I've got a surprise for you," I coaxed.

"Yeah? Well, I've got a surprise for you, too," she said.

I heard David's footsteps behind me. Karin peered around my shoulder and groaned at the sight of him. "This is going to be even worse than I thought."

"What is? Why are you acting so weird?" I asked, impatient now.

Behind Karin, my mother burst out of the car like a stripper out of a cake. One minute there was emptiness, and then there was Mom, armed with an umbrella, a shoulder bag and a suitcase on wheels.

"Mom! What are you doing here?" I clutched the baby to my chest like a shield.

"Hello, Jordan," she said through her teeth. "There's no need to shout."

Mom wore her best wrinkle-free pants suit. She'd worn that same knit suit on the two-day drive to Grammy's funeral, and once on an anniversary car trip to the Cape with my father. The suit was a luminescent orange color that she optimistically called "ripe pumpkin." If you knotted the legs and arms of that suit, it would make a perfect life raft.

She had splurged on a new perm. The frayed gray curls stood about my mother's head like sea anemones on a rock, waving slightly in the morning breeze. "Who's this?" Mom pointed over my shoulder with the umbrella.

"Uh, this is Karin's friend, David Goldstein," I fumbled. "And David, this is Grace O'Malley, my mother. He's a doctor," I remembered to add.

"A doctor making a house call! Well. And here I was, thinking that our nation's health coverage was going to hell in a hand basket." Mom sailed past me, the suitcase wheezing and tottering behind her like an arthritic spaniel on a leash.

"Meet my mother," I said to David.

Karin fluttered her fingers. "Good to see you, glad not to be you!"

"Oh, no, you don't." I grabbed Karin by the elbow. "Stay for coffee, why don't you?" I hissed.

"Not a chance." Karin set her jaw.

"What am I going to do?"

"I don't know, but think fast," Karin said. "I've been with your mom since 11 o'clock last night, when I found her weeping outside the baggage claim at the airport because you didn't pick up your cell and she was convinced that you'd been mugged in the big bad city. And hey, guess what? I had to tell her she was right!"

"Oh, no," I moaned.

"Oh, yes. I had to drive with that baby of yours screaming in the back seat like a howler monkey all the way to the airport and back. Now your mom knows she's a granny. Imagine her surprise! I know you must have told her somewhere along the line, but gosh, somehow it must have slipped her mind."

"I just couldn't do it."

"I don't mind being your stand-in," Karin said, "but it would be a lot easier if I knew my lines beforehand."

David draped his arm around my shoulders and gave me a squeeze. "Just tell your mom the truth, Jordan. There's no point in trying to hold anything back now."

"I was trying to do the right thing," I said. "I wanted to find Cam and get him to do something about Nadine and the baby before I told Mom anything."

Karin sighed. "Yeah, but sometimes the right thing isn't the best thing, is it?" She hugged me. "Good luck. I'll check in later. I still love you even if you're a complete idiot."

David hugged me, too, and kissed me lightly on the mouth. "Want me to stay?"

I shook my head. "This is already complicated enough," I said, glad to have Paris's hand wrapped in my hair and anchoring me in place. Otherwise I might have fled the scene.

❧❧

Then I was alone with Paris and my mother in my studio apartment.

Mom stood in the middle of the room, her bags on either side of her, the umbrella dangling from her elbow. "So this is it?"

"Yep. Want the grand tour? I promise it'll take less than an hour."

She didn't crack a smile. "Well, you never were one for housekeeping."

I was suddenly aware of the bed with its tangled sheets floating in the middle of the room like a cruise ship abandoned at the docks. "No," I agreed. "Cleaning house always seems so futile. The dishes are never all done and there's always more laundry."

My mother must have known I was looking at the bed behind her, but she didn't turn around. "My God, Jordan! Your bed with Peter isn't even cold, and yet here you are, frolicking!"

"Mom, it's not like I'm a widow," I reminded her. "Peter's not dead. There's no need for a proper mourning period. Look, let's not talk now. You're tired. I'm tired, too. Get cleaned up, and then we can have a real conversation. I'll go for a coffee run." I was desperate to escape.

"Where's your brother?" she demanded. "Just tell me that much. I understand this trouble concerns him more than it does you." She jutted her chin in the baby's direction.

"This 'trouble' is your granddaughter. And I'll tell you everything I know, but only after I get some coffee," I said, lifting the baby backpack from its hook on the door.

"What in God's name is that?" my mother demanded.

"A backpack for babies."

"In my day, we strapped them into strollers."

"The backpack's easier when you're shopping someplace like that little corner store. The aisles there are so narrow, Paris grabs stuff off the shelves if she's in the stroller."

Mom frowned, watching me open the metal stand on the backpack, set it on the counter, and drop Paris inside the canvas pack like an orange into a Christmas stocking. "In my day, we didn't let children grab," she noted, before exclaiming, "Jordan, that baby's going to fall right out of there and break her neck!"

"No, she's perfectly safe. Look, I've strapped her in." I backed into the pack like a horse backing into a carriage, and buckled the belt around my waist to take the weight off my shoulders. "See how easy?"

Unfortunately, I turned without folding the metal backpack stand down first. The stand caught on the teapot and sent it flying off the counter.

Mom's reflexes had always been good; I'd inherited that from her. She dropped her umbrella and caught the teapot before it hit the ground. "Oh, yes," she said. "Perfectly safe."

Paris giggled. For a minute, Mom and I smiled. Then we resumed our standoff. "I'll be back in fifteen minutes," I promised.

Kanchan was besieged this morning by customers buying doughnuts and coffee, but today, as always, she ignored the line of customers to chat up the baby. "How's life, little one?" she said.

"Her grandmother's visiting," I said, trying to sound nonchalant.

Kanchan read the panic in my eyes. She patted my hand and pushed a couple of fancy chocolate bars across the counter when I was buying the coffee. "Here! Sugar on the house!"

In all, Paris and I were gone twenty minutes. My mother was nowhere in sight when I opened the apartment door. I thought she must be in the bathroom until her head popped up over the kitchen counter. She wore rubber gloves and, when I stepped up to the counter, I could see that she'd been on her hands and knees next to a bucket of soapy water, scrubbing my kitchen floor.

"Mom! Your nice travel outfit!"

"You know what?" My mother sat back on her knees. "I had my colors done by that Belinda Little at my salon, and she says I'm a winter, not an autumn. How could I have gone so wrong?" She sniffed. "I'm dumping this suit into the free box at the church the very second I get home. Then it's blues and greens for me."

"Please, Mom. Get up! This is embarrassing! What makes you think I haven't washed the floor?"

She waved a grimy sponge the size of a toaster. "I know how much time babies take. And you can't ever have the floor too clean with a baby in the house."

"But where'd you find that sponge? And those gloves?"

"I brought them with me in my carry-on. You just never know."

I imagined my mother sponging out the tiny sinks on the plane. There would be no stopping her now. The next time I went out, she'd probably arrange my clothes by color the way she had at home when I was a child, from blacks to brights to pastels, white blouses dangling at the end of the rack like surrendering flags.

I kept Paris in the backpack while I made the coffee, then stood over my mother, arms folded, until she agreed to sit outside on the deck with me. I'd made cinnamon toast, too; Paris gummed a triangle of toast while stacking metal measuring cups on the wooden deck.

My mother still refrained from asking questions about the baby. What exactly had Karin told her? I studied Mom as we ate, trying to wrap my mind around the idea that she was now a grandmother. Even if she wasn't acting like one, she looked the part: the gray curls, the tight mouth, the knit suit, the sensible rubber-soled walking shoes.

Had distress and fatigue made her look older in just a few days? Or had she always looked this way, and I only now realized it?

Mom was describing her cross-country odyssey. Yesterday, unable to reach me for the fourth day in a row, she'd taken a cab to the Boston airport and bought a ticket on the spot. "I just had this feeling that you needed me," she said, her chin trembling.

She had called me every ten minutes from the San Francisco airport for two hours before finally giving up and phoning Karin. As she talked, I could imagine it all, even the suitcase packed with clothing that had been ironed and meticulously rolled into narrow tubes to avoid wrinkling, the tidy handwriting on the note she'd left for my father describing each plastic container in the freezer.

I was still incredulous. Mom had never traveled alone, not even to her sister's in Rhode Island, because my father had convinced her it would be unsafe. Dad had deliberately bought a house in a town "on the way to nowhere," just to keep his family untouched by city sinner ways. He was certain, therefore, that we were all easy prey.

"Your mother could carry on a conversation with a deaf mute for six hours," Dad believed, "and his ears would be bleeding from the noise while some idiot snatched your mother's purse on the sly."

"Why did you really come?" I asked her now. "I still can't believe you'd just show up without talking it over with me first!"

Mom rolled her eyes. "Why should I? Look at you. First you dump a perfectly good man who wants to marry you. Then you drive across the country and leave your family behind. Now you're caring for a baby that you say is your brother's with nary a word to me about it."

She stabbed a finger in the baby's direction. So far, she had refused to touch Paris or mention her by name. "Why should I tell you anything? It's clear that communicating with me is at the bottom of your list of priorities."

"You could have gotten an explanation over the phone," I pointed out, then immediately realized my mistake.

Mom's eyebrows lifted over her prim pale blue eyeglasses. "Certainly I could have been spared a great deal of money and agony, if only you'd had the courtesy to return my calls."

"I wasn't the only one not calling you back," I reminded her furiously. "What about Cam?" My mother, in a matter of minutes, had reduced me to a scowling, sullen adolescent.

"Cam is a boy," she sniffed. "You hope for more from a daughter. Besides, I've always counted on you to be responsible." Her voice caught and she glanced away, embarrassed. "Now, will you please just tell me what's going on? Who is this child? Karin says she's Cam's daughter." Her knuckles were white on the coffee cup.

I told her everything. Paris, meanwhile, kept climbing off the deck and I had to keep hauling her back onto it, since she was so determined to dig in the dirt and chow down on a couple of clumps of sod.

Somewhere between telling Mom about searching for Nadine in the park and the mugging that followed, I went inside to fetch a set of wooden spoons, a couple of pans, and a colander. I filled one of the pans with dirt while I finished filling my mother in on Cam's vanishing act to Nepal. Paris squealed and sprayed dirt around us like a piglet rooting for truffles.

"You spoil her," my mother observed.

"What? How? I haven't bought her a thing, other than essentials!"

"You pick her up every time that child says 'boo.' Honestly, Jordan, that baby has you wrapped around her little finger. How's she ever going to learn patience if you never say no?"

"I say no plenty, believe me. But I say yes whenever I can. I've got to make up for what Paris hasn't had." I didn't realize the truth of this impulse until I'd voiced it.

"It isn't good for children to get everything they want. That teaches them that the world is at their beck and call, instead of teaching them patience. And it's certainly not up to you to make up for anything. Least of all, this child's life. Cam's the one who's got to take responsibility. She isn't yours."

This stung. I decided to derail her with questions of my own. "So what does Dad think of you coming out here? Didn't he want to come?"

Mom grimaced. "Daddy refuses to travel anywhere that isn't a direct line between the television and the refrigerator."

I stared at her, comprehending at last. "You hatched this plan in secret and left for the airport before he woke up this morning!"

"No," she corrected. "Daddy was awake. He was out mowing the lawn when I left. He couldn't hear the taxi."

"I can't believe this! You ran away from home?" I pictured my father coming into the kitchen, his white t-shirt tucked into the sagging waistband of his shorts, skin red from the sun, the graying hair on his barrel chest matted with sweat.

Dad would come in, like he always did while mowing, to ask my mother to pour him a glass of lemonade. He would wait in the kitchen, yelling her name. Then he would check the laundry room and living room, frustrated that Mom wasn't there to pour out the lemonade and compliment his mowing. He'd finally climb the stairs and mop his brow with the damp t-shirt, thirsty and irritated, still disbelieving.

In the end, when he didn't find her, would Dad finally find the glasses in the cupboard above the dishwasher and pour the lemonade himself? And, when he did finally read Mom's note, would he try to call her, or just crumple the paper in his big ham of a fist?

"Daddy will be on his own for breakfast and lunch, of course," Mom was murmuring, more to herself than to me. "But he can certainly manage cereal, and he'll probably go to the diner for a sandwich. I've got suppers in the freezer, though, if he can just manage the microwave. Enough for a month."

"A month?" I squeaked. Where the hell was my mother planning to stay? The answer was obvious, yet unthinkable.

My mind raced. First I was responsible for Cam's disappearance, now my own mother's! "You'd better call Dad and tell him where you are," I commanded. "Right now."

Mom raised her eyebrows. They were as gray as her hair, I realized, like moths that had alighted on her pale forehead. "Your father knows where I am. If he has anything to say to me, he can just pick up the phone himself. I programmed my cell number into the house phone so that he can't lose it, and left him a note about how to dial me. All he has to do is push one button."

"If you don't call him, I will," I threatened.

"And I'll tell him all about the baby. That should get your father on a plane in no time." Mom smiled her gracious church smile.

She had me: I certainly didn't need Dad here, too, blustering and blaming.

My mother set her coffee cup down and surveyed the garden. The fog was a sheer mist tinged gold by sunlight. "With those red flowers climbing the wall, and the palm trees over the fence, this place looks like a movie set. At least some of what you told me about California was true." This last was an accusation, but mild.

"More toast?" I pushed the plate in my mother's direction, but Paris speed-crawled across the deck to intercept it. She gnawed on a second corner of toast, turning it in her hands like a squirrel fiddling with a nut. She had deposited more toast on her t-shirt than in her mouth.

I remembered the pile of laundry on the floor of my closet. How would I get to the laundromat without a car?

My mother was watching Paris, too. "That baby's knees and hands will be full of splinters if you let her crawl around on the deck," she predicted glumly. "Children die from splinters, you know. Blood poisoning before you know it."

"I can't keep her in the crib every minute."

"Why not? There's nothing wrong with confining a child for her own safety," Mom said. "You and Cam spent hours in the playpen. It's the only way I got things done. I certainly never thought of carrying either of you on my back like a papoose! That's a sure fire way to spoil a child. No, even when we went into stores, I expected you to behave."

"At seven months old?"

"At every age!" My mother bristled, then sighed. "And what sort of name is Paris? A California name, I suppose." She watched Paris play for a few more minutes in silence, then added, "She's filthy. She'll need a bath before you let her crawl around on that white rug in there."

"Oh, God," I moaned. "Don't say that."

"Why not?"

"I don't have the energy. Every bath with Paris is The Battle of Waterloo."

"Nonsense. You're just not firm enough. Let me give that child a bath, teach her to mind her manners. Then we'll get that brother of yours on the phone and sort this out."

"I don't know, Mom. Paris is as slippery as a guppy."

"I haven't drowned a child yet."

Chapter *ten*

P aris protested when I left her with my mother, and no wonder: Mom handled the baby at arm's length, gently but firmly, the way you would an unruly puppy. "Who died and made you boss?" my mother demanded, pinning the baby in place with one hand while she efficiently laid out the bath towel and fresh clothes on the bed.

I felt apprehensive, leaving Paris again so soon. But I had no car, much less a car seat, and I had a mountain of laundry and groceries to buy besides. I couldn't possible manage Paris along with the laundry bags and groceries. As I was leaving, my mother stood in the apartment doorway, Paris squirming under one arm, naked and furious.

"Jordan," she said, "I'm sorry I've intruded, but I did not spend my life teaching you and Cam the important values in order to just stand aside while the two of you throw away your upbringing and become bums."

"I am not a bum!" I protested, clutching the garbage bags of dirty clothes. "I have a master's degree! A good teaching job! And I had a decent car, until that idiot drag queen mugged me!" This last point weakened my position, so I added, "I have a life!"

"You call this a life?" my mother shouted over Paris's enraged howls. "You had a decent apartment in Boston and a fiancé, and now you've given up all that security to do what? To live in a home the size of a chicken coop? You don't even own laundry baskets, God help you!" Mom raged and slammed the door.

Two hours later, I emerged from the laundromat. I still carried garbage bags, but at least now they were filled with clean laundry instead of rank. I wondered what to do with them while I shopped for groceries.

I hadn't been able to string two thoughts together since my mother's appearance. Originally, I'd planned on popping over to the market while the clothes were in the dryer, but the hum and warmth of the laundro-mat lulled me right to sleep. I'd awakened on a plastic chair to find my chin damp with drool and an elderly woman in zebra leggings impatiently yanking my hot laundry out of the dryer.

Now I lingered on the corner like a bag lady, waiting for a shopping cart to drop out of the sky so that I could make it the three blocks to the grocery. In answer to my prayers, a horn blared from across the street. "Hey, Beautiful!"

It was Ed in his rusty Saab. Once again, I was struck by how rarely I'd thought about him. My life had been turned upside down by Paris, and now my mother was proceeding to turn everything inside out. Ed was a shadowy memory.

And David? Where did he fit into my life? Somewhere, I hoped.

I crossed the street towards Ed with both garbage bags flung over my shoulders. Very attractive. But Ed treated me like Queen Victoria, leaping out of his car to take the garbage bags and open the car door. He wore tat-tered, paint-stained overalls with a black t-shirt and had tied a red bandana around his head. In his Herculean grip, the garbage bags swung like clutch purses.

"Thanks," I told him. "What are you doing in this neighborhood? You look like a pirate, with that scarf around your head. Are you on lunch break from a job?"

"Nah. I'm modeling at the school later, but I was painting my kitchen cupboards."

"You'll pose with the paint splatters still on, I hope. You're so decorative, with all of those teal accents on your skin," I teased.

He grinned. "Absolutely."

"But that still doesn't explain why you're looking for me."

He shrugged. "Karin told me about your car, so I thought I'd help you run errands. Your mom told me where you were."

"I'm too tired to say no," I agreed, and climbed into the front seat.

Ed slipped in beside me. "I'll take that as a compliment," he said, easing the car onto the street.

"Sorry, I'm just..." I buried my head in my hands, realizing. "You met my mother?" What in the world would she think of me, booting one man out in the wee hours, only to have another show up that same morning?

"I did." Ed nodded. "Where we going? Bell Market?"

"If you really don't mind. Did you talk to my mom?"

"Not really. She seemed a little distracted."

I dropped my hands and turned to look at him. "What do you mean?"

Ed grinned. "Well, some kind of parrot was screeching inside the apartment when I rang your bell. And your mom looked like she'd just taken a shower with her clothes on."

I grinned. Discipline the baby, indeed. "I don't have a parrot."

"I know."

While I ran into the market, Ed sat in the car and read a magazine. I remembered my father doing the same thing throughout my childhood, waiting in the car with Cam and me while my mother shopped. He'd listen to the radio and curse the Red Sox, the Bruins, or the Celtics, and wonder, "What the hell does your mother find to do in there?"

When I came out again with the shopping cart, Ed popped the trunk and loaded it for me, another thing I remembered Dad doing for my mother. It was nice to have help. Despite this domestic role play, though, Ed and I skated along the conversational surface until we were parked in front of my apartment. Perhaps that, too, was marital behavior, I reflected: saying nothing of import while you team up to perform life's survival tasks.

"It was nice of you to invite me to the beach the other day," I said, fumbling with the car handle and the words at the same time. "I'm glad Karin could go with you." I took a deep breath. "Ed, things with you and Karin were never really over, were they?"

"I've always cared about Karin," Ed said. "I was a wreck when she left me."

His expression was as stolid as ever, but I could hear the pain in his voice. No way was this man over my best friend.

"You and Karin clearly have some unfinished business," I said. "We had fun, but now you should go back to her and figure things out."

"You seem awfully sure." Ed turned toward me, resting his arm along the back of my seat.

In this strong daylight, I noticed how deep the lines were around his eyes. He was in the middle of his life, tired of treading water. "I am sure," I said.

"Is it because of Karin?" His voice sounded more hopeful. "Some sort of loyalty between childhood friends?"

"Loyalty is part of it, especially because Karin still has feelings for you."

"She does?" Ed's eyes shone. "Feelings that go beyond friendly?" By the sudden urgency in his voice, I suspected that getting my permission to see Karin might have been the real reason Ed had originally sought me out this morning.

I was so relieved to be off the hook, to not be hurting Ed, that I laughed and leaned over to hug his broad, hard torso. "She does," I assured him, and kissed Ed on the neck—all I could reach–just as a car slowed beside us and stopped, the engine idling.

I turned to look at the car beside us, and met David's eyes through the open window as he hit the accelerator and sped away.

Ⓖ

It was my mother's cure-all remedy that revived me enough to sit up in bed: flat ginger ale, a cheese sandwich, and a bowl of tomato soup thick with oyster crackers. This was Mom's cure for everything from flu to menstrual cramps.

It was nearly noon. I'd been in bed for fifteen hours, drifting in and out of sleep, slightly feverish. Just a cold, I told my mother, who nonetheless called Karin.

Karin hadn't moved from her perch at the end of the bed since her arrival, and we'd been chatting aimlessly. Mom looked on from the safe distance of the wicker rocker but said little, her focus on knitting a bright strawberry hat for Paris. She had already made the baby a ridiculous pair of pink leg warmers that Paris refused to remove.

Ed had appeared, too, after Karin telephoned him. I'd never had this many people in my studio apartment at the same time. With the three of them hovering over my bed, I felt like Dorothy in Kansas, coming out of her tornado-induced coma and insisting that Oz was real.

I felt like a coma victim. I was completely exhausted. After David had driven away yesterday afternoon while I was sitting in Ed's car, I'd taken Paris from my mother under the pretense that Mom should sleep off her jet lag, put the baby in the stroller, and race-walked to the clinic. When I arrived, Enrique had told me that David was finished seeing patients for the day and gave me directions to David's house.

"Way I understood it, Doc was in a hurry to get his beefy buns over to your place." He narrowed his eyes at my red, perspiring face. "Said he wanted to help you out because you'd lost your wheels. Everything okay?"

I hurried from the clinic through the heart of the Mission and up into Bernal Heights, puffing behind the stroller as I wound my way along the steep crooked streets. David lived on a dead-end street in a house painted the deep magenta of eggplants and tricked out with lime green trim. The windows were open, and a dog yammered inside when I rang the bell.

Nobody answered. I peered into the windows and made out furniture that looked hammered together out of fruit crates and a grand piano in the living room. A dog the size of a rabbit repeatedly launched itself off the top of the sofa and against one of the windows, trying to attack me through the glass.

I sat on David's steps until the sky darkened and the air grew too chilly for Paris's t-shirt. Where had David gone? Why wasn't he answering my phone messages or texts?

I thought I knew why, and I hated not being able to explain the truth about my relationship with Ed to him.

On the other hand, the truth was murky: because I had gone to Ed's apartment after Karin's party, with every intention of sleeping with him, and done the same with David, there was the chance that David might think I was the sort of woman who made a habit out of testing out new mattresses within hours of meeting someone.

I didn't dare imagine how I'd feel if the situation were reversed. What if David pulled up in his car right here, right now, and I saw him kiss another woman? The thought made my stomach lurch.

He never did come home. Later, back in my apartment, I'd fallen asleep with Paris curled up on the pillow beside me, her hands wound in my hair.

My mother let us nap until she scrambled eggs for dinner. I noted without comment that Mom carried Paris in the backpack while she worked in the kitchen and fed the baby bits of toast over her shoulder. The toast crumbs fell like rain on my mother's new perm.

We ate dinner in silence until Mom noticed I wasn't eating, but pushing chilly bits of egg beneath my toast like dust under a carpet. "What's the matter with you?" she had demanded. "What are you trying to hide from me now?"

This was the first question my mother had asked since my return from David's. Clearly, she was determined to act the part of a respectful parent, the sort of mother who wouldn't think of imposing on her adult daughter's boundaries, other than showing up unannounced and rearranging the contents of my entire house.

By now, my apartment looked as if it were occupied by a retired librarian. As Mom cooked the eggs, she could efficiently lay her hand on the oregano right next to the pepper, and I'd found my bathrobe hanging from the hook on the bathroom door with the belt coiled in one pocket as neatly as a snake.

When I hadn't answered her question, Mom said that I looked tired. "And no wonder, the way you eat! You don't have the fixings for one complete meal in that refrigerator. I can't even tell you went shopping today! What was the point? Not one piece of meat." Mom studied me closely. "You haven't gone vegetarian, have you? Those people are always anemic."

That was my mother's idea of going native in California, I guessed: you moved West, turned vegetarian, and left all of your cares behind with those carnivorous Type A's. I got up from the counter, lifted Paris out of the high chair, and staggered towards the bathroom.

My mother caught my elbow mid-stride and took the baby to bathe her for me. "You don't look well," she observed. "Bathing a baby is one thing I know how to do."

Paris was surprisingly docile, even cheery in the tub. In the other room, I called David's cell phone number three times. I even tried tracking him down at Aunt Mary's, but the woman who answered the phone assured me that David's group wasn't scheduled to play this week.

Still, it wasn't until I'd gotten Paris into her pajamas, read her a story, and rocked her to sleep that I felt completely free to break down. I had sobbed into the pillow until Mom produced an enormous bottle of cherry cough syrup out of her magic Mary Poppins flight bag, gave me a double dose, then made me tea with honey. The combination made my teeth hurt but finally put me to sleep.

Now it was morning and I felt as if I'd hit my head on something. Objects in the room appeared as if at the wrong end of a telescope. Mom's chair was impossibly far away, and so were Karin and Ed, who sat cross-legged at the foot of my bed like meditating monks. Gradually, Karin had coaxed out the story of David discovering me in Ed's car. I wondered, though not for long, why Ed hadn't told her himself.

Now Karin reached over and rapped me on the forehead with her knuckles. "Earth to Jordan! Earth to Jordan! How are you feeling?"

"Stupid. Like the Stan Laurel of relationships." I fished fresh oyster crackers out of the box beside my bed, taking grim pleasure in the furious dry pop of each shell between my teeth. "Admit it! I'll probably be alone for the rest of my life."

Karin, Ed and my mother exchanged glances. "I will admit to no such thing," Mom said. "You're a nice, responsible, hard working girl."

"Exactly my point!" I finished off the sandwich and sank back into the pillow. "I'm a drone. A nice enough drone, but a drone. I'm the Queen of Drones, and how sexy is that?"

Especially with a scar on one breast, I nearly added, but didn't because of Ed being there, and because I knew what my mother had said, and would say again: Get over it. You're fine. Be glad you still have two.

"What on earth is the matter with you? Since when was sexy everything?" My mother glared at me over her knitting. "Is it that time of the month? Do you need an aspirin?"

"Mom! Please!"

"Well, honestly. I've never been to such a pity party."

A silence followed. Paris, who had been following the conversation like a front-row tennis fan, grabbed my spoon. I let her hold it, helping her manipulate it until one of my soup crackers swam into the spoon like a trapped tadpole.

Paris giggled and dropped the cracker back into the bowl. Soup splattered onto the bed tray that my mother had fashioned out of a cookie sheet covered with a dish towel. Mom and Karin both grabbed paper towels and blotted up the mess.

"Let's get to the point," Mom demanded then, tossing the paper towel with a pitcher's professional wind-up into the kitchen trash. "You're upset that David, a man you're just getting to know, saw you sitting in a car with this man here." She pointed to Ed, who actually blushed.

"Not just sitting," I corrected. "I was kissing his neck."

My mother studied Ed's neck over her glasses, as if evidence of the act might still be visible. Then she shrugged. "Kissing is hardly a crime. There's no diamond on your finger. After all, you've only known David a short time."

I didn't dare admit that David and I had already spent two nights together, or that I'd gotten into bed with him both times as fast as I could. Nor did I confess that I had let Ed take me home with him for the express purpose of a marathon pleasure fest, only to back out at the last minute. Sex for fun? Not for my mother. She had dated my father for a solid month before allowing him to kiss her.

Karin turned to my mother. Her dark hair was up in a severe French twist which, on Karin, only begged to be unpinned. "What I think," Karin said slowly, "is that Jordan is overwhelmed by the sudden responsibility of caring for a baby, plus madly in love with David."

I stared at her. Overwhelmed, yes. But the other?

"Madly in love?' I mouthed the words like an unfamiliar spice. "I haven't been in that kind of love since ninth grade! You know that."

My mother agreed. "How could Jordan be madly in love? Love doesn't appear overnight, tiptoeing in like the Tooth Fairy." She frowned, then settled on a sentiment echoed in greeting cards everywhere: "Love is a seedling that grows into a solid oak tree over the years." She smiled, looking pleased with herself.

I took a sip of ginger ale. Was that really what my mother thought her marriage to my father was, an oak tree? Well, every tree had its termites and fungal rot.

Ed stood and stretched. His blue jeans were tattered at the knees and his t-shirt was just as old, a thin web of cotton across his shoulders. The total effect was that of the Incredible Hulk bursting out of his clothes. "I think David probably reacted that way not because you were kissing another man, but because I was the one you were kissing," he proposed.

"Oh, my. The King of Modesty!" Karin laughed.

My mother arched an eyebrow and held her knitting at arm's length to count stitches. "Why do you say that?"

Ed looked sheepish and tugged on one corner of his moustache. "David and Karin were dating when I first met Karin at a dance club. David's band was playing there, and he had invited her to hear them. I asked her to dance. David must've felt like I scooped Karin out from under him." Ed sighed. "I did act like a heel. But I was a heel in love."

"You've said all this before, and I still don't believe you," Karin protested. "David and I were just friends. We never actually slept together. David just takes things too seriously."

"You don't get it, do you? You have a powerful effect on people," Ed said.

He gave Karin such a solemn, tender look that I studied the drowning crackers in my soup, embarrassed. Paris was sitting on the bed with me, gumming a sandwich crust; I put my hand beneath her chin to catch the drool.

My mother was unimpressed. "Not one of you takes relationships seriously enough. You treat sex like a game of musical chairs: whoever isn't quick enough, loses."

"We only sleep with people we really care about," Ed protested, his eyes still on Karin.

Oh, sure. *And with anyone else who happens to be available.* I stroked Paris's hair, trying not to catch Ed's eye.

Mom exploded. "Edward, if you and Karin really care for each other, you'll get busy building a life together. Look at you! You're what, Ed, forty-something? You're pushing fifty with a short stick! That's two-thirds of your life gone. You'll be having a stroke soon, with nobody around to wipe drool off your chin. And Karin? You've got your looks now, so it's easy enough to find company. But women's faces fall after forty, and your hips will spread from here to Texas whether you have children or not. If you can imagine sitting in a rocking chair next to this man some day and liking it, reel him in while you've got the chance."

"Mom!" I scolded.

But Karin spoke up for herself. "People live a lot longer than they used to, Mrs. O'Malley. Forty today is what thirty was in your day."

Mom snorted. "Forty is still old enough to have a bad back and an ounce of common sense."

Karin soldiered on. She'd never been afraid of anyone's parents, even as a child. "Don't you think it's good for Ed, for all of us, to find out who we really are before we make a commitment to someone else?"

On the warpath, Mom's cheeks burned red and her breath came in short pants. "What absolute drivel. You still have the same basic personalities you did when you were the size of this baby here."

Mom nodded her head towards Paris, and then something must have stopped her—what? Paris's curls? Her hands clasped on the blanket? Her tiny, perfect nose? For she smiled at the baby before continuing in a softer voice.

"Karin, you've always been bold," Mom said. "I can remember you doing handstands on our lawn for all the world to see, not caring whether your dress was up or down. And you, Jordan O'Malley, have always been sweet and serious. You may be taking a vacation from common sense right now. But no amount of experimenting in San Francisco will ever change the fact that you're basically a very nice girl who likes to make people happy."

"That's me," I muttered. "Nice."

Karin laughed. "Yeah, and I'm the little slut with the dress up around her waist."

Mom shook her head. "The point is, you did nothing wrong today, Jordan."

I nodded, momentarily accepting absolution.

"All right, then." My mother had finished the strawberry hat. She began winding up her yarn and gathering it into the flight bag beside her chair. "It's time to quit beating yourself up. Hang the blame where it belongs. If David was really so keen on being with you, he should have yanked open your car door and confronted you, instead of zooming off like a scared rabbit."

I stared at her. "But why should David go out on a limb and risk having me reject him for Ed, when he's already been there and done that with Karin?"

My mother leaned over and pulled the strawberry hat onto Paris's head, admiring her handiwork as Paris touched the hat and chortled her approval. "Nobody ever said love is dignified, Jordan. That's about the last thing we are, when we're in love."

CICO

Paris was shrieking at me from her crib, her face screwed up like an angry troll's and her pale hair standing on end in feathery tufts. I climbed out of bed and scooped her up, nuzzling her damp neck. It was only then that I realized my mother wasn't in the apartment.

Morning sunlight flooded the room. Mom had spent the night on the floor, on a blow-up mattress she had toted along in her suitcase. God knows what else she had brought with the air mattress, rubber gloves, and sponge. I recognized this mattress as something I used to lie on at the town beach; underneath the white sheet, the mattress's green canvas skin was mottled and bleached from the sun.

Where could my mother have gone at 9 o'clock in the morning without a car, in a city where she knew no one? I fussed in the kitchen, making oatmeal for Paris and me.

I tried David's cell and clinic numbers as I cooked and handed Paris utensils to bang on her high chair tray. He wasn't answering either number. Still, I felt calmer. Today I'd catch up with him, explain. A good night's sleep and Paris's morning grin had restored a sense of normalcy to my life. Or was it Mom's tomato soup and grilled cheese? All I had to do was reach Cam and David today. Then everything would be fine.

The baby and I ate outside on the deck and played in the thin ribbons of sunlight, creating helicopters out of dried leaves. Then I brought Paris inside and carried her in the backpack to keep her out of trouble while I cleaned up the kitchen. The phone rang as I dried the plates.

I jumped towards it, convinced David would be on the other end. I would be cheerful and warm, not panicked or tearful. Karin was wrong: I was not madly in love with David. Just interested.

I picked up the receiver and squeaked a hello.

"That you, Jordy?" My father bellowed from across the country. I could hear a shooshing sound on the line. The hose? He was probably watering Mom's roses.

"Yes."

"Huh. Almost didn't recognize your voice. What the hell is going on over there? Put your mother on the phone!"

"I don't know where she is," I answered truthfully.

"What do you mean? I got her damn note. Says right here in black and white, she's staying with you in Frisco."

Paris squealed, trying to wrest the phone out of my hand and give it a good gumming. I held it out of reach and spoke loudly into the receiver. "Mom's here," I admitted. "But she's out at the moment. I don't know where. And, Dad, nobody calls it `Frisco' anymore."

"Frisco, Nabisco, who the hell cares?" my father muttered. "Do you know what the crime rate is in that city?"

I didn't. My father, no doubt, had gone to the town library, his home away from home, now that he'd stopped being a regular at the bars, to look it up. This was the first time Dad had phoned since I'd left. He'd always maintained that phones were for business, not pleasure, so I was impressed that he'd actually dialed out of state.

"Dad, I'm sure Mom's fine. She probably just went out for milk or something."

I should wear an official name tag: "Family Peacekeeper," I thought, scrubbing the egg pan with resentful zeal as my father yammered on about where Mom should be and what wasn't getting done in her absence: the mail, the dry cleaning, the grocery shopping, the vacuuming. Why did I get all the flack, while Cam pulled one disappearing act after another?

"What the devil is that racket?" my father demanded suddenly.

I'd forgotten Paris, since I was so accustomed to having her yell in my ear while I did chores. "A nature show," I told him. "Parrots and monkeys."

Dad grunted. "A lot you've got to do, watching TV at this hour. You teachers and your summers off. Then your unions have the balls to demand more money! When your mother gets back, tell her to call me. Can you do that much for your old man? Or is that asking the moon?"

Did I imagine it, or did my father sound nervous? Mom could say all she wanted to about coming West to find Cam and me; it dawned on me now that she'd left for other reasons as well.

"Sure, I can do that. Listen, what's going on with you two, anyway?"

"None of your beeswax," he said. "A little misunderstanding. Just get your mother to call me ASAP."

My mother and my landlady, Louise, arrived about an hour later, while I was playing with the baby on the floor and wondering whether to call the police. Mom's face was flushed from exertion and she looked pleased with herself. She was wearing a huge necklace of bright red and yellow beads.

"Oh, hi Louise!" I said. I'm glad you two have met." I aimed to sound casual, but my voice strained tight as elastic around my unasked questions. I waited to see what explanation my mother might offer for her absence.

None was forthcoming. Instead, she gave me a look that said, *See what it feels like?* Meanwhile, Louise squealed and clapped her hands. "Oh, there's our little miracle darlin'!"

At first, I thought she meant me. But then I heard babbling at my feet, where Paris was using my leg to pull herself up to a standing position.

Louise scooped the baby up and cradled her in one meaty arm. "You precious little pumpkin pie," she murmured. "Who's happy today? Who's got a smile for Louise? Who needs a kiss?"

Ignoring Paris's wailed protests, Louise bussed the baby and played out the whole hyperbolic "this little piggy" routine on her toes. Well, at least I wasn't going to get evicted for housing a child.

My mother hung back, smiling not just at me, but at the baby. "Hello, Jordan," she said. "Feeling any better after that good sleep? It's time for a fresh start!"

"Sure, I'm better. And you look great."

I felt pinpricks of irritation at being kept in the dark about my mother's activities, but it was true: Mom looked terrific. Her perm had softened into finger curls around her face, which was pink from her recent outing, and her gaze was bright. She had erased five years since yesterday.

"Thank you," Mom said briskly. "I'm so glad you're well. We have a busy day ahead of us!" She rubbed her hands together, grinning like a cruise ship hostess.

"We do?"

"Yes! We're going to track down your brother."

"I've already tried to find him, Mom. Nothing but dead ends."

"Yes, but you didn't have me helping. Today you're driving me to Berkeley. Somebody must have a clue about your brother's whereabouts in Nepal."

Ah, I had her there. "Oh yeah? In what? I was car-jacked, remember."

Louise handed Paris back to me after one long, last, lipsticky nuzzle that left a ring of red on Paris's left ear. "Take my car," she said. "I won't need it today, and it's the least I can do." She gave my mother a look, then started up the stairs to her apartment. "Hang tight and I'll toss down the keys in two shakes."

A minute later, Louise dropped her keys down from the landing. The keys spun in the air, flashing like silver coins into my mother's outstretched hands.

"Hey, you had a phone call," I remembered, once Mom and I were inside and gathering up things for Paris's diaper bag.

"Who was it?"

"Oh, gee, Mom. I didn't catch his name. Who on earth could it have been? Your boyfriend?"

"Him?" My mother sighed and tossed Louise's keys into the air several times, like a gangster with a lucky coin. "He can wait."

Chapter eleven

"**S**o what will this little foray prove, exactly?" I asked my mother as we climbed into Louise's ancient Volvo wagon. "Other than the fact that Cam's really gone, and that we'll be damn lucky to get across the Bay Bridge in under an hour at rush hour."

"Watch your mouth," Mom said.

"What about calling Dad back? He doesn't know anything about the baby yet."

"Your father doesn't need to know everything."

Louise's ancient Volvo sagged on the driver's side, its shocks completely gone. Still, it wheezed up the hills with determination. Louise had attached a single sticker to its crooked bumper: "God sees what you're doing, and is she ever pissed!" I leaned into the corners to compensate for the car's sag, gritting my teeth each time I had to wrestle the stick shift into gear. My mood was not improving.

"So what's up with you and Dad?"

"What makes you think anything's going on?" My mother's voice sounded high and strained.

"Uh, let's see. How about the fact that you're 3,000 miles from home? You're the one who maintains the myth that Dad can't dress and feed himself."

"Have you ever known your father to press a shirt? To turn on the stove?"

"You're making my case for me."

"Never mind. I can take a hint. I'll find a hotel this afternoon."

"Mother, that's not my point and you know it!"

"Shush. The baby's almost asleep."

I glanced in the rear view mirror. Paris's head listed to one side like a sunflower and her eyelids drooped. "I just want to know what you and Dad are fighting about," I whispered.

"Your father and I don't fight. You know that."

"But you had a little misunderstanding, Dad said."

"What else did he say?"

I shrugged. "Nothing."

My mother sighed. "That's par for the course. Sometimes we go a whole day without having a real conversation. If he's not doing yard work, it's just Dad in front of his new flat screen TV, locked in battle with guests on talk shows."

It was true. Mom puttered in her kitchen or went off to church, while Dad lounged in his recliner or obsessively tended the lawn. One Saturday, I'd come home unexpectedly and watched him mow the grass in carefully widening circles around a single dogwood tree, then reverse direction and do it all over again, until the grass was as smooth as a billiard table. My mother threatened to have the lawn cemented over years ago.

"So why have you stayed with him this long?" I ventured.

My mother sighed. "Your father wasn't always a nice man, Jordan. In fact, he was an ass, those years he was drinking. But he was always present. Every night. And a good provider. You could say that much for the man. Think about Grammy, the year she died."

"Dad was good to her," I agreed. When Grammy came to live with us that year, my father was the one who converted the dining room into a replica of her mobile home bedroom, putting Grammy's scarred pine dresser right beside the rented hospital bed and gathering all of her ceramic animals on it. And it was Dad whose hand Grammy held at the end.

"The truth is that I'm lonely now, without you and Cam around," Mom said.

"What about your friends?" I asked, wrestling the Volvo through a narrow street and dodging a bicycle messenger.

My mother turned a little in the seat to look at me. "Even friends can't make up for distance in a marriage. Besides, as old as I am, there's a lot of competition for friendship: Alzheimer's, cruises, divorces, heart attacks, Florida condos. Hardly anybody in the neighborhood remembers me from before my hair turned gray. They're all dead or missing in action." She faced the windshield again and added, "I've been thinking of leaving your father."

I gripped the steering wheel, stricken. It was unnerving to have the one person I'd always depended on for everything from clean sheets to tomato soup tell me that her foundation was crumbling. Mom's foundation was my bedrock. "Why now? Why didn't you leave Dad when he was drinking?"

She shrugged. "The years Dad was drinking, all those black years, I clung to the idea that someday your father would wake up and realize how good we had it together. Meanwhile, I drove myself crazy, looking after you kids, the house, his moods. Felt like an eternity at the time. Turns out, though, that kids grow up before you blink."

My mother glanced at Paris over her shoulder and then at me again, briefly. "After you left, I got to thinking about Cam, about how I failed him, and I started worrying again about you and your health problems. You and Cam are my life, Jordy, but your father never wanted me to spend the money to see you. You chose to leave, is how he sees it, so it's your loss." She reached across the seat and touched my leg. "I had to let him know that he can't ever stop me from seeing my own children. That's just not going to happen."

I took my mother's hand in mine, afraid to look at her for fear I'd do something stupid, like cry. We covered the next couple of miles in silence, slowly winding through the Berkeley streets.

After a few minutes, Mom said, "It's not just for the baby's sake that I need to find Cam." She took her hand back so that she could clutch the purse on her lap. "It's for my own. I feel so guilty."

"Why? I don't understand how you failed Cam. Why is it your fault that he's such a screw-up?"

She flinched, and for a minute I thought she wasn't going to answer. Then Mom pulled a tissue out of the vast reaches of her purse and pressed it to her eyes. "I need to say I'm sorry for not standing up for him all those years. After you went away to college, there were a couple of bad years when Cam caught the worst of it when your father was drinking. But I suppose you know that." She glanced at me. "Cam must have told you."

"Cam never talks about it. But I knew something was going on." My knuckles were white on the steering wheel. "Why isn't Dad the one saying sorry? You didn't do anything but good, all our lives."

Mom tucked the tissue into the sleeve of her dress. "Your father was an alcoholic. He was the victim of a disease. I had my wits about me, but still I sat back and did nothing, because I was afraid. And fear should not be the boss of your life, Jordan, especially when it's your own children who need protecting. Your father should certainly make amends, but this is my journey, too."

I didn't answer, caught up in a single, crystal revelation: Cam had always run away from us, from everyone, because doing anything remotely responsible— like having a job, or even letting you know how to find him—meant to Cam that he was like Dad, the last person on earth he'd ever want to become.

Half an hour later, we reached Shepherd Jon's house. I drove straight up the driveway of the big Victorian. Val was probably gone by now, too. Paris woke when I shut off the engine. I carried the baby up the flagstone path and held her up so that she could ring the front doorbell. Paris giggled and pressed the bell hard with her thumb, like she was squashing a bug.

"This place could stand a little TLC," Mom murmured, surveying the peeling trim paint, unkempt bushes, and filmy windows. I knew her fingers must be itching for a rag and window cleaner.

"Jon, the owner, inherited this house from his parents," I reminded her. "He's not too keen on housekeeping."

My mother snorted. "Of course not. He's letting the house go to ruin as a passive revenge."

I stared at her. "Why, Dr. Freud. You amaze me."

The door popped open a crack, making us both jump. Val peered out from within the dark, musty interior of the house. "Damn," she said, staring at me in feeble recognition. "You have a baby now. That was quick."

"Yep." I introduced Val to my mother, who took the other woman's hand in hers and pressed it tightly, like a foreign dignitary visiting a host ambassador.

Val was an ambassador of sorts, as the only walking, talking representative of Cam's life in Berkeley. She looked no better than the last time I'd seen her. Her hair was matted into short, stiff yellow ropes, and her complexion had the waxy pallor of someone used to sleeping during daylight hours. On the up side, she was dressed. Val wore a faded cotton skirt, t-shirt and battered leather sandals, the hangdog sort of ensemble I associated with aging women academics.

I didn't have high hopes for this visit. But Mom used her Avon lady manners to insinuate our way into the kitchen, where she convinced Val to scrounge around for tea. The tea was surprisingly fresh and strong, a loose leaf Assam that Val spooned out of a tin on the counter. Empty boxes–cereals, crackers, pasta–littered the kitchen counter and floors, most of them torn open in ways that suggested foraging raccoons. I wondered what Val would do for food once she'd grazed her way through the rest of Jon's pantry.

Val plopped down on one of the wooden chairs at the table and began shoveling teaspoons of sugar into her teacup. I counted six before she said, "It's so good to see somebody. Thanks for stopping."

It had never occurred to me that Val, if she were here at all, might actually be happy to see us. "Have you heard from your house mates?" I asked. Too soon for letters from Asia, I thought, but Jon might have called to check on the house.

"Not a word! I feel like an abandoned dog."

"Surely not," my mother protested. "They're only roommates."

Val gave her a level look, or at any rate a less stoned look than usual. Maybe she'd smoked her way through every hidden stash at this point and run out of money to buy more. "Jon, Domingo, Melody, and Cam are more than just roommates. They're family," she said, articulating each name, each word, with the precise diction of a high school principal awarding diplomas.

"Your real family wouldn't leave you in the lurch like this," my mother asserted.

Val barked a short, unpleasant laugh. "My own father set the gold standard in abandonment."

I waited for my mother to take the same hard line on pity parties with Val that she adopted whenever I wallowed in my own personal travesties. Instead, Mom laid a gentle hand on Val's own larger, rougher one. "That's terrible," she said gently. "Without family, a person is cast adrift."

Val's eyes brimmed with tears. To my horror, my own did, too, as Val responded to my mother's mothering by recounting her Dickensian life: evil stepfather, miserable boarding school, on the streets by age sixteen. Jon had taken her in at her lowest. "I owe him my life," Val said.

Paris was starting to whine. I left my mother huddled with Val in the kitchen and wandered out to the greenhouse with Paris on one hip. The orchids were every bit as abandoned as Val, yet continued to thrive without Jon. He must have them on some sort of automatic watering system.

When the complex odors started to make me feel dizzy, I strolled around the main house and entered it again through the front door. The tables were thick with dust and a desperate cat had apparently run out of space in the litter box. I climbed the stairs to Cam's room, ignoring Paris's burbled demands to be allowed to crawl up the stairs by herself.

Cam's bed was covered with the same tired striped sheets I'd seen last time. He'd left the bathrobe my mother bought him hanging from the door. I fingered its tattered terry edges, heard something crackle in the pocket, and thrust my hand in to extract a single sheet of paper, a neon pink flyer for a Chinese restaurant.

I was about to replace it when I noticed that the back was covered with Cam's cramped handwriting. Cam's writing had always been difficult to read; it was faint and spidery, as if he were as fearful of committing his thoughts to paper as he was to committing himself to anything else in life. My heart pounded hard, but why? I wasn't going to steal anything. Only look. And Val was hardly the sort to bound upstairs and catch me snooping, especially when she had a captive audience downstairs.

I set Paris down on the floor and studied the paper. The handwriting was badly smudged and Cam's thoughts seemed barely connected. The entire first paragraph was devoted to a dentist's visit gone bad.

No pot to piss in, so forget the root canal and crown. Christ, I could buy a car for that. Had it pulled instead. An hour of fucking torture, the demonic Dr. twisting at the tooth with those damn pliers, me humming that mantra Jon taught. I may be the jewel in the eye of the lotus and all that, but this jewel is one rotted carcass. Jon says suffering and illness are directly related to the unstable nature of the mind. Smart dude. Stress guarantees thought patterns that fuck up the flow of life.

Cam rambled on from there, parroting Jon's pedestrian philosophies of life, then added, *Tooth hole's so sore I can't even eat a cracker. On the other hand, who the fuck cares about crackers? Sold my pain meds to help pay my astro dentistry debt. Bad enough your body rots, but then you've got to pay the piper too. Now Jordan's here like a busy little beaver sawing logs, dragging them into the middle of the stream and diverting the natural flow of events. Jordy's always been a busy little beaver. Me, I just want to be the stream.*

Seeing my name written in Cam's hand made the hairs rise on the back of my neck, as if he had walked into the room and spoken it. I glanced up and saw Paris, who was now gumming the foot board and grinning at me with her father's blue eyes, with my eyes.

"Take that gross thing out of your mouth," I said. The baby giggled and started race-crawling around the bedroom. I hoped there wasn't anything nasty on the rug, took a deep breath, and finished reading the page.

There were just three more lines: *Jordan wants me to join the pitiful polluted stagnant reservoir of humanity, but I'm ready to roar over the rocks, cleanse my soul, change the world, leave my troubles behind. In Nepal we'll be on the rooftop of the world, where the gods walk among us mere mortals. Everything will become clear at the Hotel Everest, all will manifest itself in its own way, if only Jordan...*

And there the sentence ended, as if Cam had drifted off to sleep, my name the final grace note to my brother's escape from his known world.

Three nights later, I lay on my bed between Paris's crib and my mother's air mattress, unable to sleep. To my right, Paris snored softly, her tiny body humped beneath the crib blankets. To my left, Mom reclined on the wheezing mattress like a fallen garden statue, her nose pointed straight up at the ceiling.

Mom was probably awake, too. We had been arguing since visiting Val about the best course of action to take, now that we definitely knew that Cam's destination had been the Hotel Everest in Kathmandu. The words of our disagreement hovered above us like moths, spinning in the dim glow of moonlight filtering in through the foggy veil hanging outside the French doors.

The gist of the argument was simple: I wanted to travel to Nepal to find Cam and convince him to come home and help me raise Paris. If he absolutely refused, I hoped to have him sign papers giving me legal guardianship. I had seen a lawyer, a friend of Karin's, to get the necessary documents drawn up. Then I had made a reservation to fly to Kathmandu.

My mother didn't want me to go. "You'll get lost," she had argued. "You don't speak the language and Nepal isn't safe to begin with."

She cited every scary story she must have found on the Internet about tourist rapes, muggings, kidnappings, and murders in Asia. "Plus, Cam probably isn't even there anymore. Or, if he is, he's not going to want to have anything to do with the baby. We have to just take care of Paris and wait for Cam to come to his senses."

I reminded her that I had called the Hotel Everest and discovered that Cam was registered there. What's more, I had phoned the American Embassy in Kathmandu, where an official had checked through passport records and told me that Cam was definitely in Nepal.

"Even if your brother doesn't stay at that hotel, you could probably catch up with him at the American Express Office," the clerk said kindly. "Kathmandu is a small town. Not like San Francisco. Everyone walks the same streets here."

I didn't believe my mother's theory that Cam would return to California on his own steam if we waited him out. If Cam had gone to this much trouble to put distance between himself and his life here, he meant this action to count for something.

I felt confident that I could locate my brother. I had different fears entirely about this trip. The first was that Cam might refuse to not only come home, but to sign the guardianship papers putting Paris in my custody. Doing so would mean admitting that he'd fathered a child. If he didn't sign those papers, I'd have no control over what happened to the baby if Nadine changed her mind about wanting me to raise her.

The second fear was more complicated: if Cam did sign the papers, what would happen if I adopted Paris, only to discover I wasn't really ready for motherhood?

My mother sighed suddenly and sat up. "This is no good. We might as well give up on sleep and talk," she said. "I can hear your wheels turning."

"What makes you think we'd get anywhere with this conversation in the middle of the night?" I sputtered. "We've been going in circles for hours."

"There's one solution we haven't considered yet."

"What's that?"

"We could both go to Nepal and take Paris with us instead of me staying here with her."

I toyed with this idea for a moment, if only for the satisfaction it gave me to imagine my brother's face when he saw our mother waltz into a Kathmandu hotel, giant flight bag in one hand, his baby in the other.

"You know we can't do that," I said. "It's too dangerous. The death rate for kids under five in Nepal is phenomenal. There's malaria, typhoid, hepatitis..."

"Shush, Jordy! You sound like your father, all gloom and doom!"

"My father, who you will call tomorrow, right?"

"I don't know. I'm still thinking that one over. Maybe after I go out for breakfast with Louise."

"You're going out with her again this morning?" I asked.

She nodded, smiling slightly. "It's the most fun I've had in years."

"How did you meet Louise, anyway? I don't remember introducing you."

"Remember that morning you went to the market with Ed? Well, I was having such a terrible time with the baby in the bath that Louise heard the racket. She came downstairs like the house was on fire. At first I did think she was a bit odd."

"A bit," I agreed.

"Still, she was wonderful with the baby," Mom said. "Played peekaboo with a washcloth until I had that child clean as a whistle, then helped me dress her. So we got to talking, you know, about me and my situation."

"What do you mean? What situation?" I swallowed hard. What had I missed?

The air mattress squeaked beneath her as Mom swiveled around to face me. I'd offered her my bed when she first arrived, but of course she wouldn't hear of putting me on the floor.

"The thing is, I'm tired of living such a pale little life, Jordan," she said. "I want a life in living color! Coming to see you was the first step."

My heart hurt, hearing this admission. It dawned on me then that one of the toughest things about being an adult was realizing that your parents were in pain, and you didn't ever know it. Though I suppose that Cam and I had, on some pale level, which is why we always steered clear of emotional interactions with either of our parents.

"Well, Mom," I said, "like you used to tell me, you have to make a plan and follow it through."

"I told you that?" Mom snorted. "No wonder you and Cam left home. Huh. Now I would tell you two something completely different."

"Like what?" I held my breath, waiting.

My mother's voice was so soft that I had to strain to hear her. "Follow what you know is true, and you'll have fewer regrets than I did, Jordy. And by the way? You need to start doing that right this minute."

"What do you mean?"

"I mean, isn't there somebody you ought to visit before you leave for Nepal?" My mother fell back onto her air mattress and pulled the blanket up to her chin. "Since you've got a built-in babysitter and all."

I stared at her for a minute, then climbed out of bed and slipped into a t-shirt and jeans. I squatted by the mattress to kiss my mother's cheek. Paris had shrugged off her blankets again and flopped onto her back like a sunbather, arms straight along her sides. I stooped to pull the baby's blankets up again before heading for the door.

"Jordan?" Mom called softly.

I stopped and turned, waiting for what I expected my mother to say, as she had every day of my childhood: *Be careful*.

But Mom didn't say any such thing. "Have fun," she said, then added, "Mind if I take you up on that offer and crawl into your bed for a few hours? My back's killing me."

David was home. I could hear a jazz saxophone blaring against background piano even from the bottom of David's hill. I wound my way through the hibiscus-scented dark to the top of the street, my arms swinging in time to the music.

Every other house and apartment was dark at this hour, but lights blazed in David's windows. Was he having a party? So much the better. I could casually slip inside, say I was just passing by. Oh, and by the way, looks like I'm going to Nepal. Got any tourist tips on temples and yaks?

The blinds were drawn. There could be two people inside his house or twenty. I hesitated on the front step, wondering how to make my entrance. I didn't have long to ponder my approach: his dog started yapping, its shadow leaping and twirling behind the window shade like a marionette dancing the Tarantella. So much for the subtle approach.

I rang the bell. The dog grabbed the bottom of the door blind in its teeth. The blind snapped and rolled up, the dog dangling from its edge as David crossed the living room to open the door.

David looked at me a moment too long. The dog released the shade and shot out the door like a cobra to grip my jeans between its jaws. "Just thought I'd drop by and see what you've been up to," I said, giving my foot a little shake. The dog hung tight. "How's it going?"

"Fine," David mumbled, then bent down to detach the dog. "Hang on. I'll just stick Jack in his crate."

I hovered on the porch like a Jehovah's Witness. From the sounds of Jack's shrill yapping and David's ineffectual shushing noises, he was clearly a better pediatrician than dog handler. At last a door closed somewhere in the far reaches of the house. The dog was still barking, but at least now the sound was muffled.

"What are you doing, walking the streets alone at this hour?" David demanded when he returned. "Or did you get your car back?"

"About that day you stopped by to give me a ride…" I began, but David held up a hand to stop me.

"Wait. Didn't mean to be rude. Sorry. Come in, come in. Hold on while I turn down the music." He left me again.

I hovered in the living room, craning my neck for clues to David's existence. If he did have a woman here, she was hiding. This was bachelor heaven. The furniture cushions were brown corduroy, the gold plaid curtains looked as though they'd been inherited from someone's basement. and an iguana lurked in an aquarium.

"I haven't done much housecleaning in the past few days," David apologized, following my glance as he returned a few minutes later. "It's good to see you, Jordan."

"Really? Even though I had to hunt you down? You've been avoiding my calls."

"Busy," David said. "You? How are things?"

He was wearing baggy red cotton pajama pants dotted with penguins and a black t-shirt. He was barefoot. I couldn't decide if he looked ridiculous or sexy as I sank onto the couch.

"Things are good," I said. "Mostly." I tried to breathe deeply and relax against the couch, only to spring forward again as something hard and thorny squeaked beneath me.

"Sorry!" David said. He fished a plastic cactus chew toy out of the cushion, shying away from any actual contact with my hip.

"That's some watchdog you've got."

"Yeah, Jack has even bitten me," he admitted. "I rescued him from an abandoned house near the clinic and can't give him to a shelter because he's so nasty."

"So he wasn't having a particularly bad reaction to me?"

"No, no," David promised. "In fact, I think Jack took a real shine to you. He went after your jeans without taking a piece of your ankle."

I sat back against the couch again. My face felt hot. I took a deep breath and said, "Look, I know you don't want to hear this, but I came to explain what happened the other day when you saw me with Ed."

"You don't owe me an explanation," he said hastily. "I should have called before coming by your place."

We weren't getting anywhere this way. David's eyes were dark with apprehension. Even his curls looked anxious, bobbing about in tight ringlets above his glasses.

I forced myself to continue. "You saw me kissing Ed, but there's nothing between us. Ed and I are just friends. He's dating Karin now."

"Ed was dating Karin before," David said. "Ed's always dating Karin. Whenever he's not dating the rest of San Francisco, that is."

His glum tone stopped me. Was David also secretly harboring feelings for Karin? God, that would be just my luck.

On the other hand, Karin had made it clear that David was just a passing idea for her. I moved a little closer to David, resting my hand on one of his knees as I leaned over to kiss him. It was a long kiss, cool at the start and then so hot my mouth felt as if it were burning.

The dog continued to issue muffled distress calls from the back of the house. We kept kissing until I didn't know when one kiss started and the other ended.

I moved on top of David and tugged both of our t-shirts up so that I could rub my breasts on his chest. He was hard beneath me and breathing fast. I removed his glasses, which by now hung crookedly over one earpiece.

Suddenly, David wriggled out from under me and moved over on the couch. He retrieved his glasses and settled them above his nose. "I can't do this," he said. "I'm sorry, Jordan."

Mortified, I glanced down to where his body had been just seconds before. The cushions were warm and I was still resting on my arms, my t-shirt hiked up over my bare breasts, which now bobbed in the air like floats at the Macy's Day Parade.

I yanked my shirt down and sat up on the couch again, so far away from David that the wooden sofa arm bit into my hip. "Sorry," I mumbled. "Don't know what got into me."

"Don't apologize!" David begged. "Look, I lied. I do want an explanation." He swallowed hard. "I want to know whether you slept with Ed."

"Why?" The word was out before I had time to think. Damn. I took a deep breath. "Never mind why. Of course you want to know. I was with Ed. Just one time. We didn't do anything, not really. I didn't even spend the night. I'm sorry I didn't tell you before. I didn't know how. I was afraid you'd think what you're thinking now, which is that I want to be with him instead of you, or that I'm the kind of woman who hooks up for the fun of it."

David stood up and paced the room, played a few agitated chords on the piano, then came back and stood in front of me with his arms crossed. "How did you find time? Just tell me that much! You and I were apart for what, a total of six hours?"

It dawned on me then. "Oh, no! I didn't go with Ed after sleeping with you! Not that same day you saw us! Only before I was ever with you, and only one time! And we didn't have sex." I didn't know how much more clearly I could spell things out for him.

"Before?" David rubbed his chin, then plopped down beside me on the couch again. "Okay, yeah. Yeah, that's better." He leaned his head back against the couch. "How long before?"

"What difference does that make?" I demanded, feeling suddenly tearful, unduly accused. I rested my face in my hands, thinking hard. Did he need every detail? Maybe he did. I would, in his shoes.

"The point is," I said, choosing my words carefully, "I only tried sleeping with Ed before there was anything between you and me. Ed is with Karin now, and I'm glad. I want to be with you."

There. Now the guy had a road map, a shortcut straight to my heart. What more could I give him?

David had closed his eyes. I poked his arm. "Hey! Wake up!"

"I'm awake," he said softly, his eyes still squeezed shut. David's long, dark lashes were the sort princesses have in storybooks. "Just in a state of emotional paralysis."

After a few more minutes, I stood up and left him. I needed to get my wits back. I wandered down the hall to the bathroom. It was as minimalist as the rest of the house: one blue towel, a shred of soap, a mirror the size of a saucer.

I glared at my reflection. I had the rosy cheeks and red nose of a boozer and my hair was matted on one side. Jesus. What a mess. Between taking care of Paris, searching for Cam, and making plans to fly to Kathmandu, I was wrung out. I started to cry and turned the shower on full blast to hide the noise, sinking down onto the floor with my head in my arms.

The bathroom door opened and David poked his head in, squinting through the steam. "Can I come in?"

"It's your bathroom." I spun out a length of toilet paper and blew my nose. The evening was getting more romantic by the second.

David closed the door behind him. "Want the water off or on?" He gestured at the shower.

"Off. Sorry. Didn't mean to waste it."

"That's all right. It's nice and warm in here now."

David turned off the water, sat down on the floor beside me, and handed me the blue towel. "I think we've got sort of a Russian Baths thing going. Steam the air, cleanse the pores, make big decisions."

"Look, I might as well sweat out the rest of my confession right here." I took a deep breath. "I went home with Ed after Karin's party for lots of reasons that had nothing to do with wanting to be with Ed, but I'm not sorry. I was trying to leave my old life behind, and I needed a dramatic finale to how I was living before. Does that make sense? Or does that screw things up between us?"

David's glasses had fogged in the steam. He took them off and wiped the lenses fruitlessly on the hem of his t-shirt. "Here's the thing, Jordan. I appreciate how honest you are. I really do. But I was into you. I mean, like really into you. And now, after seeing you kiss Ed and knowing you were with him, I don't think I can be with you. Not until there's a certain level of trust between us. I was born a century too late. When I make love with a woman, I'm usually *in* love with her. I have a low tolerance for loss. I don't know why. Maybe my dad's death makes it impossible for me to trust that someone will stick around."

David was in love with me? Was that what he meant?

I joyfully crab-walked out from under the sink and sat against the wall across from him. He was in love with me! "What happened to your dad?"

A rock climbing accident, David explained. "I was fourteen then. A long time ago. Long enough so I don't think about him every day." David flashed a grin. "Except when I'm climbing mountains, of course."

"Your mother must have a fit every time you do it!"

"Her worries are over now that my knees have given out. But I hate not being able to climb. I've lost the only connection I ever had with my father."

"I'm sure that's not true." I put my hands on his knees. "I wish I could heal you. Still, I'm glad you're not climbing. I wouldn't be able to follow you."

"Sure you could. I'd teach you." David patted my hand. "Come on. Can we give the couch another try?"

I followed him into the living room, where I let him sit on the couch first. "Where do you want me?" I asked, hesitating.

"Right here." David patted his lap.

"You're sure?"

"Yes. I just want to hold you. Is that all right?"

"More than all right." Already, I was listing towards him, as if a web had been spun from my belly to his. I sank onto David's knees and rested my head on his shoulder. We sat that way, talking more about his father, his music, my mother, Paris, and Cam. Finally, I told him about Nepal. "Do you think I should go? "

"Of course. You'd never be able to live with yourself if you didn't make one last try to sort this thing out with your brother."

David always made things sound so simple. "I don't know," I said. "I'm confused about my own motives. Part of me wants things to stay just as they are, so that I can have Paris without really taking on the full responsibility of motherhood."

"But you're too responsible," David suggested.

"I don't feel very responsible right this minute." I pressed my lips lightly against his neck. David's curls were damp from the steamy bathroom and he'd taken off his glasses. He trembled slightly. "Want to give me some Kathmandu travel tips?" I asked, putting my lips close to his ear.

"Here's one." David's arms tightened around me. "Come back in one piece."

"That's my travel tip?"

"Yes."

"Will you be waiting for me?" I pressed my face to David's neck, unable to resist his smell, his skin. I traced the length of his throat with the tip of my tongue. David tasted of salt and lime.

"I don't know," he said. "I don't think I can promise that. I need more time with you before I can let my guard down. And that seems kind of pointless in a way, doesn't it? Since you're going back to the East Coast? I'm sorry."

"It's all right," I said miserably. "I understand."

And I did, since I couldn't make promises, either. What would I do if Cam granted me guardianship of his daughter? Where would I live? How would I work? I didn't know the answers to any of those questions. So how could I possibly promise to be reliable as a lover?

David ran a hand through my hair. "God, Jordan," he whispered. "The things you do to me! And you've got such a wild mane of hair. I love your hair. Sometimes it looks like your hair is on fire." He traced my lips with one finger. "Will you sleep with me?"

I sat bolt upright. "Sleep with you? I thought you just said..."

"I mean just sleep."

"I'm not sure I'm capable of that."

"Of course you are. And so am I. Would you stay with me until I go to work?"

I thought about my mother and her breakfast with Louise. "I have to be home by eight."

David glanced at his watch. "Four whole hours," he said. "An hour more than last time. Will you?"

I laughed. "There's no place else I'd rather be," I said, thinking how rarely in my life I'd ever been able to say that.

Chapter twelve

hree days later, I flew from San Francisco to Hong Kong, and
then on to Kathmandu, where the plane seemed to hover over the
Himalayas.

David had told me that each mountain had its own personality,
and he was right. Some peaks rose gracefully above the clouds, their folds
as delicate as white skirts. Others gleamed like pink church spires, a few
stern black cones standing between them like castle turrets. Glacial lakes
gleamed sapphire against the darker wrinkles of the terminal moraines.

"The pilots don't fly through the clouds here, because the clouds have
rocks in them," the Nepalese businessman beside me confided.

The Kathmandu airport was a tiny, burnt orange stucco building with
yellow flowers draped over its roof. The customs officers examined my
backpack with Boy Scout efficiency, then ushered me through the door.

Outside, I was immediately swallowed by a sea of gleeful, shouting
taxi drivers. I chose one and directed him to the Hotel Everest, Cam's last

known address. This turned out to be a two-story brick building with tiled floors and thin, damp mattresses on wooden platforms. The family who managed it included three underfed boys with the mournful look of abandoned kittens.

Cam had already been to the hotel and gone, the owner said, showing me the guest register. "Maybe he changed hotels?" he said. "Many tourists, they change. You want a room?"

I booked a room and saw at once why tourists might switch hotels after arriving here: the rooms were cold and damp, with cement floors and pitiful lumpy mattresses on string beds. I had bought a Nepal Telecom SIM card at the airport for my cell phone; now I used it to call my mother and tell her I'd arrived safely. Then, exhausted by the journey, I fell onto the mattress and slept.

It was still dark outside when I opened my eyes. I looked automatically to my left to see if Paris was asleep in her crib. It was all I could do not to cry out when I saw that the room was empty except for a white cardboard bureau and my own dusty backpack, which bulged with clothing that my mother had insisted on ironing. My mother had issued warnings with each stroke of the iron, making me promise not to walk through dark alleys; eat in empty restaurants; or take any drugs other than the malaria, cholera, worm, sulfa, and antibiotic pills David had gathered for me in a drawstring nylon bag that weighed as much as a bowling ball.

Now I felt out of synch and sore besides. David had insisted on giving me multiple immunizations. He had promised to protect me against Hepatitis A, meningitis, tetanus, and typhoid, wincing himself as he pressed each needle against my skin.

A rooster crowed in the courtyard below. Someone in the communal bathroom across the hall started the shower and sang in German. I swatted mosquitoes and lay there, paralyzed by anxiety as I listened to the rumble of Australian, German, English, and French voices. Travelers were emerging from their rooms and waiting in line for one of the toilets down the hall. Horns were already blaring in the darkness and a cow lowed on the street between a rooster's hoarse calls.

I was in the Thamel district of Kathmandu. Thamel seemed to translate from Nepali as "Tacky Tourist Central," given my brief glimpse of it yesterday as I hurtled down the streets in a taxi with no muffler. The driver pointed out sights, but of course I couldn't hear anything he said over the ear-splitting grind of the engine, a sound that even now seemed trapped inside my own skull. There were guest houses, lodges, and hotels every twenty feet in this part of Kathmandu, along with ethnic restaurants, souvenir shops, t-shirt stands, English bookstores, and backpacking resale shops.

I could venture just half a block to the next lodge, I decided now. Then I'd check the next hotel, the next, and so forth, until I'd combed Kathmandu's maze of streets on foot and found Cam.

On the street below my hotel window, a processional band began to play a loud, tinny march punctuated by flailing cymbals as it proceeded along the road. I climbed out of bed and knelt at the window to watch. The robes of the musicians gleamed ghostly white against the final edge of night.

I dressed and plunged into air that was steamy from last night's rain. The streets were dotted with metallic silver puddles. My head throbbed. I felt hung over just from being surrounded by such a din.

Barely wide enough for two cars to pass, the street was clogged with wheels: rickshaws, bicycles, motorcycles, cars. The motorcycles carried entire families; I saw a small boy fly off the back of one as his father careened around a corner. Horns blared but nobody stopped, only swerved to miss him. Cows and dogs did their bit to confuse the traffic as well. There were no sidewalks; I pressed against the stone walls of the ancient buildings, thinking that I was more likely to get run over than find my brother in all this mess.

I stumbled into the first open restaurant and ordered Tibetan yak cheese, honey bread, and tea from a menu written in five languages. I wolfed down the thick bread, licking honey off my fingers and relishing every bite in the relative quiet of the restaurant until the woman at the table next to mine—the only other customer—launched into a coughing fit that caused her ceramic tea cup to rattle in its saucer.

She was a stringy blonde with a dancer's muscles and pretty features, her eyes so light gray that they had the silver cast of the street puddles. She wore a short denim skirt and a skimpy black t-shirt. She coughed for several minutes, finally spitting up into a napkin.

The woman glanced at me, then crumpled the napkin onto her untouched plate of eggs, and apologized in a prim British schoolmistress's accent as she lit a brown clove cigarette. She wore a dozen or so noisy silver bangles on each arm and a silver dot in her nose.

"Sorry," she said, beginning to cough again, but this time managing to stifle it with a pull on her cigarette. "Too much bloody time in India. This cough and the bloody trots, those are my souvenirs. I'll never have a normal stomach again. I'm Leslie Gallant, by the way."

I told her my name. "India must be fascinating. How long were you there?"

"Seven, maybe eight months. Long enough to know I'd skip the whole mess next time 'round the world. Bloody hell!" Leslie waved the entire Indian subcontinent away with the sweep of one hand, jangling her bracelets.

"What made you go to India in the first place?" Despite seeing the international stew of lodgers crowding my own hotel, it was still difficult for me to grasp the idea that people voluntarily boarded planes and flew dozens of hours to wander unfamiliar countries.

Most of these wanderers seemed short on money and common sense. It seemed like traveling through Asia with a backpack was less about taking a vacation than about plunging into your own personal underworld. That's probably why Cam was here.

"Why does anyone go anywhere?" Leslie was saying. "In my case, the reason was a man, a Swedish Buddhist I met on a beach in Thailand. A really yummy man child. I couldn't resist. We lived in an Indian Ashram where a guru performed our spiritual marriage. Then my spiritual husband broke my spiritual nose during one of our very spiritual knock-down fights, and I hopped on the next train out of Nirvana." She coughed again, the sound rattling in her chest like dice in a cup.

"So why did you come to Nepal? Instead of going home, I mean. Or at least resting somewhere until you're well." *Somewhere with clean water and fewer mosquitoes*, I nearly added.

"Too many places left to see. I'm on my way to Australia, where I'll find work someplace. I'm a software engineer, so that shouldn't be too difficult."

"But why Nepal?" I asked again.

She shrugged. "I'm on a sort of women's odyssey," she explained, "since I'm off men at the moment. Nepal is one of the safer countries for women going it solo. Nothing like the Muslim countries. My plan now is to score a Sherpani to carry my gear into the mountains."

I couldn't imagine this woman reaching the summit of a staircase, never mind trekking the Himalayas. "Maybe you should stay in bed for a while and eat bland foods before you go," I said. "You know. Bananas and rice. That sort of thing might settle your stomach."

Leslie snorted. "My, you're a right little mother, aren't you?"

"Nearly," I agreed, digging around in my pocket for rupees to leave on the table. This took some time; I still wasn't used to the currency, and both of my arms felt like they were on fire from the immunizations.

Leslie helped me count out the money. "What d'you mean?" She fixed her pale eyes on my face. "Not pregnant, are you?"

"No, but I'm thinking of adopting my niece."

My own bald admission stunned me. Still, in this place, where nobody knew my history, it seemed possible to reveal anything I wanted to about my life. The thing about foreign travel was that you could assume any personality you wished and try it on for size, because the odds were slim that you'd ever see these people again.

So I told Leslie about my breakup with Peter, my sudden move to San Francisco, my discovery of Cam's baby, and now my search for him. Leslie listened without comment, then generously offered to search the city with me.

"I know every traveler's favorite pit stop in Thamel," she said.

I was glad for her company, since being in Kathmandu was like being inside a kaleidoscope. I took a deep breath as we stepped outside into the flow. Rickshaws rattled past, tugged along by spry men whose muscles ran like ropes along the lengths of their thighs. Most of the rickshaws carried foreign tourists or recently butchered, bloody animal torsos.

From every alley, shadowy figures hissed temptations: "Change money? Good massage? Good fuck? Clean hashish?"

The tempo and clamor were terrifying. I kept turning my head away, looking at the sky, at the buildings, even at my feet—anywhere but at the people living their lives so openly on the street. In my New England neighborhood of white clapboard houses, we had curtains and fences to ensure privacy, and San Francisco secrets were often guarded behind walled gardens. In Kathmandu, though, there were few secrets. I saw people haggling with vendors, men shaving and urinating, a naked child vomiting. In one shadowy alley, next to one of several Net Cafes offering free WiFi to travelers, a man defecated into a trash pile.

Everywhere we went, children followed, demanding pens, sweets, and rupees. Some were no older than six, yet carried skinny babies with fly-infested eyes. The babies looked hungry, but how would you know? They dangled placidly from the arms of their brothers and sisters, occasionally grinning toothlessly in my direction.

I thought of Paris, of her lusty howls for food and of how she had been nearly as skinny as these babies when Nadine first left her at my door. Now her limbs had the plumpness of newly risen dough. Paris was a fighter, I'd always thought, but perhaps that was only because I'd gotten her soon enough. If Nadine had taken her to Oregon, would Paris have been as listless as the poor infants living here?

Depending on where they'd come from, the women of Nepal wore heavy cotton Tibetan striped aprons over dark skirts or bright silk saris, colors blazing against the dusty streets. The Hindu women had rings in their noses and the third eye, the red dot on their foreheads, while the Tibetan women from the mountain villages wore long, heavy necklaces of turquoise, some with stones as big as robins' eggs. They smoked cigarettes in a protective way, cupping their hands over pungent brown stalks. I felt big-footed and clumsy, striding past them in my clownish pants and hiking boots.

Leslie and I stopped at over two dozen budget and medium-priced tourist lodges and hotels over the next three hours. The desk clerks greeted us with wide grins and that sideways head shake that could mean yes, no, or maybe so.

A few tried to prolong the conversations, glad to have a diversion from the bookkeeping they did in huge clothbound ledgers behind tall dusty counters. I studied each guest book for my brother's name and showed clerks a photograph my mother had given me out of her wallet.

The clerks were happy to try their English with us. One elderly man with black hair short and stiff as a carpet told us that he was happy to help tourists. "I learn many things from tourists." He grinned, examining the photo of Cam, the corners of which were beginning to melt in the steamy heat. "But I have not seen your man."

"What kinds of things do you learn?" I asked.

"Oh," he bobbed his head, "I learned all about the AIDS. I am not borrowing any more t-shirts from people now, oh no." He grinned. "I know Lady Gaga, yes? And Britney Spears. She is hot. Someday I will buy an iPad and watch videos here." He gestured at his scarred desk.

The guests in these shoestring Kathmandu hotels were mostly under thirty, all of them information traders: the best beach in Thailand, the cheapest hostel in Jakarta, a German woman's mugging in Delhi. None of them remembered seeing Cam.

"He must not be on the regular tourist trail," Leslie said finally. She suggested taking a break, then trying the American Express Office after one o'clock, when the daily mail arrived. If Jon was getting mail in Nepal, that's when he would show up to collect it, she said.

"Let's go to the Monkey Temple," she said. "It's a nice walk, and you want to see something of Kathmandu other than all this bloody tourist rigamarole while you're here, right?" She hung a skinny arm around my shoulders.

I agreed. I was worn out and eager to escape the clamor of Kathmandu's tourist center.

As we started walking toward a hill that rose above the city, I wondered what combination of fate and choice had brought Leslie to this point in her life. With her posh accent and pert features, she could scrub herself up, slip into a little black dress and pearls, and take over as director of an art gallery or pose as some business mogul's trophy wife. Yet she had mentioned no family, no apartment or house.

All around us, though, were people like Leslie. Europeans, Australians, Americans, and a smattering of Japanese wandered the streets of Kathmandu, many teetering like ants beneath sugar cubes as they lugged oversized backpacks from one budget hotel to another in search of exotica at bargain rates.

"Cam must feel right at home here," I told Leslie, watching the cotton-clad, sandaled men and women who seemed to be roving through Asia on a few dollars and a lot of hope, searching for enlightenment the way surfers scan the horizon for the next wave.

"Everyone does," Leslie said. "That's the wonderful thing about Kathmandu."

The small temples we passed on every corner of Kathmandu acted as bustling business establishments. Barbers, shoe shine boys, masseuses, and even nose hair trimmers offered services on the temple steps. The secular and the divine rubbed shoulders on the streets. Even I felt like I could pray here, to the gods and mountains, to the rivers and women: to all that made up the precarious existence of humans on earth.

The street funneled us onto a rickety footbridge over a river. The water was murky with stinking sludge, yet most Nepalese ignored the bridge and waded through the turgid goo with enormous bundles balanced on their heads and shoulders. Two men even carried a brass bed, its frame strapped to their backs.

On the other side, along a road where dust rose in plumes around our faces, we arrived at the foot of Swayambhunath, the Monkey Temple. As Leslie and I hiked up its steep slopes, the clouds began to roll in. Scruffy monkeys snatched at our cameras and purses, startling me not with their gestures, but with the way their little faces crumpled in greed. We hurried past a long line of women whose voices were joined in nasal prayer just as it started to rain.

Far below, Kathmandu's red brick buildings spread across the steeply terraced green fields below the mountains like a storybook kingdom as monks in saffron robes turned prayer wheels at the temple. The painted eyes of Buddha observed us from the central stupa, where Nepalese women sat passively waiting for the rains, turning their handheld prayer wheels and facing the sky.

Watching them, I felt like a dodo bird among finches, big and awkward and scrambling to fly. What would I pray for here, if I could?

I put my hand out and turned the prayer wheel slowly, picturing Paris in her knitted strawberry hat playing on the floor with my mother, and prayed for my family to be healthy and whole.

Leslie walked me back to the Hotel Everest in the drenching rain and cast a horrified glance at my room. "You can't stay in this hell hole," she proclaimed, studying the cracked plaster walls and mossy tiled floor. "This is dreadful, and you're paying twice as much. Come share my room at Earth House Lodge."

I agreed, and left a note for Jon and Cam in case they returned. I was still planning to check the American Express office this afternoon. Later,

Leslie was going to take me to Durbar Square to visit another slew of lodges before dinner.

With its rounded doors, heavy dark beams, wooden shutters, and bamboo furniture, the Earth House looked as though it had been designed by Druids. It was crammed with travelers with iPods, paperbacks, or electronic readers in the lounge; I might as well have been in one of San Francisco's cafes.

Leslie napped that afternoon while I showered and took a taxi through the rain to the American Express office. I wore my best teacher's outfit—a black skirt and pink cotton blouse, with black wedge sandals—to give an impression of authority. I wanted to look trustworthy, as though I deserved information.

The Nepalese women in the office spoke English with a British accent. Each wore a silk sari but was made up like a Dallas cheerleader. When it was my turn at the counter, I gave Jon's name, rather than Cam's, since I thought Jon was more likely to receive mail. The youngest woman in the office, a shy girl with the sleepy eyes of a child, said that Jon had collected his mail there regularly.

"Until four days ago," she added, turning around with a stack of letters between her long fingernails to wave at me across the counter. "Then he is coming no more."

My heart sank. Where could Cam and Jon have gone? I didn't think they'd go south to India, because of the heat, but they might have decided to trek to cooler elevations.

Just as I turned towards the door, another office clerk—this one in a pistachio green sari who had powdered the part in her black hair a bright red—rapped on the counter with her knuckles. "He will be returning tomorrow," she said.

"What?" I wheeled around. "How do you know?"

She shrugged her shoulders which, tightly encased in the orange fabric of her sari shirt, looked as round and shiny as waxed Christmas oranges. "Your brother's friend, he has asked us to hold the mail in his box until he can come tomorrow," she said. "He was here with your brother, that boy in the picture, and he told me that himself."

Tomorrow, then, I would stake out the American Express office all day. I checked the hours posted on the door, thanked the women, and stepped outside. The rain had stopped and the clouds were clearing like curtains parting on a stage.

I found a quiet corner in an alley and phoned my mother. Her voice was surprisingly clear on the line. "Are you all right? I've been frantic!"

"I'm fine, Mom. And I think I can track Cam down tomorrow. Jon's supposed to pick up his mail at American Express."

"American Express!" my mother said happily. She was relieved, I supposed, to think that I would be waiting someplace so clean, so efficient, so official. So American.

"How's Paris?"

"She took her first steps alone!" Mom exclaimed. "Made it from the kitchen counter to your bed, the little monkey."

I bit my lip, overcome with an indiscernible emotion. Then it came to me: envy. I wanted to be the one to see Paris take her first solo steps! I felt cheated.

Well, I'd see her walk when I got home, wouldn't I? And by then this entire mess would be settled. I told my mother where I was staying before trudging back to Earth House.

After her shower, Leslie's hair floated about her shoulders like a yellow scarf. She had changed her clothes, too: She wore a short blue batik skirt with a pink tank top. As a final touch she'd tied a rainbow canvas belt around her tiny waist. I couldn't decide whether she looked more like a harem girl or an orphan boy.

"Time to tear up the town!" Leslie said, punctuating this announcement with her trademark hacking cough. She doubled over. "Bloody hell!"

"You'd better stay in bed," I said, leading her by the arm to her bed and propping her against the pillows like an oversized doll. "Come on, you don't seriously think you should go out, do you?" Even as I said it, I realized that I was mothering her again.

"Well, I've got to eat," Leslie wheezed when she was able to speak again. "Besides, if we go to Durbar Square, we're a lot more likely to run into your people than we are in this sty."

"I'm planning to catch up with Jon at the American Express Office tomorrow."

"What if he doesn't show?" Leslie asked. "Anyway, aren't you at all hungry? Come on! I promise to be a good girl and shovel down heaps and heaps of rice and tea."

I was famished, truthfully. "All right. Let's go."

She stopped me with an upraised hand. "Wait! You're not going like that, are you? You look like a bank teller!"

"Or a teacher?" I said. At least I hadn't worn a hair band.

Leslie cocked her head at me. "Do us a favor and change your top, anyway."

"Doesn't seem worth the bother, does it? Then I just have more clothes to wash."

Leslie ignored this and fumbled around in her own backpack. I accepted the pale blue sweater and strappy sandals she handed me. I had left Massachusetts for San Francisco because I wanted to change my life; I just hadn't anticipated that updating my wardrobe would be part of that transformation.

It was true, though, that dressing differently made me feel different. Even my posture and stride were altered, I noticed, as we meandered through the gathering darkness to Durbar Square. Because of the sandals and soft sweater, my back was arched and I held my head higher.

The evening light was lavender, which made the red buildings look bruised and tired. At Durbar Square, Leslie asked if I'd heard of Kumari, the Living Goddess. I hadn't.

She led me in the direction of an ornate temple. "She's a Hindu goddess, but always selected from Buddhist families of the highest caste," Leslie explained. "Kumari is really Tuleju, the protective spirit of the Kathmandu Valley, who got really ticked off when the King made an improper advance. She threatened to leave Kathmandu forever, but the King begged her to stay. She agreed, but only if she could come back as a prepubescent girl, so that the King would never be tempted to touch her again. The girl who's chosen as Kumari has to go through a sort of Miss Spirit World pageant to earn the title."

I stared at the enormous temple. When I examined the wood more closely, I could see that the carvings were of deer, fish, peacocks, snakes, men, and women. The people and creatures were all twined about one another in sexual positions, some loving, others so lewd and painful looking that I had to avert my eyes.

I nearly had to hold my nose, too; the courtyard stank of rotting food and fish, sewage and damp wood. Even goddesses tossed their garbage out the windows in Kathmandu, apparently.

Leslie was explaining that each girl chosen to fulfill the role of Kumari had to pass multiple tests of perfection to earn the title of "Living Goddess." The final test consisted of walking through the inner courtyard of the temple past the heads of 108 slain buffalo, candles flickering between their horns.

"Kumari can't show any fear during the tests," Leslie finished in a whisper, "and her reward for passing them is to live in this ghastly place, bestowing blessings on everyone, even the King of Nepal."

"Does she stay here until she dies?"

"No," Leslie said, explaining that, after puberty, the girl went back to her village, but as a former Kumari, didn't usually marry despite a generous government dowry. "Rumor has it that any man who marries a Kumari is bound for early death." She laughed. "Of course, staying single's not necessarily a bad thing, is it? Nothing's scarier than the thought of ending up married to the wrong bloke. Think of me and my spiritual husband."

I shook my head. "I don't know about that," I said. "I'm beginning to think it's not marriage that's so scary. It's love. Just plain, ordinary love."

For dinner, Leslie took me to a place called Marco Polo. We checked several more lodges on the way with no luck, then ducked into a low rounded doorway.

"Here we are," she said, gesturing at the red-checked tablecloths and flickering candles as if she owned the place. "If your brother and his mates are anywhere within fifty miles of Kathmandu, they're bound to turn up here eventually. It's the only place in town that serves decent pizza."

Marco Polo was small, dim, and low-ceilinged. A few disgruntled plants huddled along the windowsills. Outside, cows cruised by with puzzled faces. Despite its humble appearance, the restaurant was crammed with travelers swapping tales: lost passports, missed trains, worst bus rides, where to go next.

I drank a glass of passable red wine and listened as Leslie chimed in: Turkey, Spain, India, Bali, Thailand, Fiji. This woman collected travels the way other women our age collected shoes. Like most of these people, she had been traveling not for just a few weeks, or even for months, but for years.

The man seated next to us introduced himself as Charlie. He was an Australian who had been living on his sailboat in Sydney for four years before coming to Kathmandu for "a mountain brew stop." He was broad-shouldered; his skin was leathery; and he wore his dark hair hanging half-way down his back in a braid as tight as a curtain cord.

Charlie had been traveling the islands between Borneo and Timor to trade wristwatches and sneakers for native crafts. He sold these goods to museums and collectors, he explained, and made what he called "One tidy living."

"What do you do at sea to keep from getting bored?" I asked.

He shrugged. "Stare at the water, mostly. What I really need is a woman to keep me company, warm up me bed at night." He waggled his thick eye-brows at us until Leslie and I both laughed.

Leslie had drunk three glasses of wine in quick succession, and now Charlie was waving a fistful of cash at the waiter. "Let me buy you another jarful of the grape," he said, as a pair of small, black, shiny rocks clattered onto the table with the bills.

"What are those?" Leslie touched one of the rocks with her finger and hiccuped loudly. She was drunk, I realized, and she'd succeeded in ignoring the pizza completely.

"Eat up," I commanded, sliding two slices onto her plate. "You promised."

Leslie waved her bangles at me. "Shush, Mum." She was watching Charlie.

He was drunk, too. Or maybe just nuts. He'd collected the rocks while climbing Mt. Merapi, a live volcano on Java. The rocks were magnets, he said, adding, "I use these stones for clearing me brain." He placed one rock on either side of his head, just above his ears. "This way, the forces act to repel each another, and all of my thoughts go flying out my ears while the stones bust apart."

I laughed. Leslie gestured for Charlie to put the rocks on either side of her head, too. He obliged, gazing happily down her shirt as Leslie leaned towards him. Suddenly Leslie went pale and shot to her feet.

"I'm going to be sick," she announced and bolted from the table.

"Now that's a filly who pushes the envelope," Charlie marveled, gathering his rocks back into his pockets.

I followed Leslie into the bathroom. She was bent over the toilet, nearly headfirst in the open stinking hole. "You okay?"

"Shit!" she said. "Oh, bloody shit!"

At first, I thought she must be describing the toilet's contents. But then Leslie hung her head deeper inside. "What's the matter?" I asked in alarm. "What are you doing?"

"I lost my ring." Leslie stood up and leaned against the wall beside me. We stood there with our heads pressed against the cold tile.

I couldn't tell if she was going to laugh or cry. "How did you do that?"

"Well, I leaned over the toilet to be sick," she said stiffly, "and the ring just fell in."

Suddenly, we were both giggling. "I was only wearing the ring to see if it would tarnish," Leslie managed to squeeze out between chortles. "It was a gift for my sister," she added, and the balmy logic of this caused us both to double over, howling so that the sound echoed in the tiled chamber.

By the time we returned to our table, Charlie was gone. Leslie sat down and began eating her pizza. She'd taken no more than three bites, though, before clutching at her stomach in real pain.

I jumped up, felt her forehead. No fever. "Are you all right? Here, let's get you some tea or something. Something to get you hydrated."

"Stop being my bloody mother," Leslie moaned.

"Sorry."

To my amazement, a minute later she sat up again as if nothing had happened and sucked down the rest of the wine in her glass as noisily as a horse at a trough. "Nectar of the Gods," she said loudly. "Cures what ails you. Hey. Where did that nice man go with his rocks? He had such nice rocks!"

A few diners had stopped talking to watch Leslie. The three Nepalese waiters had lined up against the wall; they stared openly as Leslie belched, sat up, and fanned herself with the hem of her t-shirt, exposing the swell of her breasts. She propped one bare foot on the table's edge. Where were her shoes? Never mind that. Where was her underwear?

I motioned for Leslie to put her leg down, but not in time. The poor bus boy was passing our table to gather dirty dishes from Charlie's table.

He stopped and stared up Leslie's skirt, hovering in front of her like a moth trapped against a light.

Leslie dropped her foot to the floor with a thud. "What I hate about Asia," she said with a regal toss of her head, "is the way every guy stares at you. Fucking animals, men!"

As if on cue, Jon came through the restaurant door and let it slam behind him. He took in the scene at once–Leslie in her skimpy clothes, glaring at the Nepalese waiters–and grinned. "Too right!" he cheered. "Fucking animals, men!"

Only then did he notice me sitting next to Leslie. Jon tipped his straw hat at me and said, "Guess it's true what people say."

"What do people say?" I asked.

"You just never know what you'll find on the streets of Kathmandu," he said.

Chapter thirteen

Jon glided between the other tables with an actor's cocksure grace, stunning Leslie into silence. Even I had to admit that Jon knew how to make an entrance. He had a buzz cut and tendons stood out along his neck and skull. He was so tan that the white scar along his cheek stood out like a bit of kite string, and he wore a heavy turquoise necklace. In less than two weeks, Jon had transformed himself from shabby Berkeley botanist to world traveler.

"Where's Cam?" I demanded when he reached the table.

Jon seated himself across from Leslie. "Nice to see you, too, Jordan," he said mildly. "It's been a while."

"By your design," I reminded him. "I had to fly halfway around the world to find you."

He shrugged. "Take it any way you wish." He stopped my next question with one upraised hand while he spoke in fluent Nepali to the waiter.

"That's so beautiful that you speak Nepali," Leslie breathed. "How many languages do you know?"

Jon bowed his head in feigned modesty. "Eight. Well, nine, I suppose, if you count my rudimentary Mandarin."

Rudimentary Mandarin? Please. But Leslie rested her narrow chin on one hand and flipped her blond hair over her shoulder.

Jon granted us each a beatific smile, laugh lines crinkling about his eyes. He ignored me, goading Leslie into exchanging the usual traveler's tales. Jon rattled off the names of countries he'd conquered with the ease of someone reciting a grocery list. Leslie wore a rapt expression. I wanted to bite his smug chin.

"Where is he?" I interrupted. "I need to see Cam."

Jon gave me the tolerant look of a parent putting up with a whiny child at the dinner table and made a big show of consulting his watch. "Probably in bed by now. Poor Cam's stomach hasn't adapted too well to Nepal."

"Take me to him." I tried to make my voice stern, irreproachable, but instead the phrase "take me to your leader" flashed through my brain in neon green letters.

I nearly started laughing at my own ridiculous posturing. I was suddenly outside my body, beyond the confines of my own life, maybe even twirling around on the fan's creaking blades above the table.

I could see myself from this distance as my poor body desperately tried to grapple with the situation. I was a teacher in an unfashionably long black skirt, and my untamed hair sprang like a bush around my sunburned face. I was a bore and a worrier, a drudge in Massachusetts, in San Francisco, and now in Nepal, too. I was already, perhaps, a mother. What was I doing here?

Leslie and Jon were deep in conversation as I returned to my body with a thud. How long had my body been sitting here without me in it? Long enough for Jon to eat several slices of pizza and order a second bottle of beer.

Time was only a human-manufactured, false construct. Once you let go of thinking about life in hours, you stopped measuring where you were or who you were. You were simply here, being. "Now" was what time it was.

Was this what Cam had been searching for? This awareness of being so alive in the moment?

Leslie nudged me sharply in the ribs. "You've got something to tell Cam, don't you? Isn't that why you need to see him right away?"

Jon raised a pale eyebrow. From my newly acquired, more objective perspective, I could view him more clearly. Jon's serenity was a sham. Beneath the table, he jiggled one foot, nearly upsetting his beer. He wasn't any less a worrier than I was.

"Whatever it is, it'll have to wait until our boy Cam's awake," he warned, then stood up and tossed his napkin onto the table. "Or you can just tell me, and I'll get a message to Cam. But wait! Don't break my suspense just yet. Excuse me a moment." He left the table, headed for the restroom.

"I see why you wanted to find Jon," Leslie breathed. "He's really something."

"He's something, all right," I muttered.

I steeled myself for Jon's return. But, as the minutes ticked by, my perspective continued to shift. When Jon walked back across the dining room, he looked suddenly older and more vulnerable. He had lost weight and his shaved head gave away his true identity: he was an unhappy man poised on the thin lip of middle age. Jon was just another seeker like the rest of us.

After he was seated again, I said, "I brought some paternity and custody papers with me for Cam to look over. I want to talk to him about adopting his daughter if he has no interest in her."

Jon shook his head. "You've got noble intentions, Jordan, but scary Karma. This is the wrong time for Cam to be dealing with this. He needs to feel good about himself, about his contributions to the world, before taking on family responsibilities. He's here to volunteer on a conservation project with me, through RCDP Nepal."

I threw my fork onto the table. The tines hit one of the plates with a ringing sound, making Jon jump. Good. "I don't give a hoot about Cam's self esteem! He has a child to think about now! And what about that sixteen year-old girl he left holding the bag?"

Jon raised his eyebrows. "Sixteen, huh?" He sighed. "Well, if she's smart, that girl will drop her baggage off with a decent adoption attorney and get herself some cash. And what about you? Why would you choose to be saddled with a child, when you obviously are struggling yourself?"

"I didn't choose," I said, stung. "Nadine left the baby with me."

"Yeah!" Leslie seemed to wake up suddenly; she tossed her arm around my shoulders in an unexpected show of support. "That girl knew Jordan would make a kind, loving auntie."

The smug look had vanished from Jon's face, replaced by alarm. "What are you talking about? How would Nadine even know you exist, unless you stuck your nose where it didn't belong and tracked her down?"

"That baby is my niece," I said. "She's at my apartment now. I have no idea where Nadine is, but she left me the baby and a note, saying that she wants me to adopt her. You're right, I am struggling. But I am not going to let this baby down. That's why I need to talk to Cam."

Jon studied me thoughtfully. I wondered again what stake he had in protecting Cam. No matter. I rested my fingers lightly on his muscular forearm. His arm was cool to the touch, like a kitchen counter.

"Please," I said. "Just take me to Cam."

"It's not that easy," Jon said. He twisted the empty bottle in front of him. "Cam's not in Kathmandu."

"Where is he?"

"I left him in a village a few hours' walk from Pokhara. And Pokhara is a few hours by bus from here."

I looked to Leslie for confirmation. She nodded, so I turned to Jon again. "Why isn't he with you?"

"He wasn't well enough to travel. Anyway, I just came into Kathmandu to collect my mail, do some banking, set myself up for the long haul. Cam's with Melody and Domingo."

The hairs on my arms were prickling with alarm. "Is he really that sick?"

Jon hesitated, then said, "Sick enough. He's had a high fever for over a week, and he's not holding down much food."

"Jesus," I said. Tension clogged my throat. "When are you going back?"

"Tomorrow."

"I'm coming with you."

Jon gave me a level look. "Yes," he agreed. "I guess you are."

❦

I woke early and threw things into my backpack. Leslie was lying on her bed with arms outstretched, her hair a pale web of knots on the pillow.

"I'm feeling some serious pain," she whispered. "Bloody hell, what a night."

I knelt beside the bed. "The clerk downstairs says there's a British doctor here who treats travelers. I wrote his address in your journal. I want you to get well and be careful, at least, if you won't go home."

Leslie stroked my cheek with one finger, her eyes solemn. "You're a good little mother, you are," she said, then pulled a braided silver bracelet off her wrist. "Here, I want you to have this." She lifted herself up on one elbow and slid the bracelet over my hand. It gleamed against my arm.

I kissed her cheek. "Thank you. Now it looks like I've been somewhere." I handed Leslie a piece of paper with my address in San Francisco as well as my parents' in Massachusetts. "Stay in touch." I hugged her hard, near tears.

"Now, now. No blubbering. You'll always know me," Leslie promised.

I gave Leslie one last hug before running downstairs. Jon was already waiting outside in a rickshaw. We headed for the bus station just as the sun started erasing the shadows draped across the narrow streets of Kathmandu.

Jon wore a yellow singlet and the briefest dungaree shorts, an outfit nearly identical to that of our rickshaw driver's. His arms were brown and hard and smooth. He grinned as he helped me hoist my backpack onto the floor of the rickshaw, then climbed onto the cracked leather seat beside me.

"Hang onto your panties!" he warned.

I clutched the seat as we rocketed through the cobblestone streets in the canopied cart drawn by a toothless old man. We were soon traveling on one of Kathmandu's outer roads, where the morning commute traffic was just kicking into high gear.

I caught brief glimpses of the steeply terraced hills outside the city. The rice fields fell in soft green folds around distant medieval buildings. Footpaths unraveled across the hills like brown twine. The gilded pagoda roofs of temples caught fire as the sun rose higher in the sky, and I started the last leg of my journey to Cam.

Chapter fourteen

The bus was so crowded that Jon and I had to sit separately on the way to Pokhara. It would be a blessed relief not to have to make conversation with him, I thought, until the enormous Hindu woman sharing my seat started waging a space war. Her broad buttocks strained her sari as she opened and closed her thighs like fireplace bellows. She advanced her bid for sole occupancy by spitting red betel juice onto the floor every few minutes, turning the tips of my sneakers bright orange.

I rode with my hip flattened against the hot metal side of the bus, alternately worrying that my backpack would fly off the roof, where it had been tied with the other luggage, and panicking over the driver's blatant disregard for petty road obstacles like pedestrians and farm animals.

Hindi music screeched from a speaker above the driver's head and a three-dimensional plastic portrait of Ganesh, the elephant-headed Hindu god, glistened in rainbow hues above the dashboard. Ganesh lay in his mortal mother's arms and gazed down upon us with dewy eyes.

At the back of the bus, Jon was jammed in place by a group of Nepalese men who hung from the overhead bars, smoked cigarettes, hawked spit, farted, and fell asleep with their bodies draped across any seat they chose. At the next stop, the carsick woman beside me vomited into the hem of her sari. Jon grabbed my hand and tugged me out the back door of the bus.

"Oh, no," I said, as he pointed at the bus roof and held a hand out to haul me up a short ladder.

Jon shrugged. "Suit yourself. You've probably got a whole inch of space left on that bench seat." He began to climb. I saw that my seat companion was now fully inclined against the window, her face pressed flat as a raw steak on the glass, and decided to follow.

Except for a few Nepali teens sucking on cigarettes with petulant looks, we had the bus roof to ourselves. I settled into the nest of tarp-covered luggage.

We began a steep ascent through a graduated series of flooded rice terraces. At one point we passed a group of men swinging sledgehammers against the rocky hillside. Women worked in the fields behind them, their children as quick as hens in the dusty roadside. The kids waved and Jon waved back with both hands high above his head, grinning. I clutched the ropes securing the luggage and hoped the driver knew his knots.

In Pokhara, we caught our backpacks as the driver tossed them from the bus roof, mine almost knocking me flat, then started walking. The town was a welcome relief after noisy Kathmandu. With its mountain views, palm trees, and calm lake edged with cafes and small hotels, Pokhara felt like a resort.

Before hiking farther up into the mountains, we stopped briefly at a Tibetan restaurant overlooking the lake, where we shared a plate of rice and lentils. Jon encouraged me to use my cell phone here to call my mother, since there wasn't any reception in the village where we would be staying. I did, and praised myself afterward for staying calm, for focusing only on the fact that I would be seeing Cam that night. I didn't want to tell my mother that Cam was sick until I knew for sure how bad it was.

Jon was companionable now that he had resigned himself to my company, other than flaming on about Nepal's devastation by tourists in the past few decades. He raged on for several minutes about this, until I held up a hand to stop him.

"You can't expect a country to stay completely disconnected from the rest of the world," I said. "What makes you think anyone wants to live in such grinding poverty forever? Why should the Nepalese women keep hauling water in buckets, when so much of the world has faucets?"

He scoffed. "Oh, we've raised life expectancy in Nepal, all right, from 40 to maybe 55. But at what cost to the land? Or to the planet, for that matter?"

He had a point. But I was saved from agreeing by the appearance of a young mother dressed in a sari, who stopped by our table with her three children. At first I thought she was begging. Then I realized that she held a half dozen coral and turquoise bracelets for sale.

She and Jon negotiated in Nepali while the solemn children studied the food heaped on our plates. The youngest was a toddler who clutched a yellow wildflower and held it out to me tentatively, pointing at my plate. I gave her the leftover food and accepted the flower. Her older siblings crowded around the plate, too, the three of them squatting to eat with their hands, completely silent as they slid the food into their mouths.

I thought of the classroom parties in the elementary school where I taught, of the mothers bringing plates of treats for birthdays, Christmas, Valentine's Day, St. Patrick's Day, Easter. Inevitably, I ended up throwing out half the food, scraping entire plates of cookies and doughnuts into the vast rubber barrels. My students consumed more food during one party than these kids would see in a month.

Eventually, Jon gave the woman a handful of bills in exchange for the bracelets. When she'd left, I leaned forward to look them over. "Those are beautiful."

He handed them to me. "They're yours."

Startled, I looked up and met his eyes. "Why?"

He shrugged. "I only bought them because she needed the money. What would I do with them?"

"All right." I put on one of the bracelets and tucked the rest of them into my backpack. "Christmas shopping is almost done."

He laughed, and we started walking again.

The trail out of Pokhara was a roller coaster path through green rice terraces. It was hotter here than Kathmandu and the humid air hung like a damp blanket across my shoulders. I kept a bandana handy to mop sweat from my face.

Jon continued to make conversation, but I was too distracted by worries about Cam to pay much attention. If my brother was really sick, how would I ever get him down out of the mountains to a clinic? My sides cramped as I kept pace with Jon, who had a burro's stamina and fancy footwork.

We walked for hours, stopping occasionally to rest our packs on stone walls erected just for that purpose. The only other people on this trail were porters carrying goods in enormous conical baskets strapped to their fore-heads and resting on their backs. One group ferried cooking utensils and bedding as they trotted past us uphill. The last porter in line had strapped a wooden table to his back; I could only speculate that this was some sort of household moving company.

The loose trails were hard on my feet and ankles despite my thick-soled hiking boots. I couldn't imagine how the porters managed the rocky ground. They were either barefoot or wore the same inflexible plastic flip-flops I'd bought in Kathmandu and then abandoned because wearing them was like having bath toys strapped to my feet.

By mid-afternoon, it had started raining. Jon whipped a poncho out of his shorts pocket and draped it over his head and shoulders without miss-ing a beat. Karin had loaned me a poncho; I'd thoughtlessly crammed it into the bottom of my pack and had to stop to burrow for it. Finally, Jon took pity on me and held things I removed so that I wouldn't have to put my books and clothing down on the soupy ground.

"So why do you know so much about Nepal?" I asked, struggling to twist the poncho around once I realized I'd put it on backwards. "Have you spent a lot of time here?

"Yes." Jon regarded me for a moment, smiling at the rubbery trap I'd made out of my own rain gear, then said, "After college, I was a do gooder like you. I went with the Peace Corps to Africa first, then to Nepal with a non-profit. Our group in Nepal was building a road. I thought I was doing the right thing, making it possible for people here to travel more easily. You know, more access to doctors and fresh fruits and vegetables. That sort of thing."

But, once they'd built the road, Jon explained, the trucks from India and Kathmandu could drive right up into the village. "The villagers were getting plastic shoes and shampoo and fresh vegetables, sure. Progress, but only in a way."

"Why only in a way?" I popped my head through the poncho hood like a snapping turtle darting out of its shell.

"Soon, it became abundantly clear that people living higher up in the mountains who used to come down to the lower villages to sell things they'd made or grown themselves couldn't compete with what was trucked up from the city. They began to suffer because of the road we'd built."

We resumed walking after Jon helped me zip my belongings back into the pack. "Did you leave then?" I asked.

"Yep. I thought that if I was going to make bad decisions no matter how good a guy I tried to be, then I might as well make buckets of money and have fun instead. So I became the king of marketing and got addicted to all those things Westerners can't do without. I made money to spend it. I even got married, but my wife wanted to be a mother and I couldn't see bringing kids into a dying world, so that was the end of that. When my parents passed on and left me the house and a little money, I repented my evil ways. I moved home so that I could give up working and focus on community service."

"Have you ever been back to that village?"

Jon grinned. "That's where we're staying, in fact. And it gives me hope."

"Really? Why?"

"Because that road we built couldn't withstand the monsoons, the avalanches, the dust storms, or anything else Nepal dishes out. Our brand new macadam was buried beneath a rock slide within a year. People went back to walking the same old paths, and everything is as it was."

"And that's a good thing, right?"

He shrugged. "I guess there was nothing for me to repent after all," he said, and upped his pace suddenly. "Come on. It'll be dark soon. We'd better hurry and get you someplace dry."

I muddled along behind Jon for another hour or so, blinking furiously to keep the water out of my eyes and slip-sliding along the steep trail.

At one point, we crossed a swollen, crashing river on a swaying rope bridge that looked too frayed to hold a squirrel. Jon skipped across the wooden slats. I clung to the ropes and inched my way across.

Two hours later, just when I thought I'd collapse from exhaustion, we veered off the main trail and onto a footpath that led us into a village of a dozen stone houses gathered around a muddy courtyard.

"Home sweet home!" Jon shouted over the rain, pointing out a white-washed house with bright blue trim. "This is the hostel where RCDP volunteers stay while we work."

I looked up at a hand-painted sign across the top of the door. It read "Shiva Tourist Lodge" in crooked blue letters. The sign dangled from a single chain, thwacking the side of the house in the stiff breeze. Far below, the valley was filled with thick clouds moving through the air like boats at full sail.

"And what kind of work are you doing, exactly?" I realized that I'd never asked him to be specific.

"The volunteers maintain a village nursery under the direction of a government director, though I have to say he's been more absent than present," Jon said. "That's one reason I came—to pick up some of the slack until they get a new director for the project. We help grow tree seedlings and distribute them throughout the villages. Nepal's forest cover has been dwindling as the population grows and people keep cutting firewood without replanting. The erosion around here has been terrible as a result."

Before passing through the heavy wooden door to the lodge, we took off our ponchos and shook ourselves like dogs. My boots slurped and my pants stuck to my legs. I removed my shoes and wished I could do the same with my pants. The kitchen fire felt wonderful despite the black smoke filling the room. A young Nepalese woman in a shabby brown dress tended the fire. She took one look at Jon and me, giggled, set a kettle on the flames, and disappeared through another curtained doorway, taking Jon with her by the hand.

"A port in any storm," I muttered, and studied the room. The kitchen was furnished with an enormous table and several mismatched chairs. A man sat alone at the table playing solitaire with a tattered deck of cards. The man wore nothing but a pair of cut-offs. His arms and chest were furred with a black mat of curly hair. He wore a silver cross the size of a fork on a thick chain around his neck.

Where was Cam? Jon had evaporated before I could ask him which room was my brother's. There didn't appear to be a hotel office. I looked around for clues, feeling like a game show contestant: Which door would lead to Cam? Which to the office? What language should I speak to this man to make myself understood?

I cleared my throat and said hello in English, since the man's sleek dark hair and pale skin made his origins impossible to determine. He didn't answer. I persisted. "Can you please tell me where the hotel office is?"

The man answered in English laced with a thick Spanish accent. "There is no hotel office here. This is not a hotel."

"Well, isn't this a lodge of some sort? Don't volunteers stay here?"

"Many people pay to stay here." He shrugged. "I am no volunteer. I am only staying here to visit the hot springs. I want to be healthy."

The Spaniard certainly looked as though he were succeeding in that quest. The man's chest and arm muscles rippled beneath his skin. This would have been appealing, had he not also exuded the musty stink of an animal in its own cave.

"Look," I said, exasperated. "I'm looking for an American man named Cameron O'Malley. Do you know which room he's in?"

The man dealt out a series of cards in rapid succession: ten, nine, eight and seven of hearts. He was cheating at his own game of solitaire.

"He is here," the man said solemnly. "Up the stairs you will find him, in the men's loft. The ladies are across the hall from there." He pointed at the center door leading out of the kitchen and went back to his cards.

The kitchen was separated from the rest of the house by a striped curtain hung in the doorway. I pushed the cloth aside and forced my aching legs to climb the steep wooden stairs.

I'd never felt so tired. There were probably twenty stairs, but it felt like two hundred. I dropped my pack in an empty corner in one loft room, where a pair of young women—both of them with short, spiky hair dyed the pink color of cotton candy—lay reading, legs tucked into sleeping bags.

The wooden platform bed was built to sleep six people but had no mattresses. One of the women smiled and greeted me—her accent was heavy and German—but quickly returned her eyes to her electronic reader.

I crossed the hall in my bare feet. The floor was warm up here because of the kitchen fire. The rain hammered on the tin roof, which leaked like a sieve into various metal pots placed in strategic spots along the floor. The pinging symphony drilled into my skull.

The second floor was even smokier than the kitchen, despite the curtain across the stairs. In the men's loft, the only light emanated from a flickering kerosene lantern at the far end. There wasn't even a platform bed here, only the wooden floor. It was nearly covered with sleeping bags and wool blankets.

A head protruded from inside a heap of blankets on the left side of the room. I recognized Cam's tangled pale hair, the only part of him that I could see, and called his name from the doorway. He didn't answer.

I approached slowly, watching my brother closely for signs of movement, suddenly terrified that he'd died up here without anybody noticing. But no: Cam's hands were moving. He made shadows dart this way and that against the wall, the way he had when we were children entertaining ourselves at night: *This is a wolf eating a rabbit, this is a princess trapped in the jaws of a lion.* Preparing ourselves for epic lives, we giggled our way through preposterous shadow plays, using flashlights after our mother hushed us and told us to go to sleep.

"Cam?" I stood directly behind him. My brother faced the wall. He held something in one hand, a small plastic cube with an abstract metal sculpture inside it.

"Cam?" I repeated. The wool smelled like a combination of urine and wet goat. I moved to stand between my brother and the wall. "Cameron!" I said sharply.

He shifted his weight slightly and squinted up at me. "Ruth?"

Who was Ruth? I got down on my knees next to the lantern and touched his forehead. Cam's skin was hot and dry, almost papery, and his blue eyes had lost their luster and were sunk deep into the sockets. He had a raging fever. His face was covered with a short, scraggly beard, and the slender stalk of his neck protruded from a deep valley of sharp collarbones.

How long had my brother been sick? I couldn't remember what Jon had said; my own eyes were threatening to close and my muscles were on fire.

"Cam? It's me, Jordan," I said gently.

Cam stared at me without comprehension. I began to panic, my own breath coming in short, dry gasps. "Cam," I said again. "It's Jordy. I'm here."

He rolled onto his back, offering up the plastic cube in the palm of his hand for my inspection. "Treasure," he said.

I still didn't know if he recognized me. "Cam, do you know who I am?"

My brother nodded, then turned his gaze back on the cube. "This pyramid lets the old souls come to you," he said, his speech slightly slurred. "But be careful. If you hold it more than a few minutes, you get a headache." He set the cube down on the floor and closed his eyes.

What the hell was he talking about? I studied the room, trying to calm myself. The only window was covered with plastic which rattled with rain. There were more books than gear, and a few t-shirts and bandanas were draped over a wash line.

Whose were they? Little in the room seemed to belong to Cam, other than a small heap of clothing next to his nest of holey blankets and a tin cup like a prisoner's. The cup was empty. When did he last have anything to eat or drink?

I reached out and shook Cam's shoulders. "How long have you been here?"

My brother opened his eyes again and grinned crookedly. I inhaled sharply at the sight of Paris's face mirrored in her father's. "Now, that's an interesting question, isn't it? How long we've been here?" He started humming an unrecognizable tune.

"You need a doctor." By now, I was talking more to myself than to Cam. "How long have you had this fever? When was the last time you ate?"

Cam stared at me, his gaze nearly vacant but for the reflection of the flickering lamplight. "My fever's going down again now. Before, I was shaking so bad, it felt like my bones were going to fly out of my skin. Weird stuff. I was, like, hallucinating and shitting blood." He shuddered. "I can't eat until I've starved the bugs out of my body. Fasting's the only way to drive them out. I'm staying up here to avoid temptation." He sighed. "Did you know they make apple pancakes here? That's the first thing I'll have when I'm cured."

"You're not going to cure yourself this way. You'll just dry out like a locust shell."

Cam shook a bony finger at me. "Don't take care of me. I'm on a mission. I have to take care of the world before it will take care of me."

I reached out and touched his forehead again. His fever must be 103, at least. Between that and fasting, Cam could very well be hallucinating, drifting in and out of a trance state. It was nearly dark now; I would have to wait until morning to descend the mountain again into Pokhara. There must be a clinic there, and I could get cell service, call my mother. I had to let her know that I'd found Cam. I could call David, too. He would know how to help my brother.

Cam had fallen asleep. I needed a bathroom desperately. I made my way back down to the kitchen. The Spaniard was still playing cards. I decided to try my own luck rather than ask him, and passed through the curtain covering the door to the right. The long room behind the striped cotton was furnished with several chairs, a small table occupied by a battered Scrabble game, and a platform bed.

Domingo and Melody were lying on the bed side-by-side without touching. Domingo snored with the uneven, guttural sounds of a faulty lawnmower. Melody heard me enter and sat up slowly, straight-backed as a zombie rising in a coffin. She looked like the living dead, too, with black circles beneath her eyes and a cauliflower complexion. She stared at me as if I were a ghost.

"You're Cam's sister," she said.

I wanted to ask her questions, but first things first. "I'm looking for a bathroom," I said.

Melody nodded slowly, as if there were nothing surprising at all about me jetting all the way to the Himalayas to find a bathroom. "There isn't one," she said.

This was not good news. "So what do I do?"

She pointed through the kitchen door. "You have to go outside. Head for the stone wall near the river. There's an outhouse, but don't try it. It's overflowing because of the rains. Everyone just goes behind the wall. Left side of the wall for pissing, right side for everything else. Watch your step. Not everybody follows the rules."

"You're kidding."

"Welcome to the Kingdom of Nepal." Melody granted me the shadow of a smile.

With a wince, I slid my feet back into my cold, sodden hiking boots and ventured forth. The rain had slowed to a drizzle, but by now it was completely dark. The river crashed angrily against its banks nearby. With my luck, I'd probably fall in and be dashed against the rocks before I even had a chance to pee.

The outhouse appeared suddenly in the mist, a crooked gray shack with a metal roof. I sidestepped to the right of it and squatted behind the stone wall, taking in the outlines of the village houses huddled on either side of the river. The water glinted a metallic gray, occasionally sending up a white plume. Something stank of sulfur and minerals. The hot springs, maybe. A couple of water buffalo wandered along the river banks, snorting and then breaking into a trot, tossing their heads.

Back inside, Melody was in the kitchen. I took off my boots again and set them near the fire. Melody handed me a cup of tea, but her eyes wandered and I knew that she was looking for Jon.

I cradled the mug in my hands, hoping the water had been boiled, and glanced at the Spaniard. He was softly cursing over his hand of cards. Apparently he'd failed to beat himself at his own rigged game. "What's wrong with Cam?" I asked Melody.

Melody wore a gray sari that had come partly unwound and dragged on the floor. She hoisted herself onto the edge of the table and perched there with her broad flanks nearly on top of the cards scattered on the table. The Spaniard gave her rear a push, but she ignored him. "I don't know. Domingo and I have been helping Jon in the orchard, but Cam's been sleeping for like five days. When he's not puking, that is."

"Ouch. Poor guy. What does he have?"

"Probably the same parasites we've all got, only worse," she said. "Jon wanted to check out another government volunteer program near Chitwan, something to do with orchids, so we stopped there for a while. The mosquitoes are bad in the lowlands at this time of year, and the water is even worse. We purified the water but every one of us got sick anyway. Except Jon, of course," she added. "He drinks right out of the rivers, and look at him. Amazing."

Pretty hard to look at a guy who's never around, I thought, but there was no need to belabor the obvious to Melody. At least Jon didn't leave her behind with Val. Where Jon was concerned, that probably counted as a major life commitment.

"Has Cam seen a doctor?"

Melody shook her head. "He's fasting to rid himself of the parasites." She pinched a handful of her own sari-covered stomach in disgust. "We all fasted, but I'm the only one who still managed to gain weight."

I couldn't see how parasites would be driven out by fasting, but maybe they knew something I didn't. "Why didn't any of you take Cam to the doctor, if he's so much worse than you are?"

She gave me a puzzled look. "Cam has no interest in doctors. He wants to beat this thing on his own."

"What is *wrong* with you?" I asked, exasperated. "That's idiotic and cruel. You don't just let somebody lie around with a 103-degree fever for five days!"

Melody bristled. "What did you expect me to do? Carry Cam down the mountain when he'd just fight me the whole way? Don't start giving me shit just because your brother is so fucking determined to make things harder for the rest of us! If it were up to me, I would have made him stay in Berkeley to deal with things there. Jon's the one who insisted that Cam needed to do this, too, to prove that he was worthwhile or something. I think Jon was afraid to leave him on his own."

"Sorry. You're right. This isn't your problem." I set my mug down on the table. The Spaniard immediately picked up my tea and drank it, slurping noisily.

"Didn't your mother teach you any manners?" I flicked the man's hairy cheating wrist with two fingers so hard that the tea splashed out of the cup and onto his hand.

"*Putana!*" the man yelped, setting the mug down. He narrowed his eyes at me, then lost interest and picked up his cards again.

Melody grinned. "Meet Fernando, our resident bastard," she said. "He's hanging out here until it's cool enough to go back to the beach in Goa."

Without taking his eyes off the cards, Fernando reached over and pinched Melody's hip. "You," he said solemnly, "are a big pest whore."

Melody rolled her eyes.

"So how do I go about renting a room in this place?" I asked. "Or do I have to volunteer?"

"You pay either way."

"You pay to volunteer?" I was incredulous.

She shrugged. "Nepal needs the money. Ostensibly, the money is supposed to go to the lodge and the people in the village, but I have my doubts. Anyway, you pay the girl who works in the kitchen. It's the equivalent of ten dollars a day for all meals included and a bed in the loft. Everyone calls her 'Didi.' Domingo and I are sleeping downstairs, but there's room in the women's loft. You can wash at the pump outside, in the courtyard, or bathe in the hot springs along the river."

I thanked her and climbed upstairs again to check on Cam before I settled in for the night.

Cam heard my footsteps and stirred to a half-sitting position. "Jordy? How's Mom?" he croaked.

I sat down beside him and studied his face, surprised that he would ask about our mother. Maybe Cam knew how much she worried about him and felt guilty despite his own best efforts to forget that he even had parents.

"She's on the outs with Dad." I hesitated, thinking I might add something about Mom taking care of Paris right now, then decided against it when a deep cough rattled Cam's chest. We could talk about Paris when Cam felt better.

"Mom is always on the outs with Dad," he wheezed then. "That's her M.O."

"This is serious. She left him this time," I said. "She's with me in San Francisco."

I thought of my mother, and of Paris, too, who at this hour was probably in her high chair, happily gumming a bagel or scooping up oatmeal with her fingers. I turned the knob on Cam's lantern slightly to see Cam's face better. The raindrops sounded as big as golf balls on the metal roof above us.

"Mom really left Dad? Yeah, I'd say that's different," Cam agreed softly, and drifted off to sleep again.

I settled on the floor beside him and leaned my head against the wall. Lulled by the drone of the rain on the roof, I didn't even change out of my damp clothes before falling asleep beside my little brother.

❧

Cam was still sleeping soundly when I managed to unfold my stiff limbs the next morning. My mouth tasted like dead water buffalo.

I found the well in front of the inn. Water gushed from an iron pipe. The mountain water was icy, but I forced myself to hang my head beneath the spray, gasping, and scrubbed beneath my t-shirt before brushing my teeth, trying not to swallow any water. Probably too cold for parasites here, I reassured myself, just as I was startled by a white horse wandering through the courtyard with a bell tied around its neck.

As the animal reached the edge of the courtyard and nosed among some tall weeds, the young Nepalese woman who had tended the fire last night jumped out from behind the stone wall and grinned at me, revealing a Jack-O-Lantern's scattered arrangement of teeth. In this light, I could see that she was only a girl, really, still in her teens, but with an old woman's hunched, narrow shoulders.

The girl introduced herself as "Didi." When I smiled, she pointed at my comb. I gave it to her.

To my surprise, Didi offered to comb my hair. Her touch was delicate and she hummed as she worked, exclaiming now and then over my hair's texture and color. Or perhaps she was only commenting on the knots? There was no way to know, but I thanked her anyway.

The young woman then led me into the kitchen, where she offered various breakfast options by pointing out scraps of food on the unwashed plates. I chose apple pancakes, thinking of Cam, and hot tea.

While I waited for the food, I tried my cell phone, but Jon was right: there was no coverage here. There didn't appear to be anyone using a computer, either. Probably no Internet access. Damn it. How would I reach my mother, tell her that things were okay?

Not that they were, really. Maybe it was better if I couldn't speak to her yet. I'd try hiking to a nearby village to call her later.

The pancakes had a smoky aftertaste, but otherwise were thick and grainy and delicious. Didi and I managed to communicate through sign language. She taught me some Nepali, too, giggling at my pronunciation.

Meanwhile, I wondered where Jon was. Had he spent the night here? Only Cam and I had been in the men's bunk room; on the way downstairs, I'd ducked into the women's room to get a change of clothes and my travel kit, and saw Fernando curled against one of the German redheads beneath a muslin sheet, his head cradled between her small freckled breasts.

After breakfast, Didi went to work in the kitchen, squatting to scrub the dishes in a rubber bucket full of cold water. I climbed the stairs with a mug of tea and a bowl of oatmeal for Cam. To my horror, I found him quaking beneath his pile of blankets, shaking so hard that he had to clutch the wool to his chin to keep the blankets around his shoulders.

I knelt beside him to force a few sips of tea between his lips, but Cam was shivering too violently. The liquid flowed out of the corner of his mouth, shiny on his dry skin.

I tried to sit my brother up, to spoon a little tea into him that way and get it to stay down, but Cam was too heavy for me to lift. I finally laid him down again and thought hard, biting my own lip as Cam's mouth shivered open, exposing his swollen tongue and yellow teeth.

Cam's breath stank of sulfur, which made me wonder whether he had been drinking from the hot springs. But wasn't there also some parasitic infection that could be diagnosed by those rotten egg burps?

I ran into my room to dig through my backpack. My mother, always paranoid about bees and wasps crawling into soda cans, had packed half a dozen straws in a plastic bag. I took one out and pocketed it.

Back in Cam's room, I tugged my brother to a half-sitting position, leaning him against my lap. Then I put the straw in the teacup, sucked some of the liquid up, and held a finger to the end of the straw as I moved the tube to Cam's mouth.

I used my free hand to squeeze Cam's lips into an "o," inserted the straw, and lifted my finger a little at a time off the end of it, tapping the straw shut every half second so the liquid would travel just a few drops at a time down my brother's throat. I'd added a good amount of sugar to the tea; I hoped this might revive him. It was clear that I wasn't going to be able to get him to a clinic in this condition.

I fed the entire cup of tea to Cam this way, moving the straw back and forth between the cup and his mouth. I didn't want to shock his system by giving him too much at once; I decided to give him one cup of tea, then wait half an hour. Perhaps next I could try him on some runny oatmeal with salt.

Cam needed to be hydrated enough so that I could leave him here tomorrow while I went back to Pokahara to find a doctor and a pharmacy. I couldn't bear to do it tonight; I didn't like the idea of walking alone down those tricky mountain paths—the thought of the bridge made me shudder—from the village and back. Plus, the trip would take eight hours. My muscles were still so sore that the idea of hiking that distance even in daylight made me wince. But what other choice did I have?

I sighed and leaned my head against the wall. Was Cam shivering less? No, just a moment between spasms. I hoped David would be able to diagnose Cam by phone. He might even be able to suggest medications available at one of the pharmacies in Pokhara I'd noticed along the main drag. Or I'd see a doctor at one of those tourist health centers. But wouldn't a doctor want me to get a stool sample, bring it in? Thinking of everything I had to do—and of everything that might go wrong in a country like this—made me suddenly feel light-headed and nauseous.

My head ached, probably from the altitude. I had no idea how much time had gone by, but Cam was still shaking and sweat poured down his face and neck. Helplessly, I watched my brother twitch and rock on the floor, his head jouncing on my legs, while I waited for the tea to work its magic.

Then another possible remedy occurred to me: I slid Cam's backpack across the wooden floor and eased his head onto it from my lap. I lay down beside him and, as quickly as I could, lifted his blankets and rolled beneath them, trying to keep my face away from the filthy wool and hoping Cam had nothing contagious. I pressed my body against his, immediately feeling the burn of his skin through our clothes.

Soon, the combination of the tea and my body heat did the trick. My brother's shivering subsided. I lay my head against his shoulder and heard the beating of Cam's heart beneath the blankets. Maybe the worst was over.

Chapter *fifteen*

C am drifted in and out of consciousness during the next twenty-four hours. His sleep was punctuated by a raspy cough, and he left the bed only to crab walk into the corner of his room on all fours and use the pot I'd borrowed from Didi. I stayed with him, descending the steep wooden stairs only while Cam slept to empty the pot and ask Didi to prepare foods I could give my brother in small doses.

My brother was clearly too sick to go anywhere or to be left alone. During his worst spells over the next two days, I forced him to eat and drink a little at a time, then slept with my back curled against his, rolling away whenever his fever broke and sweat seeped like rain from his skin. At first I also tried pressing a cold damp cloth to his head, dipping it into a small tin pan I'd filled with water, but Cam irritably tossed his head and the cloth always slipped away.

Didi offered various healing potions of her own. I accepted them on faith, muddy-looking pastes that stank of herbs I didn't recognize, and mixed them into Cam's oatmeal and tea to disguise the taste. She also helped me learn vocabulary: "*chiura*" for beaten rice, "*phul*" for egg, "*tsampa*" for a gruel made of toasted barley flour, "*dal bhat tarkari*"for lentil soup, and "*thukpa*" for a rich beef broth with pasta strips.

The few villagers who passed the house whenever I was outside pumping water at the well in the courtyard paid me little attention, other than a grinning "Namaste" accompanied by a slight bow. I saw little of the other lodgers, either. The girls seemed to be volunteering with Domingo, Melody, and Jon; they set out early each morning and came back sweaty, sunburned, and covered in dirt, their fingernails black crescents from mulching, weeding, and pruning the small trees. I still hadn't been down to see the nursery and orchards.

My second afternoon at the lodge, I came outside to wash in the courtyard and saw Domingo and Melody washing after their day's labor. Afterward they put on white cotton clothing and performed yoga exercises in the courtyard.

The villagers gathered to watch. The Nepalese women were hunched beneath firewood on their backs or balanced children on their hips; they tittered with hands over their mouths at the odd sight. The older children invented their own yoga antics, knocking into each other and falling to the stones, while the men leaned on walking sticks and spat betel juice on the ground.

Of course, I knew that I must make almost as entertaining a spectacle with my fancy toiletries kit. I soon gave up on taming my hair, which in this damp, hot climate sprang out from my head in corkscrew curls. I soon gave away my makeup and earrings as well. All of that seemed so superfluous here. All I had left was a wooden comb and my toothbrush, its bristles now a brilliant rust color from the iodine tablets I used to purify my drinking water.

Hour melted into hour. I couldn't tell whether Cam was any better or not. He didn't seem to be any worse, yet I couldn't bear the idea of leaving him to find help. I waited for a sign that he was mending or getting worse so that I'd know what to do; meanwhile, I grew increasingly disoriented by the fragmented schedule of caring for him.

I woke on the third night to discover a white thumbnail moon tacked to the black sky over the mountains. Another time, I scrambled out of the blankets to get dressed for breakfast and discovered Domingo and Melody eating dinner. The violent lightning storms usually began some time in early afternoon; the heaviest rains typically fell just before dark. I sat or lay beside Cam by the hour, watching the changing light and the shifting patterns of rain through the spattered plastic across the window.

∞

The fourth night, I was roused by the sound of hail on the tin roof. I breathed in the heavy mildewed air of the leaky stone lodge and experienced a sharp, almost physical memory of lying next to Cam in the bedroom of the summer cottage on Frye Island in Maine.

Our last summer there—the summer before I started junior high and my father decided to sell the cottage—my brother and I built an entire fairy city out of twigs and stones on the tiny, dappled beach below the cottage. Day after day, we added towers and turrets and walls, embedding the outer walls with tiny blue stones from the lake.

Cam and I talked then about how we'd soon be old enough to run away and live in a foreign land with no rules to follow, no jobs to do, no family but ourselves, no clocks but our stomachs. Now, at last, it seemed as if Cam had succeeded in doing that, and I'd followed. But I felt like an unwilling playmate; I just wanted to go home.

I sat up in the dim morning light, hail thundering in my ears, and shifted my weight to cradle Cam's head in my lap. All around us, previous lodgers had tacked magazine photographs to the walls. One ad for "tenderly Korean Airlines" showed an Asian woman serving a drink to a Western business traveler.

Above that hung a faded world map, where a former lodger had circled our position on the globe in ink and written, "You are here. Now what?"

Now what? Now purgatory, I thought, something I'd never imagined while making all of those urgent preparations to get on a plane and find my brother. I drifted off again, still sitting up, and woke when the sun fingered the edges of the plastic-covered window. The plastic was oily and pink in the new dawn light. There was no sound outdoors. What had awakened me?

Blearily, I rubbed my eyes and scanned the room, and was shocked to see a monk in scarlet robes bowing towards us, his hands pressed together, Jon hovering just behind him. I hoped the monk wasn't offering Cam his last rites. Both men disappeared before I could gather my wits together and confront them.

Cam, meanwhile, finally had cooled off and was sleeping peacefully. I eased his head onto a pillow I had made out of one of my shirts, then settled in beside him and slept, too.

The next time I opened my eyes, I was lying alone and sweating in a pool of sunlight. Cam sat cross-legged near the window, meditating with his open hands relaxed on his bony knees, his eyes closed. I sat up and waited to speak until he opened his eyes several minutes later.

"You're up!" I observed, pulling on my sneakers. "How do you feel?"

He smiled at me peacefully. "The fever's down and my headache's almost nil. What a relief. My head's been in a fucking vise grip these past few days. What'd you do, Jordy, call in the Marines?"

"No Marines. Only me. Hungry?"

Cam shook his head and patted his sunken belly. He had put on the t-shirt and shorts I had washed for him and dried on a line strung across the room. Cam had also made an effort to comb his hair. "Not yet. You go. Eat and get some air. You look like shit."

"Ditto."

Cam offered me a crooked grin. "At least we're a matched set," he said before closing his eyes again.

His breathing soon became so regular that I wondered if he'd fallen asleep. I glanced out the window. By the cloudless blue of the sky, it must be mid-morning. I gathered my things and went downstairs, where I washed at the courtyard faucet and then sat in the kitchen while Didi boiled water for tea and eggs.

I had brought my calendar down to the kitchen. Five more days until my flight out of Kathmandu. Time was running out. But how could I possibly broach the subject of Paris with Cam? Was he well enough? He'd have to be. I didn't have a choice.

I trudged back upstairs carrying a bamboo tray loaded with a bowl of oatmeal, a plate of apple pancakes, two hard-boiled eggs, and two cups of black tea. It had been so hot and smoky in the kitchen that my eyes burned and sweat streamed between my shoulder blades.

Cam was still meditating, palms cupped loosely on his knees, eyes shut tight. His fingers were long, like mine and our mother's and Paris's, but his ragged, untrimmed nails were embedded with a week's worth of dirt. I resisted the urge to run back downstairs for a pot of hot water for his hands and simply divided the food in half. If I were going to catch whatever illness or parasites Cam had, I'd already done the damage by lying next to him these past few nights. No point in worrying about germs now.

I studied my brother closely, debating how to raise the subject of Paris and her welfare. Cam might say he felt better, but he still looked unwell. His eyelids were a bruised purple and his pale skin was flaking around the corners of his eyes and mouth. He was so thin that the flat planes of his cheekbones shone through his waxy skin.

"Hey," I said. "Open your eyes. Time to quit contemplating Nirvana and start eating it."

Cam obliged, smiling at the sight of the knife and fork. "Utensils! How civilized."

"God knows, it's a losing battle around here." I held a plate out to him, but Cam's hands remained on his knees, trembling slightly. "Come on," I said. "Enough fasting. You need to build back your strength. And these are apple pancakes, see?"

"Sorry. No can do. I feel like I'm going to puke." Cam unfolded his legs and stretched out on the blankets.

Guiltily, I ate two of the pancakes and swallowed some black tea. Then I bundled a shirt beneath Cam's head to raise it a little before spooning oatmeal into his mouth. To my surprise, he ate without resistance, chewing with the methodical, steady rhythm of a ballplayer with a chunk of tobacco.

Again, I saw Paris's tiny profile superimposed on her father's gaunt, handsome face. My heart ached for her, and for my brother, too, because he wanted to deny himself the joy of knowing his child.

"You and your daughter look alike when you eat," I told Cam. "She has your cheekbones and the same fierce terrier look when she's mad or when she's eating. She's a lot neater than you are, though," I joked, wiping his chin with a cloth Didi had sent up with the tray.

I put a straw in his tea and Cam slurped the hot liquid up noisily, giving no sign that he'd heard me say anything.

"You're not really feeling any better, are you?" I fretted. "I should get you to a clinic now that you're well enough to travel."

"I don't need a doctor. It's just Delhi belly, Jordan. Every Asian traveler's lament. Had the same thing last time I was in India. Calcutta! What a cesspool! And I am better. I couldn't even see straight yesterday." Cam rolled over onto one elbow. "Guess I have you to thank for that. Where is everyone, anyway?"

"At the nursery, I suppose. I think Jon must be living down there. I've hardly seen him." I pushed the tray aside. "What bugs me is that nobody tried to get you any medical help. You could have died, Cam. You were seriously dehydrated."

He shook his head. "Don't blame them. They knew that I came here to get centered, sort of start my life over. They were respecting my solitude."

"Unlike me."

"Right." He fiddled with the tattered hem of a blanket. "So why are you really here, Jordan?"

"Like you don't know." I sighed. "I came to talk to you about Paris."

"Who?"

"Your daughter. That's what Nadine named her."

"Stupid name."

"Look, are you going to talk seriously, or not? Because, if not, I've got better things to do than sit around here wiping your face."

"Sure. I'm all ears." My brother laughed, a sharp bark. "It's not like I'm going anywhere."

I nodded. I was running out of time; I had to talk to Cam now, about all of it. "Well, first of all, you should know that I initially came to San Francisco not only because I needed to put some distance between myself and Peter, but because I had a health scare, too, and it changed everything for me."

He stared at me, his blue eyes enormous. "What sort of scare?"

Even after so many months, it was difficult for me to say it. "The Big C. Breast cancer."

"Are you kidding me, Jordy? When? What happened?" Cam tried to sit up, groaned, and settled for a half-reclining position against the wall behind him. "My gut's sore," he said gruffly, waving a hand when I looked alarmed. "I'm fine! But what about you?"

"I'm fine now, too, but it was a hairy ride for a while."

"Tell me," he said, his blue eyes focused with unnerving intensity on my face.

I had to struggle to keep my voice calm. Being with my brother during these past few fractured days had led me to keep remembering the time
he saved me from drowning for love under the ski jump. Now that he was
better, or at least coherent, I wanted another turn at sanctuary. But Cam
couldn't give that to me yet.

"The tumor was small and contained," I said. "I had a lumpectomy
and the prognosis looks good. The tissue margins were clear all around the
affected area after the radiation."

"Jesus," he said. "You must have been scared out of your mind. Does
Mom know?"

"Of course she knows!" I said, then bit my lip before I could hurl accu-
sations at him about his absence. "Anyway, that was one thing I wanted to
talk to you about before you took off. But now we need to think about the
baby."

"The baby?" Cam looked puzzled, as if he didn't know any babies.

I took a deep breath to tamp down my irritation and said, "Your baby,
Cam. She's at my apartment. Mom's taking care of her while I'm here with
you. Nadine left her with me when she went north to go apple picking. She
wants me to adopt her. I've been trying to find you to ask what you want
to do."

Cam's expression became guarded. "Ah. So that's it. You're here to ask
for the other half of the friendship ring."

"What?" I said, then remembered: I'd had a friendship ring once, a
silver heart broken in half.

That must have been in eighth grade. Cam, still in elementary school,
had pleaded with me to let him wear the other half of the ring, but I'd
laughed and given it to a girl in my class, a girl I hardly knew but desperately wanted to impress. I couldn't recall the girl's name, and I never got
the ring back. But I could clearly visualize Cam's pale face as he sat on the
foot of my bed, begging to wear it.

"Why would you want to wear your sister's ring?" I had snarled, kicking beneath the covers in adolescent fury at Cam until I caught his bony
chin on my heel and he started to cry. "What kind of moron does that?"
Cam had wept harder then, his nose running. He didn't ask me for the ring
again.

Now, my brother held the other half of something I wanted. But he
didn't say anything more about that. Only fished around beneath the

blankets, came up with a pen, and held out his free hand. He did this without meeting my eyes. "Well? Where do I sign on the dotted line? I presume you came armed with the necessary legal documents."

"What makes you say that?"

"I know you, Jordan." Cam waved the pen at me like a sword. "You're such a Girl Scout, always prepared."

It irked me that he was right. "You're being awfully cooperative all of a sudden. Why?"

He waved a hand in my direction without speaking, dismissing the question.

It was the gesture of someone in a hurry. I started fuming all over again. How could Cam just lie there and abandon all accountability? He was giving up on his own daughter's welfare, throwing away her future without a fight! I wanted to slap him.

Instead, I stood up and got busy. I folded the blankets I'd been using, brushed my hair and collected my toiletries kit to take outside. This was a survival tactic I'd learned in so many classrooms with misbehaving kids: act calm, and you create calm.

It would help if I could do something normal, like take a shower. I'd splurged the day before on a bucket of hot water for 20 rupees and lugged it behind the lodge. There, sheltered by a stone wall, I dunked my head and sponged off my body, my skirt spread about me like a tent. It was better than nothing. Afterward, though, my skin still felt encrusted with sweat and dust.

"Are you ready to admit that Paris is your kid?" I asked.

"I always figured she was," Cam said, his voice still flippant. "I'm willing to admit that, so long as I don't have to pay the piper for a kid I had no intention of bringing into this fucked up world. She's my baby, and now she's yours. Finders, keepers."

"I wish you wouldn't talk like that," I said.

"Like what?"

"Like an eight-year-old."

My brother lazily rolled his head from side to side. "No need to keep squawking. I'll sign the papers and you can go home and run the PTO or whatever. You'll have a baby without the hassle of a control freak husband. And Mom can finally knit those fruity hats for somebody in our own family. Pressure's off for all concerned."

I reached over and grabbed a hank of my brother's greasy hair, pulling Cam's head back so fast that his eyes snapped open in surprise. "Cut it out!" I hissed. Then, horrified by my own action, I immediately released him.

"Of course we need to make a big deal about this!" I shouted. "This is your kid we're talking about, Cam. Not some used car. You can't just sign her over to me without thinking hard about the consequences. Nothing's ever going to be the same again if we do this. Not for me, not for her, not even for you! How can I know you're serious about giving her up, if you won't even look at me when we're talking?"

"I don't want to look at you," he said, so quietly that I had to lean forward to catch the words. "Whenever I do, I see what you think of me."

I studied him for a moment, unable to answer. My brother's irises were yellow and marbled pink; his breath was foul. He had the look and stink of a dying man. "Oh, Cam," I said at last. "I'm not your enemy. I'm just trying to help you and the baby."

"Then why all the fuss?" he said. "I already said yes. I know it's the right thing to do. And isn't this what you wanted, Jordy? To get yourself a baby? Pay me for her, if it'll make you feel better. I could use the dough."

I started pacing, suddenly unsure. "I don't know, I don't know! I love you. And I already love Paris, probably because I can see you and me when I look at her. But I don't know if this is the right thing! Nadine's in trouble, but you could be a good father! Can't you just come home for a little while and give it a shot? You could live with me."

Not that I had a place to live in anymore, I remembered suddenly. I was going to sublet the studio apartment in San Francisco until the end of August, and after that, what? Peter had the condo and all of my boxes were in my parents' garage. Did I really want to move back in with my parents? If I didn't, where would I go? I thought of David and Karin, then, and realized that I didn't want to go back to the East coast at all.

"No," Cam was saying. "That's the one thing I won't do."

"Why not live together?" I pleaded. "We'd make a good team. We always have."

Cam still wasn't looking at me. His profile was sharp, an older man's hollow cheeks. "There's no way I can go back to the States until I know I'm clean for good," he said.

"Clean? What do you mean?" I asked.

"Nadine and I were using together," Cam said.

217

"Oh, so what?" I asked impatiently. "What's a little pot?"

He laughed. "That's what you think I was doing?"

"Weren't you? You always did."

"Yeah, well, then I stopped the pot and did heroin."

I suppose that, on some level, I had known this, yet it was still a shock. I put a hand to my throat. "Oh, Cam. Why?"

He brushed away the question. "Once you try smack, I think the bigger question in your mind is why everybody isn't using," he said, laughing a ragged little laugh. "It's bliss, Jordy. You feel this rush at the base of your spine that keeps moving up your body until it explodes like fireworks in your head. Then everything is better, even your dreams—colors, images, sensations. No more anxiety or fear, no guilt or other desire."

"What made you stop?"

"I don't know that I have, not entirely," Cam said. "No, don't look at me like that. It's the truth. I quit partly because I was afraid of dying, I guess. On the other hand, even death seems like it could be a good trip when you're high. Then I met Jon—he saw me lying on a street near the university—and he gave me a place to stay and kept me away from a particular circle of friends in Berkeley. He wanted me to engage in the world instead of sleepwalking through it, is how he put it." He frowned. "You really didn't know I was an addict?"

"Jon didn't tell me any of this."

"I thought you might have guessed by now."

"No," I said, struggling to breathe normally, to look at Cam as my brother, not as a stranger.

"Well. Now you do." Cam's smile was crooked, but it was there. "The thing is, Jon was an addict for years, back in New York City. He got away with Hep C and a determination to help other addicts. Domingo, Melody, Val, me: we all owe our lives to him. No methadone, no nothing. Just cold turkey. He locked all of us in our rooms at some point to keep us clean. And that's why he didn't want me anywhere near Nadine, because she was a user, too."

"What about here in Nepal?"

"Heroin's only available in Kathmandu, really," Cam said. "Don't worry." He held up a hand when he saw the panic in my eyes. "I'm determined to stay in the village, help out in the nursery. That's the main reason

I didn't go back to Kathmandu when I got sick. I had to be here, away from everything."

All of it made sense, now: Cam's lifestyle since college, his poverty. "All right," I said. "Then I'm proud of you. It was the right decision for you. But what about Paris? I love her, but I've never been anybody's mother. Do you really want me to have her? I might really mess up! I mean, don't you ever wonder if Dad's inside us? Have you ever asked yourself that?"

"Only about a million times," Cam said. "I never like the answer." He tugged a bandanna out of his pocket and coughed into it, his shoulders shuddering, then balled up the cloth in one fist and tossed it into a pile of dirty clothes across the room. "Remember Dad's birthday cake?"

"Of course." My face was wet, but I didn't know when I'd started crying. Cam and I were seated across from one another, cross-legged, the way we'd always done on the floor of my bedroom closet whenever Dad was drinking. Maybe that's what had made Cam mention it, because we'd sat just this way inside my closet, hiding after Dad's birthday dinner all those years ago.

Dad had come home from work via the Town Tavern. Mom had made his favorite dinner, roast beef and Yorkshire pudding. But Dad was too drunk to manage himself at the table. He sent his dinner plate skidding onto the floor and only laughed at the muck splashed on the rug, the table legs, his knit pants. Mom made us sing anyway as she brought in his birthday cake.

Then Dad blew out the candles. As he did, the candles sputtered and he threw up onto the rich swirls of frosting.

My mother had tossed out not just the cake, but the crystal plate it was on, too, snapping the plate in half against the kitchen counter before tenderly wrapping it in a brown paper bag. "So the garbage men won't cut themselves on the glass," she'd explained, adding that the plate had been a wedding present from her mother.

"On that birthday, Dad was the same age I am now," I said. "Isn't that a weird thought?"

Cam looked at me blearily, his forehead suddenly beaded with sweat. His fever must be on the rise again. "Dad might have been your age then, but he never evolved past junior high. Want to know why I dropped out of college?"

I nodded and pulled a clean bandana out of my pocket for him. "I figured it had something to do with your girlfriend. You slid off the family radar screen right when you two broke up."

"Right." Cam mopped his forehead. "That day I had my last blow-out party at home? The one with the band? That girlfriend was trying to get it on with Dad in the garage. Had him up against the wall, doing some squirrely dance in her coin skirt."

"What!" I rocked back on my heels.

"Yeah," he said. "She'd gotten her hands on some acid, then all that booze. She was the one who took my hand and led me into the thorny woods of pleasure chemicals, come to think of it. Anyway, I made the mistake of telling her she was acting just like my old man on a bender, so she decided to get back at me. Birds of a feather should fuck together, is what she said when I found them."

"But that doesn't explain why you were so pissed off at Dad," I said.

"Doesn't make sense to me now either," Cam said. "I guess I was ticked off that Dad didn't try to stop her. Just stood there like an old ram tangled in a thorn bush."

"Dad probably didn't know what the hell to do," I said, before realizing that Cam had broken down. The tears came fast, but without a sound. "Oh, no," I said softly. "Here I am defending him again instead of you, huh?"

"Doesn't matter," he said, wiping his face on the back of one arm. "Not your fault that I'm cracking up, Jordy." He wiped his face again. "I still don't feel right. I'd better lie down again. Here. Give me the papers. Let's take care of business so I can catch some sleep."

"You sure?"

"Absolutely." Cam blew his nose on the bandana and took a deep breath.

I slid the papers out of the plastic pouch in my backpack and handed them to him, biting my lip as Cam signed his name without bothering to read anything first. "We can always tear these up later if you change your mind," I said, as Cam handed the papers back to me with his tiny scrawled signature.

"No way. If I die up here, I don't want anyone raising my kid but you."

"Jesus, Cam. Don't say that, not even as a joke!" I stood up and supported his shoulders as he eased himself to the floor again. "You need a blanket? Anything else?"

My brother shook his head, curling his body so that his bony knees nearly touched his chin. I could see the ridges of Cam's spine beneath the thin t-shirt. Soon his breath was regular, punctuated only by a slight, wheezing cough.

"Don't you dare die," I whispered, folding the papers and putting them in the plastic pouch for safekeeping. "Not when I just found you again."

◌◌

I sat beside him until I was certain Cam's fever was going to stay down. We would talk again this afternoon, I decided. If he was so hell bent on staying in Nepal, I'd have to convince him to accompany me to Pokhara for blood tests. If I got Cam as far as Pokhara, he might even talk to Mom on the phone. Could she persuade Cam to come home with me? Surely we could find a rehab program that would be better than going cold turkey here in the Himalayas.

Slightly cheered by this possibility, I traipsed downstairs with my towel and kit. I'd just finished brushing my teeth with tiny squirts of purified water from my own bottle when Didi approached. She took my arm and gestured, speaking too quickly for me to understand the words. She wanted me to follow her.

We walked past stone houses with flat roofs stacked high with firewood. After a few minutes, the houses thinned out and we were in the fields, following a muddy track along the river. The mountains stretched flat against the bright blue sky, tufts of snow swirling upwards from the peaks like gauzy white scarves.

What did the world look like from that height? I would be invisible from the peak of one of those mountains. Visible or not, I was aware of my insignificance to the future of the mountains, the trees, the rocks, the villagers I saw. That thought was oddly liberating.

I slowed my pace and took big gulps of air. Didi turned around and gave me a shy smile, her teeth flashing white and square against her brown skin in a way that reminded me of Karin.

God, what I wouldn't give to talk to Karin or David right now. Even my mother! I'd never felt so isolated. Strange, since I'd just spent the past three nights sleeping in the same room as my brother. On the other hand, I knew from my relationship with Peter that the loneliest days are the ones where you keep company with someone you love who can't hear you.

After a few minutes, Didi stopped and pointed. I caught my breath. We were on a slight rise, overlooking some sort of shrine. Buddhist flags fluttered white from every branch of every tree, the sound of cloth like the wings of a thousand birds taking flight. Stone cairns were stacked along the paths. The waist-high, hand-built rock towers overlooked the water like soldiers of faith.

A few women were washing clothes along the river, which from this distance looked like a lazy snake covered with bright insects. On the opposite side, women worked the terraced rice fields, using water buffalo to draw heavy wooden plows and following them to drop seeds in the furrows.

Didi headed down the river bank and stopped just above the water's frothy edge, pointing out a pool formed by a semi-circle of stones. The half-circle reached a radius of fifteen feet or so from the river bank.

"*Taato*," she said eagerly, still pointing. I recognized the word: hot. This must be one of the hot springs. I raised the towel, and she grinned and nodded before leaving me to bathe.

At David's suggestion, I had brought along a bar of biodegradable soap. I took it out of my kit, stripped off my clothes and draped them over the branches of the nearest bush. Then I made my way gingerly down the stony river bank and slid into the pool.

The air was hot, but the water was much hotter. It smelled of salt and metal. Beyond the pool's rocky perimeter, the river crashed and sang, rising in angry tufts above the larger rocks. Those must be boulders brought down by avalanches from the mountains, I decided, since they were so much larger than any of the others.

I settled into the water and rested my head against a rock. When I was seated on the pool's silt bottom, the water bubbled at chest height. My limbs relaxed, buoyed by the salty water. An enormous crow cried out above me and tumbled through the air on the warm breeze. I followed the bird's progress for a moment, then plunged my head beneath the hot, swirling water.

The minerals stung my eyes and nostrils, but I stayed beneath the water's surface, letting myself go limp and floating to the surface on my stomach. The pool was deepest at its center, about three feet. I let the river's current toss me about, face down, twisting my head now and then to grab another breath before plunging my face back into the warmth. It felt so good not to think, not to do, just to be.

Eventually, I sat up again and watched a flock of crows scribbling the sky above the river. The birds' cries were harsh, anguished.

I heard footsteps behind me, then Jon's voice. "Isn't it amazing that the Nepalese even have a crow god? They call him *Kag Basundi*."

"Do you mind?" I sank lower into the water and crossed my arms over my breasts.

"Mind what?" There was a smile in his voice. "Mind that there's a crow god? Of course not. I think there should be a god for every thing, not a God for all things."

Jon walked around the pool to the rocks separating it from the river and balanced there above the frothing water. He wore the same singlet and shorts he'd worn out of Kathmandu.

He shed his clothes, tossing them onto the riverbank, and slipped into the water to sit cross-legged in front of me. The fine hairs of his torso glinted silver against his brown skin.

No tan lines, I noted, and Jon was nearly as thin as Cam. Yet, his slender frame looked strong. I tried not to look at his penis, or at him, but that would mean turning my head away and admitting that Jon had once again succeeded in unnerving me. And so I glared, noting the swing of his stiff penis in the water, the long tendons in his muscular legs, the sinewy arms.

Infuriatingly, Jon grinned. "Don't worry, Jordan. Just because a man has an erection doesn't mean you're obligated to do something about it. Though it would certainly be my pleasure to help you enjoy your time in Nepal." He stretched one leg out in the water and brushed his foot against my calf. "How are you? You look like you've lost weight. Haven't been sick, have you?"

I shook my head. "Cam has, though. Oh, I forgot. You knew that already. You knew Cam was sick when you left him sweltering away upstairs alone in that smoky lodge. You even knew that Cam was using heroin in Berkeley."

"Hey, I helped your brother make the choice to get clean. And when he got sick here, I offered to bring him down the mountain when I went to Kathmandu. It was his choice to stay. I honored it."

"You almost honored him dying up here in the mountains," I said, exasperated.

Jon shrugged. "That would have been Cam's choice, too."

I lashed out at him with one foot, but Jon was too quick for me, grabbing my ankle before I connected with his ribs. "You idiot!" I said furiously. "You don't just let people die!"

"Even when that's what they want, more than anything else in the world?" Jon cocked his head at me. "Let's just agree to disagree. Anyway, the truth is that I've seen people in much, much worse shape than your brother. Cam wasn't in any real danger. And he didn't just have me here to look after him. He had Domingo and Melody."

"Domingo and Melody? Sure. They're about as helpful as my fourth grade students."

Jon leaned his head back against the boulders separating the pool from the river, his Adam's apple bobbing in his thin neck. "You're right. A shame those two have gotten so lost inside themselves. I didn't expect that. But you never know what will happen to people over time. Will they regress? Progress? Flip out completely?"

"How can you be so dispassionate?" My fury was abating, possibly because the hot bubbling water was making me feel limp. "You talk like people are rats in a very tricky maze. An experiment that you've designed just to see what they'll do to get themselves out of a corner."

He laughed. "Believe me, if I thought I could do that, I would."

This was a pointless conversation, I realized suddenly. What made me think I could possibly understand how Jon strung his thoughts together? And why should I care?

I stopped talking—a relief, now that my brain, too, seemed to be soaking in hot water—and tipped my head back against the rock again, my arms still crossed to protect my breasts from view. Thick clouds were beginning to gather around the mountain peaks.

After a few minutes, though, I couldn't help it: I had to ask him more questions. Really, why did someone like Jon make the choices he did?

"I just want to know why you convinced Domingo, Cam, and Melody to follow you here to the end of the earth, if you were only going to abandon them? I mean, why not just leave them in Berkeley with Val? Would've been a whole lot cheaper. I'm assuming you paid their way."

"Not all of them. Melody has a trust fund." Jon slid into the deeper water and floated on his back. "I didn't convince them to come," he said. "That's not the point of anything I do. I presented the opportunity to do volunteer work and they followed their own intentions, with my support. Cam came here to get clean before he faced the fact that he's a father. Melody and Domingo chose to follow us after hearing me talk about the inner peace and beauty here. There's no hiding from nature in Nepal."

That much we could agree on. In the past few days, I'd gotten used to going outdoors at all hours to wash or relieve myself beneath an expanse of sky. Last night, the sky had been clear enough for me to see a glittering net of stars thrown over the world as I stepped gingerly around the stone wall to pee. This morning, the sunrise was an orange ribbon laid flat along the horizon. I went out to fetch water and was stopped by the sight of mist rising over the valley.

As the damp air had cleared, a sudden ray of sunlight angled out of the clouds and lit up the small figure of a woman making her way down the steep hillside below the lodge. The woman's hair was done up in braids trimmed in red wool, and she was herding a small flock of goats into the valley, singing to them as the animals darted around the rocks. An emotion had come over me that had left me nearly in tears. It was only later, back in that hot, humid room next to Cam, that I could name it: wonder.

Jon had drifted over in the pool and was now close enough to touch. I ignored him. He didn't own the river. Besides, if he had felt any attraction towards me, he had done a good job of disguising it, other than that temporary erection.

"This is a beautiful country," I admitted. "It's the sort of landscape most people see only in dreams."

I felt Jon's leg brush against mine again. Again, I stalwartly ignored it, the way I'd overlook the accidental touch of a man on the subway.

Eventually Jon sat up. I stayed on my back, floating. Let him look. So what if he saw my scar, the evidence of flesh diseased, removed, discarded.

I focused on feeling cradled, caressed in the water. I didn't mind my scar, not here. Instead, I concentrated on imagining how my body would look from the air, as a whole, the way the crows saw it: strong brown limbs, the V of dark hair between my legs, the pale torso with heavy pale breasts, the fan of hair floating around my face.

I carried a sleeping tiger within this body. Best to see the beast, acknowledge it, and let it roam where it might, since only then did you know what you were truly capable of doing.

"Are you staying in Nepal?" I repeated.

"I'm thinking about it," Jon admitted. I could feel his eyes on my breasts, my belly, my sex.

"But won't you miss your house? Your home?" I was genuinely curious. "You must be attached to Berkeley, if you grew up there." *Attachment.* That was the name of Jon's sleeping tiger, I decided.

"Attached?" Jon mulled over the word. "I suppose I am, and that's why I forced myself to leave again. Whenever I see someone, or something, as beautiful, I try to analyze the object of my desire and break down its elements."

"I don't understand."

"For instance, my house provides comfort, and I've got a pretty good collection of paintings," he said. "There are the orchids, too, and the memories of my parents. Then I tell myself that the house is only a collection of boards and glass, the artwork is only bits of color on paper, the memories are flawed. You see? If we examine the objects that we desire, we inevitably find out there's nothing to become attached to." His gaze was still fixed on me.

"But what about the people we love?"

"Same thing. Think about a man you love, and consider his elements: His teeth, his hair, his arms and legs," Jon said. "Those features might attract you. But, when you get right down to particulars like the foul taste of his mouth in the morning or the stink of his gas, you can see that every person is imperfect and every blissful moment is temporary. That's the Buddha's first Noble Truth: all realms are permeated by suffering. His second Noble Truth is that the dissatisfaction inherent in our existence is caused by our own spiritual blindness, which prevents us from recognizing that the things we crave are temporal. You can only reach Nirvana, the end of this cycle of wanting and being disappointed, through the cessation of such craving."

I laughed and sat up, deciding to ignore my impulse to cover my breasts. "That's it in a nutshell? Your philosophy of life is to quit wanting?

Sounds more Puritan Wasp than Buddhist to me. In any case, it's utter bullshit. You're just bailing out of trying to achieve anything difficult."

"I never claimed to want to achieve anything beyond feeling the rhythms around me."

"Heavy. Incomprehensible, but heavy."

Jon smiled and pointed to one side of the plant. "See that plant?"

"Which one?" I searched the shore. "There are plants all around us."

"Exactly. Only by focusing on an individual plant can you understand the struggle of a single life."

Jon scooted over so that we were facing each other, sitting so close together that our knees touched, the water bubbling around us at chest height. He reached out and turned my head until I was looking slightly left. "There? You see? That single plant that has taken root between those two smooth stones? The plant with three black leaves among the green?"

"I see it."

Jon released my face, but I kept it averted, staring at the plant. I was acutely conscious of our legs touching, of my breasts buoyant in the water. I couldn't look at him.

"Now focus on a leaf." His voice was soft, suggestive. "One single leaf of that one single plant."

"Which one?"

"The choice is yours, don't you see? Select a leaf, and become it. Become that leaf shuddering in the breeze, clinging to the stem of that plant."

"I once had the esteemed role of a tree in my elementary school play."

Jon wouldn't be derailed. "Look at the leaf," he coaxed. "Feel how the nature of that leaf's existence is as tenuous as yours. It's an obvious meta-phor, but one that would escape most anyone struggling to survive life in the U.S.A. We live mindlessly, putting ourselves on automatic pilot to get through our days. Think about it. You probably got up at the same time every day before work, had your coffee and cereal, did your job, and came home blind tired. Maybe you rented a movie on the weekend or went out to dinner. Meanwhile, the climate is changing every minute, terrorists are planning their next strike, entire nations are dying of AIDS, and people are going hungry in some countries while, in others, people shovel dirt over plastic bags of uneaten food."

I dared to look at him. Jon's face was close to mine. Almost close enough to kiss. I knew he was thinking the same thing. "You're right," I agreed evenly. "That was how my life went, once upon a time. One oblivious step after another. Then I thought I was going to die, and learned life's biggest lesson: nothing is forever, so if you're going to do anything, do it now. Instead of slowing down, I wanted to speed up and leave no desire unexplored."

His brown eyes didn't leave my face. "What do you mean? This?" He lowered his eyes and reached out to stroke the scar on my breast. "Was that your life lesson?"

"Yes." I tried to smile, but couldn't. "Having cancer taught me that my days are numbered. It was a good lesson, but a hard one. I want to stay this awake to the beauty of every moment and not be lulled back into complacency ever again."

"Ah," he said softly. "So you've started over, trying to get your life right this time. No more hamster wheel."

"Or cage," I agreed, and tipped my head to stare at the sky again.

"Maybe you and I aren't so different after all," he said.

I thought about this as I continued watching the clouds gather. It was going to open up and pour buckets on us any minute. The black foothills humped their backs beneath slate clouds that were settling on them like pigeons. I willed myself to stand up and get dressed, to make my way back to the lodge before the rain began and made walking the rocky trails difficult. But common sense wasn't enough to pull me to my feet.

It seemed that every moment of my life was worth examining. Was that good or bad? Too much navel gazing, and I'd turn into one of those aimless backpackers trading stories about India and Bali. On the other hand, they were engaged in the world, the whole world, in ways I never had been.

Was it possible to do both, to contribute to the world while merely observing it? To be content in the moment, but plan for the future? Could you follow your heart without losing all common sense?

The only thing I knew for sure was that I wanted to be fully conscious of my life, to measure time by growing with the people I loved, in a place I could call home, while reaching out to others who had less. I would raise Paris and I would teach other people's children. I would continue to help my brother find his way.

I thought about Cam's shame and fear and fury driving him into drugs, and the courage it had taken him to kick the habit. I remembered the joy in my mother's voice as she told me that Paris had taken steps on her own, and her goofy fruit hats for babies. I closed my eyes briefly and saw David raising himself up on one elbow in bed to kiss me. There was a whole world to explore just in David's eyes. I wanted them all in my life.

"I don't know," I said slowly. "Sounds to me like you exhaust yourself looking for ways to deny all the joy that life has to offer. I don't want to drop out of my existence in order to become more aware of it."

Jon's eyes had darkened to nearly black, reflecting the clouds. "Okay, so you're not my soul mate. But you come awfully close." He glanced down at my breasts again.

I felt myself flush, my face even hotter, if possible, than it had been from the steaming water. "How can you say that? I stand for everything you've left behind: attachment, desire, connection. I've stalled out a hundred million miles away from Nirvana."

"Miles are the poorest measure of a journey," Jon said, cupping my scarred breast in one hand. Then he released it and did the same with the other. I didn't move. I longed to ask him if both of my breasts still weighed the same. But of course not. They never had.

The long soak in the hot water and the conversation had left me feeling as languid as a plant swirling in the current. I watched Jon fondle my body, at first from this mental distance, and then with a growing heat as he played with my nipples, stroked my belly, and got up on his knees to nestle his cock between my breasts. He stayed there for a few minutes, absolutely still, his buttocks just beneath the water, his stiff cock braced against me.

My body drifted with the swirling current against his. When I made no move to separate from him, Jon slid one hand between my legs and began rubbing his cock slowly, ever so slowly, between my breasts. I enjoyed the sensation until I looked up at his face.

Jon's eyes were closed, and I remembered Karin's description of making love on those fishing nets with the waiter in Mexico, of how afterward she had felt as if she'd made love not with any one man in particular, but with all of Mexico. Was Jon thinking about me? Or was I his Nepal, another step towards his Nirvana? His face was a mask of concentration, his mouth a tight line.

I pushed Jon away from me, not quite hard enough to knock him over. I thought about David, about his warm dark eyes, gentle hands, and kind smile. I didn't want to be with Jon. He was a man who made me separate body and mind. I wanted to be whole, and to be loved as such. I didn't want to make love to an idea, but to a friend who also happened to be my lover.

I stood up, steam rising from my skin as the water spilled from my breasts, belly, and thighs back into the churning pool. I was the tiger, uncurling, flexing.

"Just because a man has an erection doesn't mean I'm obligated to do something about it," I reminded Jon, and leaped onto the river bank, stranding him on his knees.

Chapter sixteen

I forced my leaden limbs into my clothing and ambled up the path from the hot springs, carefully retracing my steps to the lodge. I had reached the outhouse and was about to pass it when I was startled by something in my peripheral vision.

I paused to study the object more closely. At first I thought it must be a scarecrow tossed inside the tilted shack, a bundle of rags on sticks with the limbs at odd angles. Then I realized it wasn't a scarecrow at all, but my brother: I recognized the t-shirt and skinny arms. I broke into a run, shouting his name, but Cam didn't move.

My brother was curled on his side on the outhouse floor, shivering so violently that his eyes had rolled back in his head. His shorts were pulled up to the waist but he'd soiled them. He must have been on his way to the outhouse, but lost control of his bowels. Now his bare legs were covered in feces. Worse, some of it looked bloody.

I wanted to run to the lodge for help, but didn't dare leave him. The rain was starting to fall in sheets, now, curtains of water across the field. I flipped my brother over onto his back, grabbed his wrists and began hauling him towards the lodge, shouting as I struggled, retching every few steps from the smell and look of him, terrified that my brother might die as I slid him across the ground.

Nobody came. Cam grew heavier with each step, until at last I was barely inching him along. His white arms and legs picked up the mud and his shirt pulled up around his armpits; he looked like a giant grub worm making its slow way across the earth. A maggot, I thought hysterically, my brother's a maggot, and at that I was finally able to scream.

I'd reached a path leading between the village houses. An elderly Nepalese woman and her young daughter ran out of their hut. The three of us draped Cam over our shoulders and carried him. I was in the lead, Cam's face next to mine. He made no sound, but his eyelashes fluttered against my cheek. At least he was still alive.

When we got him into the lodge, the two women trilled in excited Nepali to Didi. The girl helped me strip off Cam's clothes and dampen cloths in her bucket of dish water to wipe the worst of the mud and feces off his skin. Then she laid another wet cloth across his forehead, gesturing wildly and speaking so rapidly that I could understand nothing. The words were a wall of sound and I leaned against it, my own body so fatigued now that I could scarcely stand.

Domingo and Melody appeared, rubbing their eyes. Fernando came downstairs smoking a cigarette. I took one look at the Spaniard's powerful torso and shrieked at him to help me carry Cam into the living room and lay him on Domingo and Melody's bed.

"Cam stinks like a goat," Domingo whined. "Why can't you put him..."

I halted his protest with a look, and Fernando carried Cam into the living room. We all began piling blankets and sleeping bags on him from every corner of the house to stop the shivering. Then Didi and I began trying to make my brother more comfortable. She rubbed an herbal paste on his chest, filled a bucket with cold water and gave me a rag. I dipped the rag in the water again and again, applying the cool cloth to Cam's forehead and chest while I rubbed his wrists.

"It's like I've got ice in my veins," Cam moaned through clenched teeth, "and a knife through my temple."

At least he was semi-coherent. But I couldn't get Cam to swallow any water or tea; whatever I gave him just came back up in a rush, soaking the sheet and mattress. At one point he vomited blood. I gave up trying to replenish his liquids for the moment and ran upstairs for my first aid kit. David had provided me with everything, even sulfa drugs and antibiotics. But what good was medicine without knowing the diagnosis?

I listed Cam's symptoms in my head: high fever, vomiting, bloody stools, shortness of breath. Those would be included in virtually every Asian traveler's lament from Delhi belly to typhoid fever, from hepatitis to simple gastroenteritis. I crushed four aspirins into half a cup of tea. If nothing else, I could at least alleviate the fever, I thought. But Cam spat out the mixture.

I had no choice but to get to a clinic. Preferably a clinic with a well-stocked pharmacy and a doctor trained to treat foreigners. I asked Melody if there was anything nearer than Pokhara, but she shook her head. "You've got to go down the mountain," she said. "Four hours' walking. But at least it's all downhill."

Four hours of walking downhill meant at least five coming back up. Could I walk that far in a day? It was already mid-afternoon. That meant I'd have to walk back in the dark. This was a terrifying thought. The foot-paths all looked the same to me.

What's more, how could I leave Cam for that long? Didi couldn't watch him alone. She didn't speak any English. Domingo and Melody were wit-less. Who else could I trust?

Jon! I had to find Jon and get him to stay with Cam. He could draw me a map to get to Pokhara, too, or maybe even help me find a guide. But where was he?

"Jon?" Didi asked.

I must have said his name aloud. When I nodded, Didi tugged at my sleeve, bidding me to follow. Her silver tooth flashed and she hastily knot-ted her hair into a bun at the nape of her neck, looking suddenly regal as she took long strides through the kitchen and out the back door. I trotted to keep up.

"You know where Jon is?" I asked.

She said something in Nepali and nodded. I kept pace with her as we went back through the village, this time veering away from the river and entering a grove of deciduous trees planted in neat rows. Some of the trees were taller than I was, while others were mere seedlings, no more than knee-high. This must be the nursery Jon was overseeing.

We plunged through the rows of trees, our footsteps silent on the mossy path beneath our feet. Even in the lashing monsoon rains, this would be a peaceful, fragrant place, I thought, catching sight of amaryllis growing at the bases of several trees, the brilliant red tube flowers like flames licking the dark wood.

We finally reached a small clearing. There were raised garden beds here—vegetables, flowers, and more tree seedlings—and a greenhouse. To one side of the clearing was a lean-to shelter made of yak hides. Wood smoke streamed from its center hole.

"Jon?" I looked at Didi, who nodded and turned heel. I hoped she was returning to the lodge, to keep an eye on Cam for a few minutes. I ran toward the teepee, hesitated for a split second at the curtained doorway, then ducked inside.

It took a moment for my eyes to adjust. There was a fire, small flames surrounded by stones. An iron grill lay across it. A tea kettle, also black iron, sat on the grill like a fat, contented hen. Herbs hung from a drying line, as well as a few articles of clothing. And, opposite the fire, Jon lay on his side, his face peaceful in sleep, the lines erased in this soft light. His shoulders were bare, but he'd covered the rest of himself with an animal hide. For someone who'd sworn off attachment to possessions, this man knew how to cozy up a house.

"Jon!" I shouted, crossing the dirt floor to shake him. "Jon, wake up! I need you!"

He sat up with a start. "What the hell?" He squinted at me, his gaze quickly becoming more focused as I described my brother's condition in detail, wringing my hands.

I felt the tears stream down my face but ignored them. When I'd finished and taken a long breath, Jon pulled me close in a quick embrace and said, "I'm so sorry, Jordan. I really thought Cam just needed more time for his system to adjust. But, if the fever's been coming and going with this kind of regularity and this intensity, it's probably malaria."

"Malaria! You don't know that," I said, trying to tamp down my own alarm. "Cam's symptoms fit every tropical disease in the book."

Jon rubbed his chin. "But only malaria has a regularly appearing fever generally proceeded by violent chills. And only malaria lets up enough to let you feel normal between spells."

He leaned over to collect a t-shirt from the tidily folded stack of clothing next to his pallet. "If it is malaria, we need to know what kind it is. And you can't know that without taking a blood sample to the clinic."

"But how would Cam get malaria in the mountains?" I was still puzzled. This was the one disease I hadn't considered. "I haven't seen a single mosquito."

"Right," he said. "But we traveled through India before arriving in Kathmandu, remember? And then across the Nepal lowlands by bus. There's plenty of malaria in that part of the world, especially during rainy season. Most Nepalis are immune to the common types of malaria, but Westerners are susceptible to it even if they're taking the usual prophylactic doses of chloroquine."

I wanted to scream. The clock was ticking. "I don't need a lecture! I just want you to help me!"

Jon had pulled on his t-shirt and a pair of shorts. Now he stood up and wrapped his arms around my waist, steadying me against him. "I want you to know the real deal before you go to the clinic, in case you get some temporary Western do-gooder doc who doesn't know his ass from his elbow."

"Do you think Cam will be okay if it's malaria?"

"As long as we get him the right medicine in time."

"You need to stay with him while I go to the clinic," I said, desperate now to be on my way.

"Of course I'll stay. Jordan, contrary to what you've always thought, I'm not a complete asshole." Jon took my arm, leading me to the door of his teepee. "Be ready to leave in twenty minutes," he commanded. "And wear long pants."

"But..."

"Shhh." He put a finger to my lips. "It's all going to be fine, Jordan. You, Cam, everything. Don't worry so much. It isn't all up to you to save him."

In my exhausted, frantic state, the next few hours were like a fairy tale, the kind of story designed to scare any child out of sleep: the black skies, the lashing rain, the tossing trees, the hasty departure from the dying prince's side. And, in this story, the wicked witch was the sleeping prince's last hope: an ancient, cackling, popcorn-toting madwoman who put me on the back of her knobby-kneed mule and gave me a ride to Pokhara.

Jon appeared at the lodge shortly after I'd changed into long pants. He checked on Cam, who had fallen into a deep, fever-induced sleep. My brother's face was bright red. Even his ears were glowing, and his t-shirt was soaked through. Jon helped me lift Cam and change his shirt.

Then, before I fully realized what was happening, Jon had passed a needle through a match flame and was pricking Cam's thumb with it. He collected the blood in a tiny jar, capped it, and tucked the jar into my front pants pocket, all without a word. Cam didn't seem to notice any of this, though blood continued to seep from the pinprick. I fished a bandaid and antibiotic cream out of my backpack and bandaged his thumb, then kissed my brother's slick forehead.

Minutes later, the old woman appeared with her mule. Jon spoke to her in fluent Nepali, making her laugh and slap him on the shoulder before she accepted a handful of bills he gave her from his own pocket.

"Look, I can pay for her to guide me," I insisted, drawing Jon aside. "And anyway, I've been thinking that maybe it's better for you to go. You at least know the way. You probably even know how to ride a horse." I didn't want to admit that I was terrified of riding alone into the mountains with this crazy crone.

Jon kissed me briefly on the cheek. "You're the one with people to call," he reminded me. "By the way, this isn't a horse."

"Thank you, Sherlock." I hauled myself up onto the back of the mule behind the old woman, who stank of whiskey. Probably that was what she was swilling out of the filthy plastic container tied to her belt, I thought, as the woman let out a startling belly laugh and switched the mule into high gear.

We bounced off through the rain, me with my teeth clenched so that I wouldn't bite my tongue. I clung to the old woman's tiny waist to keep from pitching off the side of the mule, trying not to remember the passage I'd read in a guidebook about Nepali helicopter pilots refusing to fly corpses. If I died, my body would be left for the Yetis.

The old woman turned now and then to offer me whatever was in her plastic jug as we jounced on the rocky paths and skidded down the muddy ones, shaking her head in wonder when I declined. Her method of disciplining the mule was erratic, perhaps because of her alcoholic haze. She alternately tossed the animal bits of charred popcorn, so that it had to trot and snort down the path to fetch them, and switched its flanks until the animal gave an irritated toss of its head and kept pace with her sharp commands.

We stayed on something like a path. I recognized one of the narrow bridges, as well as a certain curved stone wall near a stream. Once, though, the old woman took a shortcut, barreling beneath trees so low that we had to lie nearly flat against the mule's back to make it beneath a tangle of branches.

A little later, I saw a series of shapes zigzag ahead of us through the fog. I thought they were children because of their size and speed. Then the shapes darted toward us and I saw that they were giant, whistling, squeaking pheasants.

We made it to the Pokhara clinic before dark. The doctor was a balding Indian man whose posture was bent and crooked, as though he'd suffered a severe accident and been entirely but imperfectly rebuilt. However, he greeted me in a crisp, reassuring British accent, and listened patiently while I described the course of Cam's illness.

"I also have this," I said, giving him Cam's blood sample out of my pocket. My clothing felt immediately lighter; I'd been acutely conscious, during my journey, of the weight of my brother's blood in its fragile container.

The doctor accepted the blood sample without a word and disappeared into a back room, presumably to view it beneath his microscope. He emerged a few minutes later, shaking his head. "Sorry. Inconclusive," he said. "However, if this is Stage I malaria, it is indeed not surprising that the parasites are not visible. Your brother, he has been sick for how long a time?"

I did a quick calculation. "About seven days." My knees trembled; I sank into one of the plastic chairs.

"The most likely possibility here is also, unfortunately, the worst case scenario," the doctor mused, drawing his dark eyebrows into a frown. "The type of malaria most common in the Nepal lowlands is *Plasmodium falciparum*."

He went on to explain that over half of his clinical cases of malaria fell into this category; nearly all people who died of malaria were infected with this strain. "Not many parasites of this type of malaria need be present in the blood for your brother to feel the symptoms, so it would be difficult to detect without repeated testing." He thought for a minute. "But you say your brother has a severe headache and also convulsions?"

I nodded, scarcely able to swallow. "He shakes so hard, his eyes roll back in his head and his teeth chatter. He's like an epileptic."

"Ah. Then we will give him the combination medicines," the doctor said. He unlocked a metal cabinet behind him. "Even without the exact diagnosis, it is better to err on the side of safety. Unfortunately, I have only quinine, none of the better synthetic chemicals used in your country. There are side effects. But we have little choice. To treat this malaria before much organ damage is done, we must be working at top speed."

He rummaged in his cabinet. I noted the thick layer of dust on the shelves and hoped the bottles of medicine weren't outdated. The doctor wrapped the tablets in white paper, gave them to me, then rocked on his heels for a moment before he went to another drawer and counted out another series of tiny pills into a brown envelope.

"What's this?" I asked as he handed them to me.

"A drug that will decrease your brother's folic acid levels and inhibit reproduction of the parasites. I am hoping the combination of drugs will give your brother the best chance to beat the disease. But I am afraid this is too expensive a treatment?" The little doctor looked suddenly as mournful as a spaniel. He told me the price. I didn't even blink at the number.

I fished out my wallet and counted bills into the man's hand until the smile returned to his face.

There was no sign of my mule taxi. The old woman had indicated that she would return for me. I perched on a rickety bench outside the clinic and watched for her while I dialed the airline and changed my flight. I gave myself another week.

Then I phone David, hoping that he could confirm or add to the information I'd gotten from the doctor. He didn't pick up his cell. He must be playing a gig, or perhaps he was in the ER.

"Where are you?" I blurted when David's voice mail picked up. "God, you don't know how much I wish I could hear you sing tonight! Right into the phone!" I hesitated, hating my own imploring voice.

"Anyway, this is Jordan, in case you hadn't guessed," I rambled on. "I'm calling you from the tourist trails of Pokhara, wondering about love, malaria, and motherhood. I know you think I'm untrustworthy. I can't blame you for that. But I've thought about you every day that I've been gone. Just wanted you to know."

I hesitated again, then plunged ahead with a description of Cam's symptoms, the village, and what medications the doctor here had given me. "I'll come back to Pokhara in a couple of days, I hope, and I'll be able to pick up my phone messages then. Let me know if there's something else I should be doing for Cam, if you have a minute."

I hesitated, wanting to ask David so much more. Instead I hung up and dialed my own apartment.

My mother answered on the first ring, sounding wide awake. "You've no idea how worried I've been!" she said.

"Actually, I think I do."

As calmly as I could, I told her about Cam's condition, relaying the same information I had to David, though editing down my brother's symptoms as much as possible. Why worry my mother, when there was nothing she could do at this distance?

To my relief, she seemed satisfied. "It sounds like you've got things well in hand," she said. "Thank God you didn't listen to me, Jordan. I'm so glad you're there."

"Me, too," I said, and meant it. I just wished that I didn't feel so terrified about Cam's fate resting in my hands.

There was still no sign of the old woman, so I asked my mother how things were there.

"Oh, I'm fine. Fending off your father, who's threatening to get on a plane and come out here to fetch me home, and the baby, too, now that he knows about her."

"How did he take it?" That was one conversation I was glad I'd missed.

"You can probably imagine."

Yes, I could. "But he accepts Paris as part of the family?"

I could sense my mother smiling. Thousands of miles away, yet I could still feel it. "Your father says that he can't live without me. Nothing else matters, he says."

"He probably wants you to come home and make him lunch," I joked.

Her tone turned almost dreamy. "Dad even promised to cook once a week, or we'll go out. Can you imagine?" She laughed outright. "Your father actually wants to take me to a restaurant!"

"That is progress," I marveled. "And how's Paris?"

"Happy enough, but she misses you."

"She does not!" I closed my eyes, picturing the baby, smiling a little at the thought of her weight in my arms.

"Every day, we look at the photograph of you I keep in my wallet."

My throat ached with longing. "Thank you. Is she gaining weight?"

"Oh, yes, this child is thriving," Mom said. "And that pediatrician friend of yours, David, has stopped by a few times to confirm that."

My face felt suddenly hot, remembering the nonsensical, rambling message I'd just left on David's voice mail. "He came to the apartment?"

"Oh yes. Between you and me, though, I think it's his way of finding out whether you're home yet," Mom said. "Speaking of which, when are you scheduled to fly in? Two more days, is that it?"

I hesitated, then decided to be truthful. "I had to change the flight, Mom."

Alarmed, she wanted to know why. I assured her that there wasn't anything urgent. "Cam just needs more time to rest, and I want to be here for him."

"Good. I'm sure you'll get him to come to his senses and make him come home."

"Mom, I don't think that's going to happen right away..." I began, but Paris suddenly shrieked in the background. My stomach tightened. I imagined how she'd look, standing in her portable crib, the tufts of light hair rising from her damp pink forehead as Paris woke in a fury, willing her strong little body over the crib railing now that she could balance upright on her own.

"You hush," my mother murmured.

From the breathlessness in her voice, I knew she'd probably scooped Paris up and was cradling the phone against one shoulder, rocking the baby while we finished our conversation. "This little gal's a tough nut to crack when it comes to sleeping through the night," Mom said. "She's got a will of iron. Luckily, she knows Grandma means business."

"Good," I said. "Get her all trained for me, will you?" I rushed to end the conversation before Mom could ask anything more about Cam.

I sat on the bench a few minutes longer, feeling completely spent. By the time I looked up, the old woman was there, leaning against her mule's hindquarters and hacking spit onto the road. The rain had stopped and I could see the first pinpricks of stars.

Even the darkness smells green here, I thought, as I crossed the street and slung my leg over the mule's back as easily as if I'd been born to it.

❧

With nearly a full moon and a sea of stars to guide us, the return to the hill lodge was less terrifying than it might have been. The old woman seemed more coherent in the night air and did nothing more alarming than mutter to herself as we rode. I was so tired that at certain points I rested my head against her wooly sweater, feeling the strong muscles beneath my cheek.

Once, the crone reached back to pat my knee with a soothing murmur. Bats squeaked overhead, darting through the trees. I heard the occasional bleat of a goat as we passed small houses hidden deep in the forest.

Cam was still sleeping in the downstairs living room when we arrived three hours later. Jon sat in the only chair next to Cam's head, reading a book by lantern light. Melody was there, too, curled by Jon's feet, her head resting on his knees. I stumbled across the room and handed Jon the medicine, murmuring instructions. My hair and clothes were soaked and I smelled like a mule.

"How is he?" I asked.

"About the same." Jon nudged Melody away from his legs so that he could stand. "Fever's still high, but no more seizures." He expertly tipped Cam's head back, pushed the quinine pills down my brother's throat with one sharp thrust of his forefinger, and then held Cam's mouth shut.

"Doesn't he need water with those?" I asked.

"Nah. He'd just toss it up. Better this way." Jon stroked Cam's throat with two fingers until my brother swallowed, as if Cam were a cat, then repeated the whole routine with the other tablet. To my amazement, the pills stayed down.

"What's this other stuff?" Jon asked, inspecting the second envelope of pills.

"Something that keeps the malaria parasites from reproducing."

"Never heard of doing that," Jon grunted. "Who'd you see?"

"An Indian doctor in the clinic closest to the lake. A little man with a crooked body."

Jon looked pleased. "Good. He's been here for years. Oxford trained."

Cam shivered slightly. I lay down beside him on the bed.

"Good girl," Jon said. "Melody, get up there on Cam's other side." Melody did as she was told, her eyes wide. With the two of us pressed against him, Cam's trembling subsided.

"Is he going to be okay?" Melody whispered.

I turned onto my side, resting on one elbow so that I could see her over Cam's chest. Melody looked like a terrified child made to wait in line for an amusement park ride she didn't want to go on. The whites of her eyes were blue with fear and her lips were pressed together.

The anger I'd felt towards her for ignoring Cam evaporated. In its place rose sympathy for Melody, this nearly middle-aged woman who had followed a man halfway across the world in the hopes of finding peace or, who knows, even love.

I reached across Cam's chest and touched Melody's bare arm. Her flesh was cool and dry, the opposite of Cam's damp heat. "He'll be fine," I assured her, needing to believe that myself, too. "Don't worry. Sleep if you want."

Melody did as she was told, slipping quickly and quietly into slumber, her forehead smoothing and her eyelashes resting like spiders against her plump cheeks.

Jon was back in his chair, resting his face on one hand and snoring slightly. He looked the way my father did when he slept, his face creased in thought, his posture still upright, as if the slightest noise would startle him into action.

But there was no more action we could take. I lay back, too, and contemplated the giant spider webs along the beamed ceiling. An insect, some sort of flying beetle, hovered there, oblivious in its industrious buzzing that it was surrounded by sticky traps on all sides.

There was little difference between that beetle and mere humans, I mused. None of us really knows what lies on the other side of today.

Chapter seventeen

Over the next two days, we took turns staying with Cam around the clock: Jon, Melody, myself. Even Domingo and Fernando took a few shifts. Cam's skin gradually cooled and he began to hold down liquid and soft foods. Finally he was strong enough to sit up and eat on his own.

During one of my trips outside to wash that second day, I left Melody with Cam and came upon Fernando sitting outside on the steps. He was counting his gems, literally laying out glittering diamonds, rubies, emeralds, and sapphires he'd picked up in India. Fernando poured the stones out of their tiny velvet bags, letting them mix like colored gravel in an aquarium. I had no idea if the gems were real, and said as much to Fernando.

"*Por supuesto*, they are real," he purred. His shirt was open to the waist; now he picked up my hand and pressed it against his slick, bare skin. "You can trust me, no? Was I not the one who carried your *pesado* brother to his bed?"

I picked up a handful of sapphires and let them run through my fingers, just to feel them. I'd gone shopping for gems exactly once in my life, when I looked for an engagement ring with Peter. Part of me had been disappointed that Peter didn't surprise me with a ring of his own choosing, a ring he'd put inside a fortune cookie or on my pillow the day he proposed.

Instead, Peter had carefully scheduled a mutually convenient time for us to meet at a jeweler's in Brookline. We sat on metal stools in the back room while the jeweler showed us hundreds of diamonds, starting with the smallest, dimmest chips and moving up through the grades to better diamonds.

We'd settled on a high quality, two-carat diamond set in a plain gold band. "It's the sort of ring every one of your friends will want," the jeweler had assured me.

I had loved that ring; I'd even bought a special stand to keep it on by the sink, so that I wouldn't risk dirtying the stone while cooking or cleaning. The ring, and the husband to go with it, were what I had been waiting for all my life. But what was that diamond, really, but just another rock like these?

"So what will you do now?" I asked Fernando.

"Guard my jewels, what else?" he said, and guffawed when I shook my head and went inside.

Still, I couldn't find it in my heart to really hate him. Like the others, Fernando had done his part for Cam. My brother was surrounded by a makeshift family, all of us doing what we could to pull him through.

Cam finally opened his eyes for good that third day, his body free of fever. All evidence of pain was gone except for the circles beneath his eyes. We all happened to be gathered in his room when he woke and said, "Yo, what kind of weird dream is this?"

☞☜

Cam and I walked to the river together when he was well enough to eat and drink on his own. It was just three days until my flight home from Kathmandu. The mountain peaks gleamed around us like crystal pyramids, their glacier skirts shadowed lavender and pink where they fell to the earth's green surface.

We waded into the hot springs in our shorts and t-shirts. We dunked our heads like retrievers and then came up, sputtering, our noses full of the metallic water, our hair slicked back in an identical way from our foreheads.

I studied Cam's eyes, so like mine, so like his daughter's, and thought of the night Paris had croup, of my terror at the thought that I'd lose her, of the slight wheezing weight of her on my shoulder in the steamy bathroom.

Our mother had held me, had held Cam, through fevers and colds, accidents and tearful fights, through the years. As children, being loved by our parents and caregivers helped us find the courage we needed to join the world and think we could survive. I looked at Cam, who now rested his head against a stone thick with moss, and thought sadly that Paris would never know her father the way I did.

I had to try one more time. "Come home with me. Just for a little while. I'll buy your ticket."

"Not yet." Cam lifted a hand and let it fall flat on the surface of the water between us, splashing my face.

I splashed him back. And then we were laughing and paddling at top speed, until a pair of egrets hidden in the tall grass along the river's edge shot into the air like spirits rising.

"When?" I asked, once we were at rest again and the water had calmed.

"Someday." Cam grinned, but the smile didn't reach his eyes. "I'll visit when you've got a husband and four kids besides mine. And a mortgage and a minivan. Oh yeah, and a job to pay for all that."

"And a dog? Can I have a dog, too?" I was thinking of David's little mutt.

He considered this. "Yep. You can have a dog. As long as you promise not to name the dog after me."

I contemplated the gray flannel clouds just beginning to gather around the mountain peaks. "And you? What will you do?"

There followed such a lengthy silence that I sat up again to study my brother, whose face was calm. Perhaps he hadn't heard me. "Cam? You okay?"

"Yeah. Just thinking. See, I'm not like you, Jordan. I don't have a plan. Or want one. I just want to get away from everything I ever was before this moment."

"Not everything you were is something you should leave behind," I said gently.

"No, but mostly. I've been a coward. A shirker. I let Dad make me into who I was, and blamed him for it, didn't I? I blamed Nadine for getting pregnant. Hell, whenever I couldn't make decent falafel, I blamed the chick peas."

Cam dunked his head and came up shaking it, so that water droplets sprayed all about the pool. Then he wiped his face and said, "I've been clinging to the nihilist view that nothing I do matters, since life's a bitch and then you die. Thought I'd have some fun, maybe see a little of the world. But now I think that might not be enough."

I was afraid to push him too hard, but couldn't help myself. "Why not?"

"I don't know. Or can't explain." Cam slicked his hair straight back from his forehead. "Let's face it, I probably would've bitten the big one if you hadn't turned up to save my ass. I was determined to stay up in that room and let my body do whatever the hell it wanted. My body could keep breathing or not. Keep thinking or not. Keep pissing or not. It was like I was in this trance, you know, separated from my body, and I could see little pieces of my little worthless life."

I smiled. "The old life-flashing-before-your-eyes trick?"

He smiled back, and this time his eyes danced. "Yeah. Only in my case nothing flashed, and I realized that nothing I'd ever done in my life amounted to squat. I tried so hard not to be like Dad that I wasn't like anything. I was just a shadow."

Cam stopped talking and dunked his head beneath the water again, then came up and wiped the water from his face with both hands. There was no way to detect tears on his dripping, sharp-boned face, but I knew that Cam was crying.

He said, "I'd given up on myself. And then you showed up in the middle of my really boring slide show of life, Jordy. I tried to convince myself that you only came to get yourself a baby, you know, to get those papers signed."

I laughed. "Right. I just happened to stop by the Himalayas. Jesus."

"I know." My brother's smile was slight, but it was there. "When you kept on hanging around when I was sick, I realized you might have come to Nepal for me, too."

"Of course I did, idiot," I said. "What else could I do?"

"You could have left me." Cam looked at me, blue eyes unflinching.

"No, I couldn't." I poked his chest with one finger. "Mom would kill me if you died. So now come on home, why don't you, and earn me a medal."

Cam studied my hand, lying there near the crook of his elbow above the frothy water, and then he leaned down and kissed it. "I can't, Jordan. Not yet," he said. "I need to figure things out. I'm going to work up here in the mountains for a while, live clean, save a few trees. Then maybe I can come home again."

"Okay," I said, taking his hand in mine. "But hurry up."

Cam left the hot springs before I did, saying that he was tired. I lay my head back on the rocks and tried to feel good about our conversation. Instead, what I mainly felt was bereft. How could I leave Cam here, when I felt as though I had just found him? How could I face my mother and Paris, knowing that this missing person in our family wouldn't be standing beside me?

I had to have faith that Cam would stay true to his mission here, and come home eventually. For a moment, I breathed a silent prayer of thanks to Jon, who had looked out for my brother and saved him when the rest of us could not.

At last, feeling as wrinkled as a Shar-Pei dog, I climbed out of the water and shook myself dry. It had been mild all day, but I knew the air would rapidly cool as the sun sank behind the mountains. I gathered my towel and started traipsing back along the path, head down.

"Hey! There you are!"

My head shot up. I squinted against the sun and saw the figure of a man. Back lit like this, I couldn't make out his features, but I knew it was David. I started running toward him, slipping a little on the damp trail.

"You can't be here!" I said, nearly skidding to a stop in front of him and flinging my arms around his neck. "How did you even find me?"

He held me about the waist, not drawing me close, but not pushing me away, either. "Your mother told me where you were, and said you'd changed your flight. I knew that you wouldn't really tell her the truth about Cam, because you wouldn't want to scare her. So I came to see if you needed help. I wanted an excuse to come back to Nepal anyway."

A pair of Nepali women passed us, bundles of laundry on their heads; they cast sidelong glances at us and giggled.

"Namaste," David said, nodding his head at them and pressing his fingertips together with a little bow. The women giggled harder and hurried along.

"You came all this way to check on my brother?"

"I did," he said. "I was worried. I hope you don't mind that I came."

"No, of course not." Still, I took a step away from him. David was a good person; it was plausible that this kind, compassionate man would travel to Nepal for this reason, especially because this was a country he knew and loved so well. He had worked here; he probably still had friends in Nepal among the aide workers.

The realization began to set in that David hadn't come for me after all. This wasn't a movie or a fairy tale. This was simply the case of a man doing the right thing.

"It's nice to see you," I said. Conscious of the rapidly falling temperature and my wet hair, I wrapped the towel around my head like a turban.

David burst out laughing. "You look very royal that way."

Annoyed, I said, "Have you seen my brother yet?"

"Yes, just now. I stopped at the lodge."

I didn't bother asking him how he had found the lodge or the village. He had been to Nepal many times; besides, my mother probably told him. I started walking. David fell into step beside me, his hands in his pockets.

"How does Cam seem to you?" I asked.

"Good. He seems fine," David said, glancing at me. "How about you? Are you okay?"

I stopped on the trail so suddenly that David bumped into my shoulder. "My health is fine," I said. "I'm over the altitude sickness. I've been purifying the water."

He looked confused. "I'm glad," he said. "Why are you angry?"

I barely refrained from stamping my foot. "Because I was so excited to see you—you know how I feel about you, you must know, after that idiotic phone message I left you a few days ago—but now I can see that you're here for all of the right reasons, none of which have to do with me."

He laughed and reached for me, pulling me close to him while I was still sputtering. He kissed me hard on the mouth. I didn't put my arms around him, but it didn't matter: it was as if my whole body were being embraced, even absorbed by his. Lips and chests, hips and thighs, even our knees were touching. I felt as if we were surrounded by a vast space, here in the mountains, holding each other in thin air, no gravity necessary.

David pulled back. "How about that? Was that the right reason to come to Nepal?"

I sighed and put my head on his shoulder, finally wrapping my arms around him. "The best," I said.

When I said goodbye to Cam, he was digging an irrigation trench, a bandana wrapped around his hair. He looked lean, but tan and healthy again.

"You will write to me, and you'll come home soon," I said.

"Promise me you'll tell the baby our stories," he said.

"Tell her yourself," I answered, and kissed him.

Cam hugged me briefly, his embrace so rough that it knocked the air out of my body. Then he began digging as if the life of every tree and plant in the nursery depended on how well he determined the course of the snow melt coming off the mountain. He was focused on a future he could control for the moment, and that was a good start.

David was going to stay on in Nepal for another week. His goodbye kiss was deep, and he held onto me for a long time before letting go. "Will you still be in San Francisco when I get back? Or am I going to have to fly to Boston?"

"I'm thinking of staying in California," I said.

He smiled and kissed me again. "Hurry home, then."

Jon insisted on accompanying me to Kathmandu, making some vague excuse about the mail. It was early in the morning when we left; the sun was as mild and yellow as a Chinese lantern. I gave Didi my magnetic backgammon set as a goodbye present. She grinned and slipped a turquoise necklace over my head, the beads as big and blue as a robin's eggs.

Jon and I made the descent to Pokhara on foot, sliding a little on the muddy trails just below the village, where mushrooms had sprung up beneath the trees like entire villages of tiny elf houses. By the time we arrived, sweaty and hot after the jolting crowded bus ride from Pokhara to Kathmandu, it was early evening.

We ate dinner at Marco Polo. There was no sign of Leslie; I wondered if I'd ever see or hear from her again. The pizza tasted unnaturally heavy, after the rice and lentils I'd been living on, and the cheese was as sticky and unpleasant as glue. The incessant restaurant music assaulted my senses, too, after the quiet of the lodge and the mountains.

But the beer was cold, and Jon was good company, pacing the conversation carefully, seeming to sense that I was nervous. Finally I thought to ask him what he planned to do next.

"Never say what you're planning to do," Jon reminded me. "That just invites the gods to play with you." He reached into his pocket and handed me a key. "I want you to have this."

"What? Your house key?" I asked. "You want me to look in on things, make sure Val's okay?"

"That, yes. And I want you to have access to the house in case you ever need a place to stay," Jon explained. "You might not want to go back to the East Coast, with everything you have going on in California, right? And this will at least give you a place to take the baby if you need more space while you figure things out. Your mom is welcome, too."

I was stunned, holding the key in my hand. "But why not just sell the house? You'd have more cash, fewer hassles."

Jon shook his head. "Not interested. Besides, you never know. I might need a place to crash. Cam might, too," he added. "I have a feeling he'll be home before long."

By the light of the candle on our table, his balding forehead gleamed like the head of an old man. Seeing the sunburned skin made me think of the retired men who used to sit on the town common across from my childhood home. The men would line up like pigeons in the sun and sit there all afternoon, occasionally bringing out chess boards that they balanced on their knees. Jon wasn't an old man yet. But you could see the reach of age across his face.

"Thank you." I took the key and pocketed it. "You might find my entire oddball tribe camped out there when you come home," I warned. "I seem to be collecting people these days."

"There are worse things," he said, and smiled.

When my cab to the airport arrived in front of the restaurant, I kissed Jon on the cheek, glad to have found the goodness in him.

∽∾

The second leg of our flight, from Hong Kong to San Francisco, was delayed for several hours. I stayed in the waiting area and watched women mud wrestle on television. The women looked as joyous as children flinging mud at each other after a rain.

Three muddy matches later, the airline gave up on getting the plane off the ground and announced that we would have to fly out the next morning. I was bussed along with the other passengers through Hong Kong's downtown, a smoggy cinematic city of glass towers and bright neon signs, to a posh business hotel, the sort with a phone in the bathroom and a soft white robe laid out on the bed. I made good use of the enormous, sparkling bathtub, then ordered a grilled fish through room service with a bottle of white wine.

By the time I'd finished the fish I had somehow emptied the bottle as well, watching Seinfeld reruns dubbed in Chinese. My messages to my mother and Karin were long and slurred as I vented my frustration about never being able to reach anyone by phone.

"San Francisco might have been swallowed up in an earthquake, and how would I even know, since nobody ever answers my texts or calls?" I said as I recorded my new arrival time on Karin's machine.

The next day, I tried hard to recollect exactly what I'd said in my phone messages as the pilot on my flight out of Hong Kong announced that he, too, was having trouble getting us across the ocean.

"We seem to be hitting some severe turbulence," the pilot carefully explained, first in Chinese, then in French, and finally in English. The man's tone was rational, even chatty, the sort of tone anyone would use during an emergency to keep others from panicking.

The sort of tone designed to send everyone into a panic, I realized, as the plane fell silent and the tiny Chinese businesswoman beside me pulled a string of rosary beads out of her briefcase and ran them through her immaculate fingers.

We were so far into the flight that we must have been hovering somewhere over the deepest canyons of the Pacific. But I didn't panic or pray, either. I stared out of the window as the the plane lurched, sank, recovered, and sank again.

We were flying above the clouds, a bouncy pink, wooly mat, and the wings of the plane were tipping this way and that. The tiny flaps on the wings opened and closed like fish gasping out of water. We might crash, or we might not. It wasn't up to me.

There was no way to know if this was another tiger sharpening its claws, ready to spring for my life, or whether the beast would once again yawn and go back to sleep until next time. For there would be a next time. That was one truth we all had in common.

I rested my head against the seat and pictured the pair of egrets that Cam and I had startled out of the tall yellow grass near the hot springs. If the plane crashed, that was how I wanted to imagine my soul fleeing my body, freed at last to circle the heads, the lives, of everyone I'd ever loved. I would watch over them all.

But we didn't crash. There was a cackling sound over the loudspeaker, something in Chinese, and then in French, and then, more jubilantly still, in English, as the captain announced, "Our small difficulties have been resolved."

The rest of the journey was uneventful. I slept, ate, and read a pile of magazines, catching up on world news. San Francisco, it seemed, was still there.

After the sprawling chaos of Hong Kong, San Francisco looked like a toy town from the air, with its rows of neat colorful houses lining the hills. When I was finally walking down the long airport hallway to customs, I felt as though I were floating. That out-of-body sensation stayed with me until I was through the gate and into the terminal.

Then, when no one appeared to greet me, I felt just how solidly my feet were on the ground, how heavy my backpack was on my shoulders. I struggled out of its straps and rested the pack beside me. I was too tired to walk another step.

Instead of moving forward, I stepped to the side of the hallway out of the crowd, dragging the pack with me, and rested my back against the wall. I would wait a few minutes and then get a taxi home. Obviously, none of my messages had made sense to anyone; either that, or I'd gotten the arrival time wrong. It could even be a different day entirely. I had completely lost track of the calendar.

I closed my eyes and took a deep breath, trying to create space in front of me, a field instead of a crowd, a stream instead of a hallway. It didn't work. I was too keyed up.

I opened my eyes again and let in the crowd, the noise, the close smell of too many bodies in one place, everyone rushing to be somewhere else.

I saw them before they saw me. Karin came first, her mass of dark curls flying as she walked, pulling Ed by the hand. He was talking, trying to calm her down, his eyes on her back.

Then my mother appeared, just a few steps behind them, her bulk dividing the crowd like a rowboat separating weeds, her blue eyes alight, her step quick behind the baby stroller. Paris was in the stroller, her feathery tufts of blonde hair caught up in a pink ribbon.

Their eyes searched for me everywhere, until I stepped into view and held my arms open to them all.

Acknowledgments

Every writer needs a muse. I am lucky to have so many.

Nobody has taught me more about independence and perseverance than my elegant, clever mother. My husband Dan, too, has taught me a great deal—about the nature of creativity and the value of luxuriating in love between bouts of hard work. It's amazing, really, what software engineers and writers have in common.

Our children—Drew, Blaise, Taylor, Maya, and Aidan—have shown me that there really is such a thing as unconditional love. They are all passionate, creative, intelligent, witty people who ought to be the poster children for anyone wondering whether parenthood is worthwhile.

Richard Parks, my gallant and loyal agent through many years, submitted this novel to publishing houses in its original form many years ago. His belief in the book, and in me as a writer, gave me the courage to revise this book and publish it on my own, and to publish other books in more traditional formats.

And, finally, my wise and loving LIW—Elisabeth Brink, Terri Giuliano Long, Ginnie Smith, and Susan Straight—thank you, thank you, for always being there, whether I wanted to fix a sentence, whine over a rejection, or celebrate a publication.

If you want to be a writer, open your heart to the muses who surround you, and the words will flow.

Made in the USA
Middletown, DE
12 November 2014